AFTERWORLD
ROAD TO REDEMPTION
Copyright 2022 © Olivia Boothe
Copyright 2022 © Victoria Liiv
https://oliviaboothe.com
www.vicwritesbooks.com

Book cover design:
TrifBookDesign
https://trifbookdesign.com/

Internal layout:
Lunar Morrigan Arts
Giulia Calligola
https://www.lunarmorriganarts.com/

AFTERWORLD
ROAD TO REDEMPTION

OLIVIA BOOTHE
VICTORIA LIIV

For those who reach for the stars.
Never stop dreaming.

AUTHOR'S NOTE

Afterworld: Road to Redemption is a dark apocalyptic paranormal romance, meaning it includes some triggers, such as graphic violence, explicit sexual scenes, and other mature situations. For a more comprehensive content/trigger list, visit www.oliviaboothe.com/afterworld.

While Afterworld can be read as a standalone and has a resolution, this is a planned series, and the book ends with a Happily For Now.

Also, though not required, for an enhanced reading experienced, you can read the short prequel, Afterworld: Losing Salvation available as a FREE download by signing up for our Newsletter on StoryOrigin: Afterworld - Losing Salvation

Hope you enjoy Kate and Jax's love story.

Reader discretion is advised.

WHEN THE WORLD ENDED

My grandmother believed in God. As a devout
Christian, she did everything in her power to guide me
in her footsteps.
The Bible. Mass. Penance.
I practiced it all.
At age fifteen, when that invisible, mysterious force
couldn't save my parents, I decided religion was a
farce. A crutch. Something people held onto when they
had nothing else left to believe in. No force existed out
there, listening to our prayers, watching over us with
love and good intentions.
Religion was for the weak, for those who couldn't cut it
on their own.
Now, nearly two decades later, I've come to understand
how wrong I was.
But believing in something is not the same as having
faith in it.
God exists; He just doesn't give a fuck about us.

FROM THE PAGES OF KATE JONES'S JOURNAL
YEAR 2032

*Behold, I have given you authority to
tread on serpents and scorpions.*

LUKE 10:19

CHAPTER 1
KATE

A reminder of how cruel Hell truly was crawled out of the boarded-up Chinese takeout place on the corner of Eastern Parkway and Bedford Avenue, in what used to be the trendy, hipster part of Brooklyn. The letters of the Chung Kitchen restaurant sign hung loosely off the brick building, the paint faded, looking browner than red. One of the C's swung as a strong gust of wind blew, the *creaking* of the mangled metal echoing down the desolate street. Fallen leaves dragged across the sidewalk, swirling past the abomination clawing at a piece of bloodied flesh between its teeth.

Crouched behind the steel roof of a torn down glass bus shelter, I spied on the ghoulish creature from across the street, watching as it tore a cat—or at least, what used to be a cat—into pieces. Then, as if it was tracking something, it sniffed the air and stumbled in the direction of the next small eatery.

Seemed this devoured and I shared a similar goal tonight— to find food. Difference was, cat wasn't on my menu—well, at least not yet, thank goodness—but the small shops lining Eastern Parkway had been practically cleaned out weeks ago.

What little remained was ravaged by rats or rotten. While he was in search of his second morsel, I had yet to find anything.

Creeping its way past another fast-food joint, E-Bite, it kicked through a wide, somehow-undamaged window next door. The glass shattered with a loud *crash*, making me crouch lower, dread spider-walking down my spine. Fuck. The sound would likely draw more of its kind. But that wasn't even the worst of my worries. The sun was setting, and that's when the real baddies came out to play.

Peeking over my hiding spot, I watched it continue to rummage through the debris. The crunching of broken glass was accompanied by a low, guttural growl as it suddenly peered over its shoulder. I sunk back down. Fucker must have sensed something was watching it. Perhaps it caught my scent.

Hank let out a soft whine beside me.

Patting the German Shepherd on the neck, I whispered, "I know, buddy. Just a little longer."

We didn't usually cower from the devoured. They were fairly easy to kill, as long as you avoided those two-inch claws and teeth. A bullet through the brain normally did the trick, but I was running low on bullets and needed them for the real threats.

Mentally adding ammunition to the laundry list of supplies I needed to scrape up, I shook my head and pursed my lips. My supply runs were expanding beyond what I could cover on foot in one day, not to mention I was running out of holy water and had recently lost contact with my source.

Canned or dry food were always on the list, along with kibble for Hank and batteries. Painkillers, toilet paper, and antibiotics were the real high-ticket items. I could always trade those for food on the off chance I ran into other survivors. Doubtful I'd find any medicine this side of town, though, unless I went on a scavenger hunt through some of the high-rise apartments, but everybody knew those were death traps. If I came across some soap and tampons on this run, I'd call this hunt a success—

especially the tampons. Aunt Flow didn't stop coming over just because the apocalypse hit.

I glanced down at my watch. Thirty minutes until sundown. Shit. I bit my lip. Seemed this supply run was gonna turn into a bust, anyway. If we didn't get a move on, we'd be trapped out here after dark with little protection. Checking the mag of my Glock, I counted four bullets. Barely enough to take down a nightcrawler.

Hank's hackles raised. He, too, understood we were running out of time. Peeking over to where the devoured stood, my chest filled with relief. Seemed it had forgotten about us and had found something else of interest deeper inside the store. Pointing a finger to my eye, I signaled to Hank to watch me. His tail wagged.

Good dog.

Adjusting his tactical vest—his previous handler must have perished while out on a mission and had left Hank fully geared—I put a finger to my lips and gestured for him to be quiet and follow. We needed to be quick and stealthy to get out of this sweet little pickle with minimal damage. With one last glance, I decided now was our chance and creeped past the building the devoured had turned into, keeping well to the other side of the road and moving as quick as I dared. Hank padded next to me, his head lowered, keeping close and impossibly quiet.

His years as a service dog always came in handy. I couldn't be more grateful for the day he found me.

Just when I thought we had cleared the risk zone, the devoured rushed out of the shop with a roar. It must have caught our scent and now had its black eyes locked on us. Standing in front of the rundown cellphone store—where I'd managed to resource a package of batteries and some bubble gum a couple of months ago—I raised my firearm and aimed.

The roar turned into gurgles and groans as it awkwardly waddled toward us through fallen leaves and shards of glass. A deep, threatening growl rumbled from Hank as he stepped in front of me, barking in warning. Still pointing my weapon at the beast, I patted my hip with my other hand, ordering Hank to step back.

I didn't trust the manner in which the devoured hobbled across the street—something in the way it moved caused my spine to stiffen. His black eyes assessed us, and I realized this wasn't the typical, mindless creatures we normally faced. If it was nimble enough to catch a cat, it could bolt at us unexpectedly. My gun remained pointed at its head, and even after so many times, my finger trembled over the trigger.

I had seen enough of those things to know there was nothing human left under the grey, mutated shape. Even though this one still walked upright on two bare, bloodied feet, its hands were awkwardly long and ended in sharp claws. Black pus oozed from odd growths all over its skin. With a face resembling that of a twisted goblin rather than anything human, I should have felt less compassion.

Still, this hellish creature had been somebody's son before, perhaps somebody's husband. Someone had cared and loved it. They might have seen it turn, get twisted, and kill. Someone might have seen it tear through the flesh of their three-year-old daughter with claws sharper than blades. That someone might have stood frozen instead of pulling the trigger.

I'd never make that mistake again.

Without warning, the devoured sprinted in our direction. The gun went off with a loud *bang*, but the shot missed. Dammit. This one moved too fast. Feet still planted on the pavement, I fired off another round, clipping its shoulder. Thrusting the creature backward, the impact surely caused a nasty wound, incapacitating it long enough for Hank and me to hightail it out of there.

With only two bullets left, I decided not to waste them on a wounded devoured—his mates would make a quick meal of him.

Holstering my handgun, we made haste toward the Brooklyn bridge. The sun was practically below the horizon now. We'd made camp at an abandoned brownstone on Myrtle Street, but there was no way we'd make it back there without attracting unwanted attention. We needed to find a place to hole up for the night, ASAP, and far from where the nightcrawlers could track us back to our safe zone.

We made sure to keep to the shadows as we hurried toward Manhattan, past more broken shops and trashed apartment blocks. I'd done a sweep of the neighborhood a week ago, mapping out the least infested areas, but after finding a devoured in an area that should have been clean, we couldn't take any chances.

The Brooklyn Bridge was now more a Brooklyn-climb-across than an actual bridge. The structure had collapsed in an explosion two months after the first outbreak. A military unit had trapped a large number of infected on the bridge, hoping to stop the spread of the virus, but all that did was contaminate the river and destroy the bridge.

There was still a way to cross over—people had patched the gaps on the bridge with wooden boards. Part of the crossover was very narrow, but you could hold on to one of the tangling wires, which I gripped for dear life as I scaled it. Hank never seemed to have trouble, but he had four paws to balance on. After that, the bridge widened, and we had minor difficulty hurrying past charred, hallowed out car husks.

The moon shone brightly tonight, which made it easier to spot the nightcrawlers. Unlike the devoured, these nasties didn't start out human. Nah, these motherfuckers literally crawled out of the pits of Hell. They traveled in packs, patrolling the streets every night, hunting. What the virus didn't kill, they were sent to finish off.

Except, they didn't always kill their catch… not at first.

Ear piercing howls erupted into the night, followed by high-pitched whoops and squeals. They reminded me of what I imagined hyenas sounded like in the Serengeti, but more marrow-splintering. Lightning-fast and with jaws that could crack a man in half, no one stood a chance against one, never mind a pack of them.

Bullets could take one down, but you'd need to empty a clip into their cavity. I had two bullets left, a machete strapped to my thigh, and my last vial of holy water in my pocket. I probably had enough to slow one of those things down, but not enough to kill it.

Their whooping calls grew closer, but I wasn't sure if they were coming from behind or from up ahead. Either way, we were sitting ducks out on the bridge. Picking up the pace, Hank and I bobbed and weaved through the graveyard of cars and mangled steel, then he stopped.

"What is it, buddy? This isn't the time to chicken out."

Hank looked unsettled. He paced sideways with his tail tucked between his legs, letting me know he didn't wish to go farther.

The yelps grew even closer now. We'd run out of time.

Shit. Shit. Shit.

I looked around for a place to hide, but there wasn't anything we could crawl under where those beasts couldn't sniff us out.

"Damn it, Hank," I whispered harshly. Our only other option was to climb down to the water's edge and submerge ourselves in the Hudson River with the hopes to mask our scent. Hank let out a low whine. "Yeah, well, we don't have much of a choice now, do we?"

Kneeling, I took his beautiful, furry face in my hands and looked into his eyes. "We can do this, Hank. Just for a little bit, okay?” With a hand gesture, I commanded him to go down first.

As I climbed over the side of the cracked road, a loud scream broke through the night. Human. Female. Hank scurried up to meet me, ears propped, eyes hyper-focused. He was trained to identify when a human was in danger—that was how he’d found me when I’d been cornered by a horde of devoured.

I knew he was scared, but his training was kicking in. “Hank, whoever it is, we can’t help them. I don’t have enough bullets.”

He whined.

“We can’t go.”

This time, he huffed at me. He wasn’t asking. Drawing in a deep breath, I gripped the handle of the machete and made sure the holy water was easily reachable. “You’re gonna get us killed, you know that?”

He huffed before racing back up the fallen debris to the broken road of the bridge. Another scream split my eardrum, this one more pained. I already knew what we were going to find. With any luck, the nightcrawlers had made their kill and moved on.

As I followed Hank, we came to a stop behind a half blown-up military tank. Voices could be heard several yards away. Hank lowered to the ground, ears twitching as he listened. Not wanting to give away our position, I reached into my backpack for the mirror I’d swiped from a pharmacy a few weeks back.

Using the mirror to spy on the situation, a hand flew to my mouth the instant I spotted the man sitting atop a horse. No, not a man but Death itself. Hands trembling, I struggled to ease my breath. My heart pumped so hard, I could feel it press against my rib cage.

It was him...

One of the four Horsemen.

A pack of nightcrawlers had surrounded who appeared to be a young girl, probably no older than fifteen. Panic-stricken and with tears streaming down her face, she held on to an injured arm as she paced in a small circle.

"Please... no," she cried.

Perched on a pale, skeletal-looking horse, the Horseman approached the girl, the hood of his black cloak obscuring his features. Although his face was hidden, I was able to see his breath billow like a snowdrift, as if it were below freezing outside. "She will do," he uttered in a voice so deep and calm, it iced my blood.

From behind him, a Minotaur-looking creature stepped into the moon's silvery light and the girl let out a guttural scream that could have shattered glass if any of the burn-out cars scattered about had any.

Hank rose on all fours, a deep growl rumbling in his chest. Gripping his vest, I had to hold him back from bolting after the girl. "Stay," I gritted. If we went out now, we'd be minced meat. He was a well-trained service dog and could take a human down in one breath. I'd even seen him take down one of the devoured, but a nightcrawler was a different story. And there were five circling the girl.

Not to mention the Horseman. I'd only seen him once when shit hit the fan eighteen months ago, but I'd not been this close. Fucker hadn't looked nearly as terrifying then. Now? I could barely move. My entire body vibrated.

No. I couldn't allow myself to be paralyzed by fear. I couldn't allow another helpless girl be—

I shook my head, smudging away the images of that dreadful night—the night my soul was ripped from my body. If I lost myself to the grief now, then all would be for nothing. Hank was right. We needed to do something.

Pointing to my eye, I got Hank to focus. "Okay, buddy, we only have one chance at this. Like we practiced." Whispering a couple of simple but targeted commands into his ear, I tightened his vest and put protective goggles over his eyes.

While out on supply runs, Hank and I had developed a diversion strategy. Sometimes I lured the devoured away and he would swoop in and take the loot, while other times he was the diversion.

Tonight, I would be the prey.

Strapping on the set of balls I needed for this, I slid out of my hiding spot, keeping my palm low in a signal to Hank to stay put until I was ready. The instant I stepped into view, all five nightcrawlers stared in my direction, those awful whooping calls grating my nerves. But I smiled. I couldn't show fear.

I refused to give these assholes what they wanted.

"Whoops. Sorry for crashing the party, boys." With my gun aimed at the Horseman's head, I added, "How about you let the girl go and maybe I'll let you live." It was more of a bluff than a real threat, but they didn't know it.

Unrushed, the Horseman tipped his head toward me, and from behind the shadows obscuring his face, his eyes glowed blood-red. I swallowed hard. That gaze promised me more than death. *I'd definitely hadn't thought this plan through.*

With my free hand still hanging by my thigh, I gave a very subtle flick of two fingers, signaling to Hank. The plan was for me to lure the nightcrawlers and the two head demons away from the girl, then Hank would rush in and guide her to safety.

As I voiced the plan in my head, it felt less sound and more insane. Even if I managed to get the *crawlies* to come after me, what then? How was I supposed to outrun five huge, muscly, jaw-snapping, teeth-grinding beasts?

"Well, gentlemen? What will it be?" I kept stalling, wanting to give Hank enough time to sneak around to a good vantage point.

Red Eyes whispered something inaudible to his Minotaur minion, who then unsheathed a monstrosity of an axe from behind his back. The demon must have stood a good eight to nine feet tall and was built like a bulldozer. He could probably pummel a grisly to the ground with his fists. He belted a visceral roar into the night that rattled the broken steel frame of the bridge.

The crawlies whined and whooped, their calls sounding like animalistic laughter. Unsure of what was happening, I gripped my gun tighter, making sure not to lose aim. From the corner of my eye, I saw movement in the shadows.

More nightcrawlers appeared, as if summoned by the night itself.

Yeah, I'd definitely not accounted for that. About a dozen more of those snarling beasts had been unleashed, which meant they'd seen through my ruse and were not planning to leave the girl unguarded to come chase after me. Panic surged through my blood as I thought about Hank.

If I knew anything about that dog, he would risk his life to save that girl. I didn't know how he'd lost his last handler—and it was stupid to think dogs could feel guilt—but something told me Hank felt his previous owner had died because he wasn't able to save them. Now, he was atoning for that mistake.

Blowing out a low whistle through my lips, I signaled for him to abandon his last command and return to me. There was no sight of him.

Fuck.

The crawlies stalked closer, pushing me westbound. Dammit. I didn't want to leave Hank. I whistled again but still, there was no sign of him. With another war cry, the Minotaur set his pack of dogs after me, leaving me little choice but to run. Reaching for the vial of holy water inside my jacket pocket, I doused myself in the liquid as I bolted. I knew there was no chance out running those creatures, but I knew the holy water would keep them from tearing into me at least until it dried off.

In the commotion, I lost sight of the Horseman. I scolded myself for not firing my gun. I had finally had the son of a bitch within a close shot, and I'd blown it. Hell knew when I'd get another chance. Rushing past debris and trying to put as much distance as possible between me and those animals, I came to an abrupt halt, almost tripping, when one leapt up and over me, landing a mere stone's throw in front, blocking my escape.

The beasts formed a circle, sniffing the air as they drew closer. Holy water alone wasn't enough to repel the creatures. In order to activate its magical properties, a prayer or holy verse needed to be recited. I never thought the time I'd spent pouring over scriptures with my grandmother would come in handy one day, but then again, I never actually believed the end would arrive with fire and brimstone.

Somehow, the words spilled from my lips on instinct. *"Even though I walk through the valley of the shadow of death, I will fear no evil, for You are with me; Your rod and Your staff, they comfort me. You prepare a table before me in the presence of my enemies; You anoint my head with oil; my cup overflows—"*

The nightcrawlers whined and whooped in agitation. Snarling, they bared their jagged, pointed teeth, black saliva dripping from their mouths. Catching the scent of the holy water, they squealed as the stench of blessed water scorched their noses.

Unstrapping the machete from the scabbard around my thigh, I said, "That's right. Touch me and you'll burn to ash!"

All of a sudden, a blinding light appeared out of nowhere, followed by a loud *bang* and a deep rumble under my feet that made the ground shake. Shutting my eyes to shield them from the light, I wobbled and fell backward from the impact of the crash.

The air froze in my lungs when I finally opened my eyes. Crouching inside the circle with me was another impossibility in this new world of impossibilities. With white wings expanding a good fifteen to twenty feet wide, a man rose to his feet. Well, not exactly a man, but what I could only imagine was an...

An angel.

Even among the ugly horrors of this world, he made you believe beauty still existed and he was the embodiment of it all. Clad in white and gold leather armor, he appeared majestic, powerful. His skin was luminescent, as if light itself flowed through his veins. A weapon flared in his hand—a sword made of fire.

In the blink of an eye, he swung the sword, slicing through nightcrawlers like they were butter. Shrieks exploded through the air as he gracefully danced with the skill of a deadly assassin. I'd never seen anything quite like it.

Quite like him.

It felt like my feet had sprouted roots and were now permanently attached to the ground. I couldn't move and could barely breathe as I stared at him in complete awe. Then a nightcrawler escaped his blade and stalked toward me, snapping me out of my daze. Tightly gripping my machete, I swung it at him, but the creature didn't flinch, it only snarled louder. I felt my body stiffen, but I shook my head, quickly knocking myself out of the stupor. I would not freeze. If this was how I was going to die, then I would die fighting. Right as I was about to charge, Hank leapt out from the shadows, growling with such ferocity I almost didn't recognize him.

Challenging the nightcrawler, he stood between me and the beast, refusing to let it near me. But the demon was three times Hank's size, with teeth sharper than razor blades. The creature charged and a scream erupted from my chest. The nightcrawler swiped one of its paws, clawing Hank's right side and knocking him sideways against one of the beat-up cars.

"No!"

Fury ripped through my muscles as I sliced the machete through the air, landing each blow against the nightcrawler's neck. It roared and lunged at me, hitting me in the chest with its head and flinging me back several yards. I landed against the broken pavement with a hard *thud*, every bone in my body cracking on impact.

Rolling to my side, I yelped as a stabbing sensation shot through my rib cage. I watched through tear-blurred vision as the creature shook its head, the cuts I'd inflicted a mere nuisance. Teeth bared and eyes flaming with pure evil, it sprung toward me. I managed to push up to my elbow, but the pain knocked me back down.

Accepting my fate, I closed my eyes and let Isabella's memory bring me peace. Her beautiful chocolate-brown eyes, her dark curls, her soft, little hands. Her smile that stole my heart every single time.

I'm coming, baby...

Holding my breath, I braced for the attack, but it never came.

Piercing white light flashed before my eyes as warm liquid splattered against my face. When the brightness subsided and I opened my eyes, the breath I'd been holding burst from my chest. The angel stood before me, his sword flaming. The nightcrawler's head lay severed at my side and that's when I realized I was covered in the beast's blood.

The angel's armor, as well as his face, was smeared with nightcrawler blood. Twice now, he'd saved me. The sight of him holding that sword and his glorious white wings spread wide arrowed through me and a myriad of emotions swirled in my chest. Ever since my parents' death, I had done nothing but hate on God and His false promises. And when Hell broke loose, unleashing every torment from our wildest nightmares, I grew convinced only hate existed in this world.

Had God finally remembered us? Was He finally sending us His saviors?

The angel's eyes shimmered, and a sense of peace enveloped me, healing my bones and calming the pain webbing through my body. Fresh tears ran down my face—not tears of loneliness and desperation, but tears of love and happiness. The memory of everything I'd lost was no longer the weight holding me down, but the wings lifting me up.

Hope lit inside me like a torch. Perhaps we could win this war. Perhaps all was not lost.

As I rose to my feet, that hope was violently stolen from me as a frenzy of hysteria stampeded through me the instant I saw the Minotaur rush toward us.

But I saw him too late. The creature swung his axe with such force, it knocked the angel down in one swing, hacking off one of his wings.

Horror vise-gripped my spine and my voice choked in my throat. All I could do was tremble as the Minotaur swung a second time, hacking off the other wing. The angel hollered, his bone-cracking cry echoing through the Heavens. As the Minotaur raised his axe for the final blow, an explosion rippled through the air as if a cannon had been fired. Several more explosions followed, then water rained down over us.

The Minotaur hissed as the water burned his hide.

I looked up and wondered who'd shot the holy water over us.

He roared as it took off, disappearing into the night, along with any remaining nightcrawlers. Snapping out of my terror, I rushed to the angel. Blood the color of the sun poured from his wounds. Turning him over, I cradled his head in my lap.

Wiping the nightcrawler blood from his cheeks, I said, "Tell me what to do. How do I help you?"

"Daughter of Eve, my time has ended. Now you must take arms."

"I don't understand."

Dipping a finger into his blood, he brought it up to my forehead and made the sign of the cross. "Blood of my blood. Flesh of my flesh."

"What are you doing?"

"Katherine Elizabeth Jones, in the name of the Father, and of the Son, and of the Holy Spirit, I anoint thee. No weapon that is fashioned against you shall succeed, and you shall confute every tongue that rises against you in judgment. This is the heritage of the servants of the Lord and their vindication from me, declares the Lord." He lifted his sword and the flame snuffed—all that remained was the glimmering blade. "Take my weapon, Daughter of Eve. Join your brethren and tell them more are coming. You have not been forsaken."

Wrapping my hand around the hilt, I stared in awe as the heat of his energy passed from him to me through the sword. The veins in my arm lit up with the same light I'd seen in his. When I finally looked back down, his eyes had dimmed. All life was gone from his body, but before I could even grasp what had just happened, his flesh turned to dust in my hands and blew away until nothing was left.

I remained on the ground, chest heaving, heart beating so hard it ached. I hung my head but was suddenly jolted to my feet by the squeal of tires braking. Quickly strapping the short sword to the knife holster on my thigh, I turned toward the approaching vehicle.

Looking like it'd just escaped a *Mad Max* movie, the BMW came to a screeching halt in front of me. It must have come from the eastbound side, where the bridge wasn't as torn up and was still attached to the mainland. The passenger window rolled down as a piece of rusted paint flicked off in the breeze, and the driver lowered the red scarf covering the bottom part of his face, revealing the man's striking features. Even with his jaw covered in a short, scraggly beard, he was arresting.

"Get in," he shouted, knocking me back into this world. He gestured for me to jump into the car.

The sight of another human drove a small smile to my lips, but it also gave me pause. Telling the good guys from the bad wasn't always easy, and aside from the girl on the bridge, I hadn't seen any survivors in weeks. Handsome or not, this guy was either a scavenger wanting to take advantage of a bad situation, or someone as stupid as me, trying to rescue a poor soul.

A chorus of yelps and whoops sounded off in the distance, filling my blood with alarm and sending my pulse galloping. Perhaps now was not the time to second-guess this guy's intentions.

"Well?" he pressed, his thick eyebrows climbing up his forehead. "You coming or what? Holy water's not gonna hold long."

The explosion. The holy water that had rained down and sent the beast running. He'd been the one who'd shot those water cannons?

I turned back to where the angel had fallen. What happened tonight? Ever since the world ended, the only things I'd seen roaming the streets were the spawns of Hell. Not once had I seen an angel or any divine being reveal themselves. There had been no signs that help was on the way. No signal that God was coming to judge the living and the dead. We'd been left behind to die on a land scorched by evil.

So what had changed?

I looked down at my hand, the one that had glowed with internal light. What that angel said about there being more on the way, had he meant angels? And he'd known my name. How was that possible? I peered back up to the Heavens and watched the moon shine brilliantly, her beauty everlasting. No matter how awful things got down here, she always put on her best dress and brightest smile, as if mocking our suffering.

Without another second to waste, I adjusted my backpack and accepted Mad Max's invitation.

BLOOD SACRIFICES
AND DEMON SUMMONING?

Fucking fantastic.
Dark and mysterious right from the get-go. Reeling you
in and poisoning your mind.
And that's exactly what the sect did—fill me with their
toxic vitriol.
I had no choice.
Lame excuse, I know. Everyone says they had no choice.
I was just too young, too stupid, and too fucking blind.
So, I helped their cause until I realized what they were
up to—but by then, it was too late.
The blood sacrifices I could deal with, even the
Summoning I could cope with. But raping countless
innocent women in the name of the Devil?
Fuck that.

FROM THE PAGES OF JAX CONSTANTINE'S GRIMOIRE
YEAR 2031

Learn to do good; seek justice, correct oppression; bring justice to the fatherless, plead the widow's cause.

ISAIAH 1:17

CHAPTER 2

JAX

"Buckle up, angel. It's gonna be a bumpy ride." Before making sure my unexpected passenger did as I said, I floored it. The car roared louder than I would have liked while trying not to alert demons of my presence. Once the car accelerated, taking us past the graveyard of corroded metal and off the bridge, I breathed a sigh of relief.

Slightly glancing over at the woman sitting on the passenger seat, I bit down on the smirk twitching at the corners of my mouth. It was a mere coincidence I happened to be in the same vicinity and close enough to reach her—and thank my lucky stars for that. I'd been minding my own business—though running a little later than usual—and hadn't planned to stay out past sundown. But when did anything go according to plan these days, anyway?

In a perfect world, getting in and out of the 200 Water Street apartment block would have been a piece of cake. The world hadn't been perfect before the Summoning, and it was far from perfect now. Raiding a skyscraper hadn't been my first choice—everyone knew they were an easy way to get ambushed—but my first choice had been wiped clean before I even arrived. There weren't many people crazy enough to risk entering the building, which was how I'd managed to gather a good haul before the party started on the bridge.

The wails had been loud enough to reach up to the forty-eighth floor, where I'd been about to break into another apartment. Which meant the noise had probably roused any damned lurking in the building. Which also meant the damned would've likely heard me rummaging through people's cupboards and belongings and had come to inspect, looking for fresh meat.

I had a few getaway tricks up my sleeve, but even *I* knew I'd be a goner when the screams coming from the bridge signaled that whatever was happening outside wasn't a typical hunt. If I'd not booked it out of there that instant, I would have been stuck between a horde of the damned and a large pack of *d'shiad.*

I'd raced down the service stairs to the beat-up BMW I'd hijacked and had every intention of avoiding the ruckus on the bridge when that fucking lightshow put a stop to that plan, too. It wasn't every day the sky lit up like the fucking Fourth of July, especially after the gates had opened.

I had to see what was going on. Staying upwind and in the shadows, I'd come close enough to see the woman fly across the bridge and crash against the pavement with a sickening *thud.*

She should've been dead.

Now, I spared a glance at her very alive body in my passenger seat. By some miracle, the beast hadn't killed her, but she must've broken at least a rib or two when he launched her. I'd seen her attempt to get back up, and she'd looked like a truck had run her over.

Yet her breathing was normal, and with the way she slumped against the seat, there was no way she could sit like that without putting pressure on fractured ribs, so she clearly had no injuries.

It didn't surprise me, really. The angelic warrior had likely healed her right before the biggest *d'shiad* I'd ever seen cut straight through one of his wings. When I saw that barbaric creature raise his axe, I knew I had to do something, or I'd lose my opportunity to capture the angel alive. On instinct, I'd pulled my hand cannon and four holy-water-filled projectiles off my belt. My last ones, of course.

By the time I'd raised the weapon to aim, the *d'shiad* had chopped off the second wing. A heart-crushing cry exploded from the holy creature, and I didn't think twice. I fired the damn cannon four times, then ran for the BMW I'd hotwired.

Only one thought raced through my mind as I'd slammed on the gas; I had to get to the angel. He was my last chance at finding a way to get rid of the parasite living inside me. I needed to make it. The tires screeched as I took off toward the opportunity of salvation, but still, I arrived too late.

The angel died. I shouldn't have expected anything else when I saw the holy creature land in the midst of the chaos. Angels were impressive warriors and fought to the death to defend God's children. Still, I'd hoped he would have survived long enough to cleanse me.

Hope is a bitch.

All I got was a pile of ash and the woman in my passenger seat.

Well, the woman and the holy relic strapped to her thigh— its magic pulsing through the car like bass in a nightclub. I'd never been close enough to an Empyrean weapon to feel the vibrations, but I'd never expected the powerful energy coursing through the car to hit me like a hurricane. I did my best to concentrate on driving, but ignoring the waves of energy was damn-near impossible.

"How'd you do it?" I asked, glancing her way, trying to distract my mind from the pulsating energy force. My voice came out raspier than I was used to. Ever since my escape from headquarters, I hadn't really talked to many people. How long had it been? Weeks? Months? Other than an occasional trade run, I stayed to myself. It hadn't taken me to looney-ville quite yet, but given another week or two, I might've started talking to myself just to hear anything other than the rats scurrying around inside the walls of my hideout.

She turned toward me, and from the corner of my eyes, I saw her eyebrows pinch. "Do what?"

"How'd you summon an angel?" I knew all about summoning demons—lived for it, bled for it. Practice makes perfect, and I had plenty. Angels didn't work that way, though. I'd tried. Man, how I tried. No matter what I did, I hadn't managed to make contact. Certain holy prayers could work, but the circumstances had to be unique and dire, and I doubted any angels would heed a prayer from someone like me.

"I didn't summon him," she replied as if I'd asked her a stupid question. "He appeared out of nowhere. Hank and I were… Oh, my God. Hank! We have to go back for him."

When I didn't lay off the gas, she banged on the dashboard. "Hey, slow down!"

The woman's hands flailed as she pivoted in her seat, looking for Hank on the streets as if he'd ran after the car all the way from the Brooklyn Bridge to the corner of 6th Ave and Canal Street.

"Look," I said, "whoever you were with is most likely dead. The best you can do is let it go and worry about your own life."

"Hank is not dead!" she cried, spinning toward me. The heat of her gaze was as palpable as a hot iron. "Turn the car around."

I shifted toward her as she yanked off her seatbelt and a flash of silver around her finger caught my eye.

Fuck. She's married.

"We're not going back," I ordered. "Put your seatbelt back on."

There was nothing we could do for her husband. There'd been too many *d'shiad* on the bridge, and there was no way he was still alive. And if, by some miracle, he was, he'd be smart enough to find shelter on his own.

"You don't have to come with me," she spat. "Just stop the car and let me out."

We were on West Street, riding toward the Lincoln Tunnel. We had to get out of Manhattan—it was crazy for both of us to be this close to headquarters after dark. The Holland Tunnel was a wreck, and the George Washington Bridge was too far away. We'd have to risk the Lincoln. I wasn't going to let her out. She wouldn't make it back to the Brooklyn Bridge, anyway—she'd be dead in minutes. And I sure as hell wasn't letting my chance at that weapon slip away so easily.

"Nothing survives a pack of *d'shiad*," I reiterated. "The sooner you accept it, the easier it'll be."

For the both of us.

As if she hadn't heard a word I'd said, she reached for the door handle.

We were going a hundred miles an hour, and she thought it was a great idea to open the door? I slammed the brakes before she could endanger the both of us or kill herself jumping out of the speeding vehicle, all in the name of love.

The change in velocity took her by surprise and she flew against the dashboard, letting go of the door she'd opened. The door flapped against the wind like a baby bird learning to fly before it came to a halt. Leaning across her seat, I pulled her door closed, locking it for good measure.

"Are you trying to get yourself killed?" I didn't mean to linger that close to her. Hell, I'd meant to pull back and drive the fuck off the moment the door was securely shut, but I was unable to move. I didn't realize what triggered my personal inner-demon until I was hit by a whiff of sweat, blood, and underneath all that grime, something distinctly female.

You caught us a toy, a gravelly voice only I could hear whispered in my ear.

Fuck me.

My eyes roamed down her delicate neck to the curve of her chest. The tight top she wore revealed a generous five-star view of her breasts. Encouraged by the sight, my eyes traveled lower, drinking in her slender shape, all the way down to where she gripped the angelic blade.

The beautiful metallic glint snapped me out of my trance and I slunk back into my seat. As much as I needed that damn sword to save me, I also knew the danger it posed.

I took a few cleansing breaths, then dared a quick glance her way. I hadn't had the chance to truly appreciate her intense beauty. She was alluring—there was no doubt about that—but not just physically. She'd challenged those beasts when she'd clearly never stood a chance. The woman had balls of steel, and I liked that. Admired it.

Fierce and stunning.

The demon inside me growled, his desire broadcasting through my veins like a hit of heroin—she would be a delicious treat for him, the fix he'd been craving. Pinching the bridge of my nose, I took several deep breaths, suppressing that part of myself back to where it belonged. In the fires of Hell.

It kept resisting me.

Gripping the steering wheel, I ground my teeth for several heartbeats.

"Please, take me back to the bridge," she said, her voice trembling. "I have to find Hank."

I'd frightened her. Either she saw the hunger in my eyes or felt it. Giving into her pleas, I turned the car around.

It was easier to ignore the pulsing of the blade if I chanted something, *anything*, inside my brain. I was counting streets by the time we got back to Center, the burnt down high-rise buildings lining the riverside a harsh welcome.

I drove onto the bridge with more stealth than the first time. Flicking the headlights off, I slowed the car to a quiet purr. Moonlight shone through a thin veil of clouds, partially illuminating the way and giving me enough visibility to keep from driving into the abandoned cars. The shadows cast by the moon's pale light seemed as if they were hiding something within their depths, and there was a good chance they were. It was eerily quiet, the voice in my head coming to a curious pause as I took in the unsettling calm.

Scorched, hollowed-out cars lay strewn about, shattered glass glinting off in the moonlight. Cracked slabs of concrete and mangled steel cables added to the obstacle course. A metal pole pierced through the top of a minibus and farther back, a half blown-up military tank blocked the way.

We were almost to the spot where I'd picked her up when my passenger jumped out of the car before I came to a full stop. The woman ran off toward the center of the bridge, hollering her husband's name into the night.

"Jesus Christ, you're gonna get us killed," I gritted as I stopped the car and jumped out. With no holy water left, I had no efficient way of repelling any more of the devils. Checking my handgun, I released a frail sigh of relief. I had a few rounds of infused bullets left, but that wouldn't be enough to take down the pack of *d'shiad* that'd claimed the bridge only twenty minutes prior.

I ran after the woman as she continued to shout her husband's name toward the wrecked cars.

"Stop yelling," I whispered harshly as I joined her. "Honestly, I'd rather be stuck in a real-life Jurassic Park and have velociraptors hunting me than what's actually out here."

She shot me a pointed look but stayed quiet. I was just about to tell her that if Hank hadn't responded to her yelling by now, then he was probably not there anymore when a whimper arose from the military tank. It didn't sound like anything human, and I tried to pull her back in case it was a trap, but she bolted before I had a chance to grab her.

Damn this woman.

Following her with more caution, I gripped my gun and kept it aimed, but was forced to pick up my pace when she disappeared behind the tank.

"Hank!" Her excited voice echoed through the bridge, and I felt my entire body cringe. How the fuck had she survived this long with such poor survival skills?

"Hey, buddy, are you alright?" Her voice was calmer, but her comment caught me by surprise. Not what I expected she'd say if she'd actually found her husband. When I reached the tank and saw her crouched next to an injured, dripping wet German Shepherd, my mouth went dry.

This was Hank? A muscle in my jaw tightened. We came back for a *dog*.

"You hid in the water, didn't you?" she cooed, ruffling his fur. "Smart boy."

"We've got to go," I reminded her. Distant howls coming from the city hiked my urgency up several notches. Sounded like the pack of *d'shiad* had caught our scent. Not to mention all the ruckus she'd made had been loud enough to wake the dead.

Apparently, the howls did not spur the same sense of dread in her as the woman looked unfazed. Instead, she remained crouched next to the dog, scanning the bridge as if searching for someone else. For a moment, all I could do was stare at her in utter disbelief. A pack of the same creatures who had quite literally killed an angel before her eyes—and would have shredded her to pieces if I hadn't showed up—were racing our way and somehow, she remained unperturbed. As if we weren't about to get ambushed.

How *had* she fucking survived all this time?

The intensity of her eyes as she seemed to turn over every rock and scrap of metal with her gaze, looking for whatever else she'd lost, was remarkable. I gulped hard. I *feared* I'd have to haul her over my shoulder to drag her ass off this bridge.

Her dark hair was pulled up in a ponytail, with a few loose tendrils framing her face, showcasing her sharp cheekbones, delicate nose, and full lips. Had we not been seconds from turning into *d'shiad* dinner, her mesmerizing beauty would have taken my breath away.

Taking the dog's face in her hands, she leaned in close and stared deeply into his eyes. "Where is she, Hank? Where's the girl?"

The dog whined and lowered his head.

"What girl?" I asked, then remembered the screams I'd heard. They hadn't belonged to just my passenger—at least, not all of them. I puffed out a long breath. I knew where she was going with this.

She turned her attention to me. "Those things probably took her. We've got to—"

"Don't you fucking say it," I cut her off. "We're not rescuing anyone else. By now, she's probably already been—" I paused, realizing she wouldn't be ready to hear what I had to say. That the young woman had likely already been tortured, raped, and forced to carry a demonic child until she either died of a pregnancy-gone-wrong or gave birth to the anti-Christ.

I couldn't reveal any of that, though. Not if I wanted a chance at taking that blade. "There is nothing we can do for her," I went on. "We can still get out of here, angel, but we have to go. Now."

More yelps and whoops erupted into the night, but closer this time. The woman's eyes flashed with worry as she looked up at me.

Finally, we agree on something.

"Come, buddy. Let's go," she encouraged the dog. He attempted to walk, limping after her, but it was clear that crawling out of the water and up the broken pieces of concrete and metal had taken a toll on the animal. At this pace, we wouldn't reach the BMW before the *d'shiad* reached us.

I stopped and cursed when the first monster appeared at the far end of the bridge, letting out a thunderous roar that raised a cacophony of screeches around the vicinity.

"There you have it," I muttered under my breath. "All that noise you made summoned the alpha."

"The alpha?"

"Think of it like the super-smart velociraptor version of the things that attacked you earlier."

Sliding in next to me, she put her back against mine as she scanned the rest of the bridge. "What's with you and dinosaurs?"

"What? You never watched *Jurassic Park*?"

She sighed. "Everything before the end is a blur to me at this point."

My brow dipped and I shot her an appalled look over my shoulder. "Woman, *Jurassic Park* is a classic. And just like the raptors in the movie, there's no fighting these guys and winning to tell the story, especially without the right ammo. We have to run."

"Hank won't make it."

In other words, if someone didn't carry him, she'd die on this bridge with her dog. Even though the woman looked stronger than I'd first estimated, I knew her dog probably weighed more than half her weight, and if someone was going to carry him, then that *someone* had to be me. I stopped next to the limping animal and reached down to pick him up, but he took one sniff of me and snarled, baring his teeth.

Fucking great.

"We are on the same side, dude," I barked. I knew what he was smelling, though—all the *d'shiad* carried the same stink. I wouldn't trust me either, but I had to win his trust or we'd turn into chopped liver soon.

"Hank, it's okay," the woman said. "*He's* okay. Let him help you."

My second attempt at picking up the dog went better, but once we took off running, the soaking wet, ninety-pound German Shepherd did not make me feel better about our chances at making it to the car. The *d'shiad* had clogged our escape route. Fleeing toward Brooklyn would have been a better option.

"I'm hoping you've got some vials of holy water," I grunted as we sped toward where I'd left the car, but as we neared the stolen vehicle, a *d'shiad* jumped over the roof of the BMW, a vicious snarl twisting its monstrous face into an even more gruesome sight.

"You were the one with the waterworks," she volleyed back.

"Which is why I'm out," I muttered, not taking my eyes off the monster. I refused to let one *d'shiad* slow us down. Even as my breathing hitched, I forced my feet to move faster. I needed to focus past the stabbing pain taking root in my arms and legs.

"You know how to shoot that gun?" I nodded toward the Glock I'd seen strapped to her thigh.

"I've got no bullets."

Figured.

The alpha had gathered some company, and at least seven of his homies surrounded the car. The Minotaur who had killed the angel with his axe was nowhere in sight, which was about the only good thing about our situation.

I dropped the dog, and he let out a yelp as he landed. "Sorry, bud." I needed my hands. Gripping my gun gave me a touch of confidence. There was no choice but to shoot our way through. "I'll guide them away. You get in the car," I said.

But she had other plans. Of course she did. Because why would Ms. Death-Wish listen to reason?

The woman pulled out the angelic blade and didn't even give me a chance to take the lead. The *d'shiad* cheered at her approach, as if welcoming her challenge. Perhaps they had no clue what she held in her grip.

Though they'd soon learn.

I didn't have a clue how well she could handle the blade, but I knew she was fearless. Either way, Empyrean weapon or not, I wasn't exactly one hundred percent comfortable leaving my life in her hands, so I trained my gun on the beast closest to us, just in case.

Before I could take my next breath, her short sword burst into a fiery glow, bathing the bridge in a brilliant spectacle. The whoops and howls ceased at the sight, drowning us in deafening silence. It felt as if the night was even holding her breath, waiting to see what this woman would do next.

We didn't have to wait long.

The stars blinked in slow motion as this woman-turned-angelic-warrior sprinted toward the beasts, spinning like a killer ballerina as she sliced through demon flesh, blood and limbs flying in her wake.

After watching their pack members fall to her blade, the remaining creatures approached with more caution, staying clear when she slashed the sword with impressive speed, as if she'd trained with God's Heavenly Army.

She'd literally just been gifted the weapon, yet she fought like a—

Shit. A Guardian.

Things had just gotten a whole ton more complicated, with a heavy dose of fucked-up thrown in for funsies.

But there was no time to dwell on that little tidbit.

The creature pawing at the ground mere feet from her stood zero chances against her blade and fury. She managed to reach it before it even had a second to react, carving the monster into pieces in a blur of fluid strokes. The thunderous energy of the weapon vibrated through the air, stronger now than it had been in the car.

It was enough to give the third *d'shiad* a pause of hesitation, which cost it its life. Another thought it clever to sneak up on her from the side while she battled the fourth. I gave in to my twitching finger and showered it with bullets. It was enough to stop it dead in its tracks and gave her sword an opening.

In the glow of the sword, I saw more—way too many more—of the *d'shiad* crawling closer. I shot two, then picked up Hank and ran the rest of the way to the car. Tucking him into the backseat, I slammed the door shut. He let out a loud whine. Unfortunately, in the rush, I had not been able to prevent him from landing on his injured side.

Aiming my gun, I turned toward the sword-wielding woman and shot the beast stalking behind her. She jerked back when she heard the gunshot, then dodged the beast still trying to claw her eyes out. Winking at me as a short smile twitched her lips, she returned to battle as if she'd not been seconds from losing her life.

Well, hell if that wasn't fucking sexy.

The beast I shot shook its head and the bullet I fired fell to the ground, leaving only a slight mark on its forehead. Its dark gaze turned toward me, and its black maw stretched into a vicious snarl. I shot two more rounds, but they only made the beast pause for a beat.

"Leave it," I shouted at the woman as she kept sparring with the same beast. "There's too many. We need to go."

I jumped behind the wheel just as I spotted a beast barreling toward my driver's side. Snarling, its teeth were longer and thicker. Its muscles moved like a wave of mountains, and a mane twice as long as that of the rest of his pack flared around its massive head.

The alpha.

Fuck.

Swallowing thickly, I rushed to slam the door in its face, but it leapt onto the hood, clawing at the windshield.

Turning toward the woman, my gut clenched when I saw her trapped between two newcomers. A string of curses flew from my mouth as I emptied my clip into the beasts. After a *click,* I dropped my smoking gun onto the passenger seat.

I was officially out of ammo.

Starting the ignition, I flashed the headlights, lighting the hell around us. There must have been at least thirty more of those fuckers stalking toward us.

"Get in!" I shouted at the demon killer.

She looked around and seemed to finally realize we were seriously outnumbered. Running toward the car, she yanked open the door to the backseat and jumped in next to her dog.

Now the whole bridge crawled with *d'shiad.*

Stepping on the gas, we peeled away, forcing the alpha sprawled on top of the hood to slide off. The windshield cracked from the weight of the beast's pounding paws, scratches spider-webbing across the glass. The claw marks on the windshield made it a bitch to navigate through the horde of growling beasts.

I drove into two of them as I sped off the bridge, their bodies flying over the roof. One tried to stay on top of the car, the screeching of its nails dragging against the metal as it searched for a grip reverberated through the car. I jerked the wheel to avoid a group of three more beasts standing in the middle of the road, and the one on top of the roof flew off.

We had to get out of the city, which meant we had no choice but to brave the Lincoln Tunnel. The hollers and wails followed us all the way to 11th Ave.

I glanced at her over my shoulder. "I fucking hope this was worth it, angel."

She sat with the dog's head on her lap, running her slender fingers through his fur as she tried to reassure him that he would be okay. Clumps of his fur slew off. That was not a good sign.

The injury appeared to be more serious than I'd thought. If he'd been clawed by one of those things, we had a much bigger problem on our hands.

"It's Kate," she said out of the blue.

"Come again?" I said over my shoulder.

"My name. It's Kate."

For some reason, hearing her name stirred something inside me. She was no longer the random woman I'd rescued from the bridge—as if she really needed any rescuing from the way she'd just fought off those beasts—and that made thinking about why I'd really tried to help her harder to justify.

I shook those thoughts from my mind. "You better hope we get out of here, Kate. We're taking the tunnel." One of the *d'shiad* chasing us punched through the back window, showering Kate in shards of glass. She let out a scream as I spun the wheel, making the car whirl and knocking the beast off the trunk. It slammed into the other two beasts running behind it.

"Jesus, how fast can those things run?" she asked as the car came to an abrupt stop.

Shifting back into drive and revving the engine, I said, "Very."

I caught a glimpse of her through the rearview mirror as we sped down the highway. Kate shifted in the seat to look out through what used to be the back window. Wind wheezed through the broken glass and the cries behind us magnified.

"Fucking nightcrawlers."

"Nightcrawlers?" I asked.

"The things chasing us," she said, leaning in close to my seat. "Why? What do you call them?"

It wasn't what I called them; it was what they *were* called. "*D'shiad.* Demons spawned by Hell's unholy fire. Those particular ones are the Devil's personal hunting dogs."

"You're telling me those are actual hellhounds?"

I nodded. "And once they're on your trail, they don't let up."

She leaned back in her seat, her aroma trailing in her wake. Even with demon guts covering her body, I was still able to discern her distinct scent. It wasn't anything exotic or unnatural; just her simple, yet intoxicating female pheromones, and it poked at the animal trapped inside.

A part of me was thankful she'd sat back, but the other part of me clawed at my chest.

"What about you?" she asked.

"What about me?"

"Your name."

My name wasn't something I offered freely to perfect strangers, but I guessed after escaping a pack of hellhounds together, I could at least give her that. "Jackson. But call me Jax."

"Thank you for what you did back there, Jax."

Peering at her through the rearview mirror again, I caught her staring off through the window. Her gaze seemed lost. "You okay?"

Turning, she briefly met my gaze in the mirror before I turned my eyes back onto the road. "When you first helped me off that bridge, you asked me how I'd summoned that angel."

"Quite an impressive show."

"What made you believe I'd summoned him?"

"Angels are not allowed to meddle in human affairs unless they are sent by God, Himself, or they are summoned—some would say *invoked*, but it's the same difference if you ask me. Anyway, given the state of affairs, I doubt God had anything to do with it."

"I didn't do anything to call him forth."

"Something powerful compelled that angel to offer you his aid in battle. That, my warrior princess, is no simple feat. Not to mention the fact he gave you his sword. That makes you pretty special."

"None of this makes any sense," she said with a troubled breath. Glancing over my shoulder, I saw her wipe a tear from the corner of her eye as she stared down at her dog. He'd stopped whining and was breathing heavily. "He said more were coming. What do you make of that?"

I wished I knew, but at the moment, we had a more pressing matter. The howls weren't subsiding, which meant we needed to find a place to hole up until sunup. Problem was, those beasts had our scent; they would find us, even if we dug ourselves all the way through to China. The only way to find safety would be to seek refuge on hallowed ground. A cemetery could provide some protection, but we'd be too exposed. And not all burial sites were as holy as you would think.

The only other option was a church, but the thought made my skin crawl. It wasn't because I had anything personal against churches, but the demon prowling under my flesh would no doubt put up a fight. As its human vessel, my body would protect it from true harm, but it would still feel some of the effects of being in a sacred place and he—I—wasn't looking forward to it.

As we neared our exit, we passed a slightly crooked overhead sign with the words *Lincoln Tunnel*. Peering down at the fuel gauge, my heart sank. We had less than a quarter tank left. I made a sharp turn and hoped we wouldn't run out of gas before we made it across to Jersey.

The screeches of the *d'shiad* accompanied us all the way to the tunnel's entrance. Their cries echoed off the tunnel walls as we were sucked into the darkness. Similar to the rest of the city, the tunnel was littered with broken-down vehicles. Getting through would be a bitch. And if the way was blocked, then we'd have to trek the rest of the way on foot in the darkness with an injured, ninety-pound dog.

The air grew rancid as we rolled through the tunnel, reeking of blood and rot.

The damned. Of course.

Because why wouldn't the awful creatures be camped out inside a dark, musky tunnel? Just as the thought crossed my mind, the first of the mutated humans jumped in front of my headlights and was promptly mushed under the tires.

The wet *crunch* bounced through the tunnel, announcing our presence. "Hold on to your butt, angel," I said. "Things are about to get interesting."

He who dwells in the shelter of the Most High will abide in the shadow of the Almighty.

PSALM 91:1 - 16

CHAPTER 3

KATE

The car bounced as whatever we'd run over made a horrific *cracking* sound. "What the hell was that?" I asked, repositioning Hank off my lap so I could take a closer look out of the broken windshield.

It was impossible to see clearly in the darkness of the tunnel, but that's when I heard it. Ear-splitting squawks and shrills broke through the thick air around us. The hairs on my skin stood on end as my entire body tensed.

"A horde," Jax said as he increased speed, weaving around the wreckage littering the tunnel, the headlights illuminating the horror lurking in the shadows. "Fact it's the least damaged exit out of the city also means the damned use it as a trap to capture would-be victims. A.K.A., assholes like us needing to escape the hungry pack of dogs waiting on the other end."

"Damned? You mean, the devoured."

"Call them what you will, angel, but they're still sorry-ass souls who didn't die from the infection. I'd rather die the painful death from the disease than turn into one of those things. So, do me a favor; you ever see me becoming one of them…” He pointed to his temple and mock-shot himself.

“Ditto,” I said as I climbed over the middle console to sit in the passenger seat. Unintendedly, my gaze dropped to his thighs as I positioned myself over the seat and I couldn’t help the lump that formed in my throat. His jeans fit snuggly against his crotch and the sight of his bulge made my pulse uptick like some lioness in heat. I’d clearly not been around a man for far too long to have this type of reaction while in the middle of getting chased by demon dogs and zombies.

Setting his empty gun in the glove compartment, I blew out a cooling breath, hoping to settle the feline clawing at me from inside.

Settle down, Kate. It’s just all the adrenaline hammering through your veins.

As I buckled, a clawed hand hit my window, causing me to jerk back. “Shit. Get us the fuck out of this tunnel!”

“What does it look like I’m doing?”

“Drive faster!”

“Woman, don’t you see the obstacle course in front of us? Any faster and I’ll add our car to the pile of wreckage.”

More clawed hands hit and scraped against the car. One creature slammed into the side of Jax’s door, causing him to lean into me as we both lurched to the side.

“Motherfucker!” Jax hollered, his muscled shoulder brushing up against mine. The musky, masculine scent that wafted from the exposed skin on his neck made my entire body tense.

The enraged screams of the damned reverberated through the tunnel as more swarmed out of the shadows, forcing my attention away from my very inappropriate and inopportune thoughts.

Grabbing the door handle to keep from bouncing all over the place, I said, “How much farther?”

Jax gripped the steering wheel, his eyes wild yet focused on the road. "Caught a glimpse of the New York/New Jersey border sign a few yards back. So not much farther, provided there aren't any huge blockades—"

Just as he said that, the headlights illuminated a dilapidated wire fence about five hundred feet ahead, blocking the exit. Several devoured lurked along the walls, waiting for their trap to snag them a snack. "You have to punch through," I said, looking back to make sure Hank was still okay and hadn't been knocked around in the commotion.

"I don't know how secure that fence is. We could end up trashing the car, trapping ourselves inside."

"If we don't punch through, we're as good as dead, anyway. We don't have much of a choice."

He slammed a fist against the steering wheel. "Fuck. We don't have room to accelerate."

"Just fucking floor it!" I braced myself, holding my breath as Jax pressed hard on the gas, the engine sputtering as it struggled to reach high velocity. Jax swerved us away from a broken-down SUV, which caused us to tailspin. We hit the side of the tunnel, and my neck whiplashed, but luckily, the car kept moving, which meant we hadn't totaled it. Jax reached his hand out over my chest to keep me from smacking my head forward into the dash.

"Shit. You okay?" he asked, eyes drifting down to where his hand met my breasts.

I followed his gaze, and he snatched his hand back as I said, "I'm fine. Don't slow down."

"Yes, ma'am." Shifting gears, he straightened the car and gunned it for the fence. I let out a scream as we slammed into it, metal scraping against the exterior of the car as we tore the fence from its hinges. Two of the devoured lunged for the car, and as one landed on the hood, another scream erupted from my throat.

The creature held on as Jax exited the tunnel, digging its claws into the frame and refusing to let go. That thing was relentless.

"Do you have anything in here I can use to knock this asshole off?" I asked, looking around for something, but not really knowing what.

"Try that sword of yours."

Right. Good idea.

Unstrapping the sword from my thigh, I unbuckled my seatbelt and rolled down the window. I swung my arm out, but even with the sword, I couldn't reach. Jax swerved to try to get it to fall off, but the thing had its massive claws pierced deep into the hood.

"This is not gonna work. I need to get closer. Keep the car steady," I said.

"What are you planning?"

"Just keep us steady." I pulled myself out through the window, my ass sitting on the edge of the opening.

"Jesus Christ. You're gonna get yourself killed," Jax hollered.

"Hold my legs, dammit. I almost got him." I swung the sword and nearly lost my balance when we hit a pothole. "Fuck!"

Jax's fingers tightened on my thigh as he gripped my pants to keep me from falling out of the car. "I've got you."

The devoured bared its ugly maw at me, those black saliva-dripping fangs threatening to tear into me.

"Not me, asshole. Not today." Repositioning myself on the edge of the window, I made sure Jax had a firm grip on me before I stretched myself as far out as I could, swinging the flaming sword down on the creature with every ounce of strength I possessed. The sword cut straight through the arm nearest me, slicing it right at the elbow. The thing wailed as it flew off the car, the severed hand flailing but still attached to the car by its claws.

Disgusted, I whacked it off with the sword, then slithered back into the passenger seat. As I blew out a ragged breath, I glanced down and noticed Jax still gripped my thigh, his fingers curling inward near my center. "You can let go now," I said, though I couldn't deny the small thrill that rippled through me at having his broad hand so close to my lady parts.

"Oh shit. Sorry about that." Pulling his hand back, he ran it through his shaggy brown hair a couple of times before bringing it to the steering wheel. "Fucking hell. You're batshit crazy." He winked at me as he took the main road toward Hoboken. "I mean that in a good way. That was some Black Widow shit you pulled back there."

I raised a brow. "Black Widow?"

"Natasha Romanov," he said, glancing at me and cocking his brow.

I stared. Was he serious?

His eyes widened. "*Marvel... The Avengers...?*"

Shaking my head, I puffed out a breath as I sank into my seat. "Another movie reference?"

"Another movie?" His voice climbed an octave, his face contorted in utter shock. "Woman, do you not know who the Avengers are?"

When I said nothing, he sat back in his seat, shoulders deflated, chest caved in. "Unreal. First human I've had contact with in forever, and she doesn't even know who the Avengers are."

This grown man was sulking like a child over comic book superheroes, and I couldn't help but burst out laughing. And it was the first time I'd laughed—actually laughed—since... I couldn't even remember when. Maybe it was the adrenaline still pumping through my system, but damn if it didn't feel good to laugh.

"What's so funny?"

"Oh my God. *You.* We literally just outran a pack of Sh—whatever—you called them. Nightcrawlers. We escaped a tunnel full of the infected, and all you can talk about are dudes in tights."

"Dudes in—" he growled as he cut himself off from repeating my insult. But he wasn't truly mad. The playful rumble rolling from his chest warmed my insides in a way I didn't expect. All of a sudden, the air grew too thick in the car—and that was with my window still down.

Feeling a tad uncomfortable, I shifted in my seat.

He glanced my way. "Black Widow. Not a dude."

I smirked, avoiding his gaze.

"So, you do know who the Avengers are."

"Of course, I do," I said, turning toward him and crossing my arms. "Just feels weird talking about them like they are something *real*. Like any of that still matters. Movies. Actors. Superheroes. Feels like a lifetime ago, you know. Like a completely different world."

Coming to an intersection, he looked both ways before crossing the road. I guess obeying traffic laws was muscle memory. "That's because it *is* a different world. But we can't forget where we came from. Not if we're going to get it back."

"You really think there's a way back from all this?" I looked out the window as he slowly drove through the streets of Hoboken and gestured to the torn down brownstones, the scorched cars littering the streets. The garbage. The signs of decomposing flesh. The occasional husk of a corpse. "From all this death? All this destruction?"

"We have to rebuild."

Heat flushed my skin, bitterness building in my mouth as I sat up straighter and glared at him. "Rebuild *what*? Have you looked around? There is nothing left for us to rebuild from. There's only survival at this point. And honestly, sometimes I wonder what the point is, anyway."

He stopped at another intersection and looked at me. "Of surviving?"

I sighed and let my shoulders relax. "Of anything." Glancing back at Hank, something in me tightened with worry. His breathing had eased, but he laid motionless on the seat, his eyes partially closed. "He's in pain. I need to get him medical attention. Do you have a first aid kit somewhere?"

"Back at my place, but that's in Manhattan."

"We're gonna need to scavenge for something. I need to patch him up."

Looking up and down Washington Street, Jax seemed to be searching for something. "Right now, we need to hole up until sunrise. It won't be long until more *d'shiad* catch our scent. I need to find a church."

"Why a church?" I asked as he turned down one of the side streets.

"Hallowed ground. Demons are forbidden from stepping foot on blessed soil. A church is as blessed as it gets."

"Are you certain about this?"

"Trust me."

"Well, that tidbit of information might've been helpful when those shits first arrived here. How come I've not heard about this?"

He shrugged. "It's not an airtight solid option for protection, and sometimes it doesn't work. Demons are forbidden from doing a lot of things, but it doesn't mean they won't test the boundaries. They've made our world their playground. Out here, we play by their rules."

"Then why even bother looking for a church? Let's just find shelter in one of these brownstones." I pointed to one that didn't look too ransacked.

"No use. They will tear through brick and mortar to get to us. We need a church. With the right materials and spell, I can make it almost impenetrable."

"Almost?"

He shot me a sideways glance. "What? You prefer barely or not at all?"

Good point. I puffed out a breath as I re-tied my hair back in a tight ponytail. "So, you're a wizard?"

He laughed, and that deep rumble of his crawled through me again. What the heck was wrong with me? I'd just met this guy and all of a sudden, he was making me feel all sorts of odd things I'd completely forgotten even existed. It had to be the fact I hadn't been near a man since Roger—

I closed my eyes, smudging the memory before it could take root in my chest and guide me down a very dark path.

"I know some… things," he said. "Point is, we need to get to a church and pray there's holy water stashed somewhere, along with the church's holy relic."

I didn't even bother asking him any more questions. Truth was, as much I'd not wanted to let the past sneak up on me, it had. I usually tried not to think much about the time before the world ended and when I did, it was because I'd scavenged a bottle of wine and allowed myself the occasional glass.

The only thing that mattered now was making sure Hank was okay. As Jax continued to drive along the narrow streets looking for a church, I mentally took note of any homes that didn't look too pilfered. I was certain there was a pharmacy back on Washington Street, but by now, it'd probably been picked clean.

By first light, I'd make my way back through these brownstones. I needed to find a first aid kit. Resting my head back, I allowed myself the small reprieve. The night was eerily silent—too silent for my own comfort. Dark clouds had gathered around the moon and the winking stars were too few to offer much light. Soon we'd probably be running from more demons, battling for our lives. This recharge wouldn't last long.

A rapid beeping sound roused me out of my thoughts. I turned to Jax and saw him tapping the fuel gauge—a reminder of how badly we needed to get off the streets.

"How much longer do we have?" I asked.

"Not much. If we don't find a church in the next few minutes, we'll have to continue on foot."

As soon as he turned off Willow Avenue and onto 9th Street, I spotted a tower looming over the rest of the roofs. "There," I said, pointing at the dilapidated sign outside a small brick church. "Hoboken Free Church. Bingo."

Jax slammed on the brakes, coming to a full stop in front of the church. He squinted as he scanned the small overgrown lawn.

"What is it?" I bit out, not understanding why we weren't rushing to get inside.

"It's not a Catholic church."

"Are you kidding me? Demons care about denomination?'

"That's not it. Before the 1960s, Catholic churches were required to have a relic sealed inside the altar. Without it, the spell will be weak."

As if on cue, a knowing whoop and yelp echoed through the night, followed by a chorus of them. The menacing calls bounced off the brick buildings around us.

"Shit. They found us." Jax shifted the car back into drive. "We're fucked."

Raiding my bank of memories, I tried to orient myself, searching for breadcrumbs. I'd been to Hoboken countless times with Roger while we were dating. There were plenty of churches scattered throughout the city, many of them Catholic.

Think, Kate. Think.

Jax was about to pull out onto the street when I reached out and placed my hand on his wrist. "Wait. Save the gas. No point in driving in circles."

"We're sitting ducks if we just stay here."

"Give me a second. I think I remember where we are. There's a Catholic church close by."

The yelps grew closer and louder. As I looked up and down the street, I noticed things moving in the shadows. Dammit. We weren't only being hunted by nightcrawlers, but the devoured had probably heard us, too. Just as I was about to give up on trying to remember, I spotted a broken-down pharmacy sign down the block.

"I got it. I remember now. Down the street. There." I pointed to the pharmacy down the block.

"I don't know what you're pointing at."

"The pharmacy. Drive toward it. Five blocks, then make a left. Go."

Without another word, he pressed on the gas and sped us down the street, the car beginning to sputter. Jax tapped on the gauge. "Come on, honey. Not yet. Give daddy a little more juice."

The way he said those words made warmth pool in my belly. Pool even lower.

What the heck is wrong with me?

A block away from 5th Street, the car finally died.

Jax ripped his seatbelt off and threw his door open. "We gotta get out now. Go. Go. Go."

Flinging my door open, I jumped out and reached for the backdoor. "We have to carry Hank."

"I got him. Just get us to that church."

As Jax pulled Hank out of the backseat and hauled him over his shoulder, a nightcrawler landed on the roof of the car, flattening it. "*Shit.* My gear. It's in the backseat," he hollered as he backed away from the car.

"Forget your stuff. We have to run. This way." I took off down the street, Jax trailing behind me with Hank on his shoulder. As I came to the intersection of Clinton and 5th, a nightcrawler cut me off from making a left. On instinct, I reached for the angelic sword and sliced through the air a couple of times before it lit up in flames. The beast hissed as I swung the fiery blade. More of his pack mates surrounded us, blocking the street. My heart pounded so fast, I swore it would burst through my chest. Anticipating an ambush, I dug in my heels, readying for the attack.

But the beasts didn't move. Snarling, they simply stayed in place.

"What's going on?" I asked. "Why aren't they attacking us?"

"Where's the church?" Jax grunted, ignoring my question.

"If I'm right, it should be right around the corner on Willow Ave. But they have us completely blocked off."

"You need to take Hank, Kate. I'll create a distraction while you beeline for the church, you hear?"

"No. I'm not leaving you behind. You saved me; I'm not abandoning you here."

"Then we'll both be dead, and what's the point in that?"

"No one is dying tonight." Swinging the blade, I challenged one of the beasts, pushing it backward into the shadows. "Something is off. I doubt I'm that intimidating."

"I don't think they were sent here to kill us."

"Not gonna wait around to find out." I continued to swing the angel's sword, catching one of the beasts across its body and sending it fleeing in a wail, its body sizzling from the scorching slice. The other beasts skulked into the shadows, snarling and clawing at the ground as if held back by an invisible force.

"It's the flame. It hurts their eyes," Jax said.

"It didn't hold them back on the bridge."

"Like I said, I don't think they were sent to kill us. Otherwise, we'd be ground beef by now. Even the damned are staying back."

He was right, but there was no time to question their strange behavior. If they didn't want us dead, that meant only one thing: they wanted to capture us, and I was not about to let those devils take me. Jax stayed close as we continued to inch our way to the end of the street, pushing the beasts back with the sword's flame.

A guttural voice boomed from within the pack of nightcrawlers as we rounded the corner onto Willow. I didn't see where it originated from, but it sounded as though it came from every direction.

I turned to Jax, wondering if he'd heard it too or if I'd been mistaken. "That's not a hellhound," he said, reading the question in my eyes.

"Then what is it?"

"Higher order demon. Listen to me, you need to take Hank and run for that church."

"I told you, I'm not—"

"Kate. I'm not asking you. They want *you,* and you don't need me to tell what will happen if they get their hands on you."

"Why do you care so much about what happens to me?"

"You keep challenging me and I might forget." He winked, and the trembling smirk that pulled at the corners of his lips made my insides clench.

As he put Hank over my shoulders, I huffed out a grunt from the added weight. "How do you know it's me they want?"

"It said it."

"You speak *demon*?"

"Latin. It's a long story. If I make it out of this, maybe I'll tell it to you one day." Pulling a knife from an ankle holster, he whispered, "When you hear me say it, run."

"Say what?"

"You'll know."

With Hank drooping over my shoulders, I held the flaming sword out in front of me, waiting for some type of signal. Then Jax hollered into the night; his voice was almost unrecognizable and the words sounded foreign. Whatever he said rattled the beasts, making them whine. Growls erupted all around me, and I knew that was my cue to go.

I hated leaving him there, but a part of me needed to trust him. I took off in a sprint—well, the equivalent of a sprint with a ninety-pound dog weighing me down. Every muscle in my legs screamed for oxygen as I trekked across the street, swerving around parked cars and blown debris. The church was less than half a block away, but I worried I wouldn't make it. Growls and roars followed behind me, biting at my heels.

My knees wobbled and my chest ached. Sweat dripped from my temples and ran down my back. A beast landed on a car near me, and the clash sent a jolt through my spine, almost knocking me to the ground. Steadying myself, I kept running, not risking a look back, knowing I'd lose momentum if I did.

A part of me also feared what I would see. The thought of Jax getting mauled by a pack of nightcrawlers and a horde of the devoured nearly made me buckle. He didn't know me, yet he'd saved my life on the bridge, and here I was, abandoning him to the demons.

A scream pierced through the night.

Jax.

My gut twisted, but I kept going. If he died because of me—for me—I would not let it be in vain. I needed to get to that church. The entrance was not far from the sidewalk. With Hank bouncing on my shoulders, I made it through the broken black iron gate and onto the stoop of the church, collapsing on the stairs.

Four beasts reached the church right behind me, but they came to a clawing halt on the sidewalk as if scared to touch the iron bars. Pacing, they snarled, their red eyes glowing. Jax had been right. Hallowed ground repelled them, but for how long? They were already sniffing around the perimeter, glaring at me; their gaze telling me it would only be a matter of time before they found a weakness somewhere.

I only prayed I'd find a way in before they found the weakness. Hank stirred beside me, his ears perking up as he took in his surroundings. A low growl rumbled from him when he saw the nightcrawlers prowling around the perimeter of the church. "Easy now, boy. These guys aren't to be messed with. He tried to stand, but I held him down. "Don't move, Hank. Stay." Scratching under his neck, I looked into his pained gaze. He licked my hands and let out a tiny whimper. Even in agony, he wanted to fight alongside me. "You're sitting this one out, buddy."

Leaving him on the stoop, I stood and yanked on the handles of the whitewashed, wood doors. Locked. I banged and yelled for help, but I knew it was of no use. On the off chance there was someone inside, there was no way they'd open the doors, especially if they'd heard the commotion outside.

As I searched around the entrance for any potential entry—either through a window or another door—my chest caved. The stained-glass windows were too high for me to reach, and the other set of whitewashed doors were also locked. "Fuck."

From the corner of my eye, I watched large, shadowy silhouettes slink out from behind buildings and cars. The devoured. What if the infected weren't affected by hallowed ground? A surge of adrenaline filled my veins. There was no way I could outrun all these beasts, and definitely not with Hank on my shoulders. Panic settled in my gut as I failed to figure out an escape plan.

Damn this night.

As I walked back to the stoop, I caught a glimpse of a nightcrawler pressing on the iron bars with his snout. A small plume of smoke sizzled from where he'd touched the bar, but he didn't pull back.

These fuckers would singe their hide just to get to me. Holding the angel sword out in front of me, I challenged the beasts to cross the threshold. One seemed to take me up on my bluff. Right as he was about to lunge through the gate, a deep shout blasted from the street.

Jax emerged from the darkness, running and carrying what appeared to be a lit flare. He shouted something as he waved it over his head, but I wasn't able to understand a word he said. The nightcrawlers whined, moving away from the church as if being near it hurt.

As Jax drew nearer, something seemed off about him. His blue eyes appeared to be glowing red—the same red I'd seen in the Horseman. It couldn't be. Perhaps the glow of the flare he held reflected off his eyes? Too stunned to move, I stared, shocked and relieved at the same time that he was still alive.

"Get in the church," he yelled, his voice so deep and gravely that I didn't recognize it.

With no time to question what was happening, I said, "Doors are locked. There's no way to get in."

Reaching the iron bars, he leapt over them with ease. He dropped the flare and ran to one of the stained-glass windows. "We need to find a way through. I won't be able to hold them back much longer without holy water or the relic."

His eyes no longer flared red and his voice seemed to have returned to normal. I wanted to believe it had all been a figment of my imagination—a byproduct of Hell's demons chasing after us—but something didn't seem right.

"Kate, get Hank," he ordered, knocking me out of my troubled thoughts. He found a large rock stuck in the ground and flung it through the window, shattering it into a million shards. He threw another rock, widening the hole. He turned to me, his alarmed gaze drilling into mine. "Kate. Hank."

I rushed back to the stoop and let out a cry when I struggled to lift him. He seemed to have gone completely limp. "No. No. No. Hank, wake up, buddy." He lay listless and pain lanced through my heart at the thought of losing him, of losing the only friend I'd had since the world ended. Falling to my knees,

I tried to rouse him, but his tongue drooped to the side. "Hank, please." I whimpered, tears beading at the corners of my eyes.

Lost in a fog of anguish, I didn't even feel it when Jax wrapped his arms around me to lift me off Hank. I wailed, thinking he was dragging me away from him. Thrashing in his arms, I fought until he finally set me back down.

"I'm not leaving him." I said, running back to Hank.

"I know. I'm not asking you to. But we need to get inside, Kate. The window is too high for me to jump up. I need to lift you up. Once inside, you can open the door. I'll stay with Hank."

I stared at him.

"Kate. I promise you, I will protect him with my life. Now, please. You have to climb through that window."

I didn't know why, but I believed him. Nodding, I allowed him to hoist me up to his shoulders. He wobbled a little as I tried to balance, my boots clearly digging into his muscles, his brown leather jacket offering little protection from my weight.

"Can you reach the window?" he asked.

"Yeah."

"Can you climb through?"

Reaching for the ledge, I hissed as I cut my palm on a jagged piece of broken glass.

"Kate?"

Ignoring the throbbing pain, I pulled myself up to the ledge. "I'm fine. Just a scrape." Maneuvering over the opening, I managed to drop onto the church floor, the *thud* echoing through the chamber. "I'm in," I shouted, the wound on my hand stinging like a bitch and dripping blood onto the dusty floors. I'd sliced it open deeper than I'd thought, but then I noticed it clotted rather quickly. Strange. No time to fuss about it, though. "Meet me at the entrance."

Covered in darkness, the church was straight out of a horror movie. A place meant to offer peace gave me the creeps instead.

Eerie shadows danced over the pews as the dim moonlight penetrated the stained-glass windows, highlighting the nave. I ran down one of the aisles, dusty spiderwebs clinging to my clothes as I crossed to the lobby and finally to the double doors. Unlocking them, solace washed over me the instant I saw Jax standing on the other side, holding Hank in his arms.

He hurried in and gently laid Hank on one of the pews as I bolted the doors shut again, but not before noting the army of monsters gathering outside.

Jax limped to the altar, and that's when I caught sight of the blood dripping down his side. He held on to a rib as he reached the sanctuary. Dropping to a knee, he whispered words too soft to make out. "Kate…" he groaned, "I can't climb up to the altar."

As I reached the sanctuary, I knelt beside him and helped him sit on the floor. "Tell me what you need."

Peering at me, he tried to offer me a smile as a thank you, but it barely reached his eyes. His face was pale, lips completely drained of color.

"Jesus, Jax. You've lost a lot of blood."

"I'll be okay, angel. Just need you to get me some holy water and chrism. And find me that relic."

"Holy water? Anything this place has is probably all dried up or gone. And chrism?"

"Check the ambry or tabernacle for the chrism, consecrated oil," he muttered, nearly out of breath as he scooted back against a pew. "If there's no water by the baptismal font, we'll need to make do with the oil and the relic. Find the reliquary by the altar."

"Slow down," I said, trying to decipher everything he'd uttered. "As a child, I went to church almost every Sunday with my grandmother, but you can't expect me to know where any of this stuff is. Ambry? Reliquary?"

Howls boomed outside, the growls sounding nearer. "They are getting braver," Jax said. "Unless we strengthen the bindings, they will find a way to break in, regardless of the pain they will endure. They will sacrifice themselves to get to their prize." He looked deep into my eyes, making sure I understood that *I* was their prize.

"Why do they want me?"

"There will be time to talk about that later. For now, go check the tabernacle. It's back there." He gestured to an altar on the side of the aisle where a golden box sat. "You'll find consecrated oil inside. Please hurry."

I did as he said and found a small glass jar with red oil. Next, I checked the font, and to my surprise, found a tiny puddle of water sitting deep within the fountain. It looked full of some sediment, but I didn't care. I ran back to the tabernacle where I found an empty chalice and was able to scoop up about two tablespoons worth of dirty, holy water.

Now for the reliquary. I went to the main altar, but a shot of uneasy energy ran down my spine the moment I stepped foot in front of the stone table. Being up there felt wrong somehow, like I was violating a sacred place, even though I'd given up believing in sacred places and rituals ages ago. Not really knowing what I was looking for, I scanned the area until I found a glass-faced silver locket displayed inside a glass container.

A placard stated: Rome. Ca. 1880 St. Barbara. Virgin and Martyr. *This has to be it.* "Found it." Taking it out of the box, I held the locket and stared at its contents, which appeared to be a tiny piece of cloth. I shrugged. I truly hoped this man knew what he was doing with these items.

Kneeling back beside him, I gave him the oil, the chalice with the holy water, and the locket. He looked at them and sighed. "This is all the holy water you found?"

I nodded, my shoulders slack. I'd done my best. Picking up the locket, he said, "Second-class relic. I'd hoped for a bone fragment at least, but this will have to do."

It would, because we'd run out of time. Claws scratched at the walls from the outside. The doors around the church clattered as the beasts banged against them. The entire church echoed with the growls of the creatures roaring to get inside.

I put my hand on his shoulder. "Whatever it is you can do to protect this place, now's the time."

He handed me the chalice. "Take the holy water. Dip your finger in it and make the sign of the cross over the four corners of this church and over the doors. Go!"

Without questioning, I did as he said, starting with the eastern side of the nave. As I crossed to each side, I watched as Jax gathered himself on both knees in front of the sanctuary, but he never once touched the altar.

He stripped off his jacket and shirt, remaining only in his dark jeans, his chest gleaming red with blood. I was now able to see the extent of his injury. He'd been slashed across the chest. Still on his knees and taking the relic in his right hand, he picked up the red oil and poured it over his head, letting it drip down his body.

My eyes widened, my jaw growing slack. A ray of moonlight shot through a small window at the top of the ceiling, illuminating him like a spotlight. Heavens. He looked like an angel and a demon rolled into one.

Fanning out his arms, he kept them spread as if being crucified, his back muscles flexing under the gleam of the oil. "Oh God, the Creator of all things, by water and the Holy Spirit, You have given the universe its beauty and fashioned us in Your own image. Bless and purify Your church."

The ground rumbled under my feet as I reached the west end of the church.

"Oh, Christ the Lord," Jax continued, "from Your pierced side, You gave us Your sacraments as fountains of salvation. Bless and purify Your church."

Another rumble shook the entire church, and tiny, rocky debris cascaded from the ceiling. "Is this supposed to happen?" I shouted across the nave, but Jax went on with his chanting, his voice growing louder but coarser.

"Oh, Holy Spirit, giver of life…" Jax's body contorted, the words getting lost on his tongue. The sounds of bones breaking echoed through the chamber, and Jax let out a guttural scream as he curved into himself.

"Jax." I ran toward him, but he put his hand out.

"Stay back!" he growled, his voice deep, transformed. Straightening back on his knees, he spread his arms once again. "From the baptismal font of the church, You have formed us into a new creation in the waters of rebirth…" His voice sounded pained, his back muscles contracting. The bones of his spine seemed to grow bigger, pointed. Jax screamed again, and this time, I collapsed in the middle of the nave, helpless and confused. I wanted to run to him, to help him, but knew he'd turn me away.

Outside, the night choked with the sounds of Hell. Creatures wailed, shrieking and yowling with every word Jax spoke.

With one final breath, Jax screamed, "Bless and purify Your church!"

Suddenly, a bright light flashed through the stained-glass windows and silence fell over the church and the street all at once. It was as if all sound had been sucked through a black hole. When the light subsided, Jax slumped to the floor, his body lifeless.

I do not ask that you take them out of the world, but that you keep them from the evil one.

JOHN 17:15

CHAPTER 4

JAX

The night we spent in the church Kate found was far from peaceful. The mutts outside had shut up and most likely ran off with their tails between their nasty demon asses, but the devil sitting on my shoulder refused to fuck off and give me rest. Not to mention I was weakened by the wounds that weren't healing as fast as they should've, compliments of the church and the adverse effects it had on demons. And given as I had one fused to my soul, my inhumanly fast healing abilities were dulled.

At least Kate fell into a restless sleep soon after I deflected her questions.

Dawn arrived with a ray of sunlight shining through the high stained-glass windows above the wooden organ. The whole place lit up in red, blue, yellow, and green hues, like a fucking magical wonderland. Warmth and light chased away any of the shadows still lingering around the pillars and rows of dark wooden pews.

Masterfully painted, gold and sapphire pattern designs looked down on me from the arched ceiling just above the altar, smoothing out into a bluish sky pattern throughout the rest of the interior. Large, iron-and-glass chandeliers hung from the ceiling on black chains, reflecting the rays like a prism. The combination of glass, wood, and iron with the incredibly high ceiling and intricate arch made the church look majestic and humble at the same time. The play of light filled even my fucked-up soul with awe.

As more light poured in through the windows, a sudden sense of calm overtook me. We'd survived the night. I've never been so happy to see dawn in my whole screwed-up life. The damned might still wander the streets after sunrise, but the *d'shiad* were confined to their dark holes. We would have an easier time navigating the streets with Kate and her injured dog.

I'd promised to help her with treating Hank before I passed out from exhaustion from my own wounds, but his state didn't look promising. Even if his wound was treated, I had a feeling it wouldn't be enough to keep him from turning. We'd need the help of a priest, or at the very least, a sanctioned minister.

I looked over at her curled up protectively next to Hank. Her dark hair had come loose from the ponytail at one point during the night and strands had fallen over her face, covering her soft features. My heart did a pole vault as I took her in. Fuck me. The woman was stunning.

She'd finally relaxed, the rise and fall of her breathing a steady sound saturating the tranquility of the nave.

In all her fierceness, she was vulnerable while she slept. Kate was stubborn, absolutely competent—even though I'd doubted it at first—and fucking crazy. A force to be reckoned with, that was for sure. And she was lying right there on the cold stone floor of the church with nothing but a thin sheet I'd found in a closet to cover her up.

Stop wasting time. Give her to him so he can set us free.

I gritted my teeth and mentally scolded the abomination trapped in my body. What he offered was tempting. I'd be lying if I wasn't as eager to get rid of him as he was of me, but there was a reason I was a wanted man. There was a reason I'd left headquarters. And that's because I refused to participate in their bloodshed.

I would rip this demon from my soul, but I wouldn't damn myself to Hell to do it—at least, not any more than I already had.

Warmth swelled my lungs as I watched her sleep. I wanted to convince myself the sensation came from the slowly healing wounds across my chest, but I couldn't be certain it wasn't also because of her. Because, for some reason, I couldn't see this woman as a means to an end anymore.

Kate had unstrapped her weapons and laid the sword next to her. The golden handle glinted in the sunlight, drawing my gaze. An impression of a lion in mid-jump and an eagle taking flight were skillfully sculpted around the guard. A blue stone glimmered in the center of the pommel.

With a bullseye on my back and a demon fused to my soul, she'd probably plunge that sword straight through my heart if she knew who I truly was.

Unable to restrain my curiosity, I reached for the weapon, but when my fingers grazed the wings of the eagle, a blinding pain shot through my entire arm. *Fucking hell.* I managed to bite down a growl as a second wave of fiery agony flooded my veins. This time, I couldn't keep myself from cursing.

As I shook my hand in the hopes of getting the feeling back into my fingers, Kate's brown eyes shot open, her gaze narrowing over my hand.

I hid it behind my back. Damn this relic. Damn this whole fucked-up world. I took a deep breath and pushed the worries to the back of my mind. My racing heart rejoiced at the failed attempt to flee. I was literally fighting against two enemies— the demon anchored to my soul and the traitorous beating organ inside my chest.

Smiling as if nothing was wrong, I said, "Rise and shine, angel. We've got a long day ahead of us."

Kate rubbed her eyes as she sat up. "Where are we going?"

"To find breakfast."

As if on cue, her stomach growled, and a smile tugged at my lips when her cheeks reddened. She pushed her hair out of her face and combed through it with her fingers a few times before she gave up on smoothing it out. If playing tour guide meant I could keep looking at her for a little while longer, it wasn't such a horrible deal.

I cleared my throat and tried to look at something else, but nothing could quite hold my attention the same way. "After that, we should try to start up one of those trashed up cars," I said. "I'm sure as hell not carrying Hank all the way back to Manhattan."

Checking Hank's wounds, her hand came back with another bundle of loose fur in her fingers, her brows pinching with worry. The area was starting to turn black. That wasn't good. She scratched under his chin and whispered something in his ear before turning toward me. "Your contact is in Manhattan?"

Choosing not to mention what the both of us already knew was happening to Hank, I said, "*Everything* is in Manhattan." Remaining vague made not mentioning headquarters a lot easier. She didn't need to know. Plus, I planned to stay as far from it as possible. Clint was a smart guy; he wouldn't sit in front of the Empire State building, anyway.

She stood, her lithe body calling my attention to every curve. "As much fun as it was driving through the Lincoln Tunnel," she said, oblivious to all the lewd thoughts running through my head, "I would prefer to avoid that. Getting a car is our best option. We could take the long route across." Strapping her knife and sword around her thighs, she remained focused on the task, always battle ready. And damn if I didn't find that downright sexy.

"Either that, or find a boat," she went on. "We could try the PATH, too, but I doubt it's any better. We'd have to walk the whole way. Without bullets and holy water, I wouldn't suggest the subway system."

"I'm not all that fond of the tunnels, either." It was all I could muster as she zipped up her snug leather jacket.

That being settled, I forced my eyes to roam the stained-glass windows behind her instead of the way the leather hugged her perfectly round breasts.

A growl rumbled deep in my chest, and I couldn't be certain if it had come from me or the demon trapped inside me.

Taking a deep breath, I tried to sedate my thoughts. Fuck. I needed a shower. A cold-ass shower. Hell, after the night we'd had, both of us could probably use one. Though, my reasons had more to do with cooling the sexual heat coursing through my body than getting clean.

But the thought of a shower also brought on a bunch of other unwanted thoughts—all of which related to getting naked, and none which revolved around actually showering. I'd clearly not been with a woman longer than was healthy and the dark side of me was finding the idea of ending the streak a little too delightful.

Shower or no shower, we had to get going so I could focus on something other than her very feminine build.

As finding clean water was harder than finding a bite to eat, I decided to forget it altogether. A fresh T-shirt would have to do, and that's where I'd make a compromise. I had spares and a few cans of beans in the duffle bag I'd left in the wrecked car last night.

Still worried about her dog, Kate knelt beside Hank. "We need to treat his wounds."

Kneeling beside her, I inspected the infected area myself. There wasn't much time left before there was no coming back from those injuries. Hank needed more than antibiotics and gauze. I pushed myself up and groaned as the wounds across my chest stretched.

Kate's gaze turned to inspect me. "We need to treat yours as well."

"I'm fine." Thankfully, she couldn't see much through the ripped shirt.

I bit down on the next groan as I hovered above the dog to pick him up so we could get going. We needed to find a different way to bring Hank with us. If a damned attacked us, I'd be unable to protect Kate—not that she needed protecting, but all hands needed to be on deck.

Her nose scrunched and I knew she was about to protest and ask to look at my chest. "We can see if the pharmacy on Clinton Street has anything useful left," I said before she could interrupt me.

Her face relaxed.

Good. I was in the clear. For now.

As soon as I stepped out of the church, a knot in my chest released and I felt the telltale signs of the enhanced healing accelerating. This was the reason Hell-born creatures avoided hallowed ground—it made them more vulnerable and easier to dispose of. If we'd stayed longer inside that church, the healing properties in my blood—complements of the demon who'd taken up residence in my body—would've stayed dulled, eventually causing me to succumb to infection.

Repositioning Hank in my arms for a more comfortable grip, I sighed in relief as the pain eased up.

One less thing to worry about.

The *d'shiad* had done a number on the yard around the building. The iron fence was trampled and the massive oak across the street lay toppled on its side, roots reaching for the sky. Deep claw marks slashed across the double doors. There was nothing left of the white paint, but if I was being honest, it was a fucking miracle the wood held at all.

Other than fallen leaves drifting across the pavement and a breeze ruffling the branches on the trees in the park across the street, Willow Avenue was dead quiet.

We took off in the direction we came from last night; the dog weighing heavily in my arms. I stopped by the dented BMW that had run out of gas at the intersection, but the thing looked like scrap metal after the *d'shiad* had torn through it. It wouldn't start, even if it hadn't run out of gas.

"You mind grabbing my bag from the back?" I asked Kate as my hands were full.

She pulled it out through the broken back window and heaved it onto her shoulder. "Jesus, what do you have in here?"

"Some food, weapons, and old broadcasting equipment I thought I'd might get working. You find plenty of interesting things from a skyscraper."

She gave me a look that clearly stated that *I* was the crazy one for trying my luck with a death trap.

As we walked past the grocery store, I stopped again, gesturing to the empty parking lot. "You don't have to carry the bag if you bring over one of those shopping carts."

She rolled it over and I laid Hank inside and hauled the duffle over my shoulder. We wheeled it all the way to the pharmacy, checking the scattered cars along the way. I could already see from the broken windows that we'd find nothing of use inside the pharmacy, but it was as good a place as any to eat breakfast. I sat on top of the front register's counter while Kate rummaged through the fallen shelves for anything she could use to clean and wrap Hank's wound.

I pulled out two cans of beans from the bag and after a moment of hesitation, I took out the can of Spam I'd been ecstatic to find yesterday. I opened it and placed it under Hank's nose.

"Here you go," I muttered as he sniffed and began to eat. I took a bite of my beans, watching with a touch of resentment as he devoured the canned ham. "You better eat all of it, buddy. That was a cherished find."

Once fed, bandaged, and absolutely certain that every car in the neighborhood was trashed, I herded us toward the pier. I'd changed my shirt to one with the *I heart NY* written across it with big bold letters. Corny as fuck, but at least it was clean.

"You a New Yorker?" I asked when the only thing accompanying us was the rattling sound of the shopping cart.

"Originally from New Hampshire but moved to the city for work. NYPD, Precinct 75."

I raised an eyebrow. "You're a cop? Damn, I'm sorry for speeding yesterday, officer."

I saw a hint of a smile skid across her lips as I looked her way. "I should thank *you*. Your skillful driving was the only reason we survived the tunnel," she said.

Couldn't argue with that.

"What kept you in New York after the virus overtook the majority of its population?" I asked.

She tilted her head, focusing on a cottony cloud as she thought about her reply. Dropping her gaze, she said, "At first, I wanted to help the people who survived. After I realized there wasn't a lot I could do and that not everyone wanted to be helped, I… I just had nowhere else to go." She turned to me, and I knew what was coming. "What about you?"

Right. That's how conversations worked. You ask a question and eventually, it got bounced back at you. I wasn't ready to tell her the whole truth or any of my reasons for staying, so I forced a grin. "What can I say? I love the city and it would've broken my heart to leave." I tugged at the T-shirt I wore for emphasis, and she laughed.

"Yeah, right. You're the king of dodging questions."

There was a pause, and I wondered if she really thought there was more I was willing to offer. If she waited for a serious answer, she was in for a disappointment. I put on my best pouty face, which wasn't probably all that good, because her impression turned from amused to quizzical.

"You don't believe me? That wounds me, angel." I put a hand over my heart.

"Kate," she corrected me. "Call me Kate." With that, she gave up her probing.

Winking, I said, "I'll try to remember that."

She simply shook her head as we kept walking toward the pier with the hopes of finding a boat we could hotwire. After a couple of more blocks, we came to a sudden stop when we finally arrived at the pier. I'd half expected to find some broken down boats, not a working sports cruiser with people already on it. I raised my hands up when a gun was pointed at us.

"We're unarmed," I called out to the man behind the trigger. He looked like one of those old timers you'd find in a biker bar ready to peel off on his badass Harley. Tattoos snaked down his arm and a long beard that could rival Gandalf's hid his face. Standing next to him on the deck was a blonde woman who could be his daughter, and she placed a hand on his shoulder.

"Bullshit!" he called back, nodding at my belt where I'd tucked the unloaded gun.

I shrugged. My guilty smile probably didn't earn us any brownie points. "We're out of bullets," I said. "We mean you no harm. We just want to get across to Manhattan."

The man's eyes narrowed, but after a long pause, he lowered his weapon. "We ain't goin' to Manhattan."

Lowering our hands, we took a few cautious steps forward. The man had lowered his weapon, but I had no way of knowing who else was on that boat with him, or in the general vicinity, for that matter. Someone could've been lurking in the shadows or hiding behind wreckage with another gun aimed at our heads. "Maybe I can change your mind?"

"There ain't nothin' that can change my mind. The Devil's in Manhattan, 's no place for the livin'."

When we wheeled our cart closer to the cruiser, I noticed two kids around the age of ten peeking through the railing.

Winking at them, I said, "There's no devil in Manhattan, I can assure you." Satan was unable to enter Earth, at least for now. "The pack of hellhounds is a different story, but they won't come out before sunset. We just need a ride over; it won't take longer than eight minutes."

"We ain't goin' that way." He stayed firm on his decision, and I looked over at Kate for help.

"We could make a trade for a ride?" Kate suggested, looking at me. "You said you had food, right?"

"A few cans," I muttered so only she could hear. "It was a feast for one person, an okay haul for two, plus a dog. I wasn't expecting to give it away."

One of the kids tugged on the blonde woman's shirt. "Mom, they have a dog. Can I pet it?"

The kid stared at his mom, and the mother directed the question toward the biker, who looked at me. I raised my eyebrow at Kate.

"He's hurt," she said. "Jax knows somebody in Manhattan who can help. That's why we need a ride."

The man walked off the ramp to take a closer look at Hank. *Figured.* Seemed a hurt animal had more power to unite a group of strangers. Maybe Hank could get us on the boat and across the Hudson, too. "How'd he get hurt?" Long-Beard asked.

I tried to come up with an appropriate answer, but Kate said, "We ran into some trouble with the nightcrawlers last night."

I guess we were going with the truth.

"Nightcrawlers?" Long-Beard and his blonde lady asked in unison, their eyebrows raising up to their foreheads.

"*D'shiad*," I corrected. "The hellhounds."

"Ye'd trouble with the beasts an' lived?" he asked, his eyes roaming us over, likely searching for signs of infection. His gaze snagged on the sword strapped to Kate's thigh.

"We're not infected," I assured him. Well, except the dog, but I wasn't going to point that out.

"Ye might be right 'bout that," the biker said, turning his eyes back to the dog. He gestured at Hank with his gun. "But he is."

"He's no danger to your family. We're going to get him help." Before he got any worse, I hoped. And before he did pose a threat. "We really need a ride over. It's ten minutes out of your way, tops."

"Ye'd be able to fix 'im up? Save 'em diseased?" He studied us again, but other than Kate's sword, there was nothing noteworthy about us.

There was no way he would know the significance of the weapon—it wasn't pulsing like it had in the car, and I doubt he'd be able to feel it if it was. To him, it was just a sword, as uncommon as that weapon was. Still, his next question took me off guard.

"Yer one of those?" He turned toward the blonde, his interest growing. "Lissie, they're part of the Chosen." Believing we'd be able to cure Hank might've had something to do with his conviction.

"What?" Kate looked at me as if I held the answer, and I shrugged. This wasn't the time for that conversation.

"The Chosen," Lissie replied. "Angel blessed, hon. Look, we're heading up the river. We heard there's a colony in Albany. You can come with us. Manhattan really isn't safe."

I had no idea how two civilians had heard about the Guardians, but if them believing we had something to do with the Chosen helped us across the river, then I'd be stupid not to take it. I didn't know Kate long enough to successfully signal for her to take the bait. She was too curious for her own good, and the conversation steered too damn close to things I'd rather not discuss with her just yet. Not before I figured out what to do about that sword of hers.

"Blessed, you say?" Kate looked at them and then at me. I saw questions racing through her mind. "There's more of *us*? Jax, maybe that's what the angel meant by *more are coming*?"

Rubbing at my beard, I tried to keep my cool. "Yeah, maybe." If she thought I knew anything more about the angels than I let on, I didn't give her a chance to express it. In the hopes of getting their focus off the topic, I said, "We have canned food, a bar of chocolate, a few knives, and a broken broadcasting device. I'm willing to trade some of those for a ride across the river, granted we'll have enough left for ourselves."

The girl tugged at Lissie's shirt again. "Mom, he said there's chocolate."

Candy never failed.

However, if someone had offered me some spareribs right now, I would've taken them to the ends of the earth. An eight-minute trip across the river for a bar of chocolate wasn't a bad trade.

"Let me look at 'em knives ye mentioned," Long-Beard said, and I pulled open my duffle bag.

Several canned goods, the chocolate bar, and an army knife later, we'd managed to strike a deal. I wheeled the rattling cart up the ramp.

"Welcome aboard. I'm Lissie and that's Dave," the woman said, patting the big man, who was flipping his new knife around on the back. She looked around the small boat meekly. "It's not much, but we make do."

"Jax," I introduced myself, then pointed at my companion. "Kate. And the brave one's Hank."

Dave walked around the deck, pulling in lines and doing whatever you do to make a boat ready to leave the dock, while Lissie guided us inside the sole cabin. It was a tight space and the two children—the girl and a boy—pushed against the shopping cart to get a better look at Hank.

"Will he be alright?" one of them asked, carefully reaching out to touch Hank's nose.

"He sure will," I directed my answer at Kate. Sorrow had snuffed out the stubborn spark I saw in her eyes the previous night. This goddamn dog meant a lot to her, and I'd be damned if Hank died on my watch. Something inside me broke as I looked at her grieved expression. Hoping to distract her, I pulled her away onto the deck. Hank would be fine with the kids. As the motor under us roared to life, I came up with the silliest thing I could think of.

Puffing my chest, I grabbed a line and in my best Johnny Depp impression, announced, "I'm Captain Jax Sparrow!" Searching for any sign of a smile, my chest deflated when she tossed me a raised eyebrow instead.

"You're who?" she asked, more annoyed than anything.

A wounded breath swooshed from my lungs. "Jack Sparrow," I crooned. "He's from *Pirates of the Caribbean*, woman. It's another classic. How do you not know the classics?"

"*Pirates of the Caribbean* is a classic?" she asked. "What about *Titanic*? Or *Dirty Dancing*?"

"Ah, so she's not so clueless about movies, after all." I placed a hand over my heart. "I'll never let go," I mock-whispered the most famous line from any movie ever made.

She rolled her eyes. "You're embarrassing me." But a small smile crept onto her lips.

"Come on, you know it's funny. Plus, at least now I know your taste in movies. You're into the cheesy, romantic, heartbreak kind."

There was a brief silence, and a shot of guilt speared through me when her eyes misted over. "My husband and I used to watch all kinds of movies together. He loved *Titanic* and—" She stopped mid-sentence, a haunted look crossing over her face. I realized that was the first time she mentioned him. I hadn't thought much about the ring on her finger after we'd found Hank.

Whatever had happened to her husband clearly had a strong impact on her. The slight smile I'd managed to pull out of her fled as memories overtook her. I wanted to comfort her but didn't have a clue what people said during moments like this. 'I'm sorry for your loss' seemed insignificant and cold, not enough to relieve the hurt in her eyes.

"I'm going to check on Hank. We're almost there." She walked off, leaving me to struggle with my own emotions.

When I entered the cabin again, I saw they'd made a nice bed for Hank using blankets.

"That's the least we could do," Lissie said, as a sad smile crossed her face. "We had a pup before all this madness. She was the happiest little thing. Cocker spaniel. The illness took her. We had to—" A tear rolled down her cheek, and she wiped it away. "We had to put her down. There was nothing we could do. I really hope you'll find help for Hank. There's enough cruelness in the world."

"We'll do whatever we can," I assured her.

"If you're ever in Albany, find us. It'd be nice to see another friendly face," Lissie said when we prepared to get off the boat.

"If it's anything like you say, I'm sure you'll be fine," Kate said.

I had no idea what they'd talked about while I was still outside; I just hoped it wasn't anything more about the Chosen. I didn't need her to run off and join the resistance. I also didn't need any more questions, though I doubted there was a way to avoid that for much longer.

We got off the cruiser by the Golf Club on 11th Avenue and trekked on foot toward Central Park in relative silence. I checked a few of the abandoned cars by the roadside, but I had to face the facts that the BMW had been a rare find.

I knew Clint took a route through the park once every couple of days. We'd made a rendezvous by the Bow Bridge once I realized he somehow managed to get his hands on bullets and holy water on a regular basis. Normally, I'd go there once a week at midday with something of value to trade.

But we'd just given away half of our food supplies and an army knife. I wasn't going to barter with the rest of the food, and the only other thing left in my bag was the broadcasting equipment I'd found. I doubted Clint would find it interesting, so I hoped the trust I'd built over the last few months would buy us the information we needed.

I sat under a gazebo with a view toward the stone bridge, and Kate looked around curiously.

"If he's not here in two hours, we'll need to find a place to stay for the night and come back tomorrow," I said, motioning her to sit.

"Why do you think this man can help?" Kate asked, studying the leaves swimming around in the water below.

"Not a man, a boy at most, but he's resourceful and has to have direct contact with a priest from the amounts of holy water I trade with him."

Kate's eyes widened. "Wait, your contact is a *child*?"

"Don't go all cop on me. It is as legal as it gets these days." I crossed my arms over my chest. The wounds from last night had likely already shrunk to thin lines. The itch had stopped bothering me a while back. "I think he's around sixteen, but his age hasn't really come up."

She jabbed my side with her elbow. "I'm not going all cop on you."

When I turned to meet her gaze, her lips curled into a soft, sensuous smile that was meant to put me at ease, but all it did was draw me closer. For a brief moment, I imagined what it would feel like to kiss that mouth, to taste the sweetness of her breath. Heat flared across my chest and further down below my belt.

Her sultry brown eyes grew wide and her lips parted just slightly. An invitation, perhaps? Christ, if I kissed this woman right now, there was no way it would end there. The beast prowling inside me growled, hoping I'd open his cage door.

This was a mistake. Shit. But it would be a glorious fucking mistake. She sucked in a small breath as I leaned in, but just as quickly as the tension had built, she cut it with a knife.

Turning from our almost-kiss, she said, "How's a priest supposed to help, anyway? No one's been able to find a cure. And if he can somehow heal Hank, can't humans be healed too?"

I tugged down on my pants, loosening the tightness around my groin. Staring out over the park, I took in the beautiful, yet eerie, quiet. "I don't hold all the answers, angel. But if there's any hope your dog can be healed from a Hell-born virus, that priest is your only chance."

Two hours passed and Clint didn't show up. We stayed an hour longer at Kate's insistence, but eventually we had to look for shelter. All the high-rise buildings alongside Central Park were far from ideal. We were as close to the Empire State Building as I dared get, so we trekked away from Midtown.

We scouted the blocks next to the park and settled on a dirty white building across the street from a funeral chapel, while still being close enough to Central Park. I would've stayed in the chapel as it was hallowed ground and would have been safer than any apartment we could find in Manhattan, but Kate had seemed reluctant when I suggested we'd check it out. Staring at the crooked entryway of the funeral chapel, she seemed lost, her eyes full of shadows and clouds. I didn't have the heart to make her enter. It could've been a reminder of her dead husband, and the last thing I wanted was to bring that up again.

The thought of her being married jabbed at my heart for whatever fucked-up reason. I tried to put it on the darkness inside me, but I knew *he* wouldn't care about a ring or any vows that might've been exchanged.

Fuck. I shouldn't have cared, either. I only needed the relic— the one I couldn't fucking touch without frying my nerve endings.

Being close to the chapel was better than nothing. With any luck, the *d'shiad* would avoid this street when they came out to play after sunset.

We left the shopping cart in the apartment lobby and used the service stairwell to hike up to the upper floors. With Hank draped over my shoulders, we scouted the first two floors but everything was wrecked. When we exited out into the hallway on the third floor, things looked more promising.

We tried the first couple of apartments, but the doors were locked. The third door opened without resistance, and both Kate and I released a collective breath. Even though the glass doors at the entrance had been smashed and the first two floors looked like garbage, the interior of this apartment was impeccably tidy, as if the end of the world hadn't caught up with it yet.

Kate and I both looked at each other, our eyes hopeful that whoever lived here wouldn't be too unkind to strangers. After waiting another twenty minutes for sundown, we decided who ever lived here probably wasn't showing up tonight. I checked all the rooms and confirmed the entire apartment was empty and safe. I locked the door and barricaded it with small bookcase, closed all the blinds, and rummaged through my bag for a sage kit I'd been carrying around ever since I left the cult and its ways behind.

Kate, who'd walked through the rooms touching tabletops and checking the empty refrigerator, lit candles throughout the space, then met up with me as I lit up the top of the sage with a lighter and softly blew out the flame. Orange embers played at the top of the smudge stick and smoke billowed.

"I purify this place of any evil and negative intentions and call upon protection and security. I command all the evil and non-benevolent beings within this space to leave. You are not welcome here. I command you to leave and go to the light."

"That's not a Christian ritual," Kate commented as I walked around spreading the smoke around in all the rooms, chanting a few more times.

I extinguished the stick and packed it away in my bag again.

"There are several ways to deflect evil," I explained. "Christianity is only a small part of the equation. Think of religions as vehicles in which to navigate the path to the truth. No matter what vehicle you use, the path is fixed. It always leads to the same destination."

Her expression transfixed, and she studied me curiously. Jokes weren't the only thing in my tool kit.

"Is this going to help against the nightcrawlers?" Kate asked, looking around the space, unconvinced by my explanation.

"It is not as strong a protection spell as the one I did at the church, but it's better than nothing. We just gotta stay off their radar." I rummaged through my bag and pulled out a can of chickpeas and corn. "Dinner?"

She nodded and blasted me again with one of those radiant smiles that literally turned my insides into jelly. Damn. I couldn't remember the last time a woman had made me feel that way. Probably never.

"How do you know all these things?" Kate asked, following me into the tight kitchen as I looked for bowls. I found them on a shelf above the sink.

I tried to come up with a way to explain it while keeping the cult out of it. "I grew up with a shaman for a mother," I said eventually, a thread of guilt wrapping around my heart for giving her the misguided truth. "Tried a few things myself."

I clenched my teeth for lying and divided the corn and chickpeas between the two bowls and handed the bigger portion to her, hoping she'd stop probing.

When she didn't immediately take it, I raised my gaze. Her eyes were fixed on me, waiting for further explanation. Her studious stare made my insides lurch, and the voice I hadn't heard the whole day woke up, growling through my thoughts.

"Look, I am not proud of my childhood," I went on. "There are things I wish to forget. Let's just eat." When I held the bowl her way again, she took it.

She went to check on Hank again after dinner. I had transferred him over to the couch. He'd been whimpering and growling at me when I touched him, but so weakly that the growls came out like soft rumbles. It didn't look good. I wasn't certain he'd survive tomorrow night if Clint wasn't at the bridge by daybreak.

There was an alternative way to save Hank, but I wouldn't even use it on a willing soul, and definitely not on a helpless animal. I was good proof this shit didn't work all that well. I was able to control my fucked-up companion, but Hank could get possessed and never return to himself again.

Not gonna happen. Clint has to be there.

I was still sitting at the dining table where we'd eaten our meager dinner when a dripping sound caught my attention.

What the—

Turning around in my chair, my eyes widened at the faucet in the kitchen when another droplet leaked from its mouth and fell into the basin underneath. Interesting. None of the houses I'd stayed in or searched through ever had any running water. Drinking water came from scavenged bottles or from any freshwater reservoirs I'd stumbled upon. I was so used to the fact that indoor plumbing was a rarity that I'd stopped checking the taps all together.

I pushed myself away from the table, the chair legs scraping against the linoleum floor, the sound snatching Kate's gaze away from the dog. Thinking we couldn't possibly be that lucky, I stood and walked to the sink, feeling Kate's eyes skating over my shoulders.

I took a deep breath and let it out slowly before I pulled the handle up. A continuous flow rushed out, clear as day. Laughter bubbled out of me. Whoever lived here was way more resourceful than we'd thought. They must have rigged some type of water collection device on the roof and connected it to the pipes.

Honestly, I didn't care how it worked. Only that it did.

"Looks like we have water," I said, closing the tap and looking back at Kate over my shoulder. "Dibs on the shower."

A small smile graced her face. "Whatever happened to ladies first? Where are your manners?"

"I'll remember that comment next time we enter another underground passage. You can go first all you want."

Her smile grew and sugary heat wrapped around my heart, making me woozy. What the heck was wrong with me? I was so close to finally being free and my own traitorous heart wanted to tie me up all over again. *Focus.* I had to fucking focus.

Get what you need and cut her loose.

Granting her first dibs on the shower, she rushed into the en-suite bathroom while I looked through the closet in the bedroom. Everything was neatly packed or on hangers. On one side hung two dresses, a leather jacket I figured Kate would love, plus a few T-shirts and jeans that might fit her. I pulled out a pair of sweatpants from the other side, gauging their size, but then my mind began to wander.

It slithered across to the bathroom door. I imagined Kate inside the shower, completely naked under a spray of water, droplets sliding down her skin, caressing those well-rounded breasts I hadn't managed to get out of my head. The thought of the water sliding further down, soaking her between her legs, made my cock tighten. Thinking about the soapy water dripping between her thighs, right where I wanted my tongue to be, had me nearly breaking down that bathroom door and joining her in that shower.

Shit.

By the time I heard the spray stop, I'd worked myself up to a fucking raging hard-on. When she came out—skin glistening, cheeks rosy, and only a tiny towel covering her curves—I pushed right past her and locked myself in the bathroom.

"There's clean clothes in the closet," I coughed out through the door. I hoped to God she'd be wearing something decent once I came out.

Two candles lit up the space. The bathroom was a small, white-tiled square. A toilet and a sink on one side and the shower on the other. Kate had folded her dirty clothes in a neat pile on top of the toilet seat, and I dropped mine on the floor. The smell of shampoo and shower gel filled the space, feminine and strong, doing nothing to ease the situation between my legs.

Take her, the gravelly voice pressed, providing me with plenty of different ways to do it.

Fuck no, not like that.

Stepping under the showerhead, I was hoping to be hit by a spray of cold water, but what came out was lukewarm and of no help at all.

Next to the bottle of shower gel that had made the bathroom smell like flowers and sunshine was a bar of soap I was more comfortable using. Rubbing it over my skin, I scrubbed off all the grime and oil from last night. My hand stopped at the edge of my shaft, where I paused for only a short, hesitant second before gripping my eager cock.

Yeah, better get this over with.

A groan escaped my lips as I stroked myself. The buildup felt good, but not nearly as good as I wanted, or as good as it would feel if I were buried deep inside her.

I leaned against the tiles with my hand still pumping my dick when the water spray stopped. Shit, we'd used up all the water. Not wanting to leave my mess all over the tub, I stepped out and leaned over the toilet instead, continuing to jack-off as I conjured up images of a naked Kate laying underneath me, legs spread wide as I watched my cock slide in and out of her pussy.

Fucking hell. I shut my eyes tight and clenched my jaw to keep from grunting like an animal. My sack grew heavy and tight as I neared an explosion. More images of Kate materialized in my head. Her on all fours as I took her from behind, my cock deep in her asshole. Her on her knees, taking every inch of me in her mouth until I made her gag.

Fuck.

I milked myself faster and harder until I came into the damn bowl, grinding my teeth so tight to keep from moaning out loud that I might have cracked my molars.

Taking several breaths, I waited until the storm subsided, then flushed.

A bath towel hung from a hook on the door, and I tied it around my waist. Taking one look into the misted-up mirror, I grimaced at my disheveled face. I had to do something about my bushy beard. This place had everything, so why not a razor? Going through the drawers under the basin, I smiled when I found an electrical trimmer, and the battery was full.

Must be my lucky day.

Put to death, therefore, whatever belongs to your earthly nature: sexual immorality, impurity, lust, evil desires and greed, which is idolatry.

COLOSSIANS 3:5

CHAPTER 5
KATE

Still wrapped in my towel, I paused in front of the full-length mirror beside the closet. I almost couldn't recognize myself. I'd been so eager to jump in the shower—eager to finally wash all the filth and blood off me—I hadn't bothered to look at myself in the vanity. Afterward, I rushed out to give Jax a chance to shower and forgot.

How long had it been since I'd taken a moment to look at myself? Raising a hand to my face, I padded fingers around my hollow cheeks and sunken eyes. The skin around my eyes crinkled more than I remembered, and my forehead had gained a few lines as well. I swallowed hard as I took in my shoulders and arms. I'd definitely lost several pounds—probably close to thirty—but I'd gained some lean muscle.

Had to be all the walking and climbing.

My mouth dried up when I thought about opening the towel and looking at my naked body. I shook my head. What was wrong with me? Why did I even care? I'd never worried too much about my image before, so why was I scared of what I might look like now?

The answer came as I heard the water shut off.

Jax.

Something about him made my skin tingle and I couldn't quite put my finger on it. Despite the fact I'd only met him recently, I felt a connection, some type of attraction, to him. Yet another part of me felt weary, suspecting he hid something. He always sidestepped my questions, especially after everything that happened the night before. That protection prayer he cast on the church was unlike anything I'd ever seen, yet he refused to talk about it, refused to tell me where he'd learned to do that.

Still, trusting him came unusually easy. Was it his corny-ass humor? The sparkle in his eyes when he looked at me? Or maybe it was gratitude that drew me to him. He'd saved my ass. *Twice.* And now he was helping me find Hank the aid he needed by going back into the middle of the hell we'd barely escaped.

He had no reason to do that. While there was safety in numbers, it was harder to find food for three mouths than it was for one. Maybe he was just as relieved as I was at finding another living, uninfected person. Perhaps he, too, was tired of being lonely, of only listening to the sound of his own voice. Or maybe that tiny fire stoking inside me was lighting up inside him as well.

The notion steamrolled through me, making me queasy.

After Roger passed, the thought of being attracted to another man never crossed my mind, not in this new world. And not after the love Roger and I shared. We'd been high school sweethearts, each other's one and only.

Then the world ended, taking him from me, and with it, any awareness of who I was as a woman—of what I'd once been. There'd never been a me without Roger.

A lump formed in my throat. Could I possibly ever feel anything for another man beyond gratitude? Or would the guilt wrapped around my heart never let it beat again? Guilt for even thinking about another man after losing my husband. Guilt for wanting to feel beautiful when the world looked like shit. Guilt for thinking about how incredible it would be to have sex again when Hank was outside in the living room, dying.

Heavens. That thought cleaved my soul in two. I couldn't lose Hank, not like this. I needed to focus. To remind myself that everything else worth living for had already been ripped from me. All I had was Hank and my thirst for vengeance.

Letting go of the nonsensical thoughts, I dropped the towel and took one quick glance at myself. Aside from the visible rib cage, the rest of my body wasn't so bad. I still held on to some roundness around my hips and my thighs had some muscle from all the trekking around the city. Then I looked at the forest between my legs and cringed. Geez, I'd really let myself go. But who thinks about these things when demons have taken over the world and you're fighting for survival?

Realizing Jax would be getting out of the bathroom soon, I hurried to slip into a pair of clean underwear and a sports bra I'd found in one of the dressers. Black jeans and a white tank top finished off my borrowed outfit. Well, not like I'd be returning the clothes, but I did say a silent thank you to whomever had left this place so nicely stocked.

I lowered my head, thinking that perhaps the reason this place was so stocked, yet empty of any living person was because whoever had been squatting here had met their end. I chose to think they were on their way to Albany to meet up with the boat people instead.

Right as I finished that thought, the bathroom door opened. I spun toward it and my body went rigid, lips parting with an inward breath.

Holy trinity... I'd seen this man shirtless at the church, but that had been a whole different experience. This was...

Sin wrapped in a towel.

His broad chest and tight abs gleamed from the moisture of the shower. My eyes traveled to his narrowed waist, that male V arrowing down to where dark hair disappeared below the terry cloth.

Realizing I'd stared longer than was appropriate, I hurried to raise my gaze, only to find his lips curled into a cocky smile. "See something you like, angel?"

Heat flushed up my neck and into my cheeks. Turning my back to him in a panicked flurry, I fumbled through my words, "I'm sorry. I didn't mean to stare."

He chuckled with that deep throaty sound that caressed the parts of me I thought were long dead. "I was only teasing you. No need to turn around. Not like my cock is hanging out or anything."

Covering my face with my palm, I shook my head. *Thanks. Not the visual I needed right now, Jax.* This conversation could take a steep dive down a dangerous path if I didn't steer it somewhere else. "How was the shower?" I asked.

"You tell me. You used up most of the water."

Spinning back toward him, I gasped, "Did not. That was like, the shortest shower of my life."

Those blue eyes twinkled, and that mischievous smile of his wouldn't relent. "Certainly was for me, but honestly, I'm not complaining. I'd not showered in—"

"I know. We both stunk. Even a short shower felt like paradise." As I met his gaze and took in the rest of his face, I noticed he'd trimmed his beard down to a manageable short scruff, revealing his striking features. He was all angles, and now that the scraggly beard was gone, his fleshy lips were no longer hidden. They twisted into that wolfish grin of his and made me gulp. He had to stop that nonsense or I'd lose my mind soon.

He rubbed his short beard. "Trimmers are in there. You should take advantage while they still have a charge."

My neck cambered. "Take advantage?"

He raised a brow and pointedly flicked his gaze down below my waist. When I figured out what he meant, my eyes widened in horror as heat rose up my neck again. "Oh. My. God. Are you always this… indiscreet? And how could you possibly know if I haven't already taken care of myself? And what business is it of yours, anyway?" I sputtered.

He shrugged, laughing as he moved toward the closet. The scent of soap drifted off his skin as he crossed in front of me. Mother of God, why did he have to smell like rain and mint? He'd clearly not used the same soap as I had.

"Just helping out a friend," he went on. "Never know when the right occasion might pop up. You'd want to be at your best." Peering at me over his muscled shoulder, he winked.

Oh, he was clearly enjoying making me uncomfortable. The prick. Crossing my arms over my breasts, I said, "You assume too much, *friend*. There is no right occasion, not anymore. Nor anyone I'd care to be my best with."

Was that a shadow of disappointment I saw darken his gaze?

Without a retort, he looked down, then shifted toward the closet and pulled out a black T-shirt and a pair of dark jeans. As he turned back to me, he went to pull off his towel.

"Whoa, whoa, whoa," I yelped, putting my palms up.

With a hand on the corner of the towel ready to yank the damn thing off, he said, "You can leave the room, angel. Or you can stay and watch. Up to you."

I was about to take him up on his second offer when something caught my attention. How had I not noticed it when he first stepped out of the bathroom? Stepping closer to him, I reached up and put my hands on his chest, not even bothering to ask permission to touch him as I ran my fingers over his pecs—and not catching on how intimately close we stood.

The warmth radiating from his skin traveled up my arm. He was soft and hard, and I may have forgotten how to breathe as I marveled at what lay under my fingers.

"Angel, I… um, I didn't mean…"

But I could barely hear what he said because all I could think about was how in the universe had his chest healed so fast. The wounds were completely gone, as if they had never happened. Not even a single scar.

"Kate, listen—"

Hands still on his chest, I peered up at him. "Explain. Now. And no jokes this time, Jax. I need the truth."

His Adam's apple bobbed, the vein at the base of his jaw thumping wildly. His playful smile flattened to a hard line as his hooded gaze confessed he had yet another secret.

I closed my eyes and blew out an exasperated breath. "Jax, you were injured by the same creatures that attacked Hank, yet you're not infected."

"Not everyone gets infected or dies."

"True, but no one else heals at lightning speed like this, either."

He put one of his hands over mine, but he didn't remove it from his chest.

"Jax, you can trust me."

"You wouldn't understand."

With an unyielding stare, I pressed, "Try me."

Pulling away, he spun from me, his back muscles moving in ways I didn't know could make my insides quiver. He placed his hands on his waist. "I'm different, that's all."

I huffed, my feet digging into the floor. Why was he so hesitant to tell me the truth? Yeah, we'd only met a day ago, but after everything we'd shared in such a short amount of time, couldn't he offer me something? I mean, why bother keeping secrets in this godforsaken land? What was the point?

"That's not enough, Jax."

He didn't turn around. "It has to be."

I couldn't see it, but I felt the wall go up. He'd closed up on me and there was no climbing over that. I doubted I could even crack it with a wrecking ball.

"I can't accept that." I walked out of the bedroom.

"I'm sorry," he called out a second later, stopping me mid-step down the hall. Staying silent, I let him finish. "There are just some secrets better left buried."

There was pain in his voice, maybe a plea of some sort. As if he wanted to tell me more, but couldn't. I wanted to run back into that room. And do what, exactly? Throw my arms around him? Comfort whatever demons lay buried inside him? I had my share of dark secrets, and I wasn't ready to share them either, so why was I pushing him to tell me his? Maybe I was being unreasonable. Too tough.

But my feet didn't move. Whatever feelings were brewing in my chest for this man needed to be stamped out. My life was messy enough, and I didn't need to add all this sentimental shit now. I'd been through the agony of losing loved ones, so why would I willingly put myself through that turmoil again? Because that was the truth, wasn't it? No matter what, if we cared for someone, eventually, we would lose them.

I growled at myself. *So why is it so hard to walk away from him?*

"Kate? You still there?"

Damn it. First, he pushed me away, and now he wanted me to stay? Things were already messy, and I hadn't even slept with the guy.

"I need to check on Hank. We'll talk later." It was an escape, but not a cop-out. As hard as it was to leave him in that room, I did need to check on Hank.

I found Hank right where we'd left him, on the small sofa in the living room in front of the TV. Sitting on the floor beside him, I pressed my nose to his. It was dry, which wasn't a good sign. "Hey, buddy," I cooed softly. "How's my boy doing?"

Hank opened one eye, his gaze glossy. When I pulled back the lid, his sclera was bloodshot—a sure sign the infection was spreading. Unlike humans, animals only got sick if attacked by one of the devoured or a nightcrawler, and they seemed to get sick a lot slower than humans for some reason. Which was a good thing. It was buying us time to get him some help.

When the sickness first spread across the globe, no one knew—or at least, no one wanted to believe—that the virus was Hell-born, brought upon us by Pestilence himself, the first Horseman of the Apocalypse. Even eighteen months later, even after everything I'd witnessed, it still sounded like make-believe, but it was the truth.

Everything the Bible had predicted had come to pass.

Had we accepted that sooner, we could have healed people with holy water, maybe could have even saved thousands, if not millions. Still, humans either died a quick death or turned just as quickly, regardless if they got sick from the airborne virus or from an attack. There was no turning back. You were gone in a day.

A tear trickled down my cheek as I watched my best friend shiver. I didn't know how I could find the strength to keep going if I lost Hank. Wanting to cuddle with him, I found the strength to pick him up and brought him to one of the bedrooms. Lying beside him on the queen-sized bed, I placed my head by his and wrapped an arm around him.

"Just like back home, buddy."

He let out a long, soft breath and licked his mouth—his way of telling me he felt calm and was ready to sleep. "Go on, buddy. Momma won't let anything happen to you."

A short time later, a soft knock on the bedroom door roused me from a sleepy haze. "You awake?" Jax whispered.

Raising my head off the pillow, I nodded to the shadowed form of his body.

He gestured for me to follow him. "Come on. I found us a treat."

Rolling off the bed with as little movement as possible so as not to disturb Hank, I stood and padded out barefoot into the living room. Sitting with legs outstretched on the sofa, Jax tapped the seat next to him. I noticed he'd changed into a tight black T-shirt and a pair of gray sweatpants instead of the jeans I'd seen him pull out of the closet earlier.

"You look comfy," I said, nodding at his pants.

"Jeans were a bit snug around my junk."

Sure. As if wearing sweats had nothing to do with the fact that he looked positively inviting, dressed like we were about to Netflix and Chill. Before taking a seat, I asked, "So what's this treat you got for us?"

He arched a brow and used his hand to show me the spread he'd laid out on the coffee table. When my eyes landed on the tray of Oreo cookies and two glasses of milk, my mouth dropped open. I'd been so distracted by those gray sweatpants that I'd totally missed it when I walked in.

"Where did you—" I began, but I couldn't finish my sentence.

"I'm a good scavenger. Cookies were stashed deep in the bedroom closet, along with a can of powdered milk and some bottles of water. Guess they were saving them for a rainy day."

I plopped beside him. "That kinda makes me feel guilty about eating them."

"Don't, Kate. This is the world we're living in now. I wouldn't be shocked if someone raided my place. That's just the name of the game."

I couldn't deny that my mouth was already watering at the mere thought of having an Oreo. I'd been eating canned food for who knew how long. A piece of candy was like finding gold, but Oreos were a whole different ball game. And with a glass of milk? Forget about it.

As I reached for one, I paused. "Wait. These could be bargaining tools. I'm sure we can find people willing to trade some bullets for Oreos."

He laughed, and the deep rumble tickled my skin. It was enough to make me forget our slight fight earlier.

"Don't worry," he said. "There were two bags of Oreos. I put one in my duffel bag in case we need them to trade."

My eyes widened as I took in the full tray of three dozen cookies. "So, these are all ours?"

"Enjoy."

With a squeal, I took four cookies, my glass of milk, and sat back in my seat, crossing my legs. Stuffing a whole Oreo into my mouth, I moaned in sheer delight as I chased it with a gulp of milk. "Oh yeah. That hit the spot."

"That good, huh?"

"You know it."

"You better slow down. You want to savor every morsel. Plus, you're totally eating those wrong."

"Excuse me? There's no wrong way to eat an Oreo."

"You're thinking of a Reese's."

"Oh, man. I could kill for one of those."

"Look," he said, reeling me in. Taking a cookie, he peeled it apart and licked off the cream. Something in my belly jumped at the sight of his tongue sliding over that cookie. When he did it again—slower, and with expert precision—I felt the jolt even lower. Way lower. A sweetened warmth pooled in my center. "Now, you dunk." His hand was moving, but my mind was still stuck on the tip of his tongue brushing over the cream.

Sweet baby Jesus.

With my jaw slightly slacked, I said, "I think you need to show me that peel and lick move again. I'm a slow learner."

Peering over at me, he smiled. "You're so full of shit, angel."

I cracked up and stuffed two more cookies into my mouth before gulping more milk. It dribbled out of the side of my mouth and I snorted so loud, I nearly spit milk out in a burst of laughter.

After minutes of joking and laughing, our tummies threw in the towel. As much as our taste buds wanted to devour every last cookie, we weren't able to polish off the tray. Feeling like I'd wake up with an Oreo-induced hangover in the morning, I leaned back on the sofa with a deep sigh and inadvertently rested my head on Jax's shoulder.

"Thank you," I said. "This was a perfect night."

"You know what would make a perfect night even more perfect?" He mocked using a TV remote and pointed it toward the flat screen on the wall.

"If you could watch one last movie, what would it be?" I asked.

"That's a tough question," he mused. "I have too many favorites."

"Come on. Pick one."

"*Goodfellas.*"

I propped up and turned on my seat to face him, my brows hiked.

He pivoted toward me as well. "Please tell me you've heard of *Goodfellas*. Robert De Niro. Ray Liota. Joe Pesci? *I'm funny, how?*" he said, exaggerating Joe Pesci's heavy New York Accent. "You have to know that scene."

I scrunched my nose and shook my head. "I can't say I watched it, but I've heard of it. What's so special about it?"

He looked a bit deflated since I couldn't share in his apparent love of movie quotes. "Just good ol-fashioned movie making at its best. Maybe one day I'll get to show it to you. What about you? What movie would you watch one last time?"

As I tried to think back on all the movies I'd ever watched, one movie came to mind. Roger, Isabella, and I had sat down the night before everything went sideways and watched one of my all-time favorite Disney movies, *Frozen II*. The memory tugged on my heart, and I couldn't help the wetness that formed in my eyes.

I didn't realize tears were streaming down my face until Jax took my chin in his fingers and gently turned my face toward him. Wiping the tears with his thumbs, he whispered, "Hey. It's okay. I'm sorry for bringing that up. I didn't mean to dredge up bad memories."

Feeling embarrassed, I wiped the rest of the wetness from my eyes. "You're fine. I'm just being a big baby. And it wasn't a bad memory, quite the opposite, actually."

"You want to talk about it?"

I battled with the notion of opening up and talking about them or keeping those memories locked inside. A part of me feared that if I talked about them in the past tense, somehow the little fantasy bubble I created for myself would burst. The fantasy in which Roger and Isabella still lived. This time, I wasn't able to staunch the deluge that welled and crested over in my eyes.

"Oh, angel." Jax reached over and took me into his arms, his warmth and strength enveloping me. Roping my arms around his neck, I buried my nose in the crook of his neck and took in that smell of rain and mint and something else. Something male, raw, and dangerously arousing. He felt so damn good and, in that moment, I needed him like I hadn't needed someone before.

I needed to drown all the pain splintering through my bones. Needed to block the nightmares living inside my head, day and night. And his body promised to do just that. Even if just this once. Even if for one blissful moment in time.

Tonight, the monsters didn't need to exist.

A fist of guilt dug into my chest. How could I think about pleasure when suffering plagued the world? The emotions warring inside me were more than I could take. Why was it so hard to simply let go?

His arms loosened and I pulled away, but he reached up and cupped my cheek, fingers trailing across my jaw. Eyes darkened to a stormy blue, he studied me, asking me the question I kept asking myself. *Do I want this?*

I felt the heat of his breath. Felt my skin tingle where his fingers paraded down to my neck. I had to stop overthinking this or I'd psych myself out of finding even one small reprieve. One solitary moment of abandon amongst all the sadness. This wasn't about love or about forgetting Roger, Isabella, and the beautiful life we'd shared. This was just about finding release and comfort—even if that release and comfort came from somebody else. I needed to take advantage of the moment right now or I'd never have the nerve again.

Straddling my legs over his lap, he gasped as I pushed my hips over his, hard.

"Kate," he panted. "What are you doing?"

"What's it look like?" I asked, rocking back and forth, already feeling the pressure of his growing length. "Please don't read into this, Jax. We're just two grown adults enjoying each other's company."

His gaze melted into something darker, richer. Gone was the jokester, the goofball always trying to make me laugh. What I saw in those eyes spoke of sin and fire. "You're vulnerable right now." His voice was deep, coated in warm honey. I knew he wanted me, too—there was no denying the heat and electrified tension between us—but he was also holding back. Still, he reached up and cupped my neck, thumbs caressing my jaw, tilting my chin toward his lips. "I don't want you regretting this," he whispered. "Are you sure this is what you want?"

The heat of his hands against my skin flushed throughout every inch of my body, making me ache for his touch. "Don't you?" I taunted him as I licked my lips, but deep inside, I prayed I hadn't misread him. What if he *didn't* want this?

Feathering his lips even closer, he teased the seam of my mouth with his tongue. "I've wanted you ever since I saw you slash those beasts to shreds on the bridge." Then his mouth crashed into mine and the world faded to black. All that existed was Jax, me, and this couch. He kissed me like he'd been dying of thirst in the desert and I was his oasis. Relentless and savage, he tangled his tongue with mine, each point of contact sending shivers down my spine.

Warmth pooled between my legs, and the urgency to quell that need became torturous. Threading his fingers through my hair, he gripped tight and pulled my head back slightly. "You taste better than I fucking imagined, angel."

I bit my bottom lip, contemplating if I should tell him I'd thought about him, too. Ever since he'd touched my thigh in the car. Ever since he risked everything to save me and Hank. Since he came out of that shower, clean and smelling like sin. *Heavens.* I'd struggled not to think about anything but whatever lay underneath that towel and how his body would feel on mine.

Of how his hands would feel if he touched my…

As if hearing my thoughts, he palmed my breasts through my shirt, rubbing my budded nipples. My body moved of its own volition, matching his touch, responding in ways I'd forgotten my body could. Dropping his hands lower, I moaned when his fingers slid up under my shirt, seeking my bare flesh. He drew circles on my belly, and the proximity of his hands to my breasts had me gasping for air. I wanted more; I didn't have time nor patience for teasing. I wanted him to rip off my clothes already.

Taking matters into my own hands, I grabbed the hem of my shirt and flung it off, followed by the very un-sexy sports bra. My breasts bounced free, and as the cold air hit my flesh, my skin pebbled.

His gaze pooled with dark, male need at the sight of my naked chest. If he wanted to hold back, I'd made it impossible now. Taking one breast in each hand, he brought my nipples to his mouth, swirling his sinful tongue over them. "This what you wanted, angel?" He sucked and licked my nipples until they were so hard, he took them between his teeth, gently tugging at the delicate buds.

Fuck. He knew exactly how to please and every time he tugged on my nipples, the bundle of nerves between my legs throbbed hotter. I moaned, every strand of my DNA chanting his name. I hated the tightness of my jeans. Constricting demon pants. They kept me from spreading my legs wider. Kept me from feeling the full press of his length between my legs. Rubbing against him, I sought the sweet friction of his cock.

Reading my cues, he gripped my hips and pushed me down onto him until I felt exactly what I'd been searching for. He was so hard, and when I stole a glance downward, I got an eyeful of his tented pants. My mouth watered at the outline of his erection. Heaven help me, his size was more than impressive.

This was insane. I was really going to do this. Have sex with a man I'd only met a day before, in the middle of the apocalypse. Well, if there was ever a time to, I guess the end of the world would be it, right? No regrets.

Reaching down, I cupped him through the fabric of his sweats.

"Fuck, angel. That feels incredible."

Stroking him harder, I reveled in the feel of his masculine body as he growled his approval. He lifted his shirt up and over his head, then threw it onto the coffee table next to our leftover Oreo feast. My gaze landed on his chiseled chest and the nonexistent scars of his non-existent wounds. So many questions fired off in my head. How was it possible for a human to heal so fast? Or how he knew so much about demons and angels and protection spells. But if I let those worries invade my mind, I'd staunch the fire burning between us and right now, I wanted to be scorched to oblivion.

Tugging on the drawstring of his sweats, I tried to slide my hand inside his pants, but he put a hand over mine, stopping me in my tracks. "We go that route, and our little game ends before we really get started."

Peering into his eyes, the heat of my stare must have told him I had no patience for games. He chuckled. "Chill, angel. We're not going anywhere until sunup. We've got time to take it slow." Sliding me off his lap, he sat me on the couch, planting his knees on the floor between my legs. "Let's start by taking these off." Unbuttoning my jeans, he yanked them off with ease, as if he'd done this hundreds of times.

All that remained were the white cotton panties I'd borrowed from the drawer.

"Spread your legs." Still on his knees, he didn't wait for me to obey; he simply put a hand on each of my thighs and opened my legs as far as they could go. "Keep them like this." Slowly rising to his feet, he leaned down and kissed me, hard and slow, soft and brutal, until my lips burned from his assault.

Trailing those same famished lips over my neck and chest, he made my body rage like a pyre, demanding more, crying for more. Before I realized it, he was back on his knees, my legs still spread. With his mouth hovering over my navel, his tongue swirled a spiral path downward. Imagining what that tongue would feel like buried inside me, tasting me, put me in a trance. Wet. Warm. My sex throbbed in anticipation.

I reached for his head, burying my fingers in his hair and tugging with my silent demands. I mentally begged for him to peel my panties back, to expose me to him. But instead, he just chuckled as he used his thumb to rub at my center.

I wanted to scream, but my anguish slowly turned into saccharine delight as heat swelled in my center, his thumb summoning the pulsing vibrations that began to coil deep in my belly. "There she is," he said with a heavy breath as my clit enlarged.

All coherent thought was extinguished, lost to the ether. Memories of pain and of loss were completely gone. In the rubble of my past, I found myself again. I sat there, letting him do what he wished. I watched him through hooded eyes as he reached into his sweats and took his cock in his other hand. The undulating sensations of utter pleasure radiating from my core put me in a peaceful head space. I never wanted this to end.

"Jax, please," I cried in a soft whisper.

He heard the words that died on my tongue and moved to oblige by pulling my panties to the side, but the conversation in the bedroom pierced the bubble in my head.

The trimmers…

The forest…

Shit.

I closed my legs so fast, I nearly squished his face between them.

"What the—"

"I'm so, *so* sorry," I said.

"Did I do something wrong?" he asked.

Utterly embarrassed, I shook my head. The source of the heat flaring through my body coming from some place totally different now.

"Then what is it?"

Biting my lip, I struggled with the words until I finally just blurted out the truth, "I… I didn't take advantage of the trimmers." I covered my face with my hands.

He let out a rumbling laugh, then took my hands from my face and cupped my chin, narrowing that midnight-blue gaze into mine. "And you think I give a fuck about that?" Leaning in closer, he let his mouth roam over mine, parting my lips with his tongue and swirling it inside my mouth. "Tell me," he said in between swirls, "don't you want this?" More swirls. "Inside your pussy?" He flicked my tongue, strumming the hot wire that ran straight to my sex. "Teasing your clit. Making you come in my mouth?"

Holy Mother of the Almighty... His words pillaged through me, rendering me speechless. Of course, I wanted that tongue sliding up and down my throbbing female bits—had ever since he licked that Oreo clean of its cream like he wanted to give it an orgasm.

I nodded my answer, but still kept my legs closed.

"Then let me taste you, angel. You have no idea what the thought of licking you did to me in that bathroom. You're gonna make me beg?"

The idea that he'd thought about me, about doing *that* to me, while he showered blazed a path of tantalizing heat straight to my core.

But...

There was no way I was going to let him see my cavewoman pussy. No fucking way. Forget the fucking apocalypse. Forget that I needed this release more than I wanted food. I had to think of something, and quick. "Okay," I said, "but on one condition." I already knew this was a terrible idea.

His gaze narrowed, his suspicion swirling. "What?"

"I get to taste you first."

He cocked his head to the side, unsure of my plan. "And if I let that happen, then you'll give up on your fear of a little hair?"

"It's not a little hair, but yes." I didn't think it would, but if I got him to come first, then I could get him distracted enough that he'd forget about me. I could only hope.

Standing, he put his crotch right in front of my face, peered down at me still sitting on the couch, and shot me a crooked grin. The smug look on his face told me he thought I was bluffing. "Go ahead, angel. Show me what you've got."

Cocky ass. But I wasn't bluffing. And damn if I didn't want to pull down those sweats. His erection was already rising. Reaching for the waistband, I wasted no time pulling the fabric down to his thighs, his massive dick springing free, practically hitting me in the face.

I'd not been ready for that. He was girthier than I imagined and at least eight inches long. I swallowed, wondering if I'd even remember what to do with... all that.

Sliding my hands up his thighs, I began my tease. I lowered my mouth but didn't touch him; I simply let my breath caress the tip of his head. His dick twitched, and I could sense his eagerness build. He wanted my mouth on him as badly as I wanted him inside. As I reached the base of his shaft, I wrapped my hand around his girth and began to stroke him, long and fluid, watching his leg muscles flex with each rugged moan that escaped his lungs.

A dewy drop formed at the tip, and using my thumbs, I slathered it over his head. "Stop teasing me, Kate. I need those damn lips around my cock." He practically growled at me as he laced his hands through my hair, bringing me closer.

It was my turn to shoot him a self-assured grin, which he offered back. And right as I opened my mouth, a bark erupted from inside the apartment. Perking up, I stared into the darkness of the hallway.

"It's just Hank," he said, his words breathy. "Don't worry."

Stroking him again, I was about to slide my tongue up his shaft when another bark sounded, followed by a whine. Pulling away from Jax, I stood. "That's not a normal whine. I have to check on him."

Huffing, he hung his head back and pulled his sweats up. "Fine. We'll go check."

"Thank you. And I'm sorry." Throwing my tank top on, I ran to the room in my underwear. Hank was shivering, and I wasn't sure if he was cold or maybe having a seizure. "Oh, my God. What is wrong with him?"

Jax ran out of the room and came back with a couple of candles. He pulled back Hank's lips and examined his teeth. They'd begun to blacken. *Fuck.* This couldn't be happening. We were supposed to have more time. All the fire and sexual tension morphed into fear and panic; the heat seated in my core now sourced by guilt, not pleasure.

"Jax, we can't wait until morning."

"We have to. Where are we supposed to go at this hour? The streets will be littered with the damned and *d'shiad*. He'll make it until morning."

"How can you be so sure?"

"What other option do we have? He has to make it."

I didn't have the courage to utter the words sitting on my tongue.

What if he didn't make it?

"You need to be prepared," he uttered, as if reading my thoughts.

I shook my head, unable to accept his words. "No. No, I can't. I won't."

"Kate, if Hank turns, he won't be the same dog. He won't even be a dog anymore."

"Don't say that," I spat, harsher than I wanted. "Can't you do something? You can heal, so why can't he? Try one of your spells."

"Prayers. And it doesn't work like that. What I am, it's not something I can transfer to him. I'll look around the place; maybe I can find something to help ease the pain of his wounds."

I laid beside Hank, letting my warmth soothe him. It seemed to calm him, and the shivers stopped. A short while later, Jax came back with a tube of some gel. "What is that?"

"It's lidocaine. I found it under one of the floorboards, along with a few other first aid essentials. This should help ease the pain a little."

After applying the ointment to the large gash on the side of Hank's body where the nightcrawler had gouged him, Jax tried to get me to leave the room.

"I'm not leaving him."

"It's not safe, Kate. If he turns in the middle of the night—"

"Not leaving."

"Kate—"

"You'll be here to protect me. Please. I can't leave him."

Knowing there was no use in arguing with me, Jax left the room and came back with one of the dining room chairs. "I'll keep watch. You sleep." Grabbing the blanket at the foot of the bed, Jax spread it over me and Hank before giving me a kiss on the forehead. "Rest up."

"Isabella," I muttered.

"Excuse me?"

"My daughter. That was her name. The night before all hell broke loose, we'd been watching *Frozen II* for our weekly Friday movie night. It's the last happy memory I have of her." I didn't know why I shared that. Why that was the first thought that came to mind. Perhaps because after I'd laid my body bare for him, my heart craved a bit of the same balm he'd offered my body.

"That's the movie you were thinking about earlier?"

I nodded.

"Thank you," he said.

"For what?"

"For sharing that with me. Sleep. I'll see you in the morning, angel."

Submit yourselves therefore to God.
Resist the devil, and he will flee from you.

JAMES 4:7

CHAPTER 6

JAX

I sat my ass down on the chair and rubbed my temples, watching Kate snuggle up closer to Hank.

My gut twisted.

Yeah, I was a bit peeved that my dream of finally sleeping on a real bed was snuffed—especially after Kate's unexpected, but more than welcome, move on me back on the couch. I'd already envisioned myself sharing this bed with her, arms wrapped around her gorgeous body post what I could only imagine would have been the best sex I'd had since the world went to shit.

The *only* sex.

Talk about blue balls.

But there I was again, staying awake yet another night, keeping watch over a dog.

Hank was nice and all—before he started turning into one of the damned. I had nothing against dogs in general—hellhounds excluded—but having this beast bark at the exact moment Kate was about to wrap those cherry lips around my cock… Fuck me. The mere thought of her tongue and that fire in her eyes letting me know she'd enjoy taking me into her mouth as much as I'd enjoy being devoured by her had me ready to rip out of my skin.

Shifting in the chair, I tried taming the erection tenting my sweats.

Her dog's about to lose his life, and all I can think about is getting laid?

I shook my head. This was borderline torture. Not to mention the fucking demon inside my head wouldn't shut up.

If it were up to him, he'd have us climb on that bed and take her. Jumping to my feet, I paced the room, fists clamped tight. Fighting his urges was a constant battle, and the longer this hellion lived inside me, the closer he was to taking full control of my body.

I couldn't allow that to happen. Regardless of how badly I needed that angelic sword to finally rid myself of the demon who'd taken up residence inside me, after what just happened with Kate, I couldn't fathom ever hurting her.

Not to mention she was fighting a battle of her own, if her thrashing and turning was any indication. Turning back toward her, I followed the rise and fall of her chest. She'd fallen asleep fast, and her soft moans were now accompanied by Hank's own restless growls, the morbid symphony cleaving my heart in two.

Seeing her like that doused the fire scorching my insides. *For now.* Hopefully, we'd have another chance to revisit what happened between us.

Glad I didn't have to fight a horny demon any longer, I sat and tried to think of the coldest place on earth—anything to keep my mind from wandering to feverish, sinful places.

I had no clue when I knocked off, but I bolted awake to a furious growl erupting from Hank. Bloodshot eyes stared straight at me, and I nearly fell off my chair. Still laying on the bed next to Kate, Hank panted, his lips curled in a snarl.

"Easy, boy," I crooned, unsure if it was still Hank in there. When I looked down at my lap, I realized I was rocking a hard-on. Could it be that he sensed my intentions? Or that of my demon's?

Slowly rising from the chair, I took note of the silence inside my head. The asshole was still asleep, which meant whatever Hank sensed came from *me*. His accusing gaze tracked every step I made as I walked over to the window and pulled the curtains open to reveal the sun climbing up in the sky.

Thank heavens. It was morning again, and Hell's worst creatures had gone back to their hiding holes.

Hank's rapidly worsening state meant we had better start our day early.

"Don't look at me like that, buddy," I scolded the dog when I turned back toward the bed. "I feel like you're either going to eat me or die on me, and I am not fond of either of those choices." His gaze locked on me as I stepped closer.

"She's starting to warm up to me," I said. "You wouldn't want to be responsible for my death, now would you?"

He growled and I swallowed thickly, understanding his message. Kate was *his* and there was little room for me. I shot him a knowing stare. I had zero intentions of taking her from him. Quite the opposite; I was trying to save his ass.

I did my best to ignore Hank's growls as I leaned over him to gently shake Kate awake. "Rise and shine, angel."

Her eyes opened, taking in the room as her lazy gaze finally met mine. A brief moment after, her cheeks flushed and she covered her face with her hands. Seemed she'd just received the same flashbacks from our *couch-de-vous*. I couldn't help the smile that tugged at my lips.

I peeled her hands away from her face and was about to plant a kiss on her lips when her attention was snagged away.

When her throat bobbed, I sighed. She'd seen the same thing I had a moment earlier. Hank had worsened overnight.

He plopped his head on the pillow and closed his eyes, forgetting about me and allowing Kate to pet his head. Her jaw clenched, and I knew she was holding back tears.

"Hank's going to be alright, Kate, I promise. We need to head back to the park, sooner rather than later."

Clint had better show up and not force me to break my promise, or I'll break his scrawny neck.

"We can head out now," she said, pushing the blanket away, revealing nothing but the white cotton panties I hadn't been able to pull down the night before. The memory of the wetness soaking through the fabric did nothing to ease my morning wood.

Why, hello there ... my demon crooned.

Fuck.

I bolted away from the bed and stumbled into a floor lamp, which fell with a loud *crash*. The demon chuckled at my attempt to get away from her.

Asshole.

For fuck's sake, I thought living with the thing had been a nightmare before I ran into Kate. But now? Forget it. I was royally screwed.

Kate stared at me, eyes at half-mast as she continued to chase away the sleep still clinging to her lids. "You okay?"

"I'm alright," I grunted, stepping over the broken glass dome.

I had no idea how long I could keep the pretense of being a perfectly normal human male just here to help a girl with her injured dog. She was already suspecting something—my scarless chest was proof enough that there was nothing *normal* about me.

Needing to avoid any further questioning, I picked Hank off the bed and transferred him to the living room. His fur appeared even thinner and kept sloughing off in clumps. Poor thing had little time left, but I couldn't tell Kate that. I would not be responsible for snuffing out her hope.

I ran to my duffel bag and retrieved a can of beans. Opening it, I pushed it in front of his nose. "That's all I've got. Eat up, buddy." But Hank simply laid his head back down. A pit settled in my gut. The loss of appetite was a clear sign that things were progressing even faster.

Leftover Oreos served as my breakfast. There was no reason to let a good thing go to waste, right? As I licked the cream off the center, Kate came out of the bedroom wearing a different pair of jeans and the leather jacket I'd seen hanging in the closet yesterday. She looked sexier than I'd imagined, and I wasn't able to keep my eyes from roaming her entire body, a tingly sensation scaling up my skin.

Clearing my throat, I paused my lewd thoughts and pushed the rest of the cookies her way. "Eat. I'll scout the hallway outside."

She ignored the cookies and didn't object to me going out alone, which was worse than if she had. It would've meant she still had a bit of fight left in her. All she did was bury her hands in Hank's fur and whisper to him as I moved the bookcase away from the door and squeezed into the windowless hallway with only a kitchen knife as a weapon.

The damned and the *d'shiad* tended to wander into apartment blocks for cover when the sun rose. Difference was, the damned could always wander right back out again, while the *d'shiad* needed to wait it out. Either way, if anything was hiding in the corridor, I'd need to dispose of it before it alerted any of its friends.

A crash sounded from one of the lower floors just as I closed the door behind me.

As far as I knew, this beast hadn't sniffed us out, even though we'd only been a floor above. The sage I'd burned must've worked and masked our scent.

Descending the stairs as quietly as I could, I came to a halt on the lower landing when another crash resonated from one of the apartments. I remembered seeing the door to one of the units already torn off its hinges when we'd looked for a place to crash last night.

That's probably where this beast was, and why we hadn't heard it come in.

Stalking toward the unit, I gripped the hilt of the knife tighter. I poked my head inside the apartment and immediately spotted the female beast. Looked like she had just begun her search.

Her clawed fingers grabbed onto one of the dining chairs, pushing it out of her path as she made her way into the kitchen and ripped the refrigerator door off its hinges, flinging it across the apartment and making me flinch as it landed a mere foot from where I stood.

Fuck. She's strong.

The reek from inside the fridge was so potent, it spread across the room instantly, the stench burning my nostrils. I gagged and had to clamp a hand over my mouth to keep from puking.

But the female damned wasn't fazed in the slightest. Finding a piece of moldy cheese, she chomped on it with a growl, snorting with every bite.

I gagged again.

Distracted with her meal, she didn't notice as I creeped into the apartment. Thankfully, the stink from the fridge hid my scent, but halfway across the living room, I stepped on a fucking dog toy. Its piercing squeak halted the beast mid-bite, and the creature's inky black eyes turned toward me in an instant.

She cocked her head, eyes widening as she realized I'd make a bigger and tastier treat. Dropping the green-black chunk of cheese, she rushed toward me in a flash of teeth and claws.

Luckily for me, although deadly, these things were very stupid.

In her frantic attempt to get to me, she ran straight into the kitchen knife, which slowed her down. A shriek and a gurgle of blood exploded from her mouth, hitting me in the face.

My demon roared as I pushed the damned backward and pulled my knife out as she swiped her viscous claws at me, trying to scratch my face off. She smashed into a grandfather clock across the room. Her landing *thump* and the *dong* of the clock resonated through the apartment and out into the hallway.

Heat flared from my chest, heart pumping a million miles a minute. While the damned were birthed out of a hell-born virus, demons seemed repulsed by their own creation, and mine enjoyed killing these beasts even more than I did.

He wanted this kill. And his demand to be let loose beat hard against my rib cage.

I'd normally let it take over without question. Powered by the adrenaline rushing through my blood, he'd multiply my strength tenfold, plus give me added speed and agility. I couldn't say his possession didn't come with a perk—after all, there was a reason I'd been able to survive this long.

But there was a downside, too, and a steep one at that. Once he took over, getting him to release me was like prying yourself free from the tight coil of an anaconda.

I wasn't about to take the risk, especially with Kate only a floor above.

"Jax, everything okay?" Kate hollered from the hallway.

Case in point.

Her voice sent shivers down my back. My demon was too riled and if she came too close, I would lose the battle. "Stay back! This will only take a minute."

There was silence from the hallway, and I prayed Kate had listened. Across from me, the beast stood from the rubble and eyed me warily.

I grinned at it, my skin feeling too tight for my muscles. I couldn't deny a part of me craved the feeling of invincibility— the high of having all that power coursing through me. But that was exactly why I needed to rip this damn demon from my soul. One of these days he'd become the dominant entity, and I'd be lost for good.

"Not so eager to bolt at me now, are you?" I taunted the creature as she snarled at me.

The floor beneath her turned black from the oily blood seeping from her wound, her sunken-in shape curling defensively, her animalistic roar attempting to scare me off.

Not likely.

She continued to swipe at the air with her clawed hands as I creeped closer.

Weakened by the blood loss, she could barely stand, wobbling all over the place. When I stepped into her vicinity, she swiped at me again, and this time, I wasn't able to hold my demon back. A growl rumbled up my chest as I—*he*—grabbed onto the beast's hand and cut straight through her arm with the kitchen knife, her wails echoing off the walls.

I—*he*—took the beast by the neck and squeezed until the neck broke, a thrill vibrating through my muscles.

"Jax?" Kate's soft voice floated into the room.

Fuck. The demon hadn't fully possessed me, but I could feel him right below the surface, and the sound of her voice only made him that much more anxious to rip through my flesh. I turned toward the entrance and cursed under my breath the instant I saw her standing in the doorway to the apartment.

I lowered my gaze and hid my face from her, not wanting Kate to see the redness I knew was blotting out my irises.

"I told you to stay back." The voice that boomed from my throat wasn't mine. Deep and gravelly, it sounded anything but human.

"Jax, are you okay?"

Every muscle in my body tensed as I fought to suppress the monster trapped inside me. It wanted out so badly that my head throbbed like my skull was about to crack. Even though my back was to her, I felt Kate's presence as she came closer, her fresh, clean scent so powerful it blocked the stench coming from the fridge and the lifeless beast on the floor.

She placed a hand on my shoulder, and I flinched. Keeping my eyes hooded, I looked away, hoping the redness would soon subside. Scanning over me, she noticed my blood-streaked hand, and said, "You fought her barehanded. You could've been scratched and infected."

"I'm fine," I said, my voice still deeper than my own, but sounding less animalistic. "And I wasn't barehanded." I waved the knife around, flicking blood across the floor.

Turning from her, I grabbed a rag laying on the couch and wiped my hands before dropping it to the floor.

"Are you always this reckless?" she asked as I walked past her toward the door.

"More so since you turned up," I replied with a grunt. "You're forgetting it was your idea to go back to the Brooklyn Bridge." Stopping, I turned toward her. "And do me a favor. Next time I tell you to stay the fuck back. Stay. The fuck. Back."

She crossed her arms, the damn leather jacket barely masking the way her white tank top hugged her breasts. "What ever happened to sending me into a demon-filled tunnel first?" she asked, her tone playful, yet chiding.

My lips tugged at the corners. "Perhaps I had a change of heart."

"Yeah, well, I've been fighting those things as long as you have. And before you showed up in your not-so-shiny armor and your-not-so-white horse, I was doing just fine."

"But were you?"

She stepped closer, her eyes digging into mine. "What's with you?"

I took a step back and rubbed a hand down my face. I paused for a second, my breath hitching, something like longing wrapped in pain twisting inside my gut. I didn't know why, but a part of me wanted to confide in her. Wanted her to know

I wasn't who she thought I was. That a demon lived inside me. And the longer this thing remained, the less of a chance I had of ever ripping it from my soul.

Eventually, it would consume me until I was gone and all that remained was him.

It was why I needed her sword. Why I'd gone to the bridge in the first place. Not to save her—because, quite frankly, Kate needed no one to save her.

Except now, maybe from me.

To sever the bond between me and my demon, the spell required a magical relic from an angel—gifted to me, not stolen. I knew that, which was why I was trying to fuck this up. Because if Kate found out the truth about me—about why the demon came to possess me—she'd probably want to plunge the blade straight through my heart before ever bequeathing its power to me.

Last night was a glimpse of something we could never have. Not in this fucked-up world, anyway. And it was that realization that made me turn away from her in silence and march up the stairs to our floor.

Kate didn't ask me any more questions once we made it back to the apartment, and we packed our things in complete silence. As we exited, I took one last look at the apartment. Our two empty milk glasses were still on the coffee table in front of the couch, and a bundle of hair that had fallen off Hank covered one side of the seat, while on the other side, Kate's pair of jeans lay crumpled in the exact same spot they'd fallen last night.

Before closing the door, I ran back to the bathroom, took the batteries out of the trimmer, and slipped them into my pocket.

On the off chance we found a flashlight, these puppies would come in handy. Or they could be used to barter.

Our walk to Central Park was eventless—not that I was complaining. I'd managed to clean up before leaving and had zero desire to get covered in monster goo again.

When we arrived at the gazebo, we sat on the wooden bench and waited. The park was eerily quiet in the early morning hours. Nothing preceded the sound of leaves rustling in the wind. Every now and then, a gust would pick up an orange-yellow bundle and ruffle it around before dropping it in a slightly different location. The soft *plops* of a water-strider gliding across the surface of the lake was the only sound contesting against the ruffle of leaves. The apocalypse outside seemed to not reach here.

Kate didn't say a word and Hank was asleep in his makeshift nest. I kept to my own darkening thoughts and doubts until a different sound pierced through the park.

Footsteps.

I rose from the wooden bench and walked to the bridge. Kate wheeled the cart up next to me just as a boy came into view in between the trees, a melodic whistle trilling over the soft *thumps* of his leisurely stride. It was easy to tell the moment he noticed us. His step faltered, the melody stopped, and he took his next steps stiffer than an old man on crutches.

"Clint," I said when he came close enough. "I have a favor to ask."

The boy studied me, then his gaze roamed over Kate until his eyes landed on Hank.

The dog growled, clearly not liking the way Clint examined him.

"The fuck!" Clint unholstered his gun faster than I could've said shit and pointed it at Hank. He would have taken the shot had I not stepped in front of the barrel before his finger twitched. The magazine had to be full of holy water-infused bullets, so I'd likely survive if he decided to shoot me. Still, the demon inside me would be more than a tad peeved, and that wouldn't bode well for anyone at this moment.

"God, no." Kate moved behind me, shielding Hank with her body as well.

"Listen, Clint, you know me. Right?"

The boy narrowed his eyes.

"I need you to take me to the priest so he can purify the dog. That's all I'm asking."

"Fuck that. The beast is gone, man. There's nothing anyone can do to help it."

"Jax." Kate's voice shook.

Clint waved the gun at me, gesturing for me to move. "Get out of the way, Jax."

"No."

Gun still aimed at me, he said, "We don't take unnecessary risks. That's how we survive. A turned dog is a hell-no."

"He's not turned yet," I said, my jaw tight. This wasn't going the way I had imagined, and having that barrel inches from my chest unnerved me, the demon inside me stirring.

"Get out of—"

I took a step closer, pushed his hands to the left just as the gun went off under his twitching finger and a bullet shot into the wooden floorboards covering the bridge. In one swift movement, I wrestled the gun away from him.

"The dog needs help," I said, tucking his weapon into my belt after I put the safety on. "I can trade for information on the location of the priest you get your bullets from."

He shifted on his feet, ready to bolt. "I can't give you the location—"

"I'm not asking, Clint."

"He cannot cure the infected, Jax. Don't you think he's tried that before? You've got to shoot the dog before it turns." Clint peered around me to take another look at Hank. The dog stared back with his bloodshot eyes. Ending his misery would be a mercy, but I couldn't give up on him. I'd made a promise to Kate. "And he's hella close to turning, man."

"Please," Kate said softly.

Something in Clint's composure changed as his eyes took Kate in. He relaxed his shoulders and his defensive stance faded. I was ready to choke the kid for staring at her longer than was proper, before I realized his eyes were fixed on the angel blade strapped to her thigh and not the alluring shape of her hips.

"What's it gonna be?" I asked, my voice harsh, needing to take his attention off her weapon.

"That blade…" Clint started. "I know what that is."

Kate cocked her head, which meant questions played around in her head, and this was not the place nor the time to have this conversation. I needed to stop him before he went on about the Guardians. "Hank comes first," I said. "Once the dog is safe, we can talk about the rest."

"Hank comes first," she agreed, but the quizzical look in her eyes told me she hadn't forgotten about the kid's sword comment.

Clint stared between me and Kate for a heartbeat. "What have you got to trade?"

"Pack of Oreos, two almost-full AA batteries, and a broken broadcasting device," I said, wishing I had kept the second package of Oreos for the trade.

"That's all?" the kid asked, biting his lower lip and taking another tentative look at Hank.

I should've searched the apartment one more time before leaving. For all I knew, there might've been bottles of holy water stashed under a floorboard, or maybe bullets. "Look, you know I'm good on my word. I'll get something else, but we need to get moving or it won't matter either way."

Clint took one more look at Kate's blade.

"We good?" I asked.

He shifted toward me. "Can I get my gun back?"

"Once you get us to the priest safely."

His jaw twitched. I didn't like taking his gun; the kid needed his weapon to survive. But I'd made a promise to Kate, and I intended to keep it. Swallowing a mouthful of air, he turned back to where he'd come from and led us through the park in a brisk stride.

Unease settled in my gut about halfway through the park. That gunshot had been loud and any damned lurking around would likely come snooping.

Kate and Clint started an easy conversation I wasn't following, too busy searching for anything lurking behind the next tree. The unease only grew as we neared the edge of Central Park and there hadn't been a single damned around us.

A block later, I forced my feet to keep up with Clint's stride, every step feeling heavier than the previous. All of a sudden, I felt like I was dragging two giant balls and chains with me. My whole body rebelled against the direction we were going, and I swallowed back the lump of vomit rising in my throat.

What in the actual fuck?

My stomach clenched, head about to explode from the sudden scream bouncing inside my skull. My demonic companion thrashed inside me, fighting against my will to move us forward to our destination.

Turning a corner onto Amsterdam Avenue, I finally realized why my demon was in such a tizzy. The Cathedral Church of St. John the Divine rose up into the heavens on the other side of another park. How the fuck they had managed to conjure a warding spell that reached halfway across Central Park was beyond me, but it was damn effective.

I stopped for a breath, but the spell made it hard to take in any oxygen.

Gasping, I stared at the holy site in awestruck terror, forcing a fake smile as Kate looked back at me. Should've known the priest Clint was working with would be the one at this church.

Kate raised an eyebrow, her face covered in the questions she'd laid out the night before when she demanded to know who I was—*what* I was.

I cleared my throat and tried to come up with something to say to distract her from her burning questions. "It's only the sixth largest church in the world. It's what... a hundred thousand square feet? More than that?" I had no idea what the fuck I was saying, but it seemed to be enough to get Kate to admire the building instead of studying my reaction to it.

Kate and Clint carried Hank's shopping cart up the grand stairs in front of the five arched doorways, while I stumbled up after them.

Clint knocked on the door in a calculated, rhythmic tune, a clear way to identify any unwelcome human strangers. No *d'shiad* would willingly walk up to that door, and definitely not in broad daylight.

The door opened to a young girl, probably no older than ten.

"Back already?" she chirped cheerfully before her eyes fell on Kate, then me, and then Hank. "Is that..." Her eyes widened. "Clint, you brought an infected? Especially after what happened last time?"

"Camila, go get your uncle," Clint said to the girl, ignoring her question.

"He's at the temple."

"We can go to him," I grunted, fighting against the pain radiating from my skull.

"He's probably in the middle of blessing the water," the girl answered. "It's not a good idea to barge in on the ritual."

She was right, that was a very bad idea. The temple, where all their holy rituals took place, was the worst place for me to be, considering I was already feeling like a boulder had flattened me.

"How long do you think it'll take?" Kate asked.

"How long will *what* take?" came a deep voice from inside the church. "Who's at the door, Camila? I've told you it's not safe for you right now." A tall, slim, dark-skinned man appeared at the entrance, dressed in a black cassock.

A shadow of dread spread across his features the instant his eyes locked on mine. Clasping the golden cross dangling from his neck, he stepped in front of Camila and urged her inside. "How in all that is holy did a member of the Devil's Army get through my wards?"

Fuck.

"You are not welcome here," the priest said, eyes brimming with contempt as he stared at me.

"Father, there must be some type of misunderstanding," Kate said, climbing a step. "We mean you no harm."

"You will come no farther, young woman. This is hallowed ground, but I will not hesitate to strike you down." His eyes shifted to the left, which meant there was someone out there with a gun aimed at us.

Kate put her palms up. "I don't know who you think we are, but—"

"Take a look at the man standing beside you. Do you think I would not recognize the son of one of the leaders of the Devil's Army?"

Kate turned to me. "Jax, what's he talking about?"

I couldn't meet her gaze and kept my eyes frozen on the priest. "She doesn't know about me, *padre*. And I'm not here on behalf of my order. We need your help to heal her dog."

"Your order?" Kate's voice climbed an octave. "Jax, what is going on?"

"Why would I help anyone associated with you?" the priest snapped.

The heat coming from Kate's gaze could have incinerated me, and the fact I lacked the balls to look at her and tell her the truth bubbled in my gut like a festering boil. Taking a sharp breath, I said the only words I knew would guarantee us safe passage, but that would also carve a chasm the size of the Grand Canyon between me and Kate. "Because she's a Guardian."

We are afflicted in every way, but not crushed; perplexed, but not driven to despair; persecuted, but not forsaken; struck down, but not destroyed.

CORINTHIANS 4:8 - 9

CHAPTER 7

KATE

Before the world ended, I used to patrol past this cathedral and never once thought about going inside. Impressive was an understatement. Not only was it massive and embellished with arches and intricate details on the outside, just standing by the entrance left my stomach hollow.

Its height opened up several stories above my head. The carved stone pillars loomed over us in awe-inspiring glory, taking my breath away. It made me believe, if just a little, that God might have actually cared enough about us at one point to inspire the creation of this church.

Everything about this space, from the light grey-tiled floor to the high ceiling to the windows carved from colorful vitrine glass, worked to make my knees weak. All that stone should've weighed heavily over me, and it did, but another part made it seem light as air, because how else would all those arches and alcoves simply not crash in on themselves from the load they carried?

The church I'd spent a night in with Jax had been eerily beautiful, but this cathedral was a masterpiece in its own right.

Jax, Hank, and I were escorted through what used to be the visitor center now turned security checkpoint. Two armed guards—one male and one female—dressed in non-distinguishable black military fatigues patted us down, looking for weapons.

They confiscated Jax's gun—well, Clint's gun—but they allowed me to keep my sword. The female guard seemed reluctant to even come near it. After doing a quick examination of Hank, the guard let me push the cart past the checkpoint and toward the nave.

I followed behind Jax, watching his back muscles move under the thin fabric of the black long-sleeve shirt he'd taken from the apartment. He walked slowly, as if a mountain sat on his shoulders. Something was off about him, but I couldn't quite put my finger on it.

He hadn't said a word ever since the priest's eyes widened at the mention of me being a guardian, whatever the fuck that meant. My heart literally plummeted to my gut the moment those words came out of his mouth. I immediately thought back to the small church. Jax had shrugged off all my questions.

If we hadn't been running for our lives, and Hank hadn't been fighting for his, I probably would have pushed him to answer me.

Damn it, I should have.

But after that hellish night, I'd been mentally worn and all I wanted was a place to crash. It hadn't been until we'd showered, and I noticed those wounds had healed at inhuman speed that I'd been able to confront him again. And of course, he'd refused to tell me how that was possible. In that instant, I knew things weren't what they seemed.

Looking back, I regretted not demanding answers.

Instead, I almost slept with him.

Christ. I'd opened up about my daughter and practically offered myself on a platter to him. Meanwhile, he'd told me nothing about himself except what his favorite movie was.

What an idiot I'd been.

I tightened my grip on Hank's cart and silently cringed at myself as we continued to walk through the nave. Like an ant scurrying through the foliage of an endless forest, I felt small and insignificant, and not only because the cathedral seemed boundless, but because I knew nothing about Jax. *Nothing that mattered.* And the thought made a crackle of uncomfortable energy skate over my skin.

The priest had clearly known who Jax was—known enough not to trust him or want him inside his church.

So, who the heck was the man walking in front of me? The man I'd kissed the night before? He'd not been able to even look at me since we arrived. What was he hiding?

Okay, so maybe I only knew him for a total of two days, but we'd shared something on that couch. Regardless of the fact we were both simply starved of sex and wanted relief, for a brief moment, I'd felt connected to him.

And to now see him this cold pricked my heart.

We came to a sudden stop as we approached a crossing, the section of the church where the long arm of the nave intercepted with the short arm. This area had been transformed to fit their needs and now served as some type of combat training floor. Four pairs of people sparred with each other, practicing fighting techniques.

"Guardians," the priest offered, as he noted my awed expression. "This is where they train."

"What are they training for?" I asked. Instead of answering me, he eyed Jax, silently chastising him with a gaze that would send him straight to Hell if he could.

"Could somebody please tell me what's going on?" My head pivoted back and forth between the priest and Jax. When Jax lowered his chin, I stepped closer to him. A fine sheen of sweat glazed his forehead. "What aren't you telling me, Jax?"

"That you've been chosen to fight in my army, Daughter of Eve," a lilting voice said from a shadowed corner behind the area that used to be the altar.

We turned toward the voice and the air seemed to get sucked out of the room. Dressed in what I could only describe as skin-hugging, white leather armor trimmed with gold and red threads, an olive-toned, dark-haired man ambled toward us.

His skin seemed aglow, as if he'd just stepped off a beach in Tahiti. Eyes the color of warm honey assessed me with a glimmer of recognition. Standing at almost seven feet tall, the muscled man was devastatingly beautiful, though his presence was overwhelming.

I had the sudden urge to drop to my knees in worship.

I didn't.

Jax, however, plummeted to the floor, knees hitting the tiles with a rough *thump*. Then he fell over onto his back, clutching his chest as if fighting to keep something from ripping through him. Horrified, I fell beside him. "Jax, what's wrong?"

He didn't answer; he couldn't. All he did was grunt in agony, jaw muscles twitching as a deep, animalistic growl erupted from him. Reaching for his face, I held his gaze. "Talk to me, Jax. What's happening?"

He clenched his eyes shut as the veins under his skin bulged and darkened. "Somebody help him, please!" I shouted to the room.

The priest rushed over, pulling a vial of holy water from a pocket in his cassock. Kneeling beside Jax, he sprinkled the holy water over his body. Everywhere the water hit Jax's skin, he seemed to burn as if being sprayed by acid. It didn't make sense. Only the damned or demons reacted this way to holy water.

Jax screamed and convulsed. Two of the people who'd been sparring ran over and pushed me away as they helped the priest hold Jax down.

Shaking, I watched as the priest held the cross that had been hanging from his neck to Jax's forehead, making the sign of the cross as he chanted, *"Omni potentis Dei potestatem invoco, omni potentis Dei potestatem invoco, abrogo terra, hoc angelorum in obse quentum, Domine expuere, Domine expuere, unde abeo Dei per… venisti."*

I had no idea what he said, only that it was in Latin. He repeated the phrase three times until Jax stopped screaming and thrashing. Crawling over to where he lay unconscious, I wiped a hand over his sweat-drenched hair. His breathing slowed and the acid burns began to heal, the deep red circular wounds turning pink before my eyes. The mark on his forehead created by the cross lingered on his skin longer. "What happened, Father? What's wrong with Jax?"

"The enemy has his claws in him," the priest said as he turned and met my gaze. "Though it's going to take more than holy water and some words to free him."

"Free him of what? What happened to him?"

His lips parted to answer my question, but he paused as if unsure he should say anything. Two more of his followers approached and lifted Jax's body.

"Where are you taking him?" I asked, a ribbon of fear coiling around my spine.

"He will be safe. I assure you."

I stood, watching as four strangers took off to another area hidden behind the altar, with Jax's body hanging limply between them. My heart raced, breath sawing in and out of my chest. I'd only known him for two days, but watching them carry Jax away tore me in two, regardless of whatever secret he'd kept from me.

Because I'd kept one from him as well.

Despite whatever these people knew about Jax, the man they carried away had saved me. He'd risked his neck to bring me to this place—for Hank. Because in the last several months, he'd been the only human who'd shown me kindness. Who'd made me feel something that even resembled hope.

Tears trickled down my cheeks as I turned to the individual still standing in the sanctuary—the man who seemed to make even the walls shudder at his presence. The one whose arrival seemed to cause Jax to fall to his knees.

"We've been expecting you, Kate," he said, eyes bright like liquid gold.

I slit mine in suspicion. "How do you know my name?"

He smiled, and it appeared the sun shone brighter through the stained-glass window behind him. "You were anointed by Zadkiel, lord of the Hashmallim. One of my brethren. His mark is upon you, and I've felt your presence since."

I thought for a second, remembering the battle on the bridge and the angel who interceded and fought beside me. The angel who had died protecting me and gave me his weapon. His last words echoed in my mind.

Blood of my blood. Flesh of my flesh. Katherine Elizabeth Jones, in the name of the Father, and of the Son, and of the Holy Spirit, I anoint thee.

"The angel on the bridge, the one who gave me this sword. He was—"

"A dominion, Daughter of Eve, of the second sphere. A lordship of the lower angels. They rarely present themselves to humans, yet one of the highest not only revealed himself to you, but he died protecting you and bequeathed you his sword— an honor no other human has ever possessed." Lowering to a knee, he bowed his head and a set of immense, bronze-colored wings spread from his back. "He died to ensure that you lived. And now, I pledge my sword to you as well."

Losing my breath, I stumbled backward.

When my parents died, I gave up my faith in the divine. Since the world went to shit, I'd cursed God and His heavenly host. My husband, my daughter, I'd lost them both to a disease spawned from the depths of Hell. And for the last eighteen months, all I'd dreamed of was revenge.

Revenge against the demons who took my family. The monsters who ravaged my world and took everything I ever loved. Revenge against the angels who never came. The God who never showed.

Seeing this holy creature kneeling before me—knowing one of his kind had sacrificed himself to save me only days before—should've overwhelmed me with love and wonder, but I couldn't consolidate my feelings. I was overtaken by grief as more tears flowed down my face while a current of anger vibrated through my chest.

All the loss and pain could have been prevented. We could have fought against the demons if only God had sent His angels. If they'd only fought beside us then.

Still on bent knee, the angel looked up and tunneled his gaze into mine. "I am Mikha'el. Archangel of the third sphere, former commander of God's Heavenly Army, and guardian of this realm. Your pain is my own, Daughter of Eve," he said. "I carry the lives of every human lost. Of all the sorrow and anger brought upon a war that should have never been. I know I let you down, but the time has come to take arms once again."

He stood, towering above me as he tucked those immense, glorious wings that seemed to disappear behind some type of glamor. "I know you have questions," he said, "but first, you must eat and rest. Then, we'll talk."

I blinked, my mouth unable to form words. Could it be? Was the angel standing before me *the* Mikha'el? Had the mightiest of God's warriors knelt before me as if I were someone important? Pledging himself to me as if he owed me anything? And why had he said *former* commander of God's Heavenly

Army? He was right; I had questions, tons of them, but right now, there was something else that weighed heavier on my heart.

Swallowing thickly, I looked over to where Hank lay nestled in the cart. I cared little for food or rest at the moment. What I needed was retribution.

Perhaps the angel owed me more than he could ever imagine.

Eyes shut, Hank looked minutes from death. I couldn't have come this far only to lose my best friend, not like this. I turned to Mikha'el, eyes still wet with tears and pleading for a miracle. "If you are who you say you are, then save him."

His gaze shot over my shoulder. "Father?"

The priest stepped forward and examined Hank, pulling back his flews and checking his teeth. The gums were practically dark as coal. "We don't have much time, but he may have a shot. We need to take him to the infirmary at once."

The priest took off with the cart, wheeling Hank through a hallway adjacent to the nave, which led to another portion of the church that housed their administrative offices. The archangel and I followed at an equal pace.

As I grabbed onto the cart and helped him wheel Hank, the priest said, "When the gates opened, unleashing the four horsemen into the world, no one understood what happened, why people were falling ill to this disease. Why, all of a sudden, we were quite literally stuck in the middle of a zombie-esque apocalypse."

"Or why some people weren't affected," Mikha'el added.

"When the virus broke out," the priest continued, "scientists tried to formulate a cure. And every time they thought they'd figured things out, they failed. Then, when governments and nations fell and the world went silent, all hope for a cure was lost."

"It's a hell-born disease," I said. "How could anyone know how to fight against that?"

The priest stopped before a closed laboratory door and my eyebrows scaled up my forehead. I had no idea churches housed science labs. He noted my confusion. "Science and religion are not all that different, my child."

After knocking on the door, a short, red-headed woman dressed in a lab coat opened the door. The inside looked like a cross between a hospital ward and my high school science classroom.

"You've been conducting your own experiments?" I asked as Hank was rushed to one of the patient rooms.

"The main problem with the medical approach, my dear child, was that scientists were trying to heal the *body*."

I hiked an eyebrow, not understanding his comment. "Isn't that what medicine is supposed to do?"

"Ah, yes, but this virus corrupts more than just our bodies," he explained, a twinkle sparkling in his dark brown eyes. "This virus corrupts the soul. It's what robs humans of their humanity, what transforms us into monsters. The creatures we've been thinking are soulless zombies aren't soulless at all. And therein lies the key, the clue to solving the riddle."

"Wait, what?" Was it possible that the souls remained somewhere inside the infected humans? I couldn't help thinking back to Roger. To Isabella. "Are you certain? How did you figure this out?"

"When *he* showed up." He nodded toward the archangel standing behind me, as if he wasn't referring to the commander of God's army.

"He was the missing piece," the priest went on. "It was because of Mikha'el that we discovered the Corrupted could not be in the presence of a divine being. Higher order demons can tolerate angels to a degree, but those ravaged by the infection are repelled simply by being in his presence. It was because of this we realized that the key to healing the infected wasn't in purifying the body, but the soul."

Hank was loaded onto a metal table and his legs were hogtied to prevent him from thrashing or trying to bolt. He was also muzzled; they said it was for his safety, but I knew they'd done it for ours—in case their treatment failed. I turned back to the priest. "How exactly do you purify a soul?"

The priest prepared an IV. "The only way I know how—through God. But given the Almighty has gone MIA, the closest we could ever get to God Himself was through His heavenly host. So, we used Mikha'el's ichor—"

"Ichor?"

He sighed at my interruption. "The life-force running through his veins. We were able to create a type of antidote using angel blood."

"Angel blood…" I trailed. "Are you telling me that the cure to saving mankind has rested with the angels all along?" I turned to Mikha'el. "You could've prevented all this devastation?"

He stepped closer, the outline of his wings visible through the glamor. "Trust me. Had I known sooner—"

"You abandoned us."

Golden eyes darkened to a burnt yellow and he tightened his jaw. I swore the shadows lurking in the corners grew taller as he anchored his gaze to mine, sending shivers crawling down my neck. "I did not forsake you," he said, voice full of gravel. "We were—"

"Mikha'el," the priest interrupted.

Tremors still running the length of my spine, I turned back to Hank, threading my fingers through his fur while avoiding Mikha'el's impossibly bright golden eyes. I'd pissed off an archangel, and as much as the idea had me preening my own feathers with satisfaction, another part of me recoiled, remembering this archangel was as old as time and had fought holy wars in God's name.

"So, what's the plan?" I asked Father Ortega, ignoring the heat of Mikha'el's gaze burning holes through my clothes.

"Inject Hank with *his* blood?" I gestured toward the broody angel beside me.

"When Mikha'el arrived," he said as he started Hank on the IV, "we didn't realize the infected were repelled by angels until he joined our ranks in a battle against the Horsemen."

My ears perked up at the mention of the Horsemen. "You've seen more than one?"

"Pestilence and Death, the ones currently rounding up all the girls of child-bearing age in the city. We don't know where the other two are, but I'm sure War and Famine are ravaging other parts of the world."

"I saw a Horseman two days ago. He kidnapped a girl. It's how I ended up cornered on that bridge. I tried to rescue her."

The red-headed woman helping the priest paused to look at me. "They've taken hundreds of girls, if not thousands. We've been able to rescue some, but we've lost many of our own fighting against those demons."

"Why are they kidnapping girls?" I asked.

"You don't know much about what's happening in this city, do you?" Father Ortega asked, his voice vexed.

His snide remark hit a frayed nerve. "I've been a little preoccupied losing my family and fighting to survive the last eighteen months, Father. Forgive me if I haven't had time to brush up on End of Days current events."

His face sank, perhaps realizing he'd been unfairly harsh. "We've all lost someone to this scourge. I'm sorry about your family."

Seemed we were all shaved down to our bones. With a nod, I accepted his apology. "But now there's an antidote, a cure. We can save people."

"Not quite," he said, approaching the archangel with a monstrous-sized looking syringe, preparing to draw his blood. "The Corrupted can't be saved. Once someone completes the transformation and the body starts to decay, there's no way to reverse it. The only thing we can do is try to prevent the transformation. But even though an *infected* starts to heal almost immediately once the antidote is administered, every person we treated with the antidote healed, only to be burned from the inside out by a light brighter than the sun. In a matter of minutes, they were nothing but ashes."

My heart squeezed at his words. He was going to inject this *antidote* into Hank. "If this treatment hasn't worked, what makes you think it will affect Hank differently?"

"Hank isn't human. He hasn't reacted to Mikha'el's presence the way others do. Most go rabid, desperate to get away."

"But what if he's too tired to react?"

"Only one way to find out. Camila, bring me a vial of holy water."

I hadn't even realized the girl had followed us into the infirmary. Clint had said the priest was the girl's uncle, which was visible in the tone of her skin and shape of her nose. What took me by surprise was the ease with which she jumped right to action, as if she'd done this dozens of times.

"Holy water, holy water," Camila muttered under her breath as she ran to one of the glass-doored fridges. That's when it dawned on me: they had power. *Probably solar.* She took out a vial filled with clear liquid, and her young features set in determination as she ran back.

Camila couldn't have been older than ten or twelve, yet her demeanor was that of an older child—or one who'd witnessed too many horrors and had now grown desensitized to it all.

Still, the softness of her facial features and her small hands reminded me of Isabella, despite the age difference. She was simply a child living through hell, just like my daughter had been. Except Camila had survived where Isabella hadn't.

As Father Ortega readied to inject Hank with the angelic blood and holy water concoction, I put my hands out to stop him. "Wait. What if Hank can't tolerate it, either? What if he burns up like all the others?"

"Child," Father Ortega said. "If we do nothing, he will succumb to the infection."

"There must be another way."

"If you have any other ideas, I'm open to hearing them."

"You said the infected died because they couldn't tolerate the serum. Mikha'el's blood is too strong. Why not use a less potent concoction?"

His forehead creased in frustration, the lines around his eyes deepening. "You think we haven't thought of that? We tried diluting it, which is why we use holy water. We're not a-state-of-the-art facility capable of doing more than basic science. We barely have enough power to run the coolers."

"What about me?" I asked, taking off my jacket and fisting my hand as I offered my exposed arm to him. "My blood. When the angel who died on the bridge anointed me, he did it with his blood. I saw what it did to me and felt his essence flow through me. It glowed under my skin like rivers made of gold."

Father Ortega raised his eyes to the archangel. "Is it possible?"

Mikha'el crossed his arms and paced. "Zadkiel was a dominion. It would have been within his power to bestow such a blessing onto a mortal. Father Ortega, if Kate is right, then your prayers might have been answered."

"Can you do it?" I asked.

"I… I think so, but I will need time to test it."

"Hank doesn't have time, Father."

Taking out a new needle and syringe, he prepped my arm for extraction. "Young girl, if this works, you might have just saved humanity." As he pricked my flesh and my blood drained into the tube, I saw golden flecks swirl inside the crimson liquid.

Father Ortega's eyes widened, lips twitching with wonder as he examined the vial. "*Fascinating*. I've never seen anything like it."

"Do you think you have enough?" Mikha'el asked.

"I hope so. Trinidad, Francisco, hold Hank down." Father Ortega raised his gaze to mine. "You should probably wait in the hallway."

"I'm staying."

"The process is not without pain."

"I'm staying."

Nodding, he waited until Trinidad and Francisco had Hank restrained before injecting him with my blood and holy water mixture. The instant the priest plunged the needle into Hank's neck, Hank began to convulse, and a string of high-pitched whines and growls erupted from him unlike anything I'd ever heard.

He fought to free himself, thrashing against the metal table as the priest and his two assistants held him. I tried to calm him, to rub his nose, but he growled at me, his eyes filled with the same feral hatred of the beasts I'd seen on the streets.

That wasn't Hank staring back at me; that wasn't my best friend anymore.

The pained cries vibrating from his body tore through me. "I'm so sorry, buddy. But you're going to be okay. I promise." I touched his head, but he just growled deeper. Had he not been muzzled or restrained, I know he would've attacked me.

Unable to contain my own pain, I tried to push one of the assistants away, perhaps thinking I could somehow ease his discomfort, but I only managed to anger Hank more.

"Get her out of here," Father Ortega ordered Mikha'el.

"No. I have to stay with him. He needs me."

"Your presence is only making things harder for him. Mikha'el, now."

Before I could utter another word, the archangel wrapped his arms around me and dragged me out of the room. Even though his touch worked to ease my worries, I tried to pry myself free. It was useless; he was too strong.

Once we were back out in the hallway, he set me down and I pulled away harshly. The peace that'd seeped through the contact drew back instantly, leaving me hollow and anxious.

Pacing, I pressed on my temples. "I should be in there with him. What if he dies?"

"You are serving him better by being out here."

"He's going to think I abandoned him."

"You aren't."

I stopped and narrowed my gaze. "You mean, the same way God and His heavenly host *didn't* abandon us?"

He swallowed hard and bit down on whatever he was about to bark back. After a brief moment, he said. "Kate, things are not what you think."

"Then tell me," I challenged, stepping closer to him, my head barely reaching the height of his shoulders. "Why did God allow this to happen to us? Why does He allow children and animals to suffer? The innocent. Why?"

"This is not His doing."

My lips twitched with a humorless laugh. "He allowed this world to end and left us here to die."

Cocking his head, Mikha'el's brow pinched, disbelief ghosting across his face. "God didn't leave you, Kate. Humanity lost faith. It was you who gave up on Him. On us."

"Well, maybe we got tired of waiting for miracles. Maybe we got tired of watching people suffer and not having our prayers answered."

Before Mikha'el could respond, Father Ortega came through the door.

I rushed to him. "Please tell me Hank's okay. Father, please."

He wiped the sweat beads coating his forehead with the back of his arm, the underarms of his cassock soaked. "He's stable. Looks like we were able to stop the transformation. Your blood worked."

"I need to see him," I said, pushing past him, but he put an arm out and stopped me from entering the infirmary.

"He's sedated. We'll let you know once he's awake. Get some rest; you need it."

Muscles tight, I huffed a loud breath. "What I *need* is to see my best friend."

Eyes softening over me, Father Ortega put a palm on my shoulder. "And you will. But right now, we're monitoring him to make sure the treatment is fully effective. Please, Kate. Hank is in good hands. Rest."

"Kate, let us help you," Mikha'el added, standing beside me, the calm in his voice involuntarily easing my nerves.

I wasn't sure if he'd used some type of angelic power over me, but the anxiety plaguing me seemed to dissipate. The unwavering look in Father Ortega's eyes told me I wasn't going to convince him to let me inside the infirmary anyway, so I gave up the fight. "If you won't let me see Hank, then at least let me see Jax. Where are you keeping him?"

"He's being held in the west wing barracks, in one of the private rooms," Father Ortega replied.

Did they think Jax posed a threat? "Are you keeping him prisoner?"

"At the moment, we are just keeping him isolated."

"Is he infected?" I asked, worried what I'd witnessed in the nave had been Jax beginning to turn. He'd fought that devoured barehanded and could have been bitten or scratched.

Dammit. I'd warned him. And now the thought of losing someone else I cared about to this disease deepened the darkness already stirring inside me.

The priest wiped at the wetness on his brow again. "I think your friend should be the one to explain his situation to you."

"I'll take her," Mikha'el said.

I turned to face him, ready to tell him I didn't need an escort, but the instant I parted my lips, the words evaporated. Arms crossed, he stood with his legs shoulders-width apart, those golden eyes blazing like tiny suns. There would be no arguing with the seven-foot-tall archangel.

I nodded my agreement, then turned to the priest. "You'll come get me as soon as Hank is awake."

He agreed and went back inside the infirmary.

*Because you are precious in my eyes,
and honored, and I love you, I give men
in return for you, peoples in exchange
for your life.*

ISAIAH 43:4

CHAPTER 8

KATE

After a few minutes of walking in complete silence toward the barracks, I asked the burning question that had been eating me up since before the world ended. "What did we do to piss off God?"

The sound of our footsteps echoed down the tiled hallway, then died as Mikha'el came to a stop. "God never intended for this to happen," he said. "Samael was cast out of Heaven for betraying God's love for His creation—for humanity. The last thing He would have wanted would be for Earth to fall to this ruin."

"Samael?"

Mikha'el resumed our walk down the corridors of the church's administrative building. "You know him by many names, but his role has always been the same. He's the accuser, the seducer, and the angel of death. Samael was a seraphim of the first sphere, the one closest to the Throne of God, and he refused to kneel before Adam, the first human. To Samael, humans were imperfect creatures, unworthy of God's love. And it is because he was one of the most-high that he received such a severe punishment."

We rounded a corner and were met with more offices and hallways lined with statues of saints. "The legend of the Fall," I said, remembering Nana's teachings. "Samael is the Devil."

"Spoken about through all lifetimes in all faiths."

I paused for a beat and pivoted to face him. "So, it's true?"

He swiped a dark lock of hair from his brow. "Human stories vary, Kate. What matters is that Samael was imprisoned in Hell, never to set foot in this realm or any other."

"Yeah, well… the apocalypse happened. So much for being imprisoned."

"We're in the End Times, but Samael is still imprisoned. Preventing the apocalypse is why I'm here." He leaned in closer. "Why *you're* here."

This time it was me who stopped. "Back up. What do you mean, prevent the apocalypse? Isn't that what this is?" I asked. "The last eighteen months have been hell on Earth, *literally*."

He shook his head and started walking again, gesturing for me to follow. "With Samael imprisoned, there was no one to test humanity. His sole purpose when God created man was to test their worthiness. With no one in charge of ensuring only the worthy entered the kingdom of Heaven, God was left with only one option."

We came to an intersection and Mikha'el made a right, taking us even farther from the actual church. This cathedral was so huge and filled with so many passageways, I felt disoriented. There was no way I'd remember how to get back.

"Samael was too dangerous to be set free," Mikha'el went on. "He wanted to prove to God that humans were unredeemable. His plan was to corrupt this planet and stake it as his own."

"A fuck you to his creator."

"More or less. But Samael didn't fall on his own. His legions were cast out as well, including his lieutenants, four other seraphim, or as your people call them, the Four Horsemen of the Apocalypse. While Samael is bound to his prison, lesser demons—the angels corrupted by his hate—plus his horsemen were allowed to walk the earth, so long as all they did was test the faith of the mortals, but nothing more."

My head pounded with questions. There was no way God thought they'd simply obey His rules. I mean, even my mother had been smarter than that when it came to me, and I wasn't some supernatural being looking to corrupt a whole planet. "Please don't tell me God actually believed His rebellious angels would agree to play nice. Seriously. That's just stupid."

Mikha'el came to a halt. What I'd said clearly upset him because the shadows did that weird thing they did back at the lab, and if I had to choose between fighting this angel in battle or facing off with a nightcrawler, I'd choose the latter.

"You mistake God's mercy and grace for stupidity, Daughter of Eve. You think yourself wiser than the maker and ruler of all creation? Than the one who breathed life into your lungs? Or Isabella's lungs?" His voice was sharp and whipped against my heart, leaving an emotional welt the size of a fist.

I may have lost faith in my creator, but that didn't mean I didn't fear or respect God. Still, he had no right to chastise me. "You know nothing about me or my daughter," I said, my voice so small compared to his, I felt like a mouse, but I didn't care. "Don't you ever mention her name again."

The muscles in his jaw tensed. "God," he said, "is not a fool. He believed humans would rise above the challenge. But through his minions, Samael unleashed every form of temptation upon the earth, determined to show God how disappointing His precious humans were."

Hearing Mikha'el talk about humanity as if we were mere pawns in a chess match between God and the Devil churned the acid in my stomach. "So, He just stood idle, watching us tear each other apart at the hands of His fallen angel, *hoping* we'd eventually come around and prove Samael wrong?"

"For many lifetimes, angels were forbidden to interfere with human affairs. Such was God's faith in you that He didn't believe you needed our intervention, our help."

Turning my back to him, I walked ahead. "As I said. He stood idle while we suffered."

Speeding up behind me, he grabbed my arm and spun me around. "He let you make a *choice*. He gave you the freedom we never had. Faith. He could have wiped the slate clean at any point. Given up on you, but…"

"But what?" I spat, tugging my arm back. "Here we are, living in this nightmare. He should've just wiped the slate clean, like you said. It would have been simpler, less painful."

"No, Kate. Don't you see? *You* are His most precious creation. It wouldn't have been simpler."

"And what about you, Mikha'el, commander of God's Army and guardian of this realm? You also stood by, watching us destroy ourselves, hoping we'd eventually come to our senses?"

The archangel stepped forward, his golden eyes alight with fire as he pulled every shadow to himself. "I convinced God to send you His only son, even knowing his fate. And as he died on that cross, cleansing you of your sins with his blood, I fought beside the Guardians, those still strong in their faith, until I captured the Horsemen and sealed them behind the gates of Hell."

My chest rose and fell as I considered his words, every syllable sinking into my bones.

"I fought for humanity back then, and I will fight for it now," he went on. "Until my last breath. Because I still believe in you, Kate. In all of you. Even if you've lost faith in us."

Heart pounding, all I could do was stare into the luminance of his eyes, wondering if perhaps he was right.

Had our loss in faith led to all this?

Mikha'el nodded toward the door at the end of the hallway. It was guarded by one of the men I'd seen carry Jax away. "He's in there."

As I started toward the door, I paused, one question nudging the back of my neck. I turned back toward the archangel. "Mikha'el, who opened the gates and released the Horsemen?"

A muscle in his jaw twitched.

"You want me to fight alongside you and to have faith, but you must start with the truth. Who opened the gates?"

"The truth will set you free, Kate. But it won't be without a cost."

After the shit I'd been through the last eighteen months, I had zero patience for cryptic messages. We now all knew that God existed. That everything we had ever thought to be lies made to give us a false sense of hope weren't truly lies. But so what? None of that helped us now. I needed facts. Because once I knew who the fuckers responsible for this mess were, I'd become *their* angel of death. "Who, Mikha'el?

"The Devil's Army."

"The Devil's Army?" The blood in my veins iced, my entire body becoming a frozen block. "Father Ortega. When we arrived, he said Jax…" I swallowed deeply, but my saliva had turned to dust.

"Be careful in there," he whispered as he walked into the shadows and was swallowed up by the darkness in the hallway, as if he was made of smoke.

Well, that was ominous.

Taking a deep, cleansing breath, I donned my emotional armor. After witnessing that strange seizure-like episode that looked straight out of a horror movie and seeing how his wounds healed yet again, Jax had a whole lot of explaining to do. And I was not leaving that room without answers.

Dread spider-walked over my skin as I approached the door. I was about to face a man who'd recently found his way into my heart despite all the sadness and gloom of this world. He'd made me laugh, made me *feel* again. He'd given me a sense of hope that perhaps I didn't have to keep fighting to survive alone.

There was no way he was connected to the Devil's Army. I couldn't accept that he was responsible for all the death and destruction brought upon by the Horsemen.

There had to be a perfectly good explanation for all of this. Otherwise…

Without realizing it, my hand slid down to where my sword was strapped to my thigh. I caressed the hilt, feeling a strong vibration climb up my arm.

The disturbing thoughts birthing in my mind were interrupted by the crackling sound of a walkie-talkie. I recognized the muffled voice of Father Ortega. "Copy," the guard at the door said. As I approached, he lowered the walkie. "The room is warded, so you should be safe. I'll be out here if you need anything."

Warded? Against what?

"Okay, thank you," I said and waited for him to open the door to let me in. When I walked through, my chest filled with a hearty breath of relief. Jax stood in the middle of the room, pacing, and the minute he spotted me at the door, he didn't even give me a chance to take a second breath.

He rushed toward me and crashed his lips to mine. Wrapping his large palms around my face, he kissed me so hard and deep, he made me forget about the world for a brief moment. A heatwave spread throughout my entire body and pooled between my legs with each stroke of his tongue.

My body melded to his and my mind was possessed by thoughts too indecent for this place.

"Kate," he breathed, halting his devilishly sinful assault on my mouth. "I was so worried about you."

"I was worried about you, too," I panted as he migrated his lips from my mouth to my neck. I knew it was inappropriate to do this now, especially when there were so many unanswered questions between us. When he'd been so cold to me. When I had no clue who or *what* he was.

But I had lost my ability to think coherently when he pushed me against the closed door and his hands traveled down my body.

"I know I owe you an explanation," he said as one of his hands gripped my ass, sending a pulse of sweetened heat to my center. "I never meant for any of this to happen."

Running my fingers through his hair, I fixed my gaze to his. Heavy lidded, his eyes flashed with lust and hunger, almost making me lose my resolve to question him. But I pushed past the pleasure, past my need to have this man. "Jax, please. Just tell me the truth."

"There will be time for that," he said, claiming my lips again, silencing me from saying more. "Right now, I need to have you. To finish what we started last night."

Thoughts of his muscled body and his strong arms wrapping around me when I ground my hips into him invaded my mind, along with the heat of his arousal and the feel of his rock-hard erection.

His hands slid up my shirt and reached for my breasts. I moaned, surrendering to the idea that fighting against this need was pointless. I wanted him, more than I thought possible. Right when he was about to unclasp my bra, a knock sounded at the door.

"Kate," Camila's small voice came through. "Hank is awake." It was like pouring a bucket of ice water over my head.

"Jax, wait," I said, my voice sweet, betraying my words.

"Whoever *that* is can wait," he said, pushing his pelvis into me. The friction of his cock pressing against my center made my entire body grow soft in his hands.

"Kate?" Camila's voice sounded again, and I put my hands on Jax's chest in an attempt to stop him from making this a tougher fight.

"Jax, please. It's Hank," I whispered.

"Shit," he gritted as he pounded his fists against the door. Caged between his body and the door, I felt both the fire of his anger and the ice of his disappointment. He looked into my eyes, silently pleading with me to not go.

"I'm sorry," I said.

"You've any idea how badly I need you?"

"I need you, too," I said, placing a palm on his cheek. "But…"

"I've been an utter mess not knowing where you were," he said, cupping my chin. "Or what happened to you. One minute it feels like my chest is about to split open and the next, I'm waking up in this makeshift cell. Alone."

"They took you away once you fell unconscious. Jax, what is going on? What happened to you out there? Who are you?"

"Kate…" Camila crooned. "Do you want me to come back?"

"They were able to help Hank?" he asked.

Of course, he would take the opportunity to divert my questions. "No. You don't get to do this to me again. You're going to tell me who you are right now. Who is the Devil's Army?"

He turned from me, running an agitated hand through his hair. "Kate…"

Another knock sounded at the door.

"Go. Hank needs you," he uttered. "We'll talk later."

I stepped closer. "Talk to me now. Just tell me the truth."

He turned around, hands on his waist, features darkened as he looked at me with regret-filled eyes. "I'll tell you everything, but I need time to think, and you need to go see Hank. I promise I will tell you the truth."

When all I did was stare, he answered my unspoken question. "I'm not going anywhere without you. I'll be here. Now go."

He was right. If Hank had woken up and they'd sent someone to get me, it meant Hank needed a familiar face. I had to go to him. Nodding, I said, "Fine. But we're not done talking about this. This thing between us, it doesn't go further until I know the truth."

Camila took me by the hand as she walked me through the now candle-lit hallways of the administrative building. "How long have you all been staying here?"

"My uncle was a pastor here before the gates opened. I lived with my parents in Brooklyn before coming here."

"Where are your parents now?"

Her hand tightened around mine and her breath hitched.

"You don't have to answer. I know it's not easy to talk about those who passed."

"We've all lost someone," she said, echoing her uncle's words. "But now that you're here, we finally have a chance."

I stopped and knelt to be at eye level with Camila. "What do you mean?"

"Your sword. It's the only weapon with real power to fight against them. The Guardians all used to have them, but they were taken back before the gates opened."

"Who took them?"

She swallowed hard and her gaze lowered along with her voice. "I heard them say God took them because we stopped believing."

"And what do you believe?" I asked, standing and taking her hand as we continued toward the infirmary.

"That God is mad. Like Mom and Dad would get when I did something wrong. But they still loved me."

"You think God still loves us?"

She shrugged. "I don't know. I guess. Maybe He sent us you because he does."

"I don't think He sent me, but He's sending angels, like the one who gave me this sword and Mikha'el."

As we arrived at the infirmary, Camila stopped for a second and looked up at me before knocking on the door. "Mikha'el wasn't sent by God, Kate. He fell from Heaven."

Her words stalled my heart. Why would God's mightiest warrior fall from grace?

The door opened and Father Ortega stood at the entrance with a big smile on his face. "Kate, it worked. I think your blood actually worked."

Father Ortega walked me to the patient room where they were holding Hank. When they opened the door, I burst into tears as Hank lifted his gaze from a bowl of food and abandoned it to run to me. He jumped on his hind legs and placed his paws on my chest, inviting me to return the hug. "Oh, buddy," I squealed. "I'm so happy to see you're feeling better."

Lowering him back down, Hank spun around twice, tail wagging like a propeller. I couldn't believe this was the same dog I'd seen only a little while ago. "He looks…"

"Like he wasn't even sick. I know. It's unbelievable," Father Ortega said.

I scratched Hank's neck and let him lick my face. "Love you too, buddy."

Hank sat, staring at me with gleeful eyes, tongue drooping to the side in utter happiness. "You're such a good boy," I said, urging him to finish his meal.

Turning to Father Ortega, I couldn't help myself, and put my arms around his neck and hugged him. "Thank you. Thank you so much."

"All I did was give him an injection. It was your blood that actually saved him."

I pulled back. "Do you think it will work on humans?"

"We shall see. For now, I want to keep Hank here for more observation, just to be extra cautious."

Looking over at Hank, something pressed down on my chest. I never thought I could ever love a dog like this—as something more than just my canine best friend. But Hank was family, the only family I had left.

After ensuring Hank was comfortable on the little bed they'd made for him, I assured him he would be okay and that I would be back in the morning. Back out on the main floor of the infirmary, my stomach grumbled so loud, my cheeks warmed.

I smiled at Father Ortega, who offered to send food to the room they'd prepared for me.

"Hank's in good hands, Kate. Rest up tonight. We can talk about what comes next tomorrow."

I thanked him and let Camila escort me to my room, which was located down the hall from Jax's. I hesitated for a beat as I passed his room. I'd promised we'd finish what we started, but after he gave me the answers I needed. A part of me knew that the instant I saw him, I wouldn't be able to resist being in his arms. He had a pull I couldn't deny and being around him made me weak. And if I went in there, I'd lose my resolve.

I needed time to think, time to get my feelings in order.

So, I kept walking.

I couldn't ignore the fact that he'd kept secrets from me, information regarding his role in this mess. We needed to clear the air before going further.

Last night I'd thought being with him would be about just seeking relief, with no strings attached. But now I knew there was something more growing between us, a tether strung between our hearts. Even if we'd only known each other for a brief time, I felt the connection the instant he collapsed to the floor in front of the altar.

I was brought back to the moment I saw Roger overtaken by the disease—the moment I knew I'd lost my husband. I'd never wanted to feel loss like that again, but that fear crept into my heart when I thought I'd lose Jax, too. And that petrified me more than I cared to admit. But at the same time, I didn't want to keep doing this alone anymore. I didn't want to survive alone; I wanted Jax by my side.

If there was a chance that something real was growing between us, we couldn't build a foundation on lies.

And that included the secret that ate at my own soul every day.

No temptation has overtaken you that is not common to man. God is faithful, and He will not let you be tempted beyond your ability, but with the temptation He will also provide the way of escape, that you may be able to endure it.

1 CORINTHIANS 10:13

CHAPTER 9
JAX

I paced around the room they'd turned into my bedroom—a cage more like. Only piece of furniture in this whole space was a thin mattress on the floor, likely dragged over from the hospital next door. It left just enough room to pace around furiously.

Ever since they'd attempted to drown the *d'shiad* within me in holy water, I'd been confined to these four walls. He did not drown, though I wished those tricks worked. If they had, I would've drunk the damn blessed liquid a long time ago and freed myself of him already.

While they'd not been able to rip him from my body, they'd managed to silence him temporarily. He was hiding from the angel as much as he was fighting the protection spell around the cathedral. The holy water had worked to keep him subdued just for a while. Burned like a son of a bitch with a blowtorch. Never thought pain would make him go into hiding, especially since it always seemed to have an opposite effect.

The mere presence of the archangel sure did a number on him. What a sight. Heck, I would've bowed down to him even if my knees hadn't buckled from the demon trying to rip out of my body. To find one of God's angels working with the Guardians was something I should've expected the moment I detected the protection spell around the cathedral.

I might've even come without Kate's persuasion to get some of my questions answered. Demons only tell you so much, and Astaroth was as tight-lipped as they came. He wasn't going to spill the beans on how to get rid of him, no matter what I bargained away. Although, offering him my first-born child might have done the trick, judging by the way he urged me to fuck any moving thing.

I rubbed a hand down my haggard face. I was supposed to be sleeping, but I didn't trust the *d'shiad* lingering at the edge of my consciousness not to take over and do something I'd later regret. For fuck's sake, the place was full of females suitable for his one and only goal—the unsatisfiable need to fuck. I'd seen at least four besides Camila, and I sure as hell wasn't gonna let him touch an innocent child.

Shit, what in the world had I gotten myself into? I'd promised myself I'd only get out of bullshit situations, but now I'd walked into one heck of a train wreck. Willingly, too.

Father Ortega had no reason to trust me, and whatever he might have told Kate about me was going to be a bitch to undo. Fucking hell, I'd almost blurted out my whole miserable existence when she marched in earlier, all worried and furious at the same time.

I'd not been able to stop myself. I'd been so worried about her too, wondering where the hell they'd taken her. I ran to her on instinct the moment I saw her barge through the door and fucking kissed her as if I thought I'd die with my next breath. I knew she had questions, that she probably came to demand all the answers I owed her. But all I wanted was to feel her close to me, and I couldn't have given a shit about anything else.

Her body pressed against mine felt right and her lips belonged on mine. We'd been interrupted twice now, first by Hank and then Camila. I wasn't sure how much more of that pent-up energy I could carry around without exploding.

Astaroth didn't make it any easier on me. Hell, half of the crazed need burning a hole through my pants was his. If I'd had any resolve left in me, I would've fought him harder, but he was doing a damn good job at convincing me that we wanted the same exact thing.

It didn't help knowing that Kate was just across the hall, probably getting ready for bed. I heard her talking to someone as she walked past my room after she'd visited Hank. A hollowness built in my gut when she didn't come back to my room. Perhaps she'd been given the answers she needed and now wanted nothing to do with me.

Not like I could blame her. I was partly responsible for bringing destruction to the world—the destruction of *her* world with the terrible death of her husband and child.

I should have told her the truth back at the small church where we fought off that demon attack. Or after the shower, when she saw my wounds had healed. But then she might have plunged that sword straight through my heart.

She might still.

Even if she already knew the truth about me, I wanted her to hear it from my lips. My version. And if she wanted nothing to do with me…

I shook my head, unable to accept that outcome. Damn this.

How had this woman been able to dig her nails so deeply into me without even trying? Worst still was that I wanted her to claw them even deeper, until she buried herself entirely inside me. I'd never been one for falling in love, always choosing meaningless quick fucks over anything serious. Why would I want to fall in love, knowing what my mother had groomed me to become? Knowing what my destiny was supposed to be? Besides, no one could love me back.

When I first ran into Kate, all I'd wanted from her was that sword and nothing more. But in a matter of days, she'd managed to crawl into that hidden space that I'd never let anyone touch. Now I couldn't stop thinking about her—her soft lips, the taste of her skin, the feel of her body pressed against the hard planes of my chest.

But that wasn't all. Sure, the beast living inside me wanted me to fuck her, to own her. She was feisty, strong, and gorgeous. And after stealing a taste of her pleasure, I knew she'd drive me mad once I took her.

But still, I wanted more than that.

I'd seen what she was capable of. The way she'd stood her ground on that bridge, facing off against Hell's worst monsters. Battling alongside that mighty angel. Her fearlessness when we fought off the damned in the tunnel.

But as strong as she was, she was also tender. Her concern when she thought I'd been bitten smoothed a part of me that had always felt spiny. The way she'd kissed me on that couch, as if she'd known me forever, yet not at all, stole every ounce of breath from my lungs. Kate had seen *me*, not the monster trapped inside me and not the disgusting human I'd been raised to be.

And the way she loved Hank was powerful and pure; it didn't matter that he was a dog. She loved him with all her might, and I wanted that, too. I wanted someone to love me that fiercely.

I wanted *Kate* to love *me* that fiercely.

Fuck this. I needed to talk to her, and I was done waiting for her to decide when. She needed to know the truth, and tomorrow would be already too late. I gave up pacing and reached for the door, only to startle myself when I grabbed the handle and it turned without resistance.

They'd actually left it unlocked?

That didn't seem right.

Even more surprising was the fact there was no one guarding the door outside my room. The man I'd heard talking to Kate earlier was nowhere to be seen. Something was definitely off. When I went to walk through, I realized why they'd not bothered with locks. I stepped right into what felt like a stone wall. To the naked eye, there was nothing visibly stopping me from exiting the room, yet a tremor ran through my body when I tried to cross the threshold again. Seemed they'd cast a containment spell around the room to keep me confined.

The *d'shiad* residing inside me—perhaps motivated by the promise of sex—stirred to life and urged me to keep pushing against the ward, despite the stinging energy irritating my nerves every time I touched the invisible barrier. If they had no one guarding my room, then they must've thought the spell was strong enough to keep me inside.

Though they'd taken my gear, I knew a few sigils that could help me weaken the ward. Drawing the symbols into the air with my fingers, I pushed against the barrier and found the loose threads. It was like fighting to free myself from an electrified, fibrous membrane. Unraveling the spell thread by thread took me longer than I wanted. I got lucky that nobody came waltzing through the hallway while I worked to free myself from my room. Eventually, to my relief, I popped through the threshold.

After making sure there was no one at either end of the hallway, I tried to figure out where Kate's room was. She had to be somewhere in the vicinity, but I didn't know which room exactly. And it wasn't like I could go knocking on every door until I found the right one.

I wasn't supposed to be roaming the halls.

There was only one thing I could do. It wasn't my favorite plan, but it was the only one I could come up with this fast. Heightened senses came in handy when fighting off monsters, but in order to gain access to those gifts, I had to allow the *d'shiad* to surface. Problem was, I didn't know how strong or weak he was after that little show in the nave, so things could tip south pretty quickly if I lost control of him.

Didn't take long for his taunting voice to echo through my skull or the fiery ripple of his energy to vibrate over my skin. I drew sigils with my fingers on the insides of my wrists and one over my chest. He fought the spell, but he'd risen so close to the surface that I felt the potency of his power. And that was all I needed to accomplish my task.

With one hearty breath, I was able to inhale every scent within a few yards, including Kate's—papaya and passion fruit; the light aroma of the shower gel she'd used the night before still lingered on her skin.

Following the trail of sweetness through the corridor, I found the room Kate was staying in with ease. I stopped at the door and inhaled again, remembering how mouthwatering she'd smelled when I'd held her in my arms on the couch, and the thought of running my tongue along the length of the delicate column of her neck made my cock throb.

Squeezing the doorknob, I gave myself one last chance to turn back.

Who was I kidding? I didn't possess the strength to turn away from Kate.

My blood ran nuclear through my veins and my heart was ready to sky-rocket out of my chest as I held my breath and turned the knob. Shocked and relieved it wasn't locked either, I hurried inside, only to find the sharp point of her short sword inches from my face.

"Don't you knock?" she snapped, her voice somewhere between pissed off and startled. "You scared the shit out of me."

With my palms up in defense, I gently nudged the door behind me closed with my leg. "I stopped the practice when half the world's population died or turned into the damned." I might've lost a few other social graces along the way, although it wasn't like I'd grown up in a place that promoted courteousness. "If you don't lower that weapon, I might shit *my* pants, though."

She rolled her eyes and blew out a breath as she lowered her sword. It glinted bright under the faint light of a small oil lamp, far brighter than the poor lighting justified. "You're an idiot. I almost stabbed you."

I raised my eyes from the angel blade and immediately stopped worrying about what its glowing indicated. Still dressed in the white tank top and jeans, Kate had undone her ponytail and her chestnut-colored hair cascaded to her shoulders in thick tendrils. The oil lamp sat on a nightstand by her bed and the warm, yellow light cast a buttery glow over Kate's dewy skin.

Her brown eyes glimmered, and I couldn't help but notice the pinkish hue that caressed her cheeks or the way she bit her bottom lip enough to cause it to swell, even if only slightly. I'd pushed Astaroth back into the depths of my core, but his cursed gifts still lingered long enough for me to know Kate shared the same pull toward me that I felt toward her. I could sense it on my skin, the sexual tension between us practically crackling like static energy.

Her mouth parted and her throat bobbed as a small breath escaped her lungs. I'd pissed her off by keeping things from her, but fuck, she still wanted me. I'd come with a mission—to tell her all my secrets and to lay myself bare—but the instant my eyes landed on her, everything else faded to black. All I wanted was to kiss those fucking swollen lips until they were raw and the only thing she tasted was me.

In one stride, my feet took me straight to where Kate stood, and I didn't bother asking for permission before cupping a hand over the back of her neck and bringing her lips to mine. She didn't fight it, matching my hunger instead. Every time she swirled her tongue with mine, a current of white-hot fire shot straight to my cock. She mumbled something in between breaths, but whatever she was about to say got lost in her surprise when I pushed her back against the wall.

My hands came up on either side of her hips, and my fingers accidently grazed the edge of the sword still grasped in her hand. I bit down hard on my jaw, trying to hide the pain of the burning sting. "You might want to set your pointy object down somewhere before one of us ends up with a nasty cut," I breathed harshly, masking the real reason for my request.

Nodding, she gently thrust it onto the mattress. I wasted no time devouring her mouth, swallowing her moans as I palmed her soft breasts and bit her bottom lip. Even through her shirt and bra, I felt the hardening of her nipples beneath my touch, and it made my dick grow harder. I pressed my erection against her, and the friction drew a growling moan from my chest.

She gasped into my mouth as she felt how desperate I was for her.

"See how badly I want you?" I breathed the words over her lips.

"Is that why you came?" she asked. "To fuck me?"

Pressing my forehead to hers, I took a steadying breath. Did I come to fuck her? Was that even a fair question? "That's all I've been thinking about for the last couple of days. Ripping these damn clothes off you. Getting you hot and bothered and making you come in my mouth. Thrusting so deep into you, you'd see stars. You screaming my name."

She rubbed the pad of her thumb over my lips, and I swore if someone else came between us right now, I'd unleash Astaroth on them until they were nothing but ribbons. "Angel," I said, "you drive me insane, and I don't know what I'm doing anymore. The way I want you is utter madness, but that's not why I came, at least, not the only reason. I want to tell you everything about me. No more secrets, baby." Even as those words left my lips, I doubted I'd be able to put some space between us long enough to explain myself. I kissed her neck, tasting the sweetness of her skin. My lips climbed to her ear, and I sucked her earlobe into my mouth while working to remove her shirt. Grabbing the hem and delighting in the feel of her deliciously soft skin, I pulled her shirt upward.

"Jax," she moaned, but her body language told a different story. The palm of her hand pushed at my chest. "Wait." The slight hesitation in her voice made me realize she was about to drop a concrete wall between us.

"Don't, Kate," I said. "Don't stop this." I took her mouth in mine again and pressed my body closer to her, letting her feel exactly what she was doing to me, showing her what I wanted to do to her body. How badly I needed to be inside her, filling her until I didn't know where I ended and she began. The friction against my cock through the fabric of our clothes when our bodies collided was unbearable, and I wanted more. "I waited for you. Nearly mauled myself to death when you didn't show. Please. I'll tell you everything, but right now, I need you."

She turned her mouth from mine and pushed her palm harder against my chest. "Not like this. We need to talk."

Fuck. Before stepping through her door, I thought I was ready to hash it all out, but now the thought of opening up about my life ate at me from the inside, as if my gut was a pit full of hungry vipers. And she wasn't about to grant me any more grace.

As tough as it was to pull away from her body, I took a couple of steps back with the evidence of the fire burning through my blood visible below my waist. She tried to disguise the fact that her eyes had tilted downward toward the bulge between my legs, but I caught the moment they widened for a second before she looked away. "You're sure you want to talk first?" I taunted. Trying to deflect her attention, I cupped my cock over my pants and groaned.

Even as her lips parted slightly, she refused to budge. Her face hardened, and squaring her shoulders, she said, "The Devil's Army, Jax? Are you a part of it? Did you open the gates of Hell?" The way she said my name was completely different from the passionate moan it was before. The heat of her arousal had been replaced with a biting chill that wrenched my heart.

Kate's questions were already filled with resentment before she even knew the truth. They sounded like accusations and cut deeper than the ones my mother had thrown at me when I'd released a lamb into the wild rather than sacrificing it for one of her rituals. I'd been ten and going through a phase. I'd known punishment would follow my actions, but I'd still done it.

Kate saw the answer to her question written all over my face, saw it broadcasted in my gaze before I uttered a single word. I swallowed hard, my jaw twitching. The confusion and hurt splayed over Kate's face was far worse than the disappointment I'd seen in my mother's eyes back then.

"I *was* part of the Devil's Army," I confessed. The instant her eyes went dark, I looked away, unable to meet her gaze. I couldn't take how easily her passion for me had transformed to hatred. She'd wanted the truth, but she'd not expected it wouldn't be what she wanted to hear.

After a prolonged breath, Kate's palm connected with the side of my face, the loud *slap* echoing in the barren room as her fury searched for an outlet. Knowing there was nothing else I could say to ease the sting of my words, I remained silent.

"You son of a bitch," she yelled, slamming a fist down into my chest, then a second, and then a third as tears rolled down her face.

I did nothing to stop the blows; I deserved her punishment. Fuck, I deserved worse than that. But her knuckles couldn't inflict any real damage to my reinforced body. I wanted to at least give her the satisfaction of hurting me senseless, and I couldn't even offer her that.

I lost track of the punches I took, but I'd taken more if that's what she'd needed. She collapsed onto my beaten chest. "How could you?" she gritted, sobbing.

Wrapping my arms around her, I said, "I left that all behind when the Horsemen crawled through the portal."

She pulled away from my embrace, disgust draping over her face as if she'd been in the devil's arms. "It *was* you, then. *You* opened the fucking gates. This is all *your* fault."

"Kate, look," I said, taking a step toward her.

"Stay the fuck away from me."

I should have listened, but I was so desperate for her to hear what I had to say, and I reached for her hand.

Wrong. Fucking. Thing. To do.

She went completely berserkers on me, and her fists hit a lot more than just my ribs. I let her strike me, but the momentum pushed me up against her bed and I lost my balance, landing on my back on top of the mattress. Thankfully, I didn't land on the sword.

Her legs tangled in mine as she fell over me. In one swift move, she straddled me, looming over me like an angel of vengeance as she unleashed her anger on me. An ache started to build in places she'd hit more than once, and I wondered if the angel on the bridge had given her more than just his weapon. At this rate, she'd break my bones if she kept at it for long enough.

I let her have one more satisfying blow before grabbing her wrists. Startled, she tried to pry her hands free, but I sat up and flipped her under me, pinning her wrists above her head. "That's enough," I said, keeping my voice gentle. I had zero intentions to hurt her, but Kate was ferocious and bucked her hips, trying to knock me off her. I had to fight the urge to let a smirk creep to the corners of my mouth.

If I hadn't just confessed my sin and she wasn't on a murderous rampage, this little scuffle between us would have been crazy hot. Seeing her this fired up stoked my own flames, and I heard Astaroth growl inside me.

Don't even think about it, I warned the demon.

"You sick fuck!" she snarled. "Get off me."

"Jesus Christ, Kate. Stop." She needed to quit writhing beneath me, or I might not be able to keep the damn beast from making an appearance.

Kate wrenched her wrists again in an attempt to get free of my hold. But when that didn't work, she went for my jugular with her words. "You destroyed the world. You infected my husband. *You killed my little girl.*"

Forget my jugular. Those words burrowed through my skin and ripped me wide open across my entire cavity. Unclasping my fingers from her wrists, I pulled away and sat on the edge of the bed. The horror of what I'd done had hit me hard before, but not like this. She'd lost her family to the virus and felt it was my fault.

There was nothing I could say that could make things right. My reasons would never matter to her; they would never be enough, and they certainly would never bring her family back.

Kate curled in on herself, hiding her face from me. But I heard her cries. Could swear I even heard her heart breaking. "Why?" was all she managed to say, her voice weak.

I dropped my chin to my chest. "I wasn't... I wasn't given a choice." As much as I knew it wouldn't make a difference, it was the truth. Still, even though I hadn't directly killed her family, I'd blamed myself for all this death longer than Kate had, and her words brought my sins back to the forefront.

"I didn't mean for any of this to happen," I said quietly after Kate had calmed down.

She sat up next to me, wiping her tears.

I took a deep breath and fidgeted with my hands.

It was now or never.

"I was around five when I realized my family was different," I began. "My mother, she…we said a prayer each night, but it wasn't your usual ward off the evil and keep me safe kind of shit you'd imagine your mother to utter next to your bed before you fell asleep. Her prayers invited evil *in*. Each night, I would be trapped in hellish nightmares, seeing atrocities no child should ever be forced to witness. She took selling my soul to the devil to a whole new level. Offering off your first-born child and all that shit. I don't think she enjoyed the fear in my eyes at the thought of falling asleep, but she loved listening to the retellings of my dreams. She kept a journal with all my ramblings in it. I knew most of the things she made me do weren't right, but she was my mother."

For a moment, I was back in my childhood bedroom with my mother as she drew blood from my finger for the cursed enchantment to work. I stared into her familiar wicked eyes—those cold blackholes that never provided me with any solace. It wasn't until I was ten that I stopped longing for her affection.

I'd not realized tears had trickled from my eyes until a drop fell off my chin and onto my hand resting on my lap. "She was my mother," I repeated, tightening my lips to keep my voice from cracking. "Some mother, right?"

The warmth of Kate's skin startled me as she reached for my hand and squeezed. I dared a glance her way. Her eyes were misted over, but she kept her lips pressed in a thin line, perhaps unsure what to say to someone confessing they'd been brought up to worship the king of Hell.

I inhaled sharply, letting my eyes wander to the ceiling. Such an unremarkable white slab of plastered concrete, yet the rest of what I'd seen of the cathedral was made to impress and steal the breath from your lungs. Or perhaps it had felt that way due to Astaroth going mental and literally keeping me from breathing when that angel showed up.

"Your mother sounds… I can't imagine how hard it must have been for you," she finally uttered. "You were just a child."

Turning toward her, I took both of her hands in mine. If she was going to know the truth, then she needed to know all of it. "I didn't choose to be part of The Devil's Army; I was born into a cult. By the time I was six, I'd seen more blood than a kid that age should be exposed to. The first time I killed a man was on my fifteenth birthday, for a ritual I didn't realize would aid in world destruction. I was so eager to please, to do at least *something* right so that, for once in my miserable life, I could earn a compliment from my mother." I paused, bile rising up my throat as the memories surfaced. "I didn't have time to think about my actions until I was scrubbing dried blood from under my nails. There was so much fucking blood. She didn't even acknowledge my successful murder, didn't even look at me after it was done."

Fucking hell, the memory shouldn't have hurt the way it did. I'd made peace with it long ago… thought I had, anyway. "I've done some dark shit, Kate. I can't deny that, for a time in my youth, all I cared about was appeasing my mother and the cult."

She cupped my cheek, her eyes softening over me. "You were just a kid, Jax."

Kate's words cut to the core of my guilt. Not living by the ways of Samael was not an option I thought was possible back then, so I stayed. But I knew now that was a lame excuse. "At fifteen, I was more than a kid, Kate. I should have known better; I should've run," I said, taking her hand from my cheek. "Instead, I let them groom me into a monster."

"But eventually you left, you said so yourself."

"By then, it was too late. The damage was already done."

Kate sat up straighter, tucking hair behind her ears. "I don't know how to make sense of everything you're telling me, but what I can tell you is that you're not a monster. You chose to help me on that bridge, to bring Hank and me here."

I pushed off the bed, furious at the fact that she wasn't angrier with me. I'd just told her I'd been a member of the Devil's Army. That despite knowing what they were and what they were planning, I chose to stay. Perhaps it pissed me off that she was defending me because I didn't believe I deserved her clemency.

"But that's where you're wrong," I said, running crazed fingers through my hair. "I am a monster. I haven't told you why I'm able to heal so fast. How I was able to fight off a horde of those spawns from hell on my own. Why the priest sprayed me with holy water. Or the real reason I came to that bridge, Kate."

She stood, matching the intensity of my stance, her gaze sharp as blades. "I'm here, Jax. Go on. Tell me. I want to know."

"I came to that bridge for the angel, Kate, not for you." The moment the words left my lips, I knew with searing certainty that the rest of what I had to say could never be undone. Kate would know everything and if I left this room alive, it would be due to divine intervention.

"What do you mean?"

"War, the fourth Horseman. Or as he is more commonly known by his kin and followers, Astaroth."

"What about the fourth Horseman, Jax?"

I scratched my scalp, the nervousness raking my body making me itchy. "For the portal, or the gates to open, four offerings needed to be made. Four human vessels for the Horsemen to possess. Unlike other lesser demons, possession is the only way they can walk the earth as themselves. My mother, she was—is—the high priestess for the New York sect, and she was responsible for ensuring the sacrifice was made. I was one of the lucky men chosen for this honor. We'd been promised long before we stood in the circle of the very last ritual. The first-borns for each set of parents. That's what all those nightmares and the suffering prepared us for—"

Kate took one small step away from me, perhaps not even realizing what she'd done. But I picked up on her silent cue. Fear had begun to take root in her heart. It was instinct, it was smart.

"An amulet was hung around our necks. Each one containing a Creation Stone, the keys needed to open the gates and summon forth Samael's four lieutenants, the architects of the apocalypse. I saw them crawl through the portal, Death taking no time at all to possess Sam, who'd been groomed to be his vessel since birth. He'd accepted his destiny without question.

"I stood frozen while the dark force entered his body, and he started twitching. I knew he looked forward to this day, but even he hadn't known what the possession would be like. His chocolate skin faded to an ashen color. He stumbled and choked; he screamed his lungs out and clawed at his face until a malicious grin spread across his too-pale face. There was nothing left of the man I'd grown up with, someone I'd counted on to be my ally before he'd been brainwashed into believing sacrificing his soul to the Horseman was his *destiny*."

Kate stared at me in stunned silence. Her bottom lip quivered so slightly, most people wouldn't have noticed.

"Sam died the moment Death took over. My friend just ceased to exist. He was replaced by something no longer human, and it was the most terrifying thing I'd ever seen."

"What did you do?" she finally asked.

I'd almost done the same exact thing and accepted the fate chosen for me. "The moment the first possession took place, and I saw my best friend die, all I could think about was how fucking much I wanted to live. To really live and not just dance to the rhythm of someone else's whims and plans for my existence. After all the goddamn lectures I was forced to listen to, the blood on my hands, the connection to Hell itself, I couldn't fucking do it. I couldn't—"

Kate swallowed deeply, the skin around her eyes crinkling as she concentrated on my words. "What happened next?"

"I ran, Kate. I fucking ran for my life. I bolted from the summoning circle the instant War stepped through the portal. Nobody expected any of us to run. The room had been warded to keep outsiders from interfering, but nothing stopped me from getting out."

A sigh of relief puffed from Kate's lips as she placed a hand over her chest. "So you were able to escape."

Leaning against the stone wall behind me, I crossed my arms. "Not entirely. I ran, but I wasn't fast enough to outrun him. I don't think anyone would've. I'd been a good little boy my whole life, though. I'd listened to those damn lectures, paid attention," I said, tapping my temple. "Astaroth, like the other four Horsemen, could only take full possession of my vessel as long as I wore the amulet."

Kate's eyes drifted to my chest. She knew I didn't wear it. "You took it off."

I nodded. "Without the amulet, when Astaroth entered my body, he wasn't able to possess me—not like he needed to— but I couldn't keep him out, either."

This time, she took a step forward instead. "So, you're telling me that a Horseman, War, is inside you?"

I hung my head, and the admission cut my skin. "So far, I've managed to keep him at bay. He is contained, Kate. Hasn't fully manifested like the rest did. Like Death—"

Sam. Like Sam. Like Lionel. I didn't know what happened to Christopher. I hadn't seen Famine nor heard anything on the streets about the third Horseman. Maybe the sect kept it quiet for a reason; maybe something had happened during the possession.

"Hasn't manifested?" Kate asked, her voice shaking, along with her whole body. "Your wounds heal at unnatural speed.

And what I saw at the altar earlier, when you fell to your knees. How can you say he hasn't manifested?"

"There. There it is. That look in your eyes. The one where you finally see the monster."

"No, Jax. I'm just trying to understand. Father Ortega said you were—"

"A member of the Devil's Army," I finished for her. "I know. We were both there when he said it. And I just explained to you that I'm no longer a contributor to their cause."

"But you helped open the gates of Hell."

I squeezed my eyes shut and tried to take in a deep breath. "You're right, Kate. I am to blame for all the pain and destruction. I am the reason more than half of the world's population died or got infected. And it eats at me every minute of every waking hour."

I swallowed even though my throat felt scorching dry. Sliding down the wall, I sat on the floor, unable to look up at her. I wasn't good at this emotional shit; never felt like I could open up to somebody. But why would I? How could I trust any woman when my own mother didn't care about anything other than for me to fulfill my purpose—to be bound to a demon and release Lucifer from his eternal imprisonment.

"I should have stopped it," I said. "I tried…" The words died on my lips. "But all I cared about at the time was saving my own ass." Getting the words out didn't make me feel any better, and instead, they just left a bitter taste in my mouth. My jaw twitched as I tried to staunch the tears threatening to crest.

"Whatever the Bible says about getting rid of your sins by begging for forgiveness is bullshit," I gritted. "I've cried out in despair enough times to know it doesn't work. The memories still plague me, Astaroth is still bound to my soul, and the world still burns." I finally lost the battle with myself as one fucking tear rolled down my face.

Kate rushed forward and knelt beside me, wiping the tear with her thumb. "Jax, I'm sorry for saying what I said about the gates. I know you didn't mean to—"

I took her hands in mine. "Kate, stop. You have nothing to be sorry about."

"I see you for who you really are, Jax. And that's a kind soul who rescued me up on that bridge, not the monster your mother raised you to become and not the demon trapped inside you. You shared a full tray of Oreos with me. That's gotta mean something." She smiled, and the warmth that radiated from that simple gesture spread through me all the way down to my bones.

Cupping her cheek, I tried offering her a smile of my own, but remorse washed over me, taking away my sunshine. "How can you not see me as a monster, Kate? Your husband and daughter... You lost them because of me."

She shook her head, her eyes watering. "No, Jax. I've wanted to blame someone for their deaths ever since they died. God. The angels. The demons. This fucking world. But only because I couldn't bear the truth."

Sitting in front of me, she crossed her legs and hung her head. "When New York City fell, Roger begged me to leave. He said we needed to head somewhere less crowded, some place that was safer, but I refused. Where were we supposed to go? Up until then, the news had shown the demons were everywhere."

"Seems your husband was a smart man."

Kate burst into tears and flung her arms around my neck. "I should have listened to him, Jax. I should have listened."

I wrapped my arms around her and let her cry into my chest. "It's alright, angel. You don't have to tell me what happened."

"No. I need to," she said, pulling away and wiping at her wet face. "I haven't told anyone and I... I need to get this off my chest." She settled back. "It had been three, maybe four weeks since the world had gone completely dark, and we'd run out of food. Roger went out to scavenge for supplies. Two days had passed, and I thought he wasn't going to come back. That something had happened to him, that one of the devoured had gotten to him.

"On the third day, he returned, but I knew something was off. He didn't tell me right away, but by the next morning, a fever kicked in."

"He'd been bitten or scratched?"

"Bitten. On the leg."

Understanding where her story was heading, I broke from the inside. "Oh, Kate."

"He begged me, Jax. Begged me to kill him. That if he hadn't been a believer, he would have taken my service gun and done it himself."

"Taking a life is not easy."

"I couldn't do it. I just… I *couldn't*. That night he got very ill, could barely move or speak. He laid down in Isabella's room, and Isabella and I slept in the master. I locked the door just in case, I don't know, something happened." Kate's voice cracked and the tears trickled from her eyes again.

"Kate."

"Isabella woke up sometime in the middle of the night, like she did many nights. Except she didn't wake me up. She wanted her daddy."

Dread filled my chest at her words. There was nothing I could do against the ghosts of her past. "Kate, please. You don't have to do this."

"She went to her room and Roger… he…" Kate trembled, and I took her into my arms again. "By the time I heard the scream, it was already too late. Roger had transformed and he'd taken Isabella. I reached for my gun, which I kept under my pillow, and I ran into the hallway where he held her by the hair. Isabella screamed and screamed. I aimed my gun at him, right at his head. All I had to do was pull the trigger. I'd done it dozens of times in training and at the firing range. I wouldn't have missed. Just one shot. That's all I needed. But I hesitated."

"Kate, killing is not easy."

She squirmed out of my arms. "He had my daughter. That *thing* had my *daughter,* and I hesitated."

"He was your husband."

"No, he wasn't. Not anymore."

"What happened?"

"He bared his disgusting teeth and went to bite her, and that's when I shot him. But I was too late. He'd managed to scratch her arm badly. Two days later, Isabella—"

"Kate—"

"I couldn't do it, you know. I wasn't able to… kill her. I tied her to her bed, locked the door, and…" She took a minute to gather her thoughts. "One day I went out to scavenge for food and I got stuck out in the city for a couple of days. When I returned, my apartment had been ransacked. Whoever had broken in had found her and they… um—"

I held her trembling body tight against my chest. She didn't have to tell me the rest. She couldn't bring herself to utter the words.

"Roger and Isabella didn't die because of God," she said, "or the angels that never showed. They didn't die because you helped open the gates and Hell broke loose. They died because of *me*. Because I was too scared, because I was too selfish."

Tipping her chin up, my heart shattered when I saw the torment in her eyes. She didn't want to say it, but I knew it. I was indirectly responsible for her pain, and I wanted nothing more than to take that pain away, even if just for one moment, one second.

"Words will never express how sorry I am, Kate." I wanted to hold her in my arms forever. Make us both forget the terrible world around us. Somehow turn the clock back to that fateful day the rift cracked between the worlds and stop the gates from opening.

I didn't plan it, probably because I knew I didn't have any right to seek solace in her, but Kate must have read my mind and reached up to grab my neck, bringing my lips to hers. This time, our kiss wasn't an erupting volcano of lust and desire; our kiss was salty and wet, and imbued with loneliness and a touch of forgiveness.

I drowned in that forgiveness, and in turn, gave her the passion she craved.

*Above all, love each other deeply, because
love covers over a multitude of sins.*

1 PETER 4:8

CHAPTER 10

JAX

Kate straightened and straddled me as we both sat on the floor, our tender kisses slowly transforming into something deeper, stoking the fire of our sexual hunger. She kissed me with anger and desperation, as if needing to unleash her sorrow and aggression on me, and I was more than willing to be her punching bag.

She swayed her hips over my erection like a tidal wave crashing onto my shores. "I need you," she whispered as I slipped my hands under her shirt and ran my fingers down her spine.

"You're sure this is what you want, angel?"

"Do you want me to change my mind?"

I smirked. She was such a smart-mouth—and I knew exactly what I wanted to do with that mouth, but not yet. Kate was the kind of woman I wanted to take my time with. "Let's get this off." I grabbed the hem of her shirt, my breath hot on her skin as I licked her earlobe.

She nodded, and the instant I lifted her shirt up over her head, she let out a blissful sigh. Her hands traveled down my chest and stomach until she cupped my cock, summoning a rumbling breath from the depths of my chest.

"Jax."

My name on those lips shouldn't have sounded so good, but the way her breath hitched at the end drove me mad. I ran kisses down her neck, sucking at the skin, trying to get her to repeat it. I'd never tire of hearing her moan my name, and if tonight was all we ever got, I wanted to prolong her pleasure for as long as I could—if only to have her say *Jax* over and over again.

I worked to unclasp her bra with clumsy fingers, but I must've been out of practice for too long.

Fuck it.

I ripped the damn clasp and her full breasts spilled free. Kate was so fucking gorgeous. I was unable to contain my appetite and greedily took a breast in each hand, bringing them to my mouth.

Her little gasps encouraged me to trace my tongue over her nipples, grazing them with my teeth before sucking them into my mouth. I feasted on her, biting until both nipples were red and tender.

The way she writhed on my lap was indication enough. "You like a little pain," I murmured, fixing my gaze to hers, lips tugging at the corners. With hooded lids, she nodded, confessing her little secret. "I can give you what you want, baby."

A trembling, unsure smile stretched across her lips as she leaned in and whispered in my ear, "I want you in my mouth. Hard." *Christ.* She plucked my depraved thoughts right out of my mind.

"Get on your knees and give me your belt," I instructed, standing so I loomed over her. Her breasts swayed as she worked to unbuckle her belt and the blood running through my shaft rushed faster and hotter at the sight. She looked up at me with those beautiful, brown doe eyes and handed me the black leather belt, her hand a bit unsteady.

I knew then that she'd never done anything like this before, and a tendril of doubt wrapped around my conscience. Was this the right time to play this game? With Kate? She'd bared her heart to me, had given me the gift of her vulnerability. I didn't want to take advantage of that, but I also knew if she was suffering from internal turmoil, then this could ease some of her pain.

Taking the belt from her, I folded it in half and snapped it, making her jolt. "You're sure you want this?"

"I know I need you to help me erase the punishing thoughts, even if just for tonight. I don't want to think about the past or about anything outside these four walls. Inundate me. My mind, my body. Pleasure me. Give me pain. Just make me forget, Jax. Make me feel only you."

The desperation embedded in her eyes splintered through me. This wasn't what I'd planned or envisioned, but if this was what she wanted—*needed*—from me, then I would honor that wish.

Tightening my grip on the belt, I caressed her soft cheek with my free hand, taking my time and delighting in the feel of her creamy skin, rubbing the pad of my thumb over her lush lips. She gasped as my fingertips trailed over her jaw. I pushed her hair back, exposing her neck, trailing my fingers down the long column until her skin beaded with goosebumps.

"Tie your hair back," I said.

Taking a small hair tie from her jeans pocket, she did as she was told. Gently, I wrapped the belt around her neck, looping it through the buckle and pulling it snug, but not tight. Her body shuddered, and she looked up at me with a touch of trepidation in her eyes.

"You need to trust me," I said, wrapping the tail end of the belt around my hand twice. "If something is too much, just tell me to stop. Can you breathe?"

She nodded.

"Then lower my pants and pull out my cock."

Her eyes widened and I almost chuckled, expecting she'd give me a smart reply—except she didn't question my command. Reaching for the drawstring of my sweats, Kate untied the knot and lowered the waistband enough to pull my cock free. I wasn't fully erect, but the way she looked at me was quick to remedy that.

Licking her lips, she came forward with her mouth but was met with the pull of the belt against her neck as I held her back. "Not yet, angel."

She looked up, confusion riding the edge of the arousal painted across her face.

"Use your hands," I added.

I sucked in a sharp breath as the warmth of her skin wrapped around my shaft. She stroked me in fluid motions, slow then fast, until a dewy drop formed at the tip. Her mouth parted, eyes growing heavy as she used her thumbs to rub the wet bead over the tight skin of the head.

"*Fuck*, Kate."

She gripped me tighter, sliding her tongue along her top lip as she seemed to salivate to put me in her mouth. Astaroth growled, his will to take over clawing at my core and making my mind explode with all sorts of filth—of everything the animal wanted me to do to her.

Not a chance in hell, fucker. I made sure the message was clear. Kate was mine, and mine alone.

Tightening my grip on the belt, I tugged her neck forward, bringing her mouth so close that I felt the heat of her breath. "You want to taste it?"

"Please," she whispered, looking up at me through her thick lashes.

I nodded, granting her permission, and without breaking the connection between our gazes, she lathered her tongue along the tip of my cock as she slowly stroked my shaft. The feel of her wet mouth on me was a shot of heroin straight into my bloodstream. Watching her lick my length and run the tip of her tongue along my veins up to the underside of my head made my thighs tremble and my knees grow weak.

All I could think about was plunging my cock so deep in her mouth that I'd hit the back of her throat. As if reading my thoughts, she tried to take my full length, but I didn't fit, forcing her to use her hand as she twisted it around the areas her mouth couldn't touch.

I tried to restrain myself, knowing that if I went in too hard, she wouldn't be able to take my size without feeling pain, but then I remembered that was exactly what she'd asked for.

Wrapping my free hand around the base of her ponytail, I gripped tight, holding her in place, both by the hair and the belt, as I thrust my cock into her mouth. The harder I pushed, the more she gagged and her eyes watered. I knew the belt was digging into her skin, but I didn't pull tight enough to cut off her air.

She could have stopped me at any point, but she took every inch of my cock that fit through her perfect lips, the sounds she made a mix of arousal and pain. "You like the way I fuck your mouth?" I ground out, fighting the urge to keep going as I slowed down and released the tension on the belt.

With my cock still in her mouth, she closed her eyes and moaned as she gently sucked on the head, her cheeks wet with tears.

But I knew she wasn't crying.

I wiped the streaks coating her face and licked my fingers. "Bet your pussy's slick and throbbing."

"Maybe," she crooned with a defiant smile, then continued stroking me.

I tightened my hold on the belt, tugging her forward. "Try that again, angel."

Her eyebrows hiked up her forehead as she stared at me, and my face remained unmoving.

She swallowed hard. "It is *very* wet."

If she wanted to play this game, she would need to learn the rules quickly. Un-looping the belt from around her neck, I made sure her skin wasn't cut or bruised. Satisfied, I wrapped the entire belt around my hand and had her stand. "Take off your jeans, but leave your underwear on. Then lay on the bed and spread your legs for me."

Biting her bottom lip, she swung her right arm across her body and cradled her left elbow, caving into herself as if hiding her body from me.

"What scares you?" I asked.

"I don't know what will come next."

I tipped her chin up and kissed her, reminding her there was nothing to fear. "I want to taste your pussy, and you're going to let me. Now, do as I ask, angel."

She made it to the edge of the bed and shimmied out of her jeans before climbing on the mattress and laying on her back. I stroked my cock as I watched Kate rest on her elbows and slowly part her legs.

"That's it, angel. Just like that." Despite her nervousness, her white cotton panties were soaked, and I smiled like a self-assured prick. Now I ached to feel how silky wet she really was. "Remember what you denied me last night? That's not happening again," I began as I neared the bed and reached for her center, sliding my finger along her seam over her underwear. "I'm gonna play with your clit. Get it nice and swollen and ready to come, but I'm not going to let you come. Not until I fucking feel like it."

Back arching, she shed any remaining doubt about going further. Kate needed zero commands to spread her legs wider. She moaned as I found her swollen nub and rubbed it gently, watching as she seeped through the cotton even more. Her abdomen tightened and I knew the pleasure building around her clit was spreading. "Yeah. You like that."

"Jax…"

"Pull your underwear to the side and let me see you."

She hesitated, so I trailed the tip of the belt down her abdomen. "Kate. Let me see you."

Clenching her eyes shut, she reached for the fabric covering her dark curls and pulled it to the side.

Fuck. Me.

Everything male inside me roared to life. Astaroth screamed to rip through my chest, but the sigils I'd traced over my body did their job, and all he could do was beat his fists against the inside of my rib cage.

He could pound all he wanted; I'd never let him near Kate.

Through her curls, I saw the pink flesh of her folds and abstaining from slamming my cock inside her took every ounce of strength I possessed. If I fucked her now, I wouldn't last long. I ran the length of my index finger down her seam until I was coated in her wetness. Then I inserted it, moving to the rhythm of her body.

She writhed, closing her legs as she tried to increase the friction.

"I didn't give you permission to close your legs." Withdrawing my finger, I let her feel how empty she was without me.

"Jax, please…"

"Please, what?'

"You're torturing me."

"I know. You're desperate to come, but not yet, angel." I slid off her underwear, baring her completely on the bed. I took a minute to absorb her, to take in every ounce of her dewy skin, her gorgeous breasts, the valleys leading down to the place between her thighs glistening with her arousal.

I wanted to slide my tongue up and down that slit, to taste her, to make her come on my tongue, but pleasure was the outcome and pain was the path. Using the belt, I ran the tail end over her pussy and tapped it lightly. She shivered as the rough leather made contact with her clit. "How does it feel?"

Holding her legs open, she said, "It feels… like savoring something sweet before feeling the heat of something hot and spicy."

Another tap.

Shuddering again, she moaned, the sound deeper, less controlled.

I tapped her clit again, sliding the belt up and down her entire pussy, the leather slick with the evidence of her pleasure. Her eyes fluttered and her hips lifted off the mattress as I continued to glide the belt over her hard, little pearl.

God, I wished I could have tied her up to my bed posts—not like my place existed anymore, but damn. The thought of taking away *all* her control had me salivating. I wanted to be her only outlet.

I'd been the one responsible for her misery, and now I wanted to be the only one able to take away all the sorrow my inability to act had etched into her bones.

"Jax, Lick me. Please… I need…"

Oh, I knew *exactly* what she needed. She was almost in that headspace where the idea of pain and pleasure became one and the same. "When you feel my tongue lapping up all that sweetness dripping off you, you won't last, baby. And I'm not letting you off that easily."

I tapped her pussy with the belt yet again, this time slightly harder, and she flinched, but she managed to keep her legs open. Her clit was tender but not raw. I had no intention of inflicting any real pain—she wasn't ready for that kind of play.

This was simply a tease, a way to get her mind completely focused on me, on what her body was feeling and nothing else. None of the real darkness swallowing her up from inside was allowed here.

I delivered a few more taps, and she responded with little whimpers drenched in moans. Giving her a little reprieve from the leather, I used my thumb to caress her clit in small circles. Her entire body sighed in appreciation, her legs spreading as wide as they could go, inviting my touch. Her back arched again, those beautiful dark nipples hard as diamonds pointing straight at the ceiling.

She writhed over my finger, demanding I penetrate her. "Jax… please," she begged, and that was a mistake because I would do everything in my power to keep her begging. The way she pronounced my name, dragging out the syllable? Fuck, I could've listened to her beg all day. I could've gotten myself off just listening to her voice imploring me to fuck her and to make her come.

"Close your eyes," I told her. "And do not open them until I say so."

She said nothing.

"Kate?"

"Yes. Yes," she panted.

"Closed. Don't even think about cheating. Legs open. I want to keep looking at your pussy."

Removing my thumb, I stood back a little and inebriated myself in her beauty, my mind entering its own sinister headspace. Right now, I owned her—her body, her pleasure, her pain, maybe even her soul.

"Jax?"

"I'm here, angel," I said, climbing onto the bed and lying beside her. Using the tail end of the belt, I gently caressed her skin, sliding the leather across her chest, over her nipples, and down her abdomen, all while kissing her neck and making her skin strain with the onslaught of goosebumps. "Put your wrists together over your head."

Kate obliged, not questioning me as I used the belt to tie her wrists together. Once secure, I sat back on my knees between her legs and kissed every inch of her body, even between her thighs, but never touching her center. I kissed her mouth instead, swirling my tongue with hers, wanting her to imagine me kissing her pussy like that. Hip to hip, I knew she could feel my hard cock resting against her abdomen.

She tried shifting underneath me, wanting me to slide my cock inside her.

"They took my gear, angel. I have no condoms."

"I haven't been with anyone since Hell broke loose and before that, I'd only been with Roger."

"I'm clean, too. But what about—"

"I can't get pregnant." Eyes still closed, she turned her head, biting back the sadness about to punch through. "Isabella was—"

I put a finger to her lips. "We don't have to talk about it, not right now."

She nodded, and I distracted her by lowering my hips and rubbing the length of my cock along her entrance. I barely held on to my sanity when my hard length slid against her soft folds.

Heaven help me.

She was so wet, and the thought of plunging inside her warm heat sent Astaroth into a frenzy. Having a demon trapped inside your body was bad enough, but I had War waging a battle against my self-control. No. I would not allow this monster to take over my body, not when I was about to make love to the one woman who'd seen through all my damaged parts and accepted me despite my shitty past. Pushing up to my knees, I redrew the sigil over my chest, the magic burning a scar onto my skin in the shape of the symbol. Fuck, he'd been too close to taking over. I hissed, trying to mask the pain.

Once the burns healed, I took my fill of her naked body once again. Cock in one hand, I used the tip to circle her clit until it was so swollen, she almost lost it, but I pulled away, denying her what she so desperately wanted. She tried lifting her hips, but I used my free hand to pin her down. "You're lucky I can't tie you down to this bed."

"Jax, I can't take it anymore."

"Is this what you want?" I leaned down, spread her folds, and flicked her hard nub with my tongue. Fucking hell, she tasted like sex on steroids on goddamn crack. I licked that pussy up and down, sucking on her clit until Kate's moans echoed off the walls. Sliding my hands under her ass, I pushed her up higher, devouring her like she was my last meal.

Every muscle in her body went taut, and I knew she was ready to come. Taking her cues, I inserted one finger, then two, and finger-fucked her while licking her clit. She came in an explosion of moans and whimpers. Wrists still bound together, she brought them to my head and gripped my hair with her fingers.

I drank every ounce of her release, but I was far from done. "You can open your eyes now, angel." When she did, her face was flushed and a languid smile ghosted across her lips. "Turn around," I instructed. "Get on your knees and bend down, hands above your head."

A wicked grin creeped to the corners of her mouth. She knew what was coming, and she eagerly turned over and offered me her lovely ass. I slapped a cheek, hard, catching Kate off guard, but she didn't protest, nor did she ask me to stop.

I slapped her other cheek, loving how her ass jiggled, the skin darkening to a deep pink. Her hips gyrated, lifting her ass up higher for me, her back becoming a slope of silky skin. My mind went bonkers. Slapping her a few more times until I heard a tiny whimper, I finally spread her cheeks and buried my tongue in her entrance. I licked her until she was soaking wet all over again.

Unable to contain the pressure building in my groin, I finally pushed my cock inside her with deliberately slow strokes. Her walls gripped me with each thrust. I reached for her ponytail and tugged. "Angel, you feel so damn good," I breathed, pulling my dick out a fraction just to thrust it back in again. She was so wet and tight, I was already on the verge of coming. Her rising moans as I went deeper were music to my ears.

"That little pussy ready to come again?"

"Yes," she hissed softly.

"Say it louder."

"Yes," she replied, raising her voice.

"Yes what, Kate? I need to hear you say it."

"I want you to make me come again, Jax. Make my pussy throb."

Reaching below her waist, I found her clit and rubbed it between my fingers. She moaned, fueling my need to fuck her harder.

She spread her knees wider, giving me more access. The sounds of our bodies slamming into each other bounced around the room. "I'm gonna come. Fuck," she cried.

"Oh, baby. Not yet." I pulled out and Kate cursed my name, but I flipped her over and plunged inside her again. "I want you to look at me as I fuck you." I spread her legs wide, my eyes traveling the length of her body, and when I finally met her gaze, we lost each other to pleasure.

I unwound the belt tied around her wrists—there was no more need for games. We were just two people giving ourselves to each other. Bracing my arms on the mattress, I lowered over her and kissed her like I'd never kissed a woman. My entire body vibrated with heat as the pressure built in my chest.

Kate roped her arms around me, her nails digging into my back and her legs wrapping around my waist as I ground into her. Harder. Deeper. I couldn't get enough of her—her lilting moans or the salty taste of her skin as I traced my tongue over her neck and further down until I licked and bit her nipples.

"Can you come with me?" I asked, pinning her arms above her head, my gaze rooted to hers.

"Yes."

I pumped my hips, leg muscles tightening, toes curling as my orgasm built. Kate panted, her eyes rolling to the back of her head.

"That's it, angel. Come with me. Ah, fuck." Every fiber in my body thrummed with ecstasy as I gave her every ounce of my release and she gave me hers, but in a split-second, I blacked out. One moment I was having the best sex of my whole damn life, and the next, I was locked in my head. I felt Astaroth gunning for the driver's seat and panic surged in my gut. Thankfully, I managed to reel him in before he took full control.

I collapsed off her and onto the mattress, completely spent. "Fucking hell, angel," I panted. "That was unbelievable."

Kate remained on her back and wiped at her face.

"What's the matter?" I asked, turning on my side.

"Nothing," she said as she dabbed at her eyes. "That was just… I'd never done anything like it."

Turning her chin toward me, I kissed her lips. "That was a taste, angel. One day, when you're ready, I'll show you just how blurred the line between pleasure and pain really is."

"Thank you. I had no idea how much I needed that. I feel like I can sleep forever now." She breathed huskily as she draped a leg over mine.

A laugh bubbled up from my gut as I turned onto my back. "I'll be more than happy to be your pillow."

She placed her head on my chest, wrapping an arm around me as she let out a tired sigh. Good. I was happy to see her satisfied, content, even if just for this moment. I kissed the top of her head and cradled her closer. "Sleep all you want, angel. I'll be right here with you."

The next time I opened my eyes, the world was bathed in red. *No… Oh God, no.*

I stood over the bed. No, *Astaroth* did. I was trapped in my body as he dug his spiny gaze into Kate, watching her as she slept, her beautiful face at peace. Fuck. How did this happen? How had he managed to take control over my body despite the sigils? Despite the wards in this church?

Terror seeped through every pore. He was going to hurt her. He was going to hurt her because he knew how I felt about her. Because she was mine. Because he knew it would destroy me.

No, asshole. This one belongs to Him.

Leave her alone. She has nothing to do with this.

He pushed a lock of hair from her face, and I felt an unholy smile spread across his lips—my lips.

She's the one we've been looking for. We have her now, thanks to you.

Don't you fucking touch her!

Samael will be pleased.

Astaroth. Please. Listen to me. You can take my body. Just leave her alone.

Kate stirred and her eyes drifted open. Looking up at who she thought was me, she smiled, but then her gaze morphed into one of confusion, then fear.

My eyes. She must've seen the glowing red eyes.

Scurrying to sit, she wrapped the blanket over her naked chest. "Jax, what's wrong? What's going on with your eyes?"

Astaroth laughed, and the sound that came from my throat could make even the bravest of men cower. "There is no Jax, only War."

Kate's eyes widened, but the woman didn't even hesitate before spotting her sword on the floor and reaching for it. Astaroth jumped back the instant he saw the lion and eagle carvings on the guard.

Pointing it at us, she said, "As… ta…"

"Roth," he finished, laughing. "Put the weapon down, female. Fighting is futile."

"Fuck you. Where's Jax?" she demanded, pushing up from the bed as she kept her weapon aimed.

"Dead."

"Bullshit. Jax, are you in there?"

"Why do you care about this man? He's nothing, only a means to an end."

"Jax," she called out again, trying to ignore what Astaroth was saying.

"He doesn't even care about you, Kate. Do you know why he came to that bridge?"

Don't. Don't do this.

Kate stared, her lips trembling as she gripped her sword.

"He needed the pompous, self-righteous rat to break this curse," he said, gesturing to my body. "To rip me from his soul. But when he saw him die—and what a glorious sight that was—and bequeath you his sword, he realized his only chance at getting rid of me was the weapon. He didn't save you because of his good heart, Kate; he saved you because he needs that sword. He's only biding his time, waiting for the right moment to steal it from you."

That's not true. Not anymore. I tried clawing myself out, but Astaroth pummeled my will into powdered grains.

"I don't understand. Jax… He… We—"

"Foolish human. Love is a myth made to confuse you and to turn you into puppets. All he wants is your weapon, nothing else. Do you really think someone like him is capable of love?"

"You're lying!" she shouted, and the blade in her hand burst into a white flame. Astaroth's eyes burned from the powerful light, and he stumbled backward, shielding his face with his hand.

"Release him," Kate ordered, stepping forward. "Or I swear, I will plunge this blade straight through your heart. Something tells me that whatever the Devil has planned for my world can't happen if you're not in it."

Do it, Kate. You need to kill him—me. It's the only way to keep him from taking his full form! I fucking screamed, wishing I could crack my own skull.

Soon I will have the amulet and you will be no more, Jax. And once Samael is free, I will take her as my concubine.

"You'd kill the man you love?" he asked Kate, challenging her.

"To save this world?"

If I had possession of my lungs, I would've stopped breathing. Kate hadn't said she loved me, but she didn't deny it, either. We'd not known each other for long, but pressure the size of a skyscraper settled over my chest. I had never felt like this for anyone, ever. And the thought of the demon inside me hurting her in any way…

If she didn't kill him now, I would. I should have done it myself a long time ago.

Astaroth took advantage of her pause to lunge forward in an attempt to take her sword.

Bad idea. As if sent from Heaven, she spun from his grasp in a blur of golden light, swinging the sword at our—my, his— chest. Fuck. The searing pain traveled through every nerve ending. The force of her blow threw me back against the wall with a *crack*, and I landed on the ground with a loud *thud*.

She ran toward me, that sword still aflame, but I put my palm up.

I put my palm up—Astaroth was back in the depths of my core. "Kate, it's me. Jax."

"Jax?"

A bit wobbly, I stood, my eyes widening as I caught a glimpse of the destruction she'd unleashed on my chest. A charred slash ran from my peck to my waist. If I hadn't been a demon-hybrid with supernatural healing abilities, I'd be a dead man.

"I'm so sorry," she said as she gaped at the injury. "I didn't know what else to do. He… Astaroth, he came at me."

I stepped closer, taking her hand and placing it against the healing wound by my heart. "You did the right thing, Kate. And if he ever tries to hurt you again, you drive that blade straight through. You understand me?"

Her eyes moistened as she took in the damage to my body. When she met my gaze, she asked, "Is it true? What he said about the bridge, the angel, this sword?"

"I didn't know you then, Kate."

"You could have taken it. You had plenty of opportunities to do it. Why didn't you?"

Unable to meet her gaze, I turned away. "No unholy creature can touch an angel's weapon. I realized that back at the church, where we fought off that horde. I tried touching it and it nearly burned my hand off."

"But you stayed. Even knowing you couldn't take it, you stayed."

I spun toward her, my heart ready to gallop out of my chest. "Because I couldn't bear the thought of leaving you there by yourself. Because I saw how much Hank meant to you and for some reason, it broke my heart."

"Jax, we can find a way to rip this demon from your soul."

"There is no way, Kate, other than to kill me. To destroy his vessel. Without the amulet, he can't fully take possession of my body, and if you kill me, he will be forced to return to Hell."

"You thought that angel could help you. Maybe Mikha'el can."

"Mikha'el? As in…?"

"Yes, him."

I shook my head, a flush of anger flooding my body. Finding my clothes crumpled on the floor, I dressed. "I was a member of the Devil's Army, Kate. I helped open the gates. War is trapped inside me. I am corrupt and unholy. Unredeemable."

"Don't say that. You have a good heart, Jax. What you've shown me in just a couple of days—"

Closing the distance between us, I took her lips in mine. "After the life I lived, I didn't think this was possible, you and me. What we shared. You've given me hope, Kate. That there is still good in this world. That love is worth fighting for."

I turned to leave, but she grabbed my wrist. "Where are you going?"

"I can't be around you, Kate. Astaroth wants you, and I won't risk him hurting you."

"You said you can contain him."

"But I failed and he almost—" I couldn't even finish what I was about to say. I knew Samael's plan. I knew what he needed in order to escape his prison, and I'd be damned if I allowed him to use Kate for that. "I gotta go."

I bolted from her room without even looking back. I wouldn't have been able to leave if I'd stolen one last glance at her—and I would have regretted it my whole life.

Out in the hallway, I almost collided with a startled Camila. Eyes wide, she stared at me for a beat too long before curiosity got the best of her.

"I thought you couldn't get through the wards," she chirped, her little hands cradling a small bowl. "You shouldn't be out of your room."

I studied the contents of the bowl, which looked like some sort of meat conserve. Probably for Hank. Shit, I'd been so consumed by my own selfish needs that I didn't even ask Kate about him.

I managed to pull my lips up in a smile. "Why don't we keep that between us? Our little secret?"

She squinted at me as she thought about it. "Uncle says keeping secrets is as good as lying, and it is not good to lie."

My forced smile turned into a real one. Children really did say whatever they meant. "What else does your uncle say?"

"That I should watch out for you. You've got a dark soul. You shouldn't have been able to breach the wards." Her brown eyes studied me suspiciously from underneath her dark curls.

"I'm going back right now," I said, then pointed at the bowl. "Is that for Hank? How's he doing?"

Mentioning the dog brought a grin to her face, and she chatted happily about his miraculous recovery. First to ever come back from being infected. All because of Kate's blood.

Kate's blood.

Astaroth stirred back to life. That's when Camila stopped mid-sentence and stared up at me.

"You do…" she stuttered. "You do have a dark soul."

You have heard that it was said, 'Love your neighbor and hate your enemy.' But I tell you, love your enemies and pray for those who persecute you.

MATTHEW 5:43 - 44

CHAPTER 11
KATE

The instant Jax stepped out of my room, an arctic gale blasted through my heart. I shivered under the sheet wrapped around my body, unsure what to think about what had just happened. A sinking feeling settled in the pit of my stomach. The dread of losing him or maybe of being alone forced me to run to the door, but as soon as I reached for the knob, guilt stopped me in my tracks.

What the hell am I doing?

Placing my bare back against the wooden door, I slid to the cold floor, feeling cheap and disgusted. But mostly, utterly confused. I'd been so desperate to forget the pain and the absolute crushing despair eating at my soul, I'd traded in my conviction and need for revenge all for a quick fuck.

But how could I really see what Jax and I shared as a fleeting moment of lust when my chest literally ached, as if my heart was being squeezed dry?

He'd seen through my tough girl act. He'd given me the freedom to be weak, vulnerable. He'd offered me peace and grace. Permitted me my guilt, then washed me of it with his kisses as he traced every inch of my body with his lips.

Jax had worshiped me, yet a monster hungering to hurt me lived inside him. I wanted to believe everything would be okay, that Jax wasn't the sum of his mistakes. Although he'd shared responsibility for opening the gates, deep down, that wasn't who he was. Jax didn't want to be a part of that cult or the devastation that was ravaging the world. He had not wanted this, not any of it.

But I'd seen the demon with my own eyes, felt the vile thoughts that ran through his mind. I'd never experienced evil of that magnitude before.

How could I ignore Jax's warning? Despite his claim that he was able to control the demon, it didn't change the fact one of the Horsemen lived inside him. And it wanted to break free.

Fuck. I jumped to my feet and paced, the sheet dragging at my feet. "Damn you, Jax."

That darn goofball with the striking eyes, flirty smile, and stupid movie references had seeded himself inside my core. But what did me in wasn't any of that, was it? Not even his broad back or muscled stomach. Or the way he made me see an explosion of rainbow colors with how hard he made me come. Not the way he took away my pain and replaced it with longing and something more. Something I couldn't quite put my finger on, but that made me wonder if I'd ever known what true love was in the first place.

Angelic sword or not, he'd risked his life for me and Hank. He'd battled against War himself to keep me safe. He'd not needed to utter a single word for me to know his heart beat in tune with mine. The fire I'd seen burn in his eyes branded me with his mark, claiming me as his.

His. As if I'd never belonged to anyone else.

Christ. Was I really ready to abandon my promise to avenge Roger and Isabella for one man? A man I'd met only days before?

The question seared itself over my chest, anger boiling from within. No matter what happened between me and Jax, my hatred for the demons who destroyed my world only raged hotter. I'd sworn I'd kill each and every one of the four Horsemen and would not rest until I personally sent them all straight back to fucking Hell.

I dropped the sheet and found my clothes crumpled on the floor, dressing in a hurry like a madwoman on a deadly mission. I didn't even stop to think about what hunting down the Horsemen truly meant. All I saw was my blade slicing through their flesh like a knife through a Thanksgiving turkey.

It wasn't until I was gripping the sword in my hand and had turned toward the door with a pulsing energy scaling up my hand that it all sunk in like an iron anchor to the bottom of the ocean.

To kill War… I'd have to kill Jax.

Fuck. Well, that little detail put a wrench into my whole damn plan. My mouth dried up like the Sahara.

I was done losing people to this nightmare. There had to be another way to rip that demon from his body. And I would tear this world to pieces until I found it.

Then a thought flickered to life.

From what Jax had confessed, it seemed angels held the key to exorcizing demons.

Mikha'el had pledged his fealty and protection to me. He owed me this.

As I buckled my jeans with the belt Jax had… ah… um, *used* on me, a frantic knock came at my door. I hurried to open it, thinking Jax had decided to come back, but was startled to find Father Ortega standing at the threshold instead.

Heat spread to my cheeks. The way his eyes assessed my tangled hair made me wonder if he'd have any clue what had happened in my room only a little while ago—not like the smell of sex still lingering in the air wasn't enough to announce our sin.

Truthfully, I couldn't have cared less about having had sex inside a church—well, church grounds. At this point, I was still mad at my creator, and He was free to punish me if He wanted—not like actual Hell on Earth wasn't punishment enough for the world's collective sins. Still, the look in the priest's eyes had me wanting to crawl under the bed.

"Father Ortega, I wasn't expecting you."

"Were you expecting someone *else*?" he asked, his veiled accusation digging a thorn in my side as his beady eyes peeked deeper into my room.

"Not exactly," I lied and immediately felt like I needed to go to confession. "Is something wrong with Hank?"

"Hank is fine. But something else *is* the matter. The wards we'd raised around the church grounds appear to have weakened. We spotted a horde of the infected circling the perimeter."

I rushed back into my room to grab my leather jacket and smoothed out my hair before joining him again. "How can I help?"

"You can start by telling us where your *friend* is."

My back straightened, an icy bead of sweat swirling down the center of my spine. "Jax? Isn't he in his room? Where you locked him up."

His eyebrow hiked and he didn't need to say anything else for me to understand that he already knew why my hair had looked like a bird's nest. Gulping hard, I adjusted my jacket and forced a sheepish smile. "He didn't say where he was going. I assumed he'd gone back to his room."

"Then it is as I feared. Come with me." Without looking to see if I was following him, he strode down the hallway.

I hurried off after him, but even with my long steps, I had a hard time keeping up. "What's going on?" I asked when he seemed content rushing through the corridors without further explanation.

"We think he might have something to do with the wards being weakened," he replied gruffly. "Camila said she saw your friend leave your room earlier. He didn't look well."

"Wait," I called out after him. I couldn't believe they were blaming Jax for whatever this was. Sure, they probably didn't know about his confession—about the fact he'd been groomed and forced into that lifestyle—but I still wasn't able to stop the disbelief from coating my tone. In my heart, I knew Jax wouldn't do anything to harm these people. Certainly not the Jax I'd seen on the concrete floor with pain and regret in his eyes.

But the Horseman of War might.

Still, Jax had him contained; he'd managed to take back control. The wards being weakened had to have an explanation not related to him.

"You think Jax is responsible for this? Why would he do that?"

The priest stopped and met my gaze, my chest nearly colliding with his. "Ms. Jones, you came to my church with a member of the Devil's Army and you don't know why he'd want to hurt us?"

I clenched my fists. It was obvious he didn't really know the full story, and the way he let his accusations fly churned a tornado in my gut I was unable to rein in. "You have this all wrong," I spat with venom. "Jax *was* a member of the Devil's Army, but—"

"Not just a member, Ms. Jones—"

"Call me Kate." The harshness of my voice was unnerving, but hearing Roger's last name shocked me like being touched by a live wire. It was a stark reminder of what I'd done with

Jax. Even though I was a widow—and had been for over a year—I hadn't expected to feel what I felt for Jax so quickly, and the sudden jolt of guilt made my throat constrict.

I was extremely protective of Jax, more than I probably should've been.

"Very well. Kate," Father Ortega said with a sigh, "Jax is the son of its high priestess—the woman responsible for leading the fight against the Guardians. The one who used the Creation Stones to open the gates." He took off down the hallway again, his steps even more rushed.

I remembered the look in Jax's eyes when he talked about his mother. My own childhood wasn't always a walk in the park, but I couldn't imagine looking back at it with such terror and grief. I always had a safe place to go to; Jax, on the other hand, had been completely at the mercy of a madwoman. Yet, despite all the gaslighting and fear, he fought for his freedom.

"Jax tried to stop it," I argued with indignation as I picked up my pace. "Astaroth. War. He's trapped inside him. But Samael can't—"

We'd been rushing through the stone hallways at such speed that when Father Ortega suddenly stopped, it took my feet several more steps to get with the program. The sudden silence when both of our footsteps quieted down was pierced by the priest's startled words. "What did you just say?"

"Jax is not wearing the amulet," I rushed to explain, thinking he would know this already. He'd been the one to warn me about Jax, after all. "Without it, Astaroth can't take full possession of Jax."

My stomach dropped as a look of horror crossed Father Ortega's otherwise solemn face.

"There's a Horseman inside the church?" His voice wavered, fingers tightening around the walkie in his hand.

"He's got him under control," I said, but my words lacked confidence. I'd seen that demon in action, seen the devilry in his eyes, heard the perversity of his intentions.

"We must find Mikha'el at once. We're in far more danger than I thought." He reached for his walkie and pressed on the comms button. "Francisco, there's a Horseman inside the church. Warn the others. Find Camila and secure the girls. Over."

"Copy, Father."

"Father Ortega, tell me what's going on," I said.

"You've brought the enemy inside our walls, Kate. There's only one thing those demons want. The girls."

"Jax would never hurt anyone, let alone children. He risked his life to save Hank for Christ's sake."

He drew closer, his eyes filling with rage. "You're so certain, are you? Do you really believe that's why he brought you *here*? Open your eyes, Kate. You may think Jax is incapable of hurting anyone, but clearly, you don't know much about who he truly is. Do you know why they've been kidnapping women and girls all around the city?"

My silence made me feel like an idiot. Here I was, telling him Jax wouldn't harm any of them, yet I didn't even know why the Horsemen were hunting women.

"They are trying to impregnate them," Mikha'el's voice boomed from across the nave as if he'd been listening to our conversation the whole time. I hadn't even realized until that moment that we'd reached the main church. "Samael is unable to walk the earth unless born of mortal flesh. To free himself from his fiery prison, he must become that which he most hates."

"Why would he want that?" I asked.

"Because nothing is worse than Hell, Kate. Because once he is made of flesh, he will also have the Creation Stones. He'll be unstoppable." Standing over at the altar, Mikha'el looked more heavenly than I remembered from our first meeting. Wonder filled my lungs as I gaped at his beauty, my eyes barely able to look away from his glow, as if his skin itself was shining. It must've been the last rays of sun coming through the vitrine windows above that hit him just right and brought upon the effect as if he could light up the whole church once the night fell.

My mouth felt dry when I continued my questioning, "You all keep mentioning these stones. What are they, exactly?"

"Four gems imbued with the elements of life—water, air, earth, and fire," Mikha'el explained. "During the Holy War, the stones were crafted into keys by God Himself. In our final battle against the enemy, I used them to lock the Horsemen inside their dark realm once and for all. After that, each key was given to one of the four Guardian Houses, the mortal Chosen charged with protecting humanity on behalf of our heavenly Father."

I turned to Father Ortega. "You said Jax's mother was the one who took the stones from the Guardians. How?"

Mikha'el stepped down from the altar, and the light shifted with him, as if drawing it toward him like a magnet. For a brief moment, I wondered if he'd still keep his glow in complete darkness or if it would dim out in the absence of light. The thought was chased away once he started talking again in a voice sweet as honey. "After the Holy War, God not only entrusted the Guardians with the four keys, but He gave them holy weapons crafted from Empyrean steel—the only metal capable of killing my kind, demon and angel alike. For centuries, the keys and weapons were passed down through the generations to new Guardians." He eyed the sword strapped to my thigh.

I gulped, feeling the energy of the blade, as well as the weight of its power, resting against my leg. I was about to reiterate my question when the man I now knew to be Francisco came running toward the nave, flanked by a trio I recognized as the Guardians who'd been sparring when we first arrived at the church. "There's no sign of him," Francisco reported as he stopped in front of Father Ortega.

They must've been talking about Jax. Where the heck had he gone to? I desperately wanted to believe Jax had nothing to do with this, but now he had me second-guessing myself. This disappearing act wasn't boasting well for him.

"Are the girls secure?" the priest asked.

Francisco nodded, but there was a moment of hesitation in his demeanor.

"Out with it," the priest shouted.

"It's Camila, Father. We can't find her."

The air suddenly grew cold, and I swore the walls trembled.

"The horde is closer," Francisco went on, "but they are not alone. Two Horsemen and a pack of hellhounds are nearing the perimeter as well."

"Father, secure the church," Mikha'el said. "I will search the west wing for your niece."

"I'll come with you," I offered.

Towering over me, Mikha'el's wings fluttered, the glamor hiding them going in and out of focus. "You're the only Guardian in possession of an Empyrean weapon; they need you on the frontlines."

I didn't consider myself a guardian of anything—I'd barely been able to protect Hank as it was—but with or without the sword, I'd sure as hell wasn't going to lose another young girl.

I squared my shoulders and straightened as much as I could, wanting to seem less small standing beside his huge frame. "Up until I showed up here, I didn't even know who or what the Guardians were. But if there is one thing I do know, it's that I'm not letting those beasts put their filthy paws on that girl. I'm coming with you, and that's final."

"Very well," he said, not bothering to argue with me. I'd been prepared to volley back a few protesting remarks, but he just turned on his heel and took off toward the west wing.

"Hold up. If you want a real chance at tracking her down through this huge complex, then we're going to need Hank."

He stopped and peered at me over his massive shoulder, an eyebrow arched like a mountain peak.

"Oh, don't get your panties in a bunch. I'm sure your angelic superpowers are extremely handy when fighting off demons but finding lost girls in trouble is like Hank's catnip."

He sighed, altering his route to the infirmary, stoic and gloomy as ever.

"You didn't answer my question, by the way," I said, trailing behind the moody archangel.

"About what?" he asked, not bothering to look back.

"How the Devil's Army was able to steal the stones from the Guardians."

We stepped into the opposite hallway from where my room was before Mikha'el replied, "Within the last century, God began withdrawing the lower angels—those in the third sphere, from Earth, as well as those in charge of guiding humanity and aiding the Guardians, including the archangels."

I blinked a few times to adjust my eyes when we entered the windowless corridor. "Why did He call the angels back?" I asked.

"As our Creator, He's never needed to explain His reasons. Those of us in the lower spheres were kept out of His inner circle and simply told to follow orders, including me."

"But you're His greatest commander. His mightiest warrior.".

"*Was.*" Mikha'el's curt reply made me think he was as disappointed in our *savior* as I was. "Until I dared to question Him. And now, I'm here."

Camila's comment about Mikha'el *falling* now made sense. "God's not sending the angels, is He?"

Turning around, he waited until I caught up to him, his gaze lost in thought. "When the gates opened, I tried to intercede, gathering my forces in an attempt to bring forth my legions and send those—" he bit back what I could only imagine was a curse. "Those *archfiends* back to the rotted world where they belong. But God took away my command before we could launch the offensive. He ordered me back to the citadel to face punishment."

My eyes widened at the confession. "God threw you out of Heaven for defying Him?"

"No. I was to be stripped of my rank. After all the battles fought in His name, I was deemed unworthy of wielding His sword." He swallowed hard, the words seeming to burn his tongue with the pain of God's rejection.

"Mikha'el, I'm so sorry."

His eyes drifted toward me, gaze softening as he offered me a gentle smile. "He took my armies, but not my conviction. Not my honor. I refused to stand back and watch Earth be consumed by this evil. Stripped of my weapons and armor, I abandoned my home of my own volition, Kate, determined to fight alongside your people. But trust me when I say this, I'll challenge Samael to a battle with my bare hands if I have to, but he will not take this world."

"You gave up your home and are willing to lay your life down for us, this world that apparently, has no faith?"

"Kate, I was born of clay for one sole purpose—to lead God's army in defense of His greatest creation. Since my first breath, I've known nothing else. But it was never duty that drove me to defend you—nor God's will that compelled me. It was love. I've seen what humanity is capable of if given a real chance. I believe you can accomplish marvelous things, and I will fight to my dying breath to prove to my father that you are indeed, worthy of His love."

With those last words, he turned from me, hurrying past several closed doors. Mikha'el merely strode by without a glance at their wooden panes. As if he knew with certainty that Camila wasn't anywhere near this section of the church and that looking inside would be a waste of time.

"So, God just let you leave? The leader of His legions?"

Eyes fixed on the next bend in the hallway, he hastened to reach the end of the corridor. Seemed the only way to travel through this cathedral was at a near-run. "My dissension broke Him, but I am only one of many. Zadkiel took command of my armies. Besides, there was nothing I could have said to change His mind. He… um—" His voice broke as he contemplated his next words. Clearing his throat, he said, "I fear He lost faith in the modern world, Kate. You are not designed to follow blindly. People wanted the truth; He gave it to them."

We finally arrived at the infirmary, but as I reached for the door, my breath halted. If God lost faith, what hope did the rest of us really have? When that angel on the bridge appeared, he'd rekindled my hope that perhaps God had not left us as pickings for the nightcrawlers and devoured alike, that maybe all was not lost. But now, Mikha'el's words crushed the part of me that had kept my heart beating.

"He didn't even give us a chance to prepare for the impending doom," I said, allowing myself a cleansing, yet resigned breath. "He just let Hell break loose without warning."

"The signs have always been there, Kate, for those who wanted to see. And not just those looking to save humanity, but those who wished to see it fall."

It wasn't enough. "We were cattle sent to the slaughterhouse without mercy."

Placing a hand on my shoulder, he turned me around. "Not all faith is lost, Kate. Zadkiel is proof that I wasn't the only one who refused to watch your world burn. He gave us a weapon. He gave us *you*."

The tears that had misted over my eyes dried up. "He said more were coming. That we'd not been forsaken."

Mikha'el's lips stretched into a wide smile, and I'd not been prepared for the brightness that enveloped him. Perhaps I'd only imagined it, but his skin seemed more radiant, his eyes even more aglow with the fire of a thousand stars. Placing a fist over his heart, he said, "We will win this war, Kate."

"Let's hope you're right."

Entering the infirmary, I was immediately greeted by a joyful Hank. He spun in place, his tail wagging and tongue drooping. "So excited to see you, too, buddy." I scratched behind his ear and the relief that weaved through me when no fur clumped off was enough to fill me with newfound hope.

"He's been eating well," Trinidad said, "but clearly anxious to see you."

I threw an appreciative smile her way. Before kneeling at eye level with Hank, I said, "Ready to work?"

He huffed and sat on his hind legs, ears perked and ready to receive his orders. He was such a great dog. I turned to Trinidad. "His gear? It had been in the cart we rolled him in."

"I'll get it for you."

"And something of Camila's if you have it."

As we waited for Trinidad, a clamor of howls and yelps erupted through the walls. The sun had completely fallen, and the fact we could hear them through brick and mortar meant the nightcrawlers were closing in. A shudder ran the length of my body as Hank's hackles raised and a growl rumbled through his chest.

You'll have your revenge, buddy.

The sword strapped to my thigh vibrated, and I felt its thirst for demon blood. I turned to Mikha'el, and asked, "If the Guardians were given Empyrean weapons, how were they not able to defend themselves against the Devil's Army?'

Kneeling, he placed a hand over Hank's furry head. He whispered something I wasn't able to make out, and I wondered if he'd given him a blessing. "Without angels on earth to guide humans or protect them from the influence of the lesser demons," he began, rising back to his feet, "those seeking to open the gates of Hell were emboldened. The weapons given to the Guardians in order to protect the keys were taken back when God called upon His third sphere to return to Heaven, leaving the Guardians vulnerable."

"Fuckers waited until the Guardians were defenseless before attacking and stealing the keys."

Mikha'el cleared his throat and gave me a pointed look before he continued, his aversion to my potty mouth still intact, "The Guardians have been fighting the Devil's Army since the Holy War ended. But it wasn't until the last century when they finally held the upper hand. Eighteen months ago, they stole the last key, the Fire Stone, from the Western House."

"Western House?"

"That's us." Trinidad returned with Hank's gear and a small, worn rag doll. Handing it to me, she added, "She's had it since she was a baby."

Holding the doll in my hand jabbed at my heart. I swallowed thickly, unable to keep Isabella's memory from clawing at my skull. We would not lose another child to these monsters. Handing the doll to Mikha'el, I fitted Hank with his tactical vest and goggles. "So, this cathedral—"

"Father Ortega is the Grand Master of the Western House Guardians," Mikha'el said. "He was charged with the protection of the last key at all costs. But without their weapons, his Guardians were not prepared to fight off Edith and her sect."

"Edith?"

"The high priestess of the sect, Jax's mother."

A river of ice ran through my veins. *The Fire Stone. War.* I looked up at Mikha'el. "That's why Father Ortega distrusted

Jax. His mother stole the last key, and that's why he recognized him."

"Edith didn't steal the key, Kate. Jax was the one who actually led the team that stormed the church. It was Jax who stole the Fire Stone."

My head spun, the ground feeling like it was falling away from me. Mikha'el grabbed my arm to steady me and the instant his fingers touched me, an electric current shot throughout my entire body. Mikha'el's golden eyes brightened like fiery orbs, his gaze so penetrating it felt like he was looking into my soul, unearthing my every secret, every sin.

"Jax couldn't have…" I trailed, ignoring the intense heat of Mikha'el's eyes or I'd fall to my knees in supplication. "He said he wanted to leave the cult."

Mikha'el stayed quiet, taking in a deep breath. His eyebrows pulled inwards as he scrutinized me. Finally, he said through tight lips, "Samael is the king of lies, Kate. What else could you expect from his followers?"

Hank was ready to go. We had no time to waste, but I felt the need to defend Jax. "No. Jax is different. This is not his doing." I just hoped I was right. I held onto the image of Jax's torn face when he told his story. He couldn't have been that good of an actor, could he?

"Is it not? Astaroth is inside this church, Kate. The last battle ground for humanity." More whoops and yelps boomed from outside the church walls, filling the night with the sounds of terror. "And now Hell is at our doorstep."

I straightened up and reached for Camila's toy. He handed it over without further comment and I let Hank sniff it.

"If Father Ortega knew who Jax was and the threat he posed, then why did he allow us to enter?"

"Because of you, Kate. Because of the weapon you hold in your hand. My brother anointed you. He chose you for a reason."

"You said Guardians are strong in their faith; it's why you fought alongside them. I stopped believing long ago. I am not who you think I am. I'm no savior. I'm just a woman out for revenge."

"You were willing to lay your life down for that girl on the bridge, Kate. And now you're here, fighting for Camila. Sacrifice is the greatest act of love. And Zadkiel gave his life for you because he believed you to be special. And he gave you that weapon as a symbol of our promise to protect this realm. Our Father may have given up on humanity, but we have not."

They will fight against you, but they will not overcome you, for I am with you to deliver you," declares the Lord.

JEREMIAH 1:19

CHAPTER 12

JAX

The hallway was cool and quiet once I convinced Astaroth to leave Camila behind. Only my echoing footsteps pounded back at me, filling me with ominous dread. It was a familiar feeling, the sudden loneliness that seeped in the farther from Kate's room I got.

This time, it squeezed my battered heart even tighter.

I reached the door to my warded room and walked past it. I was not going to sit on that thin mattress in pathetic misery and wait for a death verdict, either from Kate or the rest of the church. She would come to her senses soon enough and realize I was her enemy.

When it finally clicked, she'd either confess to Father Ortega or kill me herself with that neat sword of hers. As much as I craved that justice for her, the same will to live that had spiked during the summoning ritual grabbed a hold of me again and I navigated deeper into the heart of St. John the Divine in search of my gear.

I meant it when I'd told Kate she shouldn't hesitate to kill me should I become a danger to her, but I also really, *really* didn't want to get permanently trapped in Hell. That'd be the only place for my soul once I died. If there was one thing I'd fought against the hardest during my time with the Devil's Army, it was the soul-travel I'd had to endure every night.

Hell on Earth was still better than Hell itself.

My room hadn't held any of the items I'd carried in the duffle bag. They'd stripped me of my gun and knife, too. Seemed Clint had taken his weapon back, but not because I'd remembered to hand it to him in my pain-stricken haze. It was a wonder I hadn't woken up naked in that cage of a room. They could have thought my clothes were dangerous and burned them straight off my body. Luckily for me, I only needed to find the bag.

My stuff had to be laying around somewhere and I was fervent in wanting it back—not that I was particularly fond of my sage set and the blood-smeared spare T-shirt. Plus, I didn't really have a lot of food left to feel the need to get protective over the canned stuff, but even I needed my weapons if I were to roam the streets this close to nightfall.

The hallways lacked windows, but my internal clock was certain the sun was about to set. Astaroth was distinctly aware of the fact. He was disturbingly happy about it. Not needing to fight me for control over my body now that I was away from Kate and Camila, he sat back in quiet amusement, which made the hairs on my back stand at attention and an icy river of concern swim through my veins.

The way I lost control in Kate's room scared me to the bone. And the more I thought about it, the more convinced I was of my need to leave. Kate was safe now, and so was Hank. There was nothing more I could do for them.

Except leave them be. Leave Kate.

If I was able to abandon Sam in my rush to flee the Horseman of War, then it would be a piece of cake to leave Kate.

Easy-peasy.

Totally was not going to break me apart.

Damn it. Why did I feel as if my heart was already shattering to pieces? I hadn't even escaped the cathedral's labyrinthic hallways, and I already missed her. One night with her hadn't been enough. All I could do was hope her face and voice would eventually fade from my mind, that the memory of her body against mine wouldn't torture me forever.

It was a lie I had to keep telling myself or I'd find a way not to leave this damn church.

Lost in thought, I almost didn't react in time when hurried footsteps and a hushed conversation whispered through the hallway. I tucked myself into an alcove between two pillars as far as I could go, pressing my back against the cool stone. The uneven surface scraped at my back. My feet hit the wall behind me, and a loose stone fell to the floor, the rumble louder than I liked. Holding my breath, I hoped the Guardians, or whoever the fuck else, walked this hallway, hadn't heard me.

"… have your weapon and holy water? We need to be prepared for an attack. They never wander this close to the cathedral…" The breathy voice of the speaker faded in and out as two men passed me, too occupied in getting to their destination to bother looking into my hiding place. One of them rocked a full beard better than I ever could and his shaggy dark locks flipped around his forehead as he rushed with his companion, a younger guy who appeared a bit more groomed.

I'd seen them briefly before the archangel showed up and blinded me. I didn't know their names, but whatever they were talking about worried me. The cathedral was supposed to be safe for Kate, especially once I left and took Astaroth's rotten ass and wicked thoughts with me. Only now it seemed they were being attacked. By the damned? But those beasts wouldn't come this close with the wards up. I took a deep breath and stopped dead in my tracks.

What the fuck happened to the wards?

The constant heaviness weighing me down had lessened, but I'd pinned that to Astaroth becoming resistant to the spell. Now I wondered if the reason the demon didn't buck like a wild horse in my chest was because the wards were down.

Fuck. That wasn't good. If the damned lurked so close to the church, there was no doubt the *d'shiad* would follow.

Nobody was safe.

I really needed my weapons.

Scuffing out of my hiding place with the demon chuckling inside my head, I continued through the hallway with more urgency. This section seemed to be dedicated to sleeping quarters, because the few doors I pushed open showed the same hollow rooms with nothing but a mattress or beds pushed to the corner of the room. My stuff wouldn't be in this wing, but the cathedral was gigantic, and they could have taken it anywhere. Having been inside these walls once before, I only had a vague memory of the church's layout.

I'd seen a training area for combat fighting and figured the weapons were likely kept close by. I headed back toward the nave, keeping close to the wall in case any more Guardians decided to rush past me.

I reached the spot where the hallway opened up to the combat training floor. It appeared to be empty for now, so I felt comfortable enough to slide out of the shadows and try my luck with a few doors. On my third attempt, I found their weapons room stacked with several blades and firearms. Out of curiosity, I reached out to touch one of the swords tucked into a sheath hanging on one of the four walls. Its metal handle stayed cool to my touch, the burn of Kate's angelic weapon noticeably missing.

My hand wandered over to the blade dangling next to it, but it missed the heavenly power as well. None of those weapons were blessed the same way as Kate's short sword.

Figured. If Edith was right about the angels and their weapons being called back to Heaven, then it was likely Kate was the only one carrying Empyrean steel. A part of me held hope she'd been wrong, and that perhaps the Guardians weren't completely defenseless against the Horsemen.

Unfortunately, none of the blades would be a fair weapon against a *d'shiad*, but at least they'd work just fine for beheading the damned.

I kept rummaging through their weapons cache when I found a box full of bullets.

Astaroth recoiled.

Jackpot.

They had to be infused with holy water for him to bristle like a cat about to be given a bath. I went to grab one of their guns and fill the clip when I saw my duffle bag carelessly stashed on one of the lower shelves. I pulled it out and checked the contents.

The kid had taken his payment of Oreos and batteries, but he left the rest of the contents intact. I filled my gun with the holy water-infused bullets and strapped my knife to my belt. I tried not to feel bad about taking the bullets. The priest could easily re-stock them.

It was survival of the fittest, after all. Take what you can carry and get to live another day. I shouldn't have felt like I was betraying their trust when I knew there was no trust to begin with. I needed the bullets. End of story.

I was ready to take my leave, all geared up with my duffle bag hoisted over my shoulder, when the door to the armory creaked open. On instinct, I raised my gun, now fully loaded, and pointed it at the intruder. The young girl peeking in froze, and her big amber eyes widened. My trigger-happy finger had almost shot Camila.

That wouldn't have been good.

Lowering the gun, I took a shaky breath to calm my nerves. The longer I stayed, the more I risked getting caught.

"You shouldn't be in here," she whispered harshly, her deep frown too grave for a kid. She bit her lip and stared at me with less fear now that I wasn't pointing my gun at her. That stubborn glint in her eyes reminded me so much of Kate that my heart squeezed.

"Look, kid, I don't think it's safe out here right now, especially for you. A couple of the Guardians mentioned an attack. I think you should scurry along to wherever you're supposed to be."

She remained firmly planted in the doorway, even as several whoops and hollers erupted through the church walls. She seemed unfazed by the sound of the hellhounds. "You're up to something," Camila said matter-of-factly. "Where are you going?"

I could've pushed past her with ease, but I had a feeling she'd follow—especially since she already distrusted me and quite likely knew about my demon companion.

"I'm leaving." I shrugged. "You said it yourself back in that hallway. I have a dark soul; I don't belong in a church."

"It's the cathedral of St. John the Divine, sanctuary for all, actually."

I shook my head with a small smile tugging at my lips. "I don't believe I'm welcome here. Your uncle made that quite clear when we entered, but if I meet anyone in need of sanctuary out there on the streets, I'll let them know."

She crossed her arms when I took a step forward. Lips thinned into a firm line, she remained cemented in front of my escape. "Does that mean Kate and Hank are leaving, too?" she asked in a low voice, as if dreading the answer. "I don't want them to go. I like them."

"Nah, just me." *Me and the Horseman bound to my soul— the very same one who whispers sordid thoughts in my brain.*

I needed to get the fuck away from this girl before Astaroth decided to act on any of those ideas he found so amusing.

She cocked her head, a puzzled look shadowing her bright eyes. "Why do you have to go? We have a cure now. We can purify your soul the same way we did for Hank. It's not safe out there. Uncle always says so."

The sounds of the pack nearing closer blasted louder through the walls, and the part of me that was still human wanted to shield the girl from the horrors outside. I was afraid, no matter what ritual or prayers any of us inside St. John would cast at the heavens, the *d'shiad* would break through the doors and take whatever they came for.

Kate, most likely. They had to be here for Kate, and perhaps the other women. An ever-present guilt reminded me it was all my fault, and not only because I'd opened the gates of Hell, but also because I'd guided the pack here. They must've tracked our scent and followed us.

"Your uncle can't help me." I wanted to believe he could, but I wasn't sure I could be redeemed. I needed to hurry this conversation up if I wanted to get away. It was also only a matter of time before the rest of the Guardians rushed in to grab their weapons, and the last thing I needed was for them to find me here.

"We helped Hank," Camila said stubbornly, "and he was almost turned. You haven't turned yet." She scrutinized me with her sharp eyes. "You aren't even sick."

She didn't know my dark soul had nothing to do with the infection. Worried I'd accidentally hurt her if I lost control again, I decided to leave by more force than my words provided. I strode toward her to push her aside as gently as I could, but she stumbled backward, startled at my sudden movement.

Regaining her composure, she strolled after me as I tucked into another hallway. There was no way I was taking the main exit out—it was likely guarded and for good reason. If I'd learned anything about demons it was that they were cocky. If they were going to make their push, they'd come through the front door.

"I can't let you leave…" the small voice trailed behind me.

If they came through the front door, their meager defenses might not be able to hold them back. By the sound of it, there was a whole horde out there and they'd overrun this place in minutes. Everything they'd built here, the sanctuary, it would all be lost. Camila would die; Kate would be taken.

Shit.

I stopped in my tracks. "Camila, where is the safest place in the cathedral in case of an attack?"

She bumped into me. "High in the tower. Why? Those walls have never been breached. The Corrupted can't enter."

"I need you to go there, and take anyone you meet along the way with you."

I expected her to run along right away, but she kept on staring at me, standing in the middle of the hallway like a stubborn, immovable boulder.

"I can't let you leave," Camila argued.

"I'm not leaving." The sounds from outside rippled through the walls, as if the thick stone were a megaphone. "I need you to climb the tower and hide, Camila. I'm not saying it again."

"But the cathedral—"

"Do you hear that ruckus?" I interrupted her. "The wards are down. There's no other way the dead would get this close. I felt the power of the spell when we came in, and it's gone now. That means the cathedral is not impenetrable." Even a demon could enter in broad daylight with enough motivation to drive them. I was a perfect example of that.

That's when the groans and hollers turned into *thumping*. It was hard to pinpoint the origins of the sound, but I'd give my left foot that they were banging on the front entrance. We were far enough away from the door and down a hallway that if the *d'shiad* broke through, it'd take them a couple of minutes to reach us. But that didn't mean the raising *thuds* worried me any less. All this stone around us and hollow hallways amplified the sounds tenfold.

Camila's eyes turned into perfect round circles and her head whipped around, her gaze peering down the two ends of the hallway. "You might be right," she said shakily, murmuring verses from the Bible that made Astaroth snarl.

I was torn between seeing Camila to safety and rushing through the nave to reinforce the entrance. I could take down more of those beasts than any of the Guardians.

Camila closed her eyes, her lips continuing to chant a prayer. I'd half expected her to be a frantic mess, but the girl was a small pillar of strength and calm. Still, I couldn't tell if it was truly strength or a false sense of security. Her prayers wouldn't be able to hold back a horde of *d'shiad,* no matter how much she chanted.

But I couldn't leave her to her own devices, even if that meant abandoning the main fight.

War didn't always care who was on the other side of his vengeful blows. He craved blood, the rush of the kill, and the sickening satisfaction of seeing our victims limp and lifeless before our feet. Fighting was his strongest desire and knowing a bloodbath waited just around a few bends made it hard for me to grab Camila's hand and pull her the other way.

A jolt went through my arm as her prayers manifested a small layer of protection around her—enough to make Astaroth recoil within me, but not enough for me to let go.

"How do you get up to the tower?" I asked, tugging her along.

She stumbled behind me. "It's the stairs. We're going the wrong way," she huffed, tugging back.

"Can't go toward the entrance," I grunted. "There's got to be another way."

She stopped murmuring prayers, but my hand still grew numb from the contact. I did my best to ignore it while pulling her deeper into the dark hallway. Her small fingers had a death grip on me. "It'll be okay, it'll be okay," she repeated, mostly to herself, cracking her calm shell. Underneath her show of resilience was still a little girl.

Hell, if that didn't break my heart just a little, I'd be lying. I was reminded of my younger self, repeating the same sentence in the dark. But I survived. Camila was going to survive, too.

So would Kate.

She was the strongest, most steadfast person I had ever met.

A loud *crack* reverberated from somewhere way too close. Definitely not from behind us. No, this sound came from the direction we'd been going toward. Crap.

"Is there a door there that leads to the outside?" I asked Camila as I brought us to a halt. She managed an erratic nod as she swallowed deeply.

I searched the hallway for a place to hide the little girl when I found a narrow door. Pulling it open, a mop keeled over, the sound of the wooden stick hitting the floor echoing down the hall. "Get in," I told her harshly as I shoved her and the mop back inside the broom closet and shut the door. "Don't come out unless I say so. Clear?"

"Jax, I'm scared," she cried, her voice muffled.

"If anyone else tries to open this door, shout scriptures at them. You've got to say them really loud, Camila, okay? I don't care about what the Bible says about believing being enough. Demons despise the words, so the louder you say them, the better. Yeah?"

"Okay," Camila said softly. "Are you not staying with me?"

A trio of *d'shiad* skulked down the hallway toward us, the growls growing louder and fiercer. Saliva dripped from their jowls, fangs sharp and blackened. They'd be on us soon, and Camila's scent would be too potent for them to ignore, regardless if she was tucked inside a closet.

"Someone's got to lure them away," I whispered loud enough for her to hear. "Stay put, kid. Don't open this door, no matter what you hear."

"Be careful," she pleaded through the door.

I drew my knife and cut a slash across my palm. Even though my hand shook slightly, I marked the door with a sigil. The Devil's Army used this one on all our doors when we performed rituals. It kept intruders out. Nobody could open the door, but if for some reason I didn't return, Camila would still be able to leave whenever she wanted to, though.

The sigil was designed to keep people out, not in.

Hopefully, Camila wouldn't decide to leave until I'd lured the dogs far away enough from her.

I moved away from the door with little commotion, not wanting to give away her hiding spot. Raising my tactical knife, I ran straight for the pack, knowing the element of surprise being the only thing keeping me from being mauled. The *d'shiad* hadn't expected to face the Horseman of War and halted their sprint, nearly tripping over their own clawed paws. Saliva continued to drip from their sharp fangs as their growls died down. The hallway became dead silent as the hellhounds stared at me in puzzlement, sniffing the air around me as if trying to make sense of who—or *what*—I was.

They would never attack a Horseman. Not without provocation, anyway.

I held no such reservations regarding their wellbeing. Fury built inside my chest, like coal stoked into a raging fire. Hunger for blood and carnage roiled my gut. War bellowed inside me, his cries rattling every bone in my body. His rage was pure, his need for chaos insatiable. And he made his desires mine.

War did not discriminate.

It didn't matter what I killed; he cared only that I fed his flames.

Without an ounce of hesitation, I swiped the knife clean across the neck of the closest beast, blood spurting into the air as its body slumped to the floor before my feet. I hated having a demon anchored to my soul, but the asshole did come in handy when facing a *d'shiad* without holy weapons. His power gave me the supernatural strength and agility needed to get close enough to slice through these beasts.

The first one died soundlessly, eyes wide and teeth clenched shut. The second one whimpered when my knife cut into its flesh and black blood poured all over my palm. It dripped down my arm toward my elbow as I raised the weapon higher for a strike meant for the third beast.

This one roared and bared its fangs. It wanted to bolt and bite my head off all at once, but couldn't quite decide, so it died in a bloody mess. Filled with Astaroth's will to destroy, I stabbed the miserable hell creature eight times before it stopped moving. After that, the rest of the pack held nothing back, and four more leapt at me.

I dodged two of them and caught the third in a fierce grip before it managed to plunge its fangs into my neck. The pain seared my flesh and my hollering moan echoed off the walls. The sheer force of his weight sent me off balance, and I ass-planted on the stone floor, the *d'shiad* falling on top of me. Three others surrounded me, pawing at the floor as if vying for a turn to tear into me.

Fuckers would taste the venom of my blade.

I huffed as the beast inched its deadly muzzle closer to my face. "We can talk about it now, can't we?" I groaned as I fought to keep its jaws at arm's length, hands soaked and slippery with blood, fingers still wrapped around my knife. I wouldn't be able to cut or stab it without losing my hold on its maw. "No way for a peaceful solution? I suppose your friends would not appreciate you backing off from revenge?" I asked the animal, as if I could reason with these monsters. "Negotiations are not really what you do, right?"

The beast only growled and swiped its tremendous paw toward my face. The movement caused it to move slightly farther from me, enough to grant me the opening to roll away. Only a few surface scratches scraped across my back. Now that my hands were freed, I dove the knife into the *d'shiad's* side, slicing upward and cutting it wide open. What poured out bathed me in black sticky goo, and a maniacal laugh filled the hallway, bouncing off the walls and echoing down the corridors.

Took me a second to realize the laugh had erupted from *me*.

More forms slinked from the shadows, haunches raised, growls rumbling the ground. Seemed we were in for a long night. This time, I pulled out my gun. There were too many beasts to take down with just a knife.

This fresh batch of reinforcements didn't need an invitation to attack. Horseman or not, I'd taken down several of their brethren, and now they wanted blood for blood. They stormed after me, and I was lost in a blur of red mist and demon parts. I fired my gun, the bullet piercing through a hound's eye, the hiss of his burning flesh filling the hallway. Another lost his jaw as I put the barrel to its maw, flesh melting away from the effects of the holy water.

One of the attackers lost its footing on the blood-slicked floor, impaling itself on my knife before I gutted it in half. Power flooded through my veins, healing the bite marks I'd suffered in the attack. I roared as I kicked the slaughtered beast to the side, the maddening rage sluicing through my blood like white water rapids.

Heaving, I was about to stab at the fallen animal one last time when a scratching sound caught my ears. Then a scream pierced the hallway.

Camila.

Fuck. Shaking off the bloodthirst, I turned from the mangled *d'shiad* bodies and ran toward the broom closet. I managed to reach the *d'shiad* carving his claws into the wood, and I slammed it face-first into the door. The force splattered the beast's brains across the door, cracking the wood. Camila screamed. Through the blur of another *d'shiad* jumping on me, I saw the door handle turn.

"Stay inside!" I growled, my voice like gravel. The door opened a sliver, and I pressed my back against it to force it shut while wrestling the new beast.

"Jax?" Camila whispered.

"Stay the fuck inside!" My voice rumbled like thunder, and I was certain if the growling beasts hadn't scared her, I had. The scent of fresh prey drew even more *d'shiad*. We were completely cornered, and I was the only barrier between Camila and a pack of hungry demon dogs.

The sigil was supposed to hold, but after seeing the wood splinter from the impact of the monster's skull, I wasn't sure I wanted to take a chance. Astaroth's desire for blood fed my muscles, but I was smart enough to know when I was outnumbered. The only way to clear a safe path for Camila would be to unleash his full strength and allow myself total access to his otherworldly abilities.

That also meant I'd become vulnerable to his possession. If he took full control of my body, he'd likely gift the monsters the girl and watch them devour her instead of killing his master's pets.

But if I did nothing…

Nah. I was done running.

Realizing my intentions, Astaroth banged his clawed hands against my rib cage. He'd hoped I'd give in to desperation. That to save the girl, I'd lower my defenses to access his full power and hopefully give him the ability to take control.

Not today, asshole.

As the beasts stalked closer, snarling and pawing at the ground, I tore my ripped shirt completely off my chest and, using my knife, carved a sigil straight over my heart—one I hoped would keep Astaroth from forcing himself through.

But that wasn't why Astaroth's mountainous bellows reverberated in my skull. If the sigil didn't work to keep him trapped inside me, there was something—*someone*—who could.

I smirked. This was gonna hurt like a mother, but it was Camila's only hope. "Blessed Mikha'el, archangel…" I began, invoking a prayer I never thought I'd have the *cojones* to ever use. A sickening feeling settled in my stomach, the evil inside me knowing exactly what came next.

The *d'shiad* howled, the words coming from my lips falling over their hide like acid, burning me in the process as I recited every scorching word. They stood their ground, their prize too grand, despite the threat of Mikha'el's mighty sword.

And I went on, despite the scalding heat of every syllable—compliments of the blasted demon trapped inside me, who was scared shitless of God's holy warrior. "Defend us in the hour of conflict. Be our safeguard against the wickedness and snares of the devil, may God restrain him, I humbly pray."

I fell to my knees and brought my hands together, infusing every ounce of faith and need into every single word. Kate said he was here, fighting with the Guardians. He'd not forsaken God's people. He would not forsake Camila.

Making the sign of the cross, steam billowed from my skin with every touch, but I fought through the pain as I sent the archangel my call for help. "And do thou, O Prince of the heavenly host, by the power of God, thrust Satan down to hell and with him, those other wicked spirits who wander through the world for the ruin of souls. Amen."

Astaroth roared as a blinding light appeared behind the horde of *d'shiad.*

He'd come.

And now I could unleash Hell's fury over its own wretched beasts.

246

We know that we are from God, and the whole world lies in the power of the evil one.

1 JOHN 5:19

CHAPTER 13

KATE

After giving Hank an opportunity to sniff Camila's doll, it only took him seconds to identify her scent and get to work. We sped-walked after him as he sniffed doors and crevices. Suddenly, his ears perked up, a growl rumbling from deep in his chest.

"That's not Camila he's scenting," I said, knowing the telltale signs of when he's caught a whiff of the devoured or a nightcrawler.

"He's—" Mikha'el's voice cut out as his golden eyes turned the color of liquid silver. The air around us stilled and the sound of distant, hushed voices vibrated from the shadows, words spoken in a language I could not understand.

"What is going on?" I asked the archangel, the hairs on my forearms standing up like needles.

"Your friend."

"Jax?"

Mikha'el inhaled sharply and his eyes turned gold again, lips tightening. Peering at me, he said, "He's calling for my assistance." The shadows hugging the walls seemed to shudder, as if sensing the dread in Mikha'el's voice. "The demons. They broke through."

Gripping my sword, I sucked in a heavy dose of air. "Then we must hurry."

He placed a hand on my shoulder, holding me back. "Kate, your friend is calling me to fight him."

My chest heaved for several breaths as his words found their way into my heart. "Astaroth." For Jax to be invoking Mikha'el's help, he must have lost control again. It was a desperate move, which meant he was in deep shit.

"I don't know what we'll find, but you must be prepared for the worst, Kate."

How did one prepare to find someone you cared about, who was possessed by a demon? Especially when that demon's goal was to tear that person's soul from their body.

There was no preparing, that's how. There was only rolling up your sleeves and jumping into the fighting pit. I was done losing people. If there was anything I could do to save him from the throes of this plight, I'd fight until my own blood spilled.

"Let's go," I said, muscles coiled tight, spine rigid as a steel beam, an icy grasp encompassing my heart.

Mikha'el brought forth an intricately carved golden bow that seemed drawn out of thin air.

How had I not seen that before? Guess it was part of his many illusions. "Thought you were stripped of all your weapons?"

"Stripped of *my* weapons, yes, but I made sure not to leave completely empty-handed. The arrows are not tipped with Empyrean steel. They can maim and send demons back to Hell, but they won't kill them."

Relieved, I shrugged. At least I wouldn't be the only one with a weapon.

Hank sat at my heel, waiting for a command. A part of me felt hesitant to bring him to a demon fight. I never wanted to feel that sense of despair of losing him ever again, but another part of me knew Hank would never let me go alone.

Rubbing his ears, I knelt beside him, his goggles reflecting my eyes back at me, embers of fear sparking in their depths. But I couldn't let fear rob me of my courage. Or Hank's. "Ready to kick some demon ass?"

He stood on all fours, tail held high, and gave me the widest doggy smile I'd ever seen.

"No superdog maneuvers," I warned him, but his tail only wagged.

I sighed. "Let's go," I said to Mikha'el as I climbed back to my feet.

Hank and I trailed after the archangel as he ran down corridors, our footsteps pounding around us. His impressive wings were no longer hidden by his glamor and rustled with every movement. I'd almost hoped he would teleport us—I mean, he was an angel, after all. Using portals had to be part of his special magical abilities.

"Teleport?" he called over his shoulder.

"Wait, so you can read minds, but you can't whisk us away through a portal or something?"

"I could, but it's not pleasant for humans. And I've never tried it with an animal. Fret not, Daughter of Eve, we're getting closer."

"I think we need to talk about this mind-reading thing, though. Like, can you not read my mind, please? It's rude."

We approached an intersection and Mikha'el's steps slowed. Hank's body stiffened as we stalked closer to the angel.

Raising his bow, Mikha'el drew a golden-tipped arrow from a belt quiver and nocked it as he emptied out into the middle of the intersection. His coppery wings spread wide and luminescent, the light so radiant it lit up the entire corridor.

My breath crystalized as I followed. Dozens of nightcrawlers bathed in Mikha'el's light turned in our direction, snarling, mouths dripping with saliva. Hank barked and bared his own canines, but he obeyed my command and heeled, staying close behind me.

Standing behind the wall of beasts, Jax sneered, his eyes beaming bright red and unholy. "Brother," Jax—or rather, Astaroth—said, the voice deep and distorted, "pleasure to have you join us."

Mikha'el took a step forward, aiming directly at Jax's head as he drew the bowstring and anchored the arrow along the sharp edge of his brutal jawline, sending the nightcrawlers into a growling frenzy and me into a silent panic. "You ceased being my brother the instant you took up arms with Samael."

"Still feeling vexed, are you?"

"Your betrayal isn't my burden to bear."

Astaroth chuckled. "His Majesty finally sees sense and abandons these *humans*, this banal creation, and yet you still fight for them. Why?"

Mikha'el's stance was one of pure stability and control. It was like he was made of marble, utterly unmovable as he kept his muscled shoulders and elbow raised, aligned in a perfect archer's pose. I couldn't even tell if he breathed as the fletching of the arrow brushed his cheek. "I took an oath to protect them."

I tried to swallow, but my mouth went completely dry. For a second, I thought he was about to release the arrow, but he just held his stance, waiting, it seemed, for the right moment. "Mikha'el," I breathed, "Jax is still inside there."

"The Holy City's golden warrior," Astaroth went on, unfazed by Mikha'el's threat. "Your faithfulness is *insufferable*. And all for nothing. How does it feel to be cast out?"

'That's not fearlessness you witness,' Mikha'el whispered in my mind. *'It's him trying to stall and distract me. Camila is near; I can hear her prayers. I'll keep him focused on me, and you see where she might be hiding.'*

Eyes wide, I tried not to give away the fact he'd just spoken directly into my mind. Biting down on my teeth, I mentally gritted, *'I'll give you a pass this time, but this mind-reading/talking trick of yours needs rules.'*

Ignoring me, he said, "I wasn't banished, Astaroth. Or do I not stand before you in my own flesh?" Mikha'el's voice shot down the corridor, taunting and commanding. "Can you boast the same?"

Astaroth hissed, spittle dribbling down his chin. "Make no mistake, I will be restored. Once I am in possession of the Fire Stone—"

"You know I cannot allow that." Mikha'el flexed his fingers around the bow's grip.

Every nerve ending fired off over my body. If Astaroth didn't give control back to Jax, then Mikha'el would release that arrow. "Let him go," I ordered the demon, my blade bursting into a blinding flame, "or you'll answer to me."

Astaroth pivoted his head toward me, those ruby-red eyes digging into my core. Gone was the playful gaze and mischievous mouth I'd fallen victim to. Gone was the man who'd seduced me into a craze of ravenous lips and dark desires. The memory of Jax's fingers navigating the contours of my body whispered over my skin like the touch of a rose petal, only to be turned to cinders from the hate emitting from his eyes.

"Fate is inevitable, Mikha'el," he said, eyes still chained to mine. "She's his destiny."

"He will not have her." The archangel's back flexed under his white leather armor. The only sound I heard after his last word was the whispering hiss of the arrow as Mikha'el released the bowstring, the arrow chasing its target.

My world spun in slow motion. Astaroth didn't have a chance to flinch before the arrow tip grazed the side of his face, leaving a thin gash across his cheek and embedding itself into the wall behind him. "That will be your only warning, Astaroth. Where's the girl?"

"You want the girl?" The demon gritted his teeth and flexed his neck as his wound struggled to mend. "Then come get her." Turning toward a small door to his left, he crooned, mimicking Jax's voice, "It's safe, Camila." He turned and winked, an evil smile curling his lips. "You can come out now."

"Oh, no!" I realized his plan a second too late. The instant the door creaked open, Astaroth yanked Camila out by the hair. She screamed and the splintering cry brought me back to the moment Roger took Isabella from me. A pit formed in my stomach, and I almost vomited.

"Kate for the girl. That's the bargain," he hollered over the whelps and whines of the horde of nightcrawlers. "You have until sundown tomorrow." He fled down the left corridor, dragging Camila with him.

The pack of hellhounds sprinted toward Mikha'el and me in a flurry of snarls and claws that scraped against the stone floor. The archangel already had another arrow nocked, while holding three others in his draw hand, releasing arrow after arrow—each tip aflame, lit by an internal fire—faster than I could breathe.

One by one, he took out the nightcrawlers with direct hits to the head, their bodies turning to cindery ash.

As a beast approached me, I swung my blade, cutting straight through its head, splitting it in half. Hank barked behind me, alerting me of an incoming attack. I spun around and managed to stab the beast through its eye right as it was about to take a bite out of my head.

Hank positioned himself between my legs, both of us moving in unison. It wasn't until my blade reignited into flames that every blow I delivered incinerated the demons. Mikha'el, Hank, and I glided through the swarm like choreographed dancers, cutting through hellhound flesh and bone like we'd been fighting battles together for centuries.

A roar resonated behind us, and I shuddered at the memory of that nightmarish sound. Turning toward the source, I recognized the darkened silhouette charging toward us. The Minotaur's steps thundered down the hallway, axe raised above his head.

"Kate, you need to go after Camila. I'll hold him off."

"He… He…" I stuttered, the images of the angel who'd saved me, lying on the ground, bleeding, with his wings hacked off were too fresh in my mind.

"Kate, don't worry about me. I'll find you. Now go. Camila needs you. *Jax* needs you. We can't let Astaroth take her to the Devil's Army."

His words snapped me back to reality.

I cut through two beasts as Hank and I took off after Astaroth. "Mike," I shouted over my shoulder before turning the corner.

The angel paused mid-nocking an arrow and arched a brow.

"Be careful."

He nodded. "You as well, Daughter of Eve."

With a fresh sniff of Camila's doll, Hank took off, but it seemed her scent was fresh in the air because he barely investigated before taking off in a sprint. Keeping up with him made my muscles ache, but I ran through the corridors with my heart in my throat, determined not to give up.

A bark. A growl. A rumbling roar.

Shit. I rounded a corner with alarm firing off in my blood and found myself in the middle of an open courtyard, a large maple tree standing tall like a sentinel in the middle of a grassy patch. A full moon shone brightly above, illuminating the area in platinum light. Camila sat huddled at the base of the maple's trunk, her head tucked between her legs.

Hank had his jaw clamped on Astaroth's forearm, tugging on him furiously, wanting to take him down. I knew the demon could heal, but that didn't mean he couldn't feel pain—and Hank's bite packed a punch.

But Astaroth gave Jax unnatural strength, and the demon lifted the arm Hank was tugging, then punched the shepherd in the gut. I screamed and ran toward them, my sword thirsty for Astaroth's blood.

Hank let go, falling to the ground with a whimper.

Blinded by rage, I swung my sword, but Astaroth managed to dodge my blows. He laughed at each of my failed attempts. "Come now, Kate. We both know you're quite capable of handling that sword."

"Shut up." I pointed the weapon at his chest. "I don't wish to kill you. I would rather send you straight back to Hell through the hole you crawled out of and have you rot there for eternity."

"But you won't," he taunted, stepping closer, the tip of my blade inches from his chest. "Because to do that, you'll have to kill your *precious* Jax."

"I'll do what's necessary—"

"You'll do nothing." Walking even closer, the tip finally pressed against him. I held firm, but he kept moving, driving the tip into Jax's left pec, steam billowing from the searing burn upon contact with his flesh. He bit down the scream I knew gurgled in his throat, but he didn't let up. If I didn't drop the sword, he'd impale himself on it, burying it right through Jax's heart.

My breath hitched. I should've stabbed him right then. Should've killed the fourth Horseman and somehow brought the war closer to an end. Should've taken my revenge for all the loss and pain. But at what cost? Jax didn't deserve to die like that. Jax had given me back hope. He'd shown me, that despite all the rubble, love could still exist.

I loosened my grip on the sword and Astaroth took the opportunity to knock it from my hand as he pushed me back against the stone base of a large statue of Saint Michael.

He pressed the barrel of Jax's gun under my chin. "I knew you didn't have it in you. So simple-minded, guided by your feeble heart. Or perhaps for you…" he brought his lips close to mine, the stench of his heated breath brushing against me, "guided by your greedy cunt."

I breathed harshly, my nostrils flaring at his distasteful comment.

Pressing his body closer, he ground his pelvis against me. "You're not shy, Kate. I remember every moan that escaped those pretty lips of yours. I don't know what you enjoyed more, your mouth full of cock or your pussy getting rammed."

Spitting on his face, I gritted, "You disgust me."

Amusement danced over his face as he wiped off the saliva and made a show of licking his fingers. "Yet you so willingly dropped to your knees and sucked my cock like a depraved little slut."

"You only wish it was your cock I devoured."

"You don't think I was trapped inside this head—this body— seeing, hearing everything he did to you. Everything you begged him to do."

It was my turn to chuckle. I couldn't give two flying fucks if he had a gun pointed under my chin. "Aww. It must have killed you, didn't it? To see and hear, but not be able to feel a goddamn thing because you're nothing but a pathetic, disembodied pariah. A parasite."

"Silence," he snarled.

"Must have been utter torture to watch Jax's cock dip in and out of my wet pussy and not be able to feel anything but your own quivering need. And not be able to satisfy it."

His knee slipped between my thighs and he pushed up against my center, causing me to flinch from the pain. "You have no idea what awaits you, you insipid human. Once you've served Samael's purpose, you will be mine to do as I please."

"I don't care what you do to me, you piece of shit."

I felt more than saw when Astaroth struck my face with Jax's gun. A ringing tolled through my skull and my jaw throbbed like I'd been hit with a sledgehammer. My vision blurred from wetness, and I swallowed my groan, the tang of iron coating my tongue.

"What? Not the kind of pain you like?" he teased, practically foaming at the mouth. Lifting my eyelids, I shuddered at the sight of his red, glowing eyes. Pure wickedness swam in the depths of those blood-red pools, tormenting despair their only promise.

"Not the kind of pain that had you crying for your worthless human to fuck you, hmm?" He chuckled. "Once my body is restored, I will show you what true agony is. Your body won't be able to take my fury. You'll shout my name, but you'll be begging me to stop, because, unlike him, I am not interested in your pleasure. I will drain you of all your tears and bathe in your endless suffering as I milk my cock with your tight little pussy, over and over again until there's nothing left of you. Until I've destroyed you, body and soul, and every memory you have of Jax is nothing but dust."

I had no words as the tears he swore to drain from me ran down my cheeks in rivulets. They weren't tears of pain, but of sadness. Of stone-cold grief for the man trapped inside his own body. I knew that seeing what Astaroth was doing to me right now was breaking Jax's heart; that knowing he had a hand in releasing this abomination into the world was tearing him up, fiber by fiber.

Mustering strength, I whispered, "Jax, I know you're in there. Come back to me. Please. Come back." Staring deeper into the cruel abyss of Astaroth's eyes, I touched his cheek, catching the demon by surprise.

He flinched, and for a brief second, the redness dimmed from his eyes. Stumbling backward, he shook his head, battling, it seemed, for control over Jax's body. He fell to his knees, roaring and clawing at his chest.

Rushing toward him, I went to kneel beside him. He jutted his hand out to keep me at a distance and shouted, "No." He panted, barely able to look at me. "Please, don't come any closer. I don't know how much longer I can keep him under control, Kate."

"Let me help you."

Breathless, he reiterated, "No. You must go. Take Camila to safety. Please. Leave me."

"No. I can't. Jax—"

But my words were cut off by the sound of hooves clopping. Jax and I both turned toward the iron gates of the courtyard and watched as the Horseman of Death plowed right through, bending the gates as if they were nothing but scrap metal. Mounted atop his pale, skeletal horse, he charged toward the maple tree.

Camila...

Sensing the threat to the girl, Hank shielded her crouched body with his. He barked, snarling ferociously as Death came to a halt in front of them, the horse rearing. Camila screamed as the Horseman drew a broadsword, the blade glinting under the light of the moon.

"Sam, don't!" Jax shouted and my heart fell to my stomach. The Horseman—his former best friend—would kill Hank to get to the girl.

On instinct, I ran to where Astaroth had knocked my sword, retrieved it, and charged toward the Horseman, blade aflame.

Death steered his horse toward me, swinging his sword against mine with one mighty blow. I flew backward into a stone pillar, the sound of crunching bones echoing in my ears. But I managed to fall to the ground on my feet. Still dazed, I wobbled and the Horseman saw it as an opportunity to deliver another blow.

Before I could react, a flash of brown-black fur came racing toward us. Hank leapt and clamped down on the Horseman's leg, and with strength I had no idea he possessed, managed to tug the demon off his horse.

I ran toward the downed creature, ready to plunge my sword into his chest, but while tumbling off his horse, he managed to snatch Hank in his hands. Death stood, his broad, muscled frame towering above me at over seven feet tall. His dark, hooded cloak billowed behind him like a menacing cape snapping in the wind. Face obscured by shadows, the only thing visible were his glowing, red eyes. He held the ninety-pound German Shepherd by the scruff of the neck, legs dangling off the ground like a mischievous puppy being disciplined by its mother.

Hank whimpered and I felt my heart splinter like cracked glass.

"Drop your weapon, Daughter of Eve, or your beast dies."

Without hesitation, I did as he ordered, and the echo of the metal hitting the stone floor cut through the courtyard.

Deep voice rumbling, he turned toward Jax. "Well done, Astaroth. Samael will be pleased with this one." Then he trained his gaze on me. "You're coming with me."

"The hell I am," I snarled, regretting my words the instant they left my lips.

He drew another sword from beneath his cloak, ready to gut Hank.

"No!" I screamed, but it was another voice that stopped Death from slicing his blade across Hank's belly.

"Pale Rider!" Mikha'el's voice blasted across the courtyard, his imposing tone sending a shiver down my spine.

The Horseman pivoted toward the archangel, Hank still in his grasp.

Reaching into his quiver, Mikha'el nocked his last arrow and aimed straight for Death's head. "Release the beast. Now." Body armor torn and slicked in what I could only imagine was angel blood, the archangel looked like he'd battled through the nine circles of Hell.

"Mikha'el," Death said, blowing out a hoarse breath. "Never one to disappoint. Predictable as always."

Pulling back on the bowstring, Mikha'el gritted, "Set the canine down, Beleth. I won't ask you again."

Death seemed to weigh his options. Despite their allegiances to different kings, the demon and angel resembled each other both in size and grandeur, though I couldn't truly see what Death looked like underneath his cloak. Either way, if these two decided to face off in hand-to-hand combat, it truly would be a sight to behold.

"And what of Emrandael, general?" the Horseman asked, refusing to release Hank. "You've exchanged your imperial sword for the weapon of a *sagittarii?* Hardly an equal trade. Or perhaps you've lost favor with the Almighty."

Flexing his fingers over the bow's grip, Mikha'el took a step forward. "We both know all I need is one shot to send you back to your prison."

"The time of the humans has ended, brother. Pity you chose the wrong side."

I'd been so focused on their sparring words that I'd missed the threat looming in the shadows. "Mike, behind you!"

The archangel spun around just in time to avoid the unforgiving blow of the Minotaur's axe. Death thrust Hank aside as he took hold of the reins and leapt back onto his horse. The hellish-looking creature neighed, fangs protruding from his gums.

Despite hitting the ground hard, Hank seemed to be okay, and he jumped back on all fours. Across the way, Mikha'el grunted as he dodged blow after blow, but it was clear he was struggling.

"Kate. Camila," Jax warned. Death leaned down and reached for the girl, yanking her by the arm and onto the horse before galloping away, hooves clopping hard against the stone.

I grabbed my sword and tried running after them, but it was useless—he was through the gates in a moment's breath.

"Kate," Mikha'el hollered.

Shit. The Minotaur had the archangel pinned to the ground, the axe inches from his face. Knowing I couldn't reach him in time, I whistled to Hank. He was on me in a heartbeat. I tucked the sword into his tactical vest and, with a simple command, sent him toward the battling creatures. The shepherd took off in a sprint, reaching Mikha'el in time for him to grab the sword and stab the bull-looking demon through the ribs.

The Minotaur let out a thundering roar before disintegrating and raining ash all over the archangel.

Mikha'el climbed back to his feet, wiping off Minotaur dust and kneeling beside Hank, patting him and showering him with praise. Blood-warming relief swam through my veins and the sensation overwhelmed me. I ran toward the both of them and flung my arms over Hank, then roped my arms around Mikha'el's neck, nearly knocking him backward.

Unsure what to do, Mikha'el seemed to hesitate before wrapping his strong arms around me. Being encased by an angel felt like being embraced by the warmth of the sun, and a part of me didn't want to let go. After all the horror and gore, all I desired was to feel safe.

He pressed me harder against his chest, his encompassing heat filling me with peace and security. My tense muscles relaxed, and I sighed in relief as, for the moment, all my worries seemed to flee.

'You are safe now, Kate.'

Him and his mind-reading trick.

Footsteps approached from behind us and my body jerked, expecting another ambush, but it was a team of Guardians led by Father Ortega who came into the courtyard. Torn, blood-smeared clothes covered their wounded bodies.

Limping, the priest walked toward the damaged iron gates. "What happened?" he asked, turning back to us.

"Father, I..." But I lacked the courage to continue, especially when the anguish pressing on his shoulders told me he already knew what I'd say.

"Camila..." His broken voice trailed as he looked back toward the torn down gate. He fell to his knees, tears streaming down his face.

The heavens cracked with a clap of thunder, and seconds later, globules of cold rain fell upon us. I hung my head, letting the water drench my body in her icy reproach. I'd brought the demons to their doorstep, the bloodshed, Camila. This was all because of me. Because I'd forced Jax to bring me here.

Jax...

I scanned the courtyard for him, but he was gone. In all the commotion, he'd run. An iron ball lodged in my throat. Where had he gone? Why had he left me?

"Who took her?" the priest asked.

"Beleth," Mikha'el said, placing a hand on the priest's shoulder.

"The Horseman of Death." Turning to face me, Father Ortega said, "Have you any idea what they do to girls like Camila, Kate?"

My body trembled from the cold, but also from the spiny dread drilling into my bones.

"Those monsters have been raping hundreds of young women," he went on, limping closer toward me. "Hoping to impregnate one with the seed of one of the Horseman to create the perfect vessel for Samael to be reborn into this world."

"Father, I never meant—"

His body went taut, jaw clamping down tight, his coiled anger threatening to tear me down if I didn't shut up. "They are bred like cattle, their bodies discarded like garbage when they fail to produce a viable fetus." Tears mixing with the rain, he gritted, "I swore an oath to my brother that I would protect her. That she would be safe here. Yet I allowed one of those monsters inside these walls."

"This wasn't your fault."

"Wasn't it? I allowed a known member of the Devil's Army into my home, Kate."

"You did what only a kind soul would do. You opened your heart and offered us a kindness we didn't deserve. But Jax didn't do this; Astaroth did."

"Does it matter? Camila is gone."

"Hank and I will go after her. I'll bring Camila back, I promise."

"You can't do this alone," Francisco said, stepping out of the shadows. "We've lost a considerable number of Guardians trying to free the girls they still hold captive."

"He's right," Father Ortega said. "It's a suicide mission."

"I have to try. And I'm going alone. I won't allow any more of your people to die." Strapping my sword to my thigh, I whistled for Hank and prepared to head out through the broken gates when Mikha'el stepped in front of me, blocking my way.

"I can't let you leave, Kate," he said.

I leaned on my hip. "Not you, too."

"I'm sorry."

"Move, Mike."

"It's not safe."

"I literally just fought off a horde of nightcrawlers and two Horsemen. I think I can handle myself."

"I know how perfectly capable you are at fighting off demons, but that's not why I can't let you leave."

Crossing my arms over my chest, I stared up at him. "Out with it then. Why?"

"Because you are with child."

*Guard me, O Lord, from the hands of the
wicked; preserve me from violent men
who have planned to trip up my feet.*

PSALM 140:4

CHAPTER 14

JAX

Crouched behind the stone mural of the courtyard, I battled with my willpower to flee the vicinity of the cathedral. My brain was all in on getting the fuck away from the holy grounds and the destruction I'd caused within those walls, but my heart refused to leave Kate.

It wasn't smart to linger, especially after I'd released Astaroth in order to protect Camila from the *d'shiad*, only to hand her over to him on a silver platter. He was back in his mental prison now, restless and fuming. There was no way of knowing if I could keep him at bay the next time he decided to make an appearance.

Drawing sigils on my wrists and across my chest to keep him restrained, I clamped my teeth as he roared. He tried to fight the spell, but after buckling to get free and only encountering a barrier, he settled down.

One thing less to worry about. Now, Kate.

I knew I had to leave without her, but my feet wouldn't move, my back firmly pressed against the stone wall.

Without Astaroth's power coursing through my veins, my whole body ached from the exertion of fighting to lock him back up, but none of that compared to the sharp pain in my chest. Kate had managed to break through my emotional guards and steal the piece of me I'd sealed off from the world—my heart. It was the one thing I still considered pure and unspoiled by the cruelty of my childhood—the only thing worthy of her affection. The rest of me was wretched and cursed, but my heart had stayed hopeful, striving for redemption. And it belonged to her. Good grief, every bit of me belonged to her, and I couldn't walk away from that.

I lurched when a muffled conversation on the other side of the stone wall reached my ears.

"What did you just say?" Kate asked, her voice an octave higher than usual.

"You're pregnant, Kate," the archangel said.

An electric jolt ricocheted inside my chest, and I sagged against the supporting wall. What in the world? Pregnant? She couldn't be pregnant. That'd mean—

"I'm sorry, but that's impossible," Kate fired back, her voice weaving with doubt, yet riding with a hint of bewilderment.

Yeah. It *was* impossible. It *should be* impossible.

"I can assure you, it's not," Mikha'el said.

Again, another jolt fired through me. I couldn't have impregnated Kate. Forget the fact we'd had sex literally hours ago, and there was no way she could be pregnant long enough for anyone to notice. But she'd said she couldn't get pregnant when I told her I had no protection. We hadn't really talked about the implications, but I'd assumed from what she'd told me that she was infertile. Plus, I'd been too crazed with desire to ask anything further.

Now, I didn't know how to feel. The thought of having my child growing in Kate's belly, it filled a part of me with dread. Having a child had never been in my plans, especially in a world ravaged by evil. I mean, who would want to bring a child into this nightmare?

What if the child isn't mine? It would be the only way that she could be far along enough for the angel to notice. I rubbed at the center of my chest, a tightening coil knotting deeply into my core. The mere thought of it not being mine made me nauseous. Because whether I wanted to admit it or not, deep down, I wanted that baby to be mine. As crazy as having a child with a woman I'd only met three days ago sounded, I couldn't ignore the spark of longing that fired up inside me.

"First of all," Kate went on, "I think I know my body better than you. I can't get pregnant. Never could. Roger and I, we tried. Doctors told us I had less than a .01 percent of ever conceiving, even with treatments. That's why we adopted Isabella."

"When Zadkiel healed your body with his essence, he must've healed your womb as well," the archangel said.

Could this really be possible?

Angels did have supernatural abilities—how else could he sense life inside her already? Why else would he say this if it wasn't true? He had to be right about his conviction. Even if I couldn't understand how it was possible, we would have conceived after only being together mere hours ago.

I swallowed hard. Regardless of the how, if it was true, all I hoped was that the child was in fact mine. The child *had* to be mine.

Ours... Astaroth chuckled.

Oh god, what if— No. My body was still mine when I'd been with Kate. Astaroth would've needed to be restored for the child to be his.

Right?

Fuck. I was no longer sure.

"Even if he healed my womb," Kate said, "that was two, maybe three days ago. I was with Jax hours ago." It sounded as if Kate was pacing in the courtyard, her voice stronger when she faced toward my hiding spot and slightly muffled when she walked away from me. "Not that my sexual activity is any of your business, but I guess if we're talking about this in front of everybody… It's too soon for there to even be a heartbeat. So how could you detect I've conceived?" She was in denial. Or maybe she didn't feel the same about the potential life growing inside her? What if she didn't want to have my child? I couldn't really blame her, right?

We'd known each other for less than a week. Yet the truth of that didn't make the sudden sting inside my heart any less painful.

"This is not a typical pregnancy, Kate. You have angel blood running through your veins. You were intimate with a man who has a demon fused to his soul—and not just any demon, but one of Samael's lieutenants—"

"So, you're saying that after years of infertility, after countless treatments and disappointments, after countless nights of crying myself to sleep, *now* is when God decides to grant me a child? An angel/demon-hybrid baby with a man I barely know, or worse, with a demon?"

To hear her say it like that… *a man she barely knew,* knifed me. Yeah, so we were practically strangers, but were we, really? After what we'd shared in her room earlier? That had been more than I'd ever shared with anyone in my whole life. I'd thrown the doors to my heart wide open for her.

Sure, having a baby now wasn't the greatest idea, I knew that. But regardless of the blood running through its veins, angel or demon or both, if what Mikha'el said was true, that was my child growing inside her. I didn't care if I knew Kate for only three days, I would protect that baby—and Kate— with my dying breath, no matter the circumstances.

"What I'm saying is," Mikha'el went on, "that for the last eighteen months, the Horsemen have been trying to impregnate women, hoping to produce a fetus capable of being Samael's vessel. Our kind was not meant to procreate with humans, Kate. The last time my kind tried, Nephilim were created, and things went very bad for the world of men. Many of my brethren were punished for their sin. Samael knows that the odds of producing a hybrid are extremely low. It's why the fetuses keep dying, and why the Horsemen keep kidnapping young women, even girls. They are desperate. Yet you were able to conceive."

"Even if I am pregnant," Kate said, her voice breaking. "Jax was Jax when we were together. It was still *his* body, not Astaroth's. This baby might not be the hybrid they seek."

"Your child already has a heartbeat; that's not possible for a human fetus. Whether Jax's seed was human or demon, it doesn't matter. Due to Ezekiel's blessing, you carry a child with angelic blood, Kate. It's how I was able to detect your pregnancy. The gestation period is accelerated, and the heartbeat is strong. You carry a healthy baby."

A healthy baby...

Mikha'el's words rang through me like a tolling bell. I never thought I'd ever have the opportunity to be a father. Growing up with a shitty one made me second-guess my ability to provide for a family. Even in a perfectly normal world, I wouldn't be the first choice for a best-dad award. In the post-apocalyptic shithole I'd played part in, our chances of being a happy family were even slimmer.

Still, I couldn't stop my heart from soaring into my throat or halt the tingling taking over my body. Warmth filled my chest, a feeling so strong, it left me breathless.

This is really happening. I'm going to be a father.

Unable to control my desire to see how Kate received the news, I pulled myself up and peeked over the stone barrier. She faced away from me so I couldn't see her face, but she'd brought her arms around herself, hugging her body in a way that made her look vulnerable.

Mikha'el stepped closer to Kate and put a comforting hand on her shoulder. She shuddered, then eased into his touch. My chest tightened. I should have been there for her. Should've been the one holding her, reassuring her. I almost clambered over the wall to rush to her side, but something held me back.

The knowledge that, despite my best intentions, I was still a danger to her, to the baby.

The few Guardians gathered in the courtyard scanned the area for threats while Father Ortega looked more torn up than any of the *d'shiad* I'd ripped apart in the hallway. One of them—the same one I'd seen in the hallway before the attack—looked over to where I lay hidden. I crouched and pressed my back tighter against the cool stone.

The archangel continued, "The Horsemen now know you carry the essence of our blood inside you—they would have sensed it the same way I did. Even if this child is not the one they seek, your body has the ability to carry a hybrid better than any other woman. Ultimately, you *are* who they need to bring forth Samael. Do you now understand why I can't risk you going after Camila? If they were to capture you…"

Squeezing my eyes shut, I tried not to think about the what-ifs. I knew well enough what they'd do to Kate if she was captured.

I would never let that happen. I'd never let those demons touch her. Not a fucking chance in Hell.

The courtyard was quiet for a moment. "When did you know?" she asked.

"Before, when you put your arms around me. I felt the heartbeat."

"You're one hundred percent certain?" Kate sounded conflicted, which made me crane my neck over the wall once again. The archangel placed his hand on her shoulder, and she took a deep breath, relaxing under his touch. A spark of unwarranted jealousy burned through my stomach like hot coals.

"There's no mistaking it," Mikha'el said. "You are too valuable, Kate. Zadkiel's blood runs through your veins. You are the hope for mankind's survival. Your life is worth more. Your unborn child's life—"

Pulling away from his touch, the lines on her forehead deepened. "I know what you're asking of me, and I won't agree to that. We can't leave Camila to those monsters. I won't sit idle, sequestered here, while she's raped by those demons. For Heaven's sake, Mike, she's just a child. Please don't ask that of me. I am more than capable of taking care of myself. I can go after her."

Mikha'el sighed. "Nobody doubts your abilities, Kate; that's not what this is about. We will find a way to free her. Together. I promise. But you can't go rushing into danger like that. You think the world burns now? In the hands of our enemy, you'll bring upon the true end of days."

Please listen to him, angel.

"I can't just *do* nothing," she bit back.

It was just like Kate to dig in her heels, but I hoped the archangel held more tricks up his sleeve than I did because I was defenseless against her protests. The first day I met her, I'd driven back to the *d'shiad*-infested bridge because she demanded we go back for Hank. If there was a way to convince her to stay safe, I hadn't mastered it.

"Constructing a better course of action rather than rushing after the Horsemen is not doing nothing, Kate."

She clamped her lips shut into a hard line.

"Mikha'el." Father Ortega stepped forward, cutting the silence. "As much as I understand your concerns, Kate is right. We don't have long before those demons defile my niece."

"I'm not suggesting we don't go after Camila, Father. All I'm asking is for time to conceive a better plan. We've lost people tonight. Going after the Devil's Army while we're in a weakened state is not wise. As gruesome as it sounds, we cannot risk the rest of humanity for one rescue mission."

"You mean one child," Father Ortega said, his voice trembling.

"If this is going to be humanity's last chance at survival, then let it be *our* fight," Kate added, stepping into a ray of moonlight. "Your kind abandoned us, Mikha'el, yet here we are, still fighting for our lives. I'm done waiting for a miracle. If you can't come up with a better strategy in three hours, commander, then I'm going after Camila, with or without your approval." Not bothering to gauge his—or anyone else's, for that matter—reaction, Kate whistled for Hank to follow her as she marched back inside the church.

Just before they disappeared inside the hallway with Father Ortega and a few of the Guardians in tow, she looked over her shoulder, searching the courtyard. Her eyes lingered where I lay hidden by the shadows. I didn't think she saw me, but the look in her eyes told me that she'd hoped I was there. That I'd heard Mikha'el's words.

Then she was gone. Seeing her walk away shorn my soul in half, but at least she was safe.

If there existed any possibility that Kate and I and our child could ever be together, then I needed to come up with a better plan to rid myself of my demon companion, now more than ever. I'd be damned if I didn't find a way to get back to Kate. Perhaps I'd missed something in the ancient scriptures. In the ancient spells I'd been taught since I was merely a boy.

I needed to make it back to my place and read through all my books. There had to be another way to rip this creature from my soul.

Just as I was about to push myself off the wall, something caught my attention. I peeked over. While the courtyard had somewhat emptied out, two Guardians still lingered under the big tree, studying the damage our fight had left on the grounds.

"I have a bad feeling about this woman," one of them said, lighting a cigarette and taking a long drag.

The voice sounded familiar, and then I recognized the bearded man. He was the one I'd heard in the hallway before the *d'shiad* had broken into the cathedral. The other man was unfamiliar, but their conspiratorial postures sent a ripple of unease down my back. I didn't like where this conversation was headed.

"Francisco," the other one said, "shouldn't we at least have a little faith in the Lord's plan?"

"The Lord's plan?" Francisco scoffed. "God's got nothing to do with this. Or perhaps He wanted the woman to be the end of this world. Kind of ironic, don't you think? It was Eve who got Adam kicked out of the Garden of Eden, and now another woman is going to finish us all. I tell you, Chris, it's not going to work out for the better as long as this woman is breathing. Not if she's carrying that demon child."

"I heard the Devil's Army's high priestess is the only one who can perform the ritual to bring Samael forward," Chris muttered.

"She's as wicked as they come," Francisco spat.

Edith was more than wicked. If only they knew of all the atrocities she had committed in the name of her lord.

"If you ask me, she's the one we need to put down," Chris replied.

"The priestess is kept safe by the Horsemen and their lapdogs; we'll never get close enough. Kate, on the other hand, is right under our noses."

My insides turned to stone and my blood ran cold at his words. It took every bit of restraint to not jump over the wall and strangle them both, right then and there. If either of those two assholes laid a finger on Kate, Edith would be the last of their worries.

Chris looked around the courtyard as if fearing someone would overhear their murderous conversation. Ashen-colored clouds drifted over the full moon, casting even darker shadows into the night—providing me the extra cover I needed, or he may have seen me clutching the stones for dear life, head still peeking out from my hiding spot.

Satisfied there was no else in the courtyard other than him and Francisco, Chris rolled his shoulders and relaxed. His youthful features sharpened as worry seemed to ease out of his face. "What've you got in mind?"

"I say we wait until she's by herself, and then…" Francisco mimicked cutting his throat.

"Mikha'el will have her under constant supervision, not to mention her dog won't leave her side."

"From what I've seen from this woman, I doubt she's going to wait for Mikha'el to come up with a different plan."

"What are you implying?" Chris asked, taking a drag from Francisco's cigarette.

"If there's an opportunity for her to leave the church undetected, then she'll probably take it."

"She won't be able to leave the premises undetected."

Francisco took his cigarette back and puffed a ring of smoke into the night. "Unless…"

Cocking his head, Chris seemed to follow his fellow Guardian's train of thought. "Unless… one of us is assigned to her detail."

"Bingo." Laughing, Francisco dropped the cigarette to the ground and snuffed it out with his boot before they walked back inside the church.

I didn't need to hear the rest of their plan to know what they intended to do. They would make it easy for Kate to leave. Once Kate made it out of the church, they would follow her and take her out, making it look like she got killed by one of the damned.

Kate was capable of looking after herself, and there was no doubt Mikha'el would keep an eye on her, but nobody would expect an attack from within the church. Shit, I couldn't leave knowing she was in danger.

As much as I would've loved to slit those scheming idiots' throats, getting Kate out of that place was more important. Once they were out of sight, I jumped back over the wall, crept across the courtyard, and moved back inside the church.

A weaker version of the protection spell had been put up while I'd been sulking outside, and it still hit me like a bad hangover. With my brain threatening to split open, I traced my way through the long hallways back to Kate's room, doing my best to avoid the guards stationed in key places around the cathedral.

The deeper I made it into the church, the less guards I spotted. Seemed Francisco and Chris had already executed part of their plan. By the time I reached the hallway to Kate's room, there were zero people keeping watch. Though the reason for their shoddy security job made my insides twist, right now it worked to my advantage. Staying close to the shadows, I snaked my way to her door. I was about to barge in but thought better of it. After everything that had happened, the last thing I wanted to do was startle her.

I knocked lightly a couple of times.

"Yes?" Kate called, soft and cautious.

The sound of her voice sent my heart galloping. I'd not really thought about what I would do once I got to this part of my plan. I had no idea how she would react to me. The woman standing behind that door was no longer the same woman I'd been with mere hours ago. Kate now carried my child, and I still didn't know how she felt about that.

It was now or never. Swallowing the lump in my throat, I said, "It's me, angel."

It took her a few seconds to open the door, but to me, it felt like a lifetime had passed. Eyes wild, she peeked out into the hallway as if I wasn't standing in front of her, then she yanked my arm and pulled me into the room, shutting the door behind us.

Facing me, Kate stood by the bed we'd made love in, unsuccessfully hiding a bag behind her back. The whiff of sex still on the sheets drifted in the air, and it was enough to drive me insane. I wanted to rush to her and pull her into my arms, make impossible promises and kiss her like our lives depended on it, but the little gasp she let out froze me on my feet.

A hand fell to her stomach, a gesture that seemed more instinctual than purposeful. My eyes roamed from the unsure curve of her lips to her belly, and my jaw dropped. I could've sworn her tummy had been taut just hours prior, but now a slight bump poked behind her fingers.

"Jax," Kate said, her eyes misting over.

I reached her in two strides. Dropping to my knees, I pressed my lips to the back of the hand still shielding her stomach.

A low growl sounded somewhere to my right, but I had no eyes for Hank, and seeing as I'd lowered myself to the ground, the shepherd soon found me to be no threat.

"Kate," I sighed, wrapping my arms around her waist. Her fingers threaded in my hair, and I rested the side of my face on her belly. With Astaroth subdued, my heightened senses weren't as pronounced, but I swore I heard subtle, even heartbeats pumping from within her womb, and my heart squeezed at the sound of the life growing inside her.

"Jax, I think I might be... It sounds crazy, but Mikha'el says—"

I teared up as I looked up at her. "The archangel was right."

Kate's eyes widened, her rapid heartbeat joining the much softer one coming from her belly.

"I was there," I tried to explain. "I heard him say it."

"You were in the courtyard?"

Standing, I said, "I was close enough to hear everything."

She dropped her chin. "I'm so sorry, Jax. I didn't know. I didn't think I could get pregnant."

I tipped her chin back up. "Angel, why are you apologizing?"

"Look at us. We're two people who barely know each other, living in the middle of a war where humanity stands to lose it all. How could we possibly bring a child into this damned world?"

Cupping her cheek, I took in the softness of her skin and the glow of her eyes. "Up until I heard Mikha'el utter those words, I never envisioned myself as a father. My destiny had been laid out for me since before I was born. A wife and family were never in my plans, but then I met you, Kate. You turned my whole universe inside out. I don't care if we've only known each other for three days or three lifetimes; right now, you are the only one that matters to me. You and the baby. Fuck the end of days. I will find a way to make this work. To make *us* work."

She turned away from my touch and sat on the bed, hugging her arms around her belly. "I'm scared."

"I will protect you, Kate. I promise."

"You don't understand," she said, looking up at me, her face tense. "What if this life I'm carrying… What if it's a—"

I lifted my hand to stop her. "*Don't.* Don't even say it."

"I can't stop thinking about it. All I ever wanted since I could remember was to one day be a mother, to have a family. When Roger and I found out we couldn't have children, the news broke me. It took me months to pull myself out of that dark place. Months to be okay with the fact that I would never know what it would feel like to have a life growing inside me."

I sat beside her on the bed and took her hand in mine.

"All that pain was erased once Isabella came into our lives. She was the most beautiful child I had ever seen, and it didn't matter that I hadn't carried her in my belly, she was mine. Roger's and mine, and I loved her more than life itself." Tears trickled from her eyes. "Losing a child… it's a feeling I wouldn't wish upon my worst enemy. When this fucking war took her from me, a part of me died, Jax. A part I will never get back." This time, her tears turned into a deluge down her face.

Taking her into my arms, I cradled her in my chest, wishing I could extinguish every ounce of pain from her heart. "I'm so sorry, angel."

"I can't go through that again, Jax. If what Mikha'el said is true, about the blood flowing through this baby's veins… What if I can't carry the child to term? Or what if I do, but those demons take my baby?" She shook her head. "I won't be able to survive the loss of another child, Jax. I won't."

Still holding her in my arms, I pulled her chin up, tunneling my gaze into hers. "I won't let anything happen to you or the baby. Regardless if it carries the blood of the angels or those who have fallen, I will protect you both with my last dying breath. I swear it, Kate."

A whisper of a smile ghosted across her lips, and it was the only sign I needed to believe there was still hope left for us. But first, I needed to get her out of that church. "We have to leave this place, though. It's not safe for you here."

She pulled away from my arms. "What do you mean? It's literally Guardian headquarters. Plus, Mikha'el wouldn't let anything happen to me. He pledged to me his sword… er, bow and arrow."

"It's not the angel. There are others in the church who mean to do you harm. We need to leave tonight."

"Who would want to hurt me?"

"Francisco and his buddy Chris. Fucking assholes were plotting how they were going to kill you. I heard them talking right out in the courtyard, which is why I snuck back inside. I had to warn you."

"Francisco? Why?" She seemed stunned and heartbroken.

"The baby. They see it as a liability. So, they planned to leave your door unattended in hopes to tempt you into leaving before Mikha'el came up with his plan. Once you left the premises, they would attack you outside the church walls and make it look like someone—or something—had killed you." I stared past her to the bag she had been hiding behind her back, which now sat at her feet—my bag. The one with my gear that I'd lost amidst all the chaos earlier tonight.

Her jaw tightened into a determined line as she saw the question in my eyes. "But you were already planning on leaving anyway, weren't you?"

"They took Camilla," Kate said, matter-of-factly. "I was going to get her back."

Hank let out an appreciative rumble, reminding me of his presence. He looked as steadfast as Kate. If Mikha'el hadn't been able to convince them to wait, what chances did I have? Still, I had to try. This woman had to learn some self-preservation. If I had to keep her safe by force, then so be it.

"Angel." She narrowed her eyes. "Kate," I corrected, "I don't think you're equipped to go after her alone. The whole sect of the Devil's Army is inside their headquarters—guarded by two Horsemen and who knows how many *d'shiad*. Even you and your mighty sword can't get past all that."

She stood from the bed and picked up the small duffle. "Which is why you're gonna help me."

"Angel—"

"Kate," she interrupted me, cocking her hip.

"You know, you're gonna need to hand me a manual detailing when it's okay to call you angel and when to call you Kate."

Her stern face didn't flinch.

"*Darling*," I said, hoping to get her to ease up, "you can't really expect me to waltz you into a demon-infested shithole while you're carrying my child."

She crossed her arms over her chest and looked to be unamused by my choice in nickname and refusal to cooperate.

"Do you know what the baby can mean for the world?" I continued, running an exasperated hand through my hair. "If the Devil's Army were to get their hands on you, Samael could gain a vessel to walk the Earth. Even if I was able to suppress War until then, once Samael rises from hell, everything will be lost."

Pacing, she placed her hands on her hips. "You think I like the idea of walking right into the demon's lair? Knowing what I carry inside me? But what other choice do I have? Camila was taken prisoner because of me. Because of *us*. She's only a child, Jax. We owe this to her." Peering over to where Hank sat on his hind legs, she said, "Hank is still here thanks to Father Ortega. I owe this to *him*."

So stubborn, so damn courageous. I wanted to give in to her, to give her anything and everything she asked for, just to make her happy. I also wanted to kiss the frown from her lips. Hell, I wanted to do a lot more than kiss her, but we were running out of time and what I wanted didn't matter as much as what we *needed*. And we needed to be on our way the fuck out of here.

"*Cookie*," I tried once again, hoping to tear down her defenses. She raised an eyebrow. I decided to go with it. "My sweet taste of Oreo, I can't guarantee your safety if you march right to the enemy's door."

"I want to protect this baby as much as you, but I can't, with good conscience, abandon Camila to that fate. By the time Mikha'el comes up with some plan to rescue her, it might be too late. I have to go, Jax. And I will, with or without you. Though I prefer with."

We stared at each other for a beat. "*Buttercup—*"

"Stop with the nicknames, and let's just go." She tapped her thigh, signaling for Hank, then dug her gaze into mine. "We're wasting precious time."

"What's wrong with buttercup?" I asked, mocking a wounded heart. "Didn't you ever watch the *Princess Bride*?"

"Seriously? We're back to movie references?"

"Come on. That movie only has like some of the best movie quotes, ever. *My name is Inigo Monto—*"

"I'm done. Hank, let's go."

I swiped my hand down my face. I'd been trying to ease the seriousness of our situation by hiding behind my usual defense mechanism. Giving Kate nicknames or quoting famous movie quotes would not get her from walking into danger, but it helped keep some of my fear and worries in check.

Dropping my head back, I pressed my eyes closed and tried to drown the rising storm inside me. *More like a fucking tornado.* This was why I never dared to get close to anyone. They'd either die, get turned into a demonic monster, or walk into hell on their own accord. My chest hurt at the thought of losing Kate to such an end. The pain was enough to make Astaroth scoff and bury himself deeper into the cage inside my head to get away from the nuisance of my thoughts and emotions.

Taking a deep breath, I said, "Kate, please. We can talk about helping Camila once we're out of here." But the instant my lids lifted, my stomach plunged. The door stood wide open, and Kate and Hank were nowhere to be seen.

Fuck. In less than five seconds, she'd literally snuck out without me noticing. I found her a few feet down the hallway on her way toward the courtyard.

"Hey," I whispered harshly, catching up to them. "Nice of you to wait for me."

"I did. You were just taking too long to—"

"Hush," I said, taking her by the shoulder and putting a finger to her lips. Caging her between the wall and my chest, I let the scent of her skin tickle my nose.

Her eyes grew wide. "What?"

"There's someone out there," I breathed, but as the footsteps faded away from us, I was distracted by the softness of her breasts pressing against my body. I traced an invisible line across her moist lips, feeling famished for her taste. She parted her mouth slightly, as if sensing my desire. Not able to restrain myself, I crashed my mouth against hers and latched onto her lips like they could save my soul. The taste of her consumed me and for a brief moment, I forgot we were in a church. In the middle of the apocalypse. Running for our lives. And risking everything for one stolen kiss.

Hank whined his impatience.

Detaching myself from Kate, I panted, heat flaring in all parts of my body. All. Parts. Damn if I didn't want her right now. If I didn't want to whisk her away to some dark corner and do all sorts of filthy things to that body of hers.

But we had a girl to save. "Gorgeous, please tell me you found my gun and stashed it back in my bag."

Cheeks flushed, she lifted the duffle, reaching inside and pulling out my gun. "I reloaded it with holy water-infused bullets, and I even packed some extra ammo."

"Atta girl," I said with a wide grin as I took the gun from her. "How did you get them to give you access to their weapons cache?"

"I just followed a group of Guardians as they went in. No one said anything."

I found that a tad suspicious, but wouldn't be shocked if Francisco and Chris were behind that, too. Regardless, at least I had my gear back. "Stay close to me and don't do anything heroic and reckless."

Of course, she rolled her eyes.

Keeping close to the shadows, we made our way through endless hallways with my nerves on edge. Kate stayed next to me the whole way, which eased my mind a little, but I was only able to breathe a true sigh of relief once we reached the courtyard and escaped via the downed gates.

A heaviness immediately lifted from my shoulders, and I felt several pounds lighter.

"You know where Camila was taken?" Kate asked, keeping pace next to me as we walked down Amsterdam Avenue, past abandoned cars and wrecked store fronts.

"I do."

"Where?"

"Sugar, we should wait."

Kate stopped mid-stride, Hank following suit by sitting by her feet like they'd practiced it beforehand. "Jax, we've been through this," she gritted.

I turned to face her. Kate's fists were clamped tight, feet firmly planted on the ground. Behind her, a crashed car wrapped around a bent-up lamppost and dead leaves drifted past its airless tires. A burnt front door to the apartment building across the street hung loosely on its hinges and creaked when a scurrying rat bumped against it. Shadows lurked around every corner, but the air smelled fresh, not rotten and putrid. At least there weren't any damned nearby.

But that reprieve wouldn't last long once we walked farther from the church.

"We should at least find a place to hole up until dawn before marching into the heart of the city," I said. "Wait for the *d'shiad* to retire back into their hiding holes."

I also needed time to figure out how to safely get in and out of headquarters without being noticed. They changed base after I ran away, so I wasn't familiar with their new set up, nor did I know where they actually kept the girls. I was pretty sure I could use Astaroth's senses to find them, but if I let him surface even a little, I would put Kate and Hank in danger.

"Under different circumstances, I would agree with you," she said, "but we don't have the luxury of time. Every second that passes is another potential second they could be abusing her. We can't wait until morning."

Hank whined his agreement, and I gave him a hard stare that did nothing to lower his resolve. I already knew nothing I said or did would change Kate's mind. With all the skills and quirks that came from having a demon living inside your body, mind control and persuasion still eluded me.

Yet, as much as I hated to admit it, Kate was right. Camila didn't have much time.

"Their new headquarters is inside the Empire State building," I said reluctantly.

"That's at least an hour-and-a-half trek."

"They are gonna have eyes on the main road, so we'll need to weave through some of the side streets."

She nodded and we tucked into a tight pathway between two, five-story buildings that reeked of piss and rotten eggs. A row of turned over trash bins created an obstacle course through piles of eighteen-month-old muck. I stepped into something squishy and slick, and I almost fell on my ass before I regained my balance and chose my path more carefully.

We walked in silence, careful not to alert any damned or *d'shiad* patrolling the streets. Kate took the lead, guiding us through shortcuts I had missed. Hank padded ahead of us, sniffing and scouting out areas for safety.

After almost an hour, we were able to spot the Empire State Building slashing through the moonlit sky several blocks from us. Some of its windows flickered with warm lights. *How do those assholes manage to have electricity?*

"She always aspired to obtain that skyscraper." I'd not meant to voice my thoughts out loud, but when Kate offered me an intrigued look over her shoulder, I continued, "I didn't think it was possible at the time. We'd been stuck in the basement of one of the office blocks a few streets down from the Empire State Building for as long as I'd remembered. I thought she was crazy to think we'd ever achieve any of her wicked plans. She thought I was indolent and disobedient. We never got along."

Kate slowed to walk next to me as the alley we'd slumped through widened up to another beat-up street.

"Your mother?"

"Edith," I corrected her. "She never was a mother to me." I hiked the duffle bag higher up my shoulder. "I've not been inside their new headquarters, angel. I don't know what's waiting for us once we get there."

Her steps faltered just a little before she walked down the next stinking passage between buildings. "I've been there a few times."

Neither of us added the fact that the building was preposterously gigantic and, a few times in and out was not enough to learn the nooks and crannies of the place.

"It was just you and your moth— Edith?" Kate asked when the silence between us grew heavy. "What about your father?"

"Hardly knew the man." Since today was all about confessions, I offered more than I intended. "The only time Edith ever talked about him was when I'd displeased her. 'You should've been more like your father,' she'd say. 'He'd died for the cause.'"

"I'm sorry."

I shrugged. "It is what it is."

Kate reached out and squeezed my hand. Such a simple contact, yet it relieved some of the pain in my chest. "Jax, you're gonna make a good father."

My breath hitched and words got stuck in my throat. It didn't matter, because whatever I would've said would have been interrupted by Hank's loud growl.

We both whipped our heads toward him. Hackles raised, his rumbling growl grew stronger as he neared the intersection between West 60th Street and Broadway. A terrified woman's scream pierced the night, and Hank bolted toward the sound, which must have erupted from Columbus Circle.

"Hank!" Kate didn't think twice before drawing her sword and running after him.

I strapped the duffle bag across my back and took off after them, gun at the ready, fearing what we would find.

Catching up to Kate, we rounded the corner and came to a full stop when we spotted the reason for all the ruckus.

Motherfucker.

Sitting atop his monstrous black horse, right in the center of Columbus Circle near the monument, Famine circled a girl who seemed to have been hunted down by three *d'shiad*. Wide eyed and whimpering, the poor thing looked so malnourished and frail, she could probably snap in two with the slightest of breeze.

The light cast by Kate's blade lit the streets, snagging Famine and his beasts' attention. And the instant he saw Kate step into the large roundabout, his blood-red eyes glowed brighter and a diabolical smile stretched across his handsome face.

Myth would have you believe Samael's lieutenants were horrific-looking beasts, cursed beings scorched by their sins. But what everyone seemed to forget was that these monsters were once higher order angels, some of the most beautiful creatures ever created by God. It would be easy to be fooled by their elegance and magnetism, but beneath all their glamor existed the vilest of Hell's most powerful demons.

Nothing in Famine resembled the man I once knew, the man who'd given up his body for *the cause*. The fallen angel was fully restored, and Christopher was no more.

Losing interest in the girl he'd captured, he eyed Kate with morbid intrigue, his gaze lingering on her longer than I felt comfortable. "Malphas," I crooned, stepping in front of Kate and Hank, gun aimed at his head. "You must have pissed off *someone* important if you're out here scavenging for vessels yourself. Don't you usually send lower order demons to do the grunt work?"

Lowering his hood, he revealed a mane of golden, wheat-colored hair. Pointing his monstrous staff at me—a chain with weight scales dangling from the staff end—he said, "You've done your work, human. Now step away. It's your female I want."

"Then come and get me, you piece of shit," Kate hollered.

I closed my eyes and sighed. Sometimes I wished my warrior princess wasn't always so brave.

*For You have girded me with strength
for battle; You have subdued under me
those who rose up against me.*

PSALM 18:39

CHAPTER 15

KATE

He laughed. The fucking demon actually laughed, his boisterous voice booming from every building around us. I almost wished he'd been hideous, because reconciling his angelic beauty with his unholy intentions made my head swim. From the corner of my eye, I saw shadows move around us, the nightcrawlers approaching the circle from all five points.

Jax had called him Malphas, but I knew he was Famine by his notorious black horse and the balances dangling from his staff. He dismounted the beast and stripped off his hooded cloak, revealing a bare, muscled chest. He wore only a pair of black, leathery pants and a pendant with a gemstone hanging from his neck. A set of grey, bat-like wings spread from his back, making his long hair whip around his head as he flapped them.

He looked glorious and terrifying all at the same time.

"We're at a severe disadvantage here, angel."

"No kidding. What now?"

He looked over his shoulder and nodded toward the encroaching beasts. "I'll take the big guy; you work on the hellhounds."

"There's at least twenty surrounding us."

"You have a better idea, luv? Because I'm all out."

"Son of Adam," Malphas said, snagging our attention. "Do your duty to your lord, and you shall be spared."

Jax tightened his grip on the gun. "I think I'll pass, *Fabio*. Not really digging the End of Days vibes any longer. Know what I mean?"

"The child is *his*."

Jax shrugged. "Actually, the child is *ours*."

I felt a little flutter in my stomach when he said ours. I still couldn't believe it. A gift or a curse, we'd already accepted this child was ours, and we'd fight until we took our last breaths protecting it.

"Astaroth lives inside you," the Horseman uttered, his gaze fixed on Jax. "And it is *his* essence that grows inside of *her*. You cannot take that which belongs to him. Hand her over or suffer the consequences."

"We'll take our chances, asshole," I shouted at the Horseman, fed up with the fact he kept talking to Jax as if I had no say in the matter, as if my words held no weight.

"As you wish." The demon shot up into the air, staff held high above his head, then he dove back down, slamming the staff against the ground and cracking the stone circle. A wave of energy shot out from the crater, creating a strong blast that knocked us backward a few feet. Jax and I grunted as we hit the pavement. Hank jumped back to his paws and shook off dusk from his body as if nothing had happened. Posturing for an attack, he barked, baring his teeth as the hellish creature climbed to his feet.

"Heel, boy," I called to Hank, needing to make sure he didn't decide to play pup-hero.

Rolling to a knee, Jax fired his gun, bullets aimed at the Horseman's chest. The demon dodged them, using his staff to deflect the last bullet.

"Fuck," Jax grunted. "He's not going to go down easily."

"Let me at him," I gritted, gripping my sword.

He tugged on my elbow, holding me back. "As powerful as that Empyrean weapon is, countless Guardians have fallen at a Horseman's hand. I will not have you meet a similar end."

"But you just saw what he did to those bullets. What are you supposed to fight him with?"

"Empyrean steel is not the only metal known to be a nuisance to these beings." Taking me by the shoulders, he said, "I need you to listen closely, and please don't fight me on this one, angel. I will need to use some of Astaroth's power in order to stand a chance against this guy, while you and Hank focus on fighting the beasties. And if I lose control at any time, promise me you'll—"

"Don't, Jax. You can't ask me to do that."

"Kate, I'm not asking; I'm telling you. You will plunge that sword straight through my heart."

I swallowed. There was no way. Even after everything I'd endured, I still wasn't strong enough. "Jax, I—"

With a deep kiss, he silenced my refusal to kill him if Astaroth were to take over his body. Despite the terror tearing at every fiber of my body, the touch of his lips grounded me, giving me the courage to accept whatever came next, no matter the outcome. He pulled back, breathless. "I don't know how you did it, angel, but in three days you managed to give me something I never had, something I never thought possible. I love you, Kate. It may seem silly after such a short time, but it's true. I fucking love you, and if I die tonight, it will all be worth it."

I didn't have a chance to utter a reply; hell, I barely had a chance to blink. With one last kiss, he turned from me and ran past several broken-down cars to a late-nineteenth century cast-iron lamppost that was probably one of only a handful still remaining in the city. I had no clue what Jax intended to do until I saw him reach for it, as if he planned to pull it out of the ground.

What in Heaven's name…

But I had zero time to react to what I saw because the nightcrawlers had stalked too close and one leapt at me. With a swing of my blade, I made ground beef of his neck, the flaming steel charring his flesh. I spun in place to slice through another beast when I heard Jax holler into the night with a voice so deep, the vibration rattled my knees.

He'd done just as I thought. With the herculean strength only Astaroth could have given him, he ripped the damn lamppost right from the base. Famine predicted his intentions and struck his staff down right as Jax swung the iron beam at him. The demon's weapon was stronger, and he cut the lamppost in half. Part of it broke off and *clanged* against the street between the two of them before it rolled on the uneven ground, almost tripping Jax off his feet.

He stumbled backward to avoid the piece of metal but regained his footing. Using the remaining half of the post, he struck the demon, landing a few nasty blows.

More nightcrawlers stalked me, reminding me of my own fight. Hank and I managed to dodge a few close calls, dancing around claws and fangs. I ran around the perimeter of the roundabout, hacking off limbs and heads as more hellhounds spilled from the shadows, all while keeping an eye on the battle ensuing in the middle of dozens of dried-out fountains circling the monument. Jax stood on top of a stone slab once used as a picnic bench, waving his makeshift weapon in the face of the demon, earning an aggressive blow from Famine's staff that sent him flipping through the air.

He crashed into the Christopher Columbus monument with a sickening *thump*. The marble statue shattered into a million pieces with a thundering blast as the thirteen-foot-tall column the explorer stood on crumbled in on itself, leaving nothing but rubble in its wake.

"Jax!" My heart stopped as I watched his body collapse under a mountain of debris. The distraction cost me precious seconds, and I was blindsided by a bulldozer of a beast. He knocked into my side, and my bones groaned against the force of his body. The impact sent me flying, and I landed against the side door of a broken-down car. I fell to the ground with a *thud* and every muscle in my body throbbed from the impact. My head pounded and my vision blurred as I tried to push myself off the ground.

Hank bolted after me. In a daze, I couldn't register what was happening until I heard a small scream. The girl. Shit. Pushing up on my elbows, I caught sight of her huddled behind a trash can. A smaller-sized nightcrawler crept toward her, his razor-sharp teeth dripping black saliva.

I tried to stand but fell back to the ground at the pulling-sting on my leg—a bloodied gash ran the length of my right thigh, a small piece of shrapnel protruding from my flesh. Hank licked my face, but I needed him focused on someone else right now. "Hank, I need you to help the girl, okay?" He whined as he nuzzled my nose. "Don't worry about me. I'm gonna be fine. Can you be a good boy?"

His ears perked up at my words. Always so eager to earn my praise. Pointing to my eyes, I made sure he focused before I pointed to the beast. "Attack."

He huffed, then sprinted, and my heart thundered at the implications of my command. I'd just sent Hank to fight a nightcrawler, and I couldn't stop shaking as I watched him run at full speed, his courage the size of a mountain and my love for him spreading warmth through my chest. He jumped onto a small retaining wall, then leapt off, going airborne and gaining so much lift, I thought he'd sprouted wings. Hank landed on top of the nightcrawler, digging his canines into the beast's neck.

The demon bellowed a high-pitched squeal as Hank's jaw clamped shut with the force his ancestors had granted his breed. With every muscle in his body, Hank pulled on the nightcrawler's neck, tearing flesh. After several more yanks, he managed to tear off a huge chunk of meat, sending blood spurting in all directions. The nightcrawler fell onto his hindlegs, then keeled over, dead.

My breath caught. Hank had actually taken out his first nightcrawler.

Taking a protective stance, he kept guard of the girl, barking and snarling at any beasts that dared approach, but with the dead nightcrawler at his paws, the others seemed too afraid to even get near him.

Holy fuck. Had Hank established himself as the alpha?

I didn't have long to ponder that thought as another wail caught my attention. The battle between Famine and Jax raged on, and the grating sound of metal scraping against pavement split the air. I gritted my teeth and held back a scream as I pulled out the small piece of shrapnel stuck in my thigh. I created a tourniquet with my belt, but then noticed my wound had started to mend itself at an incredible speed. Tingles raced down the torn flesh.

Once back on my feet, I was able to spy on the fight still going on in the middle of the circle. Famine slammed his staff down against a dented-up car door Jax had managed to turn into a makeshift shield. But the demon was stronger, and after three more blows, the door bent inwards and snapped into two.

Limping, Jack fell backward on his ass, the door no longer providing any protection. He was already covered in stone rubble and blood; his shirt—torn at the neckline—hung awkwardly off his shoulders and revealed a pink scar snaking down his chest that didn't stitch together quite as fast as I'd like. His movements slowed, and he didn't react fast enough to prevent the Horseman's' relentless onslaught as he bludgeoned Jax's body, blow by blow.

Jax didn't move; he didn't even flinch as the staff came down hard again, gashing his unprotected stomach. I wanted to scream but my voice faltered. On instinct, I took off after him, but the demon jabbed his weapon into Jax's chest, piercing right through his rib cage. Jax let out a guttural scream so visceral, it didn't even sound human. The demon lifted Jax's impaled body, and the sight dropped me to my knees.

"Jax!" I screamed, but I couldn't hear my voice over the sound of his pained cries.

"Brother," Famine said, staring at Jax's anguished face, but it was Astaroth he was addressing, "tell Samael we have his vessel. Soon, this world will be ours, and you too shall be restored. This pitiful human will pay for his betrayal, but we shall find you a new body and you will rain down war on all who oppose us."

Spreading his wings wide, he aimed their clawed tips toward Jax, meaning to finish him by stabbing him to death with those monstrous claws. No. I would not allow this to be Jax's end. Summoning strength from the pits of my core, I sprang into action, my mind zeroed in on one thing.

Running as fast as I could, I jumped as high and as far as my momentum allowed, my flaming sword hungry for demon blood. With one quick blow, I sliced it down one of his bat-like wings, cleaving it off at the base. The demon howled in agony, dropping his staff, Jax still impaled on it.

Famine fell to a knee, confused and angered. Bleeding, he searched the circle for his attacker, but I was smaller and moved faster. Wasting no time, I sliced my sword down hard again and cut off his second wing. After watching Zadkiel die the way he did, I knew the essence of an angel's life resided in their wings. While Famine was a demon, the fact remained that he was still an angel. Weakened and bleeding to death, he fell back on his stumps.

I approached, looming over his body. He couldn't speak, black blood gurgling up from his throat. I aimed my sword at his heart. "I'd tell you to deliver a message to Samael for me. To tell him that Kate says to go fuck himself, but this is Empyrean steel." His eyes flashed with horror, pleading for clemency. Satisfaction flared through me, knowing I'd done *that*. I'd made one of the Horsemen tremble with fear because he now knew I wouldn't be sending him back to Hell.

This blade spelled his true end.

I plunged the sword straight through his heart, blood splattering all over my face. I reached for the amulet and pulled on the chain, yanking his neck up. Staring at his eyes, I watched as they slowly dimmed from red to darkness. "The world of men has not ended, demon," I said, "but your life has. And there will be no mercy for your kind. I will avenge my people and kill every one of your brethren, even if I have to go to Hell myself and stain my hands black with the blood of your king."

And as he expunged the last of the air from his lungs and his body began to turn to ash, I smiled, knowing my face was the last he'd seen.

Hank's barking pulled me out of my blood rage, and I turned to find him licking Jax's face. With the amulet still in my hand, I rushed toward him, dropping to my knees. He laid on his side, that monstrosity of a staff piercing through his right lung. I thought about yanking it free, but unless he could heal fast enough, he'd likely bleed out. Uncertain he could recover, I decided not to pull the staff out.

"Jax," I said, swiping bloodied hair from his eyes. "Can you hear me?"

He wheezed, and I breathed a sigh of relief to know he was still alive, though barely. "Tell me what to do," I said, hot and cold waves weaving through my veins. My hands shook as I cradled his face and tears stained my cheeks.

He blinked slowly, his breaths shallow. Jax tried to speak, but blood spurted from his mouth, drowning out his words. He succumbed to a coughing fit that shook his whole body.

"Oh God, Jax."

"It's okay, angel," he croaked, more blood dribbling from his mouth. "My time has come. But you must deliver the final blow. If I die like this, Astaroth will only be sent back to Hell. You must finish me off. Only Empyrean steel can kill him."

"No. I can't. There's gotta be another way. You can heal, Jax."

"My body is too broken, angel. Please."

Gripping the sword in my hand, I screamed into the night. This couldn't be happening, not again. I looked down at him. "Listen to me, you asshole. You are not leaving me, not when you just put a baby inside me. You will live and you will be a father, and we will figure this shit out together, but you don't get to leave me right now."

But his eyes closed, and his chest no longer rose and fell. Animalistic rage burned through me as I screamed again, so loud I could have shattered the glass from every skyscraper in the city. And I didn't care if I'd woken every devoured and nightcrawler in the tri-state area. Or if fucking Death and Pestilence came for me themselves. This fucking war would end now.

Blinded by anger and pain, I went to pull the staff from Jax's chest, but a set of strong arms grabbed me from behind. Then I saw a group of shapes swarm Jax's body, and I lost it. "Don't touch him," I screamed. "Don't you fucking touch—"

Someone put their arm around my neck and applied pressure. Then, all I heard was Hank's panicked barks as my world faded to black.

I awoke in a sparse, dimly lit room several hours later, laying on a small cot. The mattress was thin and several springs poked my back. A scratchy blanket provided little warmth.

A young girl sat on a chair near the foot of the cot. "How do you feel?" she asked.

Like I've been run over by a Mack truck.

Not bothering to answer, I looked around the dingy space. This wasn't the same room from the church, and I didn't recognize the girl, either. Sitting upright, I pressed on my temple, my head throbbing. Then images flooded my brain. I gazed at the young girl again, taking in her black hair, round face, and her sharp brown eyes.

I *had* seen that face before.

She'd been at the Columbus circle. The girl who'd been cornered by Famine.

And she was the only other person in the room.

Fuck. I shot to my feet. "Hank. Jax." They weren't questions; I was just trying to make sense of the situation. Then I looked back at the girl and something in my eyes must have frightened her because she almost fell off her chair as she jumped to her feet as well.

"They are okay," she stuttered. "Your dog… he's with my brother. He didn't want to leave your bedside. Took a lot of reassurance, but he finally relented. He was hungry and needed to be let out. And your husband, he's—"

"Wait, did you say *they* are okay?"

"Yes."

"Jax?" I swallowed against the lump in my throat. "He's alive?"

"Your husband? Do you want to see him?"

I couldn't find it in me to correct her. To tell her Jax wasn't my husband. Unable to speak or I'd break into tears, I simply nodded. The girl walked me down the hall of their compound, a high-rise apartment floor. Through the windows, I could tell we were still near Columbus Circle, and we were several stories up. Daybreak seemed to loom in the distance, the sky slowly brightening from navy to a pastel blue.

Several people lined the hallway, laying on makeshift beds on the floor. Some slept while others looked up at me as we passed.

We finally came to a stop by a door at the end of the hallway. "He's in there," she said.

I blinked my appreciation and went to reach for the knob, when she added, "Thank you. For what you did for me out there. The thought of going back—"

I turned from the door. "You were held captive by the Horsemen?"

Her eyes darkened and she lowered her chin.

"I'm so sorry."

"I'm sorry for the girls who remain," she said, a haunted shadow overcasting her gaunt features.

"How did you escape?"

"My brother worked as an engineer at the Empire State Building. You know, before everything happened. He'd told me about the wind tunnels in the basement."

"Wind tunnels?"

"Liling!" a man called from down the hall, Hank trotting at his side.

"That's my brother," the girl said as Hank bolted toward me the moment he saw me.

Kneeling, I wrapped my arms around his neck and let him slobber doggy kisses all over my face. "So happy to see you too, buddy."

Dressed like a mercenary and with a rifle strapped across his back, the girl's brother looked more like a soldier than an engineer. He shook my hand. "We are indebted to you."

I grasped it firmly. "I'm glad we were able to help. My name is Kate, by the way. And this is Hank, but I guess you've already met. Thanks for taking care of him."

"Name's Jianyu, but you can call me Jian. Feel free to stay as long as you want. Our resources are meager, but please help yourself to whatever you need."

Jian resembled his sister for the most part, but his physique was wider at the shoulders and a scruffy beard covered his face. They were both thin, awfully malnourished, but the man also had dark circles under his eyes, as if he'd not slept well for days.

"Thank you for bringing me—us—here."

"Don't mention it. You saved my sister from that monster. It was the least we could do."

Instinctively, I reached for my sword, but I found the holster empty.

"You were not in the right state of mind when we found you," he said. "I had to confiscate your weapons."

"I'm going to need my sword back."

Jian nodded slowly with a soft smile playing on his lips. "Of course." It seemed like he wanted to say more, perhaps ask about the weapon, but ultimately decided against it.

"What about Famine's staff and the amulet?"

"We collected everything." Jian grabbed the back of his neck and shot me a weary look. "The sword zapped my comrades, so we wrapped it up in linen. See me after you've had a chance to speak with your… husband?"

"Jax. And he's my… Well, it's complicated."

"Everything is complicated nowadays. I gotta run. Liling will show you around." Giving her a strong hug, he said, "I'm so relieved to have you home, sister."

Wrapping her thin arms around him, she squeezed him in return. "Me too, brother."

Jian disappeared down the hall, leaving me alone with Hank and Liling. I hadn't realized I'd teared up at their reunion until I reached up to wipe the corners of my eyes. Hank licked my hand, but I was unable to snap out of the sudden wave of grief for all the families who had lost someone to this unholy war.

I needed to get my emotions together. I also needed to see Jax. "Will you keep an eye on Hank for me while I check on Jax?"

"I would be delighted. By the way, there's freshly collected rainwater in the washroom, enough to clean up a little if you want."

I touched my face, realizing I probably had dried demon blood all over my skin. "Thank you." I gave Hank a reassuring rub under his chin and told him to be a good boy for Liling while I checked on Jax. He huffed his approval of the girl, which gave me a touch of relief. If there was one thing Hank was good at, it was sniffing out bad apples.

Steadying my breath, I braced myself for what I would find behind the door. Last time I'd seen Jax, he had a gigantic staff pierced through his right lung. He'd stopped breathing, and I'd been certain I'd lost him.

My eyes widened when I stepped into the room. Head propped on what looked like an impromptu hospital bed, Jax lay with a blanket over his legs, his top half completely naked except for the crisscrossing bandages over his chest. He had demon blood caked all over his hair and parts of his face and neck, but otherwise, he looked unscathed. Still, I stood paralyzed at the entrance, waiting for a true sign of life.

Then, his chest rose as he took a breath, and I was able to release the one I'd been holding. Walking up beside his bed, I brushed a lock of hair from his brow, absorbing the warmth of his skin. *Heavens. It felt exhilarating to know he was alive.*

His lids fluttered open, and a broad smile spread across my lips when I saw those familiar sparkly blues. "Good morning, sleepy head."

"Aren't you a sight for sore eyes," he said hoarsely, returning the smile.

I chuckled. "Quoting William Hazlitt now?"

Brows furrowed, he said, "Donkey from *Shrek*. You've so much to learn, angel. And who's this William guy?"

"Someone who's been dead for over two hundred years, and no one you need to be concerned about."

He grunted and I almost burst out laughing. "God, it feels so good to see you like this, Jax."

"It feels good to see *you* too, but—"

"Hush," I said, bringing my lips to his. "There's no room for *buts* in here. Not today."

He snaked his hands through my hair, deepening our kiss, his tongue unexpectedly stoking a sudden spark of desire. He must have felt it too, because a growl of approval rumbled from his chest, and he wrapped his arms around me, bringing me down on top of him.

"Jax," I squealed as I fell. "Your wounds."

"They're healed, angel."

Looking into his eyes, I said, "As much as I hate that demon inside you, if it wasn't for his healing power, you'd be dead."

He caressed my jawline and I leaned into the soft, yet rough touch of his calloused fingers. "I can't feel him right now," he said. "I think what you did to Malphas scared the shit out of him."

"When I saw him spear you with his staff, I… lost it." I choked on my words as a tear bubbled at the corner of my eye.

Jax wiped my tear away with his thumb. "Pull up closer," he said, and as I did, he cupped my chin. "You risked your life for me, angel. I'll never forget that." He kissed me again, and this time, it was I who growled with approval.

Jax chuckled. "Seems we're both in need of each other. Is the door locked?"

"Locked? What for?"

Reaching lower, he cupped my ass. "Do I need to spell it out for you, buttercup?"

"Oh, my God. You've just recovered from having a giant staff pierced through your lung. And we're both covered in demon blood."

"Yes. I had my ass handed to me, thanks for reminding me. Look around, angel, we're in the middle of an apocalypse. The last thing I'm worried about is a little blood. I want you, Kate. Who knows how much time we have left in this forsaken world, and I want to make sure I spend every second of it worshiping you."

I smirked. "You know, relationships that start under intense circumstances, they never last."

His eyes narrowed, lips twitching. "Did… did you just quote a movie?"

Smiling wider, I shrugged. "*Annie. Speed* was one of my favorite Keanu movies."

"Wow. If I thought I was in love before, now I'm really done for." He pulled me under the blanket with him, positioning himself over me. "I want to make love to you, Kate. No gimmicks. No games. Just my heart and yours."

How could I refuse him with that beguiling look in his eyes? Jax was right. Who knew how long we had with each other? And if there was anything we needed to preserve on this scorched Earth, it was love.

I nodded, granting him permission to make me his again.

Piece by piece, he stripped me of my tattered clothing until all I wore was my bra and panties. He'd already been stripped of his clothes by whoever had patched him up, the bandages covering his chest the only thing preventing me from seeing the complete canvas of his rippling muscles. "I know we don't have long," he whispered in my ear as his hands explored the contours of my body, "before someone barges in, so I'll make it quick, angel. Quick, but worth it."

He bit my earlobe as one of his hands slipped inside my underwear. He found my center and in soft strokes, he summoned that sweet warmth that radiated to all parts of my body.

"That's it, baby," he said. "Let my touch take you to that place where only you and I exist."

I moaned, my limbs feeling like liquid. Closing my eyes, I let the heat of his breath as he trailed kisses down my chest transport me. I imagined a sun-bathed morning on a white sandy beach with a luminous glow right outside the window. A turquoise ocean gently lapped at the shore, and in the distance, seagulls squawked, looking for a breakfast treat.

Jax's lips feathered over my belly, lavishing me with tender kisses over my navel, right where a small baby bump had already started to form. My heart swelled. Could it be that I actually loved this man? That I already loved this life inside me? A life I never thought possible—that shouldn't be possible, yet there it was, growing.

He continued to use his fingers in circular motions, stealing my brief thoughts of motherhood and replacing them with something that tasted of dark chocolate and red wine. I now imagined a full moon cradled by a sea of stars, the ocean's salty breeze blowing through the window, cooling the rising heat, but the tightening at the apex between my thighs made my entire body dampen.

Sliding off my underwear, Jax spread my thighs open, and with gentle, yet firm strokes, he lapped his tongue along my seam. I quivered as each stroke brought me closer to pitching a fever.

I pictured myself sprawled on a king-size canopy bed draped in white cottony sheets as Jax feasted on me, his tongue doing things no man had any right knowing how to do, yet he'd managed to do just as he'd said—worship me. But it was he who owned me.

My back arched as I neared the peak, that moment when time stops spinning and you just wish you could make this last and last and last. But if he kept licking me like that, I was not going to make it much longer. "Jax," I breathed, "I want to feel you inside me."

"But I love the way you taste, angel."

"Jax, please…"

Positioning his body between my legs, he lowered down to kiss me. "You're so beautiful, Kate," he said as he slowly pressed his tip to my center. "Everything about you is like a dream." He pushed in with patience, letting me feel every single inch of his rock-hard, silky length. "I never want to stop feeling this—you, this love building inside me—for as long as I live."

Gripping my thigh, he brought one of my legs over his waist as he thrust faster and deeper. Crashing his mouth into mine, the heat of his hunger stoked the flames of my need. "Harder," I whispered harshly.

He obliged, the force of his strength making the bed hit the wall with loud *thumps* that echoed through the room. And I didn't care if everyone outside our room heard us or if the whole building rocked. None of the nightmares that haunted our real world could enter here.

My body felt like breaking, but I welcomed the pain, welcomed each push of his body into mine. Positioning himself on his knees, he grabbed my hips and lifted me up to meet his thrusts, then he ripped off my bra, and his feral eyes consumed every centimeter of my body with his gaze.

I was addicted to the way he looked at me, the way he drank me in. Addicted to the way he took ownership of my mind, of my heart, of my very essence.

His thrusts grew greedier as he chased his own summit, so I spread my legs wider and moaned his name, delighting in the tightening of his muscles as every sound that escaped my lips seemed to drive him crazier.

Circling my clit with his thumb, he coaxed my climax as he pumped his cock harder and harder. I gripped the sheets, practically tearing them off the mattress as I came in a wave of tremors. My release fueled his, and I gorged on the sight of his body rocking over mine. Watching him come undone was sublime, and I savored every second we spent in our little make-believe beach haven, etching it all to memory because soon, very soon, the world would come toppling down over us.

A short while later, after using the rainwater that was left inside a bucket in the bathroom to wash off the caked-on demon blood from our skin, I rummaged through the dilapidated dresser in the room, looking for clean clothes.

I was able to find two large, white T-shirts. I found Jax's sweats crumpled on the floor, and we both had to slide back into our dirty, ripped pants. At least our top halves looked presentable. As I tied the hem of my shirt into a knot at my waist, Jax looked over at me from where he was lacing up his boots. "You make it really hard to want to sacrifice myself for the sake of humanity."

I cocked my head. "Why would you need to sacrifice yourself?"

He took a few strides toward me, his hands tucked in the pockets of his sweats. "Angel, we both know what needs to be done."

Staring, I said nothing because I refused to believe what I thought he meant. I set my jaw tight and his gaze softened. Puffing a long breath, he said, "The only way we have a real chance at winning this war is by ensuring Samael never escapes his prison. And to do that we have to kill his lieutenants." He jabbed a thumb to his chest.

"No," I bit out, a lump stuck in my throat.

He caressed my cheek, but the warmth of his skin burned like frostbite because I already knew what was coming. "Had Malphas managed to kill me, I would be in Hell right now, but so would Astaroth, and that would have given that demon an opportunity to take another vessel."

"I know what you're going to say; that I should have used my sword to finish the job." I lowered my gaze. "But I couldn't, Jax."

Tipping my chin up, he said, "Though I am eternally grateful for the opportunity to have seen your face again, I would've gladly given my soul to Samael to ensure you lived in a world free of this nightmare. You spared me last night and gave me the gift of being able to touch you and kiss you again, and in a million years, I could never express my gratitude for that. But we both know as long as this demon lives inside me, no one is safe. And I can't allow Astaroth to go back to Hell, either. He needs to die. Permanently. And your sword is the only weapon capable of doing that."

I leaned in closer, refusing to allow the chasm of heartache threatening to come between us to cause an even bigger rift. "I will find another way."

"Kate, please. You need to believe me. If there was another way, I would have found it by now. When I met you, I thought the sword was the answer to my problem, that I could use it to free myself of him, and now I know it is. But there's no happy ending for me in this story. And I'm okay with that because I know my sacrifice will give you and our baby a chance at a better life."

"And it's because of this baby that we can't give up, Jax. I was once told I could never have children. Ever. And yet, here I am, carrying *your* child. So, don't you tell me there's no other way. Don't you fucking ever again tell me that I need to kill you because you're not leaving me alone in this mess. Are we clear?"

He swallowed sharply, his eyes searching mine for any hint of doubt of my conviction, but there was none. Nodding, he said, "Yes, ma'am." Though I wanted to believe him, a part of me feared he'd only said it to appease me, and I couldn't ignore the tightness that formed around my heart. If given the opportunity, Jax would sacrifice himself for me and the baby. For this world. And that made my insides twist.

"We should get going," I said, cutting the tension. "I think I know a way we can get inside the Empire State."

"How?"

"The wind tunnels."

After we'd accepted a quick meal of rice and beans—which tasted like paradise—we gathered inside Jian's command post and stood over the blueprints of the Empire State Building. The room had once functioned as someone's bedroom but had since been stripped of anything warm and comforting, replaced with a metal table and chairs, boxes stacked on top of boxes, and a mega-sized walk-in-closet that had been turned into a weapons locker.

Jian stood at the head of the table, arms crossed and surrounded by two similarly mercenary-clad individuals, introduced as Chaz and Octavia. He didn't seem convinced by my plan as he eyed the laid-out floor plans. It wasn't lost on me how fortunate we'd been to stumble upon this small resistance group, who just so happened to have a map of the Devil's Army headquarters.

Liling's brother had been the leader of this group for several months now. They'd been trying to clear the city of the devoured when his sister got captured. He'd worked as an engineer for the building's underground power plant until it was taken over by Edith, so he was extremely familiar with the tunnels. Studying the schematics, he pointed to a section in the lower basement. "This is where the abandoned bank vault is, and where they are keeping the girls. It won't be easy to gain access. We tried several times and never made it past the tunnels into the lower basement. Quite frankly, I have no idea how she managed to escape."

I turned to Liling, who couldn't have been older than seventeen. Standing at just about five feet tall and probably weighing no more than a hundred and ten pounds, if she was able to make it out of those tunnels, surely, we could figure out a way back in. "How *did* you manage to escape?"

"The vault's door doesn't seem to lock, so they have two men keeping guard at all times. They change shifts every three hours, and every three hours, one of the guards takes a handful of girls for a bathroom break right before the new shift takes over."

"Is that when you made your run, during one of those bathroom breaks?"

"I watched them for weeks, learning who was least alert, who tried to flirt with the girls, who appeared to be less of an asshole. On our walks to the bathroom, we'd pass several unmarked doors, but I always remembered seeing one marked as ventilation. My brother had talked about the wind tunnels under the building, and I figured if I could get to one of the tunnels, then maybe I could find a way out. So, on the day that Dragon—that's what they called him—took us for our break, I knew it was my chance to try. He was always trying to chat up the girls and never quite paid me any mind. As we walked back to the vault, I made sure to keep back. It was sheer luck that the door to the ventilation area was open. I ran in and just kept running, following the wind."

Jax was leaning against a wall, listening to the conversation intently, but spoke up from the shadows when the girl's eyes darkened at the memory, and she took a gulp of air. "Without electricity, those tunnels would be pitch-dark."

Jian pointed to another part of the schematics. "Most people don't know this, but the building has its own steam power plant. It was designed to provide heat and air conditioning, but when shit first hit, with a group of engineers, we tried to re-rig some of the machinery to provide electricity, not just for the building, but for the city as well. Unfortunately, soon after, those fucking devil worshippers took over."

I shared a look with Jax. The lights we'd seen shining from inside the building now made sense. His jaw twitched, and I knew he wanted to make sure I wouldn't mention the fact he had been a member of those worshippers or that he had a Horseman trapped inside.

Jax peeled himself off the wall and approached the table, studying the building's layout. "So, how do we access the tunnels?"

"The sewer," Liling said. "That's how I was able to find my way out. I'd stolen a lighter I'd seen discarded and used it for visibility. Trust me, that's not a place you want to be caught without light."

Jian piped in, "But after the rain last night, they're likely flooded. The tunnels, too."

"Not to mention you'll probably find some infected down there as well," Octavia offered as she rubbed a palm over her shaven head. Standing about a foot taller than me and heavily muscled, she looked like she could easily bench press me.

"Tavs is right," Chaz said, his whiskey-colored eyes shimmering from the early morning light shining through the window. "You'll need to wait another night until the water level drops."

"Camila doesn't have another night," I said. "We have to go today."

Jian stepped closer to me. "I know the feeling of knowing those monsters have taken one of your own… of the things they do to those girls. I want to help you, but even under favorable conditions, navigating the sewers is not easy. Even with the schematics, the tunnels are a maze. It took Liling three days to escape."

"I'll take them," Liling said, her voice firm.

Jian turned to his sister and gently grabbed her shoulders. "Sister, no. I cannot allow you to do that. It's not what Ma and Pa would want."

"I lived the horror those girls are still living now. When I left, I did it with the promise I would return for them. That I would bring help." She eyed me and Jax over her brother's shoulder. "God has answered my prayer, brother. I must take them. I'm the only one who knows the way."

After a short pause, he said, "I won't let you go alone. I will accompany you."

"I guess that means I'm coming, too," Tavs said, checking the magazine on her Glock. "I'm thirsty for some demon blood, anyway."

"Guess that makes three," Chaz added. "Wouldn't want to miss the party."

Let the groans of the prisoners come before you; according to your great power, preserve those doomed to die!

PSALM 79:11

CHAPTER 16

JAX

The number of weapons the Light Reformation Group had managed to haul together was impressive. They must've had more firepower than the cathedral's Guardians and that was saying something. Only firepower wasn't what killed the *d'shiad*—unless it was holy fire. Even though Light Reformation had figured out early on that we were dealing with hell-born creatures, their version of blessed water wasn't as potent compared to what I'd traded with Clint.

They'd been so proud of their progress with creating anything resembling holy water that I kept my mouth shut and smiled along, congratulating the discovery. If we were to stay with them after this suicide mission, we'd need to improve their blessing ritual. For now, their resources would do. We'd been a lot less prepared before we met them and having two Marines and an engineer familiar with the building join us was more than I could've asked for.

I would've preferred the girl to stay behind, but it wasn't my decision to make. I would've also preferred Kate to stay behind, but there was no chance I'd be able to convince her. So I gave up trying.

She'd saved me when she killed Famine. She was stronger than I gave her credit for and the passion to save these girls burned bright in her eyes. It was almost enough to light the way through the sewer we'd descended into.

Even though the *d'shiad* cowered from sunlight, the Devil's Army was still run by humans, and I doubted they neglected to patrol the entrance.

For the most part, the tunnel didn't reek as bad as I'd expected. Then again, the plumbing hadn't been used for months. The rainwater flooding the underground passage was clean enough to see through. It also soaked through my boots.

We had two flashlights between the six of us. Once the passageway was illuminated, we took off in the direction of the wind tunnels, Liling's shaking hands making the light from her flashlight dance around the walls.

The eerie quiet of the sewer was cut by the sloshing of us wading through knee-deep water, heightening the tension rolling off everyone's shoulders. Wanting to alleviate the uncomfortable energy, I turned toward the big guy walking next to me. "How'd you end up in New York?"

Chaz shrugged, the butt of his rifle resting against his shoulder as he kept his weapon aimed and ready to fire. It wasn't the only weapon the Marine carried. On his belt hung a Ruger and a mean-looking knife, along with all the ammo we might possibly need. But that wasn't what scared me shitless. Two hand grenades dangling next to the blade made me want to step away from him, or outright run in the other direction. I could only hope the monsters felt the same way.

"Tavs and I were sent to reinforce the city when shit hit the fan; been in the city ever since," he replied gruffly.

"Worst time for sightseeing, if you ask me," Octavia chirped from behind us. "Never thought the first time I'd see the Statue of Liberty would be from inside the tank cupola while shooting through dozens of *diseased* plugging up the Brooklyn Bridge."

Seemed like Octavia was the chattier of the two. Her weapon was ready to fire at the slightest hint of trouble as she tracked the beam from Jian's flashlight. Jian gripped his handgun as he scanned the shadows for threats.

Kate walked next to Octavia, her short sword raised in defense. If anything was to attack us, it would need to get through me and Chaz first before getting sliced by Empyrean steel or Hank's relentless jaws. Kate had told me about Hank's fight against the hellhounds. I'd missed out on seeing him take on a beast bigger than him and come out on top. He was as good a fighter as the rest of us, and if Kate was correct, he might even slow down any other hellhounds with his newly established rank as alpha.

I turned back toward Chaz. "Never thought to leave? You know, try your luck elsewhere?"

He spared me a glance before refocusing his gaze up ahead. "Our orders were to clear the city from the diseased, and the city is not liberated yet."

That was all. He didn't utter another word, just shrugged one shoulder and kept marching like a good soldier sent to war. It was better he didn't say much else. I didn't need to know any more about him—about any of them. It was better not to get attached to people these days.

Plus, if I would've kept asking questions, he might have started asking about me, and we didn't need to open up that can of worms.

They were willing to risk their lives for complete strangers, and that told me enough about what kind of people they were. Even in this world full of cruelty and trickery, they'd taken the risk of trusting us. Hopefully, we hadn't dragged them to their deaths. Still, I was thankful for their help.

We had an Empyrean weapon and I still had Astaroth's power—not that I was eager to use it—but having a couple of soldiers gave us better odds.

"Excuse Chaz's quietness," Octavia said from behind me. "He never was one for many words. Less so after the tank blew up in the middle of that damn bridge, killing most of our unit."

My throat tightened. "I'm sorry. I had no idea."

"Not your fault," Chaz mumbled.

If only that were true.

"Too many of our brothers and sisters died that day," Tavs continued as we rounded a corner.

The stench of death thickened the air, and we stopped to investigate a rotten corpse slumped against the wall. A family of rats scurried in and out of an eye socket, squealing. This corpse wasn't going to get a piece of us—it was simply dead, not damned.

I'd seen too many dead people in my life to feel anything for the poor soul, but I saw Kate wince and Liling look away in horror while covering her mouth. Hank whined quietly and Jian gagged, but the Marines showed no signs of being disturbed by the sight, nor the smell. They kept moving, focused only on their mission.

As if our previous conversation hadn't been interrupted by a dead body, Octavia said, "The air force considered us expendable and bombed the bridge. The orders must've come from the top of the command chain. Me and Chaz barely made it off before the part of the bridge we'd been on collapsed."

"We've seen the damage," Kate said softly. I'm glad she did because I was at a loss for words. I was never good at offering small comforts—although I wasn't sure Tavs and Chaz were looking for compassion to begin with. Perhaps she was sharing their story to be less of a stranger.

If Octavia was expecting to hear mine in return, she was going to be disappointed. And if I knew anything about Kate, she didn't easily share hers, either. Still, the women managed to find common ground and their hushed conversation continued while we threaded past the rotten body.

Jian sidled up next to me, and I couldn't help feeling like he wanted to ask me something. I rolled my shoulders when his curious gaze landed on me, and I could practically feel it prickle my skin.

"I saw you two at Columbus Circle," he began. "The hellion threw you around like a sack of potatoes."

Crushing my already nonexistent confidence in this mission's success was probably not his intention, but his assessment sure as hell turned my stomach.

"It's a tactic of ours," I said with a half-smile. "I let myself get beaten to death as a distraction while Kate finishes off the threat." I grinned wider, but there was zero humor in my tone. He didn't need to know last night was the first time we'd used that 'tactic' instead of running for our lives.

Jian raised an eyebrow and let out a forced chuckle. "Ruse or not, we can't ignore the fact you did have that hellion's staff pierced through your chest. And not even twenty-four hours from what should have been your certain death, here you are, completely healed like nothing ever happened, ready to battle again." His voice was laced with a touch of incredulity, but he didn't pose a question, though it was clear he was waiting for an explanation of my unnatural endurance and healing.

I gave him my version of Chaz's one shoulder shrug. "Never was one to stay down for long."

"Right. But the spear was pierced straight through your *lung*," Jian said, trying not to sound too astonished. "I pulled it out of your chest myself. Your wound was catastrophic. *Mortal*." This time, his tone was more curious than anything else. Perhaps he thought I was godsent since Kate's holy weapon was nothing short of heavenly.

He couldn't have been further from the truth if that's what he was betting on.

Chaz's shrugs seemed to work for him, so I raised my shoulder again. "What can I say? I must've been bathed in the River Styx, only held by my heel." A real grin tugged at my lips. "You can call me Achilles from now on. Jax sounds too atypical for a hero."

"*Achilles*? Yeah right." Jian rolled his eyes. Even Chaz, who'd been listening, huffed out an unconvinced breath.

The water level lowered, and the *squishing* of soaked shoes echoed off the tunnel walls. The air around us grew thicker and reeked of blood and rot.

Chaz tensed and moved ahead with practiced stealth, the distorted shadows cast by the flashlights looking like wraiths reaching their tentacles out to grab us.

Kate's sword burst into flames, drawing awed expressions from the group, except from me. That blade only lit up in the presence of *d'shiad*. Hank's rumbled growl confirmed my fear, and I gripped my gun tighter, preparing for an attack. Positioning myself in front of Kate, I tried to cover her from the looming danger, but she shoved me away.

With my free hand, I drew a rune on my wrist and over my heart to keep Astaroth confined should I have a need to reach out for his power. He stirred, making my skin crawl with thousands of tiny spiders.

My brothers are near…

I wasn't sure if he was warning me or hoping I'd rejoice.

An awareness for the two remaining Horsemen flooded through my brain as Astaroth searched our surroundings with his senses. The Horsemen weren't in the tunnel with us but were still disturbingly close. If I could feel their presence, I could only imagine they could pick up on my approach, too.

Samael's vessel is our salvation, human. The time has finally come for our king to rise.

Shut the fuck up, I told him, but he only laughed.

Jian paused to examine the map, then pointed up ahead with his flashlight. "There. The entrance to the wind tunnels is to the right of the intersection." But as we took a few steps forward, a loud hissing noise erupted, echoing down the tunnel.

Weapons drawn, we slowly approached the intersection, and as we rounded the bend, we were greeted by a giant, scorpion-like creature guarding the entrance. The stench filling the sewer must have come from it, suffocating the air.

With eight legs and a pair of appendages stretching out to grab and pierce through anything it could get a hold of, the scorpion stretched more than six feet long. A stinger that could puncture through your heart and poison you to death twitched as the monster caught sight of our group. The menacing hiss vibrated between its jaws, pincers snapping as it assessed us.

"That's an ugly-ass motherfucker," Tavs murmured with her weapon pointed at the scorpion's head. "Any idea what its weaknesses are?"

Hank growled louder and readied for a fight while Kate signaled for him to lie low.

"No fucking clue," I said when the scorpion suddenly bolted at us, forcing us to scatter. I pushed Kate out of the way and against the stone wall, while Chaz shielded Liling with his body. Hank remained at Kate's heel, his chest puffed out as he snarled at the arachnid monster.

Tavs and Chaz wasted no time showering the scorpion with bullets, but the creature's exoskeleton served as body armor.

Son of a bitch was bulletproof. The holy water coating the ammunition did nothing to damage its body.

I pulled a tactical knife from my ankle holster and pushed away from the wall as the scorpion prepared to strike at me and Kate with its nasty tail. The Marines were cornered against the opposite wall, the giant scorpion trying to chomp at them with its sharp pincers.

The stinger hit the wall where my head had been just a second earlier, crumbling the stone. Without hesitation, I grabbed the tail to keep it from snapping at us.

The scorpion recoiled and pulled its tail back as I attempted to wriggle my knife between its scales. Next thing I knew, I was flying through the air, holding on for dear life as the scorpion whipped its tail. I should have let go, but only managed to do so after it smashed my skull against the wall with a bone-breaking *crunch*.

"Jax!" Kate cried out, her voice erratic.

The monster had been busy concentrating all its energy on me, but now Kate had caught its attention. Through blurred vision, I saw Chaz and Tavs prepare to throw something that I fucking hoped wasn't the grenade from the big guy's belt. Jian pulled a shaking Liling away from the scene, back toward where we'd come.

Kate raised her sword and stared the beast down, fury flashing in her eyes. Hank snuck up on it from behind.

My vision faded in and out of focus, and jolts of pain ran through my back when I attempted to push myself off the ground. I thought I was seeing double after I blinked and saw two more scorpions approach. But when I rubbed my eyes, my stomach dropped.

I wasn't seeing double at all; this beast had fucking company, and two smaller scorpions scurried toward me.

Pulling on Astaroth's power, I stirred the Horseman awake, who answered in earnest. As I climbed back to my feet, a plastic bottle filled with holy water soared through the air. Kate sliced the bottle open with her sword, spraying water all over the scorpion. Her blade came down hard, hacking off one of its pincers.

The scorpion let out a high-pitched squeal that made my ears ring. Kate was relentless, slicing her blade through the air, chopping off scorpion limbs like a hibachi chef. Another bottle flew through the air, and this time, Chaz shot it with pinpoint precision, spraying more holy liquid over the beasts. Steam rose wherever the water touched the creatures' exposed flesh.

Still, the bastards wouldn't go down. Covered in scorpion guts, Kate landed blow after blow, but she couldn't penetrate the main appendages.

"The shell is too thick!" Kate shouted as a tail swung in her direction. She ducked just in time. Hank's teeth clamped on one of the scorpion's legs, but even he wasn't strong enough to get past the shell.

While the big one was distracted by Kate, Chaz and Tavs took on one of its siblings. It rolled itself around the ground, as if trying to rub off the holy water. Kate was handling her own with no problem, but the Marines seemed to have their hands full, so I decided to help them instead. Figuring its underbelly was its softest, most vulnerable side, I slid across the tunnel floor and dug my knife right underneath. I sliced clean through its innards, scorpion goo covering my entire body.

One down, two to go.

Jian had joined Kate, and they took turns stabbing the monster. Even covered in scorpion guts, Kate looked stunning, her movements graceful and precise, each stab and strike scraping a little more of the creature's armor.

But it wasn't enough to take it down.

Jian panted heavily, clearly winded by the vicious attack. He slumped against a wall to catch his breath.

"Get on its back," I growled, rushing at the scorpion, forcing the arachnid to raise the few legs that remained attached to its body, causing it to reveal its softer underbelly.

Jian pushed off the wall and leapt at the beast, hoping to land on its backside, but the monster was too quick, and whipped its tail, piercing Jian through the stomach with its stinger. Impaled by the scorpion, Jian's legs dangled as his horrifying screams echoed through the tunnels.

Satisfied his victim was no longer a threat, the scorpion whipped its tail again, flinging Jian against the tunnel wall. The man fell with a loud *thump*. Liling screamed as she watched her brother cover his bleeding wound with his hands, but his attempts to staunch the blood were futile. The venom would kill him well before he could even bleed out.

The scorpion's tail swooshed past Hank, and he clamped down, tugging with all his might. I stepped in the way of the scorpion pincers as it struck again and deflected the hit, thanks to Astaroth's strength. I tried pushing the monster away from Jian's body when a bullet bounced off the scorpion's armored surface, nearly taking out my eye. "Stop shooting. It's no use."

I looked toward where the gunshot had come from and saw Liling's shaking hands gripped around a discarded gun. Her eyes widened. She'd wanted to help, but the distraction cost me precious time and the scorpion slammed me against the wall so hard, I saw stars again.

Tavs and Chaz kept taking shots at the smaller of the scorpions. "Get on its back," I shouted again, shaking off rubble from my hair and shoulders. Running at the big son of a bitch once more, I danced around the scorpion's deadly pincers, trying to get close enough to wrestle it away from Jian's dying body and his sobbing sister.

"He's fucking crazy," Tavs yelled, referring to me, I guessed. The Marines had finally cornered their opponent and managed to reveal its weak spot. I didn't see them slice the scorpion open, but the squeal I heard was loud enough, tearing through my eardrums and making my insides quiver.

Liling covered her ears, the gun she'd been gripping falling to the ground. When the sound stopped, she hovered over her brother. "Jian. Stay with me. Please."

I shook my head, knowing it was already too late.

Kate struck the scorpion once more, and it pulled its pincers back in pain. Her blade finally broke through the armored shell, and dark blood poured from the wound. Frantically, it whipped its tail, knocking Kate off her feet, flinging her against the wall.

My heart sank when I heard her pained groan. Anger swelled inside me; rage unlike anything I had ever felt flooded my veins. *No more games.* I was done playing nice with this giant motherfucking bug, or whatever the hell it was. With one deep inhale, I let Astaroth push into the driver's seat.

Only to regret it a moment later. He took full control of the steering wheel as he used my body to grab onto the scorpion's mandibles and yanked them apart so hard, the beast exploded with gooey blood, guts, and shell fragments.

Filled with bloodlust, Astaroth roared, looking for something else to destroy, but all that remained were the people in the tunnel, and the Horseman did not discriminate. I tried reeling him in as he stalked toward Chaz, but my attempts were nothing but smoke.

Fuck. Fuck. Fuck.

Astaroth chuckled, thinking that if he took out Chaz, the rest of the group would be easy prey, leaving him free to take Kate. I pounded my will against my rib cage, but my feet kept moving. In the next breath, Astaroth stood in front of Chaz, gripping his throat and pinning him against the tunnel's wall.

"Stop." Kate's voice poured over me like warm honey, but I was powerless against Astaroth's strength.

She'll kill you. You know she will, I told him.

He paused, considering my words. He knew Kate had sworn she'd drive that sword straight through my heart if I ever lost control again.

I just hoped he believed her, because there was a part of me that wasn't so sure.

"Let the man go, Astaroth," Kate commanded.

Still gripping Chaz's throat, he peered over my shoulder at Kate.

Her eyes burned with conviction as she aimed that sword straight at us.

She would do it. Kate would kill me to save the girls trapped above us.

Good girl.

Do it, angel…

Standing next to Kate, Octavia's eyes widened as she took in the sight of my possessed body. "Jesus Christ," she whispered. Raising her gun, she aimed for my head, fingers locked over the trigger. "If he doesn't release Chaz, I'll smoke him."

Kate gently put a hand over the Marine's gun and lowered it. "That won't do anything."

"Who… *what* is he?"

"Astaroth," she said. "The Devil's third Horseman, War."

"Good to see you again, *angel.*"

Sword flaming, she stepped closer, making Astaroth recoil. "I said, let him go."

Hank growled, baring his canines so fiercely, I made a note to remind myself that if I made it out of this alive, I would never piss him off.

Astaroth glanced at Hank, then back at Kate before dropping Chaz. The Marine coughed, pawing at his neck.

The demon took advantage of the slight distraction and spun around quickly, trying to catch Kate off guard, but she was quicker, raising the blade to my throat. His frustration made my nostrils flare. "By now you know I will not hesitate to kill Jax to kill you. And from the fear blazing in your gaze, you also know I've already sent one of your brothers on a one-way trip to the afterlife."

"Killing me won't stop Samael from claiming what is his," he growled. "Tell me, Daughter of Eve, is this sinful world worth your human's life?"

"Is it worth yours?" she countered.

Astaroth growled before relinquishing his hold on me.

With a gasp, I took back control of my body, and as Kate dropped her blade from my throat, I wrapped my fingers around her wrist. "You should've killed him." I'd gotten too used to calling upon the demon's power during a fight, and I was certain this wouldn't be the last one of the night. Having me around would put everyone in danger. Astaroth couldn't be taken any deeper into enemy territory. "We can't do this anymore, Kate."

She peered deep into my eyes, knowing I was right, yet choosing to challenge me, anyway. "Can't do what? Keep saving your ass?"

"Keep pretending like you're not going to have to kill me. Like I can just go on living with this thing inside me while you tame it with that sword."

"You really should know by now that I make my own choices, and I'll make that one when I goddamn feel I need to, *not* when your idiot face tells me to."

Fuck. Why did she have to say stupid shit like that? Shit that made me fall even more madly in love with her bratty ass.

Taking her in my arms, I whispered, "You're the salvation I don't deserve, angel."

She wrapped her arms around my waist, resting her forehead on my chest. "Then stop asking me to fucking kill you."

I would've held on to Kate for an eternity, but Octavia's voice broke through the bliss of having her in my arms. "What the fuck just happened?"

I sighed and let go of Kate. "It's… complicated."

The Marine pointed her rifle at my head. "That's not good enough, pretty boy. I just saw you rip that fucking giant ass insect in half with your bare hands, then you went after Chaz. Start talking, now."

"We don't have to do this," I said, putting my palms up. "Please. Lower your weapon."

She pivoted her rifle and pointed it at Kate's head instead. "I don't take orders from you. And I'm not dying down here for nobody unless you tell me right now who the fuck you are. Both of you. Or I'll put a bullet in your girlfriend's head."

Hank growled, but Kate told him to lay low.

"Tavs," Chaz said, his voice hoarse. "We don't kill civilians."

Not taking her finger off the trigger, she drew the gun closer to Kate's head, sending my heart into hyperdrive. I clenched my fists as my demon banged against my rib cage. If she hurt Kate, there would be nothing left of the humans in this tunnel. I gritted my teeth as I fought to restrain myself, but at my silence, the woman jabbed the nozzle of the rifle against Kate's temple.

"The rules have changed," she gritted. "Start talking."

My chest heaved. "Fine. I'll tell you everything," I spat. "Just please. Fucking lower your rifle."

Sweat beaded on Kate's forehead and I could practically smell the musty scent of her terror.

"Tavs, do as he says," Chaz said.

She nodded slightly and lowered her gun.

My breaths came out shallow as relief wove through my muscles. "I've got one of the Horsemen trapped inside me, and the only way to kill it is to kill me."

She tightened her grip on the gun once again and pointed it at my chest. "If she won't do it—"

Kate stepped between me and the barrel of Tavs' gun. "No one kills him, but me."

"That's very romantic of you, but I ain't taking my chances with that *thing* living inside him. He turned on Chaz; who's to say he won't do it again?"

"I won't let him become a danger to any of you."

That was a lie. There was no way for her to prevent that. I took a step forward to correct her, but she shot me a razor-sharp stare that made me swallow my words.

"He's *my* responsibility," she assured the Marine.

Tavs' throat bobbed, her lips thinning to a straight line. For a long second, I didn't think she'd take Kate's offer, but then she lowered her rifle. "Don't think I won't keep my eye on you. The *both* of you."

Liling's quaking voice cut through the tension. "Please… help."

We all turned toward the young girl where she lay in a puddle of her brother's blood. The flashlight he'd been carrying laid on the ground.

Jian's chest rose with shallow breaths, blood seeping from the corner of his mouth. The poison turned his veins black, making them visible under his skin. The scorpion's venom had spread through his entire body already. There was nothing any of us could do to help him.

The blackened veins pulsed under his skin, and when his shirt was pulled up to reveal the damage, none of us uttered the truth of what we saw. The flesh around the wound was decaying.

He would be dead in minutes, if not less.

Liling gripped her brother's hand for dear life while Octavia searched her med pack, retrieving a morphine syrette.

"Jian, you're going to be alright," Liling cried.

"Not… this time, *mei mei*," Jian choked, coughing blood. "You… always were… the stronger one."

Kate dropped to her knees next to him, rolling up her sleeve in the process. When she placed the blade of her sword against her wrist, I realized her intentions.

"Kate, this is not the same as the infection." I pulled at her shoulders. "You can't cure that."

She fought me. "I've got to try, Jax."

I ran a palm through my hair. Her actions were noble, but we'd already wasted precious time. Plus, who knew if more scorpions or other monsters weren't on the way? "We need to go after Camila. I'm sorry, Kate, but there's nothing we can do for Jian now, other than dull his pain."

Liling burst into uncontrollable sobs, and my chest tightened. Losing someone you loved was never easy, especially to this war. The look in Sam's eyes the moment he died would forever haunt me, just as this moment would haunt Liling for the rest of hers.

Turning away from the siblings, Kate took several deep breaths. She seemed to struggle with her own ghosts and was unable to look on as Jian coughed up more blood.

"Save… them," he whispered, his body going slack with his last breath. The venom overtook his flesh completely, his body decomposing into rotten remains.

Chaz was the first to jump back into action. "We've got to keep moving."

Tavs tugged at Liling, pulling her away from what was left of her brother. "Is this where you exited the wind tunnels?"

With tear-streaked eyes, she looked around in the darkness while Chaz picked up one of the flashlights and pointed it at the crumbled walls. "I… I think so."

Kate turned around, wiping at the wetness under her eyes. "Take us to where those assholes are keeping the girls."

The wind tunnel was a white stone, semicircular corridor with wires and pipes running across the ceiling. Thanks to the electricity they had powering some of the building, partial lighting coming from some old fluorescent bulbs helped guide the way. Following the corridor to the stairwell was eventless. No eight-legged monsters guarded the passageway, and thank fuck for that.

Once we reached the same level as the bank vault, we skulked through the shadows, keeping to a single line, our footsteps light, breaths steady. We didn't bother with our flashlights as a yellow glow emerged from the end of the corridor, along with the sound of chatter.

`Chaz led our group, followed by me, Kate, Hank at her side, Liling, and Tavs at our tail. The area was clogged with old machinery, pallets, and boxes, offering us perfect cover. Two guards sat at a table in front of a giant metal disk—the broken vault door. Busy with a card game, neither of them noticed the shifting shadows cast by our bodies.

We seemed to have caught the guards in the middle of their shift. It would have been easy to take them down and march into the vault, but if the shift change were to come during our attempt to get the girls out, we'd have to deal with unexpected reinforcements and potentially be overpowered or trapped in.

I voted to wait for the shift change and take out the new guards, and of course, Kate voted to go in now. "The new set of guards will be alert. They could call reinforcements before we get to them. Those two are not paying any attention. We can take them out before they even see us coming."

Placing my hands on my waist, I hung my head. "And if we don't wait, we could get caught in the middle of the switch, adding more guards we would have to fight."

"We sure as hell will if we don't go right at this moment," she challenged.

I looked to both Chaz and Tavs hoping for support, but all I got from Chaz was a shrug and Tavs nodded toward Kate, clearly agreeing with her plan. I was outnumbered. Defeated, I gave Chaz a knowing look and he immediately got the message.

Pulling out a military-grade pistol with a built-in silencer, he aimed and shot the guards in one breath. The poor bastards didn't know what hit them as death whispered in their ears.

The Marines didn't waste any time dragging the bodies into the shadows and confiscating their walkies and ammunition. As the vault door was inoperable, a large, black tarp covered the entrance. We peeled back the makeshift curtain and countless weary eyes peered back at us.

None of the girls made a sound, likely fearful of whatever punishment usually followed even the slightest resistance. The room was poorly ventilated, and the stench of sweat, blood, and urine was so strong, it burned our noses. Even though Liling had said they were allowed a toilet break every three hours, some of them were in no condition to make the walk.

Cowering against walls and holding onto one another, each pair of eyes told of terrors beyond imagination. Torn flesh and bruises marring their bodies were enough evidence of their torture to boil my blood. It made me wish I'd been the one to kill those guards. Hell, I was close to unleashing my demon on the rest of the Devil's Army.

The ire burning in Kate's eyes justified my murderous thoughts, but we needed to stay on task.

"We're here to rescue you," she said. "Everything will be alright." Helping them stand, she examined their wounds, offering the girls the water we'd brought with us. Her gaze searched over each and every face, looking for Camila. I did the very same, with no luck.

The priest's niece was not in the vault.

My stomach hollowed. Kate wouldn't leave without the girl. And her not being in this room only meant one thing—she was either dead or being *used*.

Chaz tried to help a frail-looking girl, but she slid away from his touch in wide-eyed terror.

"We're military," Octavia tried to explain. "We're here to help."

"You can't help us," a low, trembling voice murmured from a dark corner in the back of the vault. "We're already doomed."

The bronze-skinned woman slumped against the far wall. Her dark brown hair was dirt-streaked and bloody. Though battered and missing several teeth, her spirit looked more bruised than her body.

"We have a way out, but not a lot of time to get to it," I said, but the woman didn't seem phased by the prospect of getting out of this shithole.

"Camila is not here, Jax…" Kate trailed as she continued to scan every terrified face. Fear shadowed her features. She'd faced off against the worst of the *d'shiad* and had killed more damned than she could count, but it was the possibility of not finding the innocent little girl that seemed to coat her in morrow-splintering dread.

"Tavs, Chaz, and Liling will get the girls out through the tunnels. We'll find Camila," I reasoned.

Kate nodded, kneeling next to the woman who'd spoken earlier. "Have you seen her?" Kate asked. "Camila is ten, maybe twelve years old. Dark, curly hair and amber-colored eyes. She must've been brought in last night."

"I saw her. Small girl, way too young for all the horrors of this place. She excited the guards but would be of no use for the devil gods. Doesn't mean they can't have fun with her while she's still pretty."

I fisted a palm and gritted my teeth. Sick monsters, all of them. And Edith allowed it to happen. She had no compassion for the women they held captive, even after they'd failed to produce a vessel for the dark king.

"Where was she taken?" Kate demanded.

The woman let out a strangled laugh. "You can't help us," she repeated her words. "We're already doomed. We're doomed. We're doomed."

Liling came over to tell us they were ready to take most of the girls to safety. Some were in too bad a shape to even walk. "That's Qadira," she said quietly while the woman fell into a crazed fit. "She's been here longer than anyone can remember. They say her name means 'full of power,' which is why the hellions had a special interest in her."

"Do you know where they might've taken Camila?" I asked Liling.

The girl pressed her lips together and nodded. "I might."

Kate's head whipped around. "Can you show us?"

Liling paused, her gaze dropping to the ground. "I… could." The hesitation in her voice confirmed my fears about where they may have taken Camila.

"You don't have to, Liling," I said. I'd been forced into situations I'd rather run away from too many times to ever do that to anyone else. "Just point us in the direction they might've taken her, and we'll do the rest. You can leave with Tavs and Chaz."

"No. I want to help."

"You *are* helping," Kate said, tucking a loose strand of hair behind the girl's ear. "What you did here, Liling… your brother would be proud."

Eyes misting over, Liling nodded, her shoulders relaxing a little.

"Go on. Help those girls get back safely."

"What about the ones who have to stay behind?"

Kate looked at me, but I had no easy answer. Traveling down those tunnels with able-bodied individuals was going to be difficult enough, especially if there were any more bugs down there. And even if I could haul a girl on my back, what about the other half-dozen girls?

"We'll have to mount another rescue, Kate. There's simply no way to get them out of here without more manpower."

She swallowed hard. I knew she wanted to fight me on this, but she also knew I was right. "Promise?" Her eyes pleaded with mine.

"Cross my heart, angel."

Chaz led the women out of the bank vault while Tavs took up the rear. We gave them the only two flashlights we had. To navigate those tunnels with all those girls, they'd need them more than Kate and I would. Plus, we had Hank. He could track a needle in a field of hay. Not to mention Kate's sword could light up any room like the Fourth of July.

Before joining the two Marines back down in the wind tunnels, Liling gave us vague directions to the basement, which was a few floors up.

I listened to the soft *thumps* of bare feet as the group of women hurried down the hall toward the entrance to the wind tunnels. Though the Marines had hid the dead guards in the shadows, whoever came down here would immediately know something was awry when they found their posts abandoned.

"Ready?" Kate asked, with Hank at her heels.

"I'm ready."

We needed to go up and deeper into headquarters to find where Camila was probably being held. The stairwell was empty when we reached it, but as we started climbing, we heard a door open a few floors up, then a gruff male voice rumbled through the shaft. "To think, even though we have electricity, they can't get the service elevators working."

A second male laughed. "Walking the stairs is what keeps you in shape, Dragon. The boss lady wants to conserve power, so only the main elevator to the top floors can work."

Fuck. The next shift. At this point, there was no avoiding a confrontation. Even if we managed to hide, the instant they made it to the vault, they would know they'd been infiltrated and would alert the rest of the army. I couldn't allow that to happen. We had to stall them from sounding the alarm, at least until the Marines had the girls in the sewers.

"What's that sound?" the first male asked.

Shit. Had they heard us? Or the girls? They'd tried to stay quiet, but the tunnels weren't designed to muffle noise.

"What sound?" the other one asked.

"Didn't you hear it?"

Kate and I held our breath at the bottom of the stairwell. With a finger to her lips, she ordered Hank to remain silent. He stood solid as a statue, waiting for his next command.

Now we just needed a plan.

"You're paranoid, Hydra. There's nothing there."

Just then, a chorus of screams erupted from the direction of the tunnels, followed by gunfire. Kate bristled, ready to rush toward the girls, but I grabbed her arm and stopped her. Camila was our mission. I had no clue what had caused the commotion in the tunnels, but they sure didn't need Dragon and fucking Hydra making an even bigger mess of things. "Tavs and Chaz can handle it," I whispered.

Kate's gaze filled with doubt, but I reassured her that those girls couldn't be in better hands. Then the beats of footsteps racing toward us echoed down the stairwell.

Time to tango.

"Hello, fellas," I greeted the two guards as they reached our floor, a knife gripped in my hand. "Why the long faces?"

Not giving them time to react, I slammed the closest one to me against the wall, stabbing him in the lungs a couple of times and pounding his head until he went lax, but the other one managed to shout into a walkie-talkie before I got to him.

"Intruders! We've got int—" A shot rang out through the stairwell, quieting the guard before he could finish his message, but the damage had already been done.

Kate stood with her gun aimed, a long breath trickling from her lips. Her hands shook.

Killing demons was one thing, but shooting a man dead in cold-blood was another. For a second, I wasn't sure what was going through her mind, but eventually, she lowered her weapon.

"You okay?"

She nodded, but her eyes told a completely different story. Still, we had bigger problems.

If that shot wasn't enough to alert the cult to our presence, then the explosion that followed from below sure would be. The entire foundation shook, tiny rocks of debris raining from the ceiling.

Whatever they'd encountered down in the tunnels must've gotten blasted with one of Chaz's grenades. Kate and I exchanged glances. They'd either been ambushed by guards or another scorpion. Hopefully, it was the former.

With both guards dead, we raced up the stairwell, two steps at a time, but as we reached the second floor, a unit of men burst through a door a few floors up.

"Repeat, Hydra. Over," one of them spoke into his walkie-talkie.

Opening the door on our landing, I shoved Kate and Hank through, then followed behind them, gently closing the door shut. The hallway on this floor was pitch-black, but that didn't mean those men wouldn't stop to check.

"Your location, Hydra? Over," the man shouted into his walkie again as he ran past our floor, followed by several more guards. Once they spotted the dead men at the bottom of the stairwell, more calls were radioed to the rest of the Devil's Army.

I turned to Kate, wishing there was enough light for me to see and memorize her beautiful face and that stubborn glint in her eyes. "When the time comes, run and don't look back."

"Not this again. I won't leave you, Jax."

Always so obstinate.

"We need to create a diversion to keep them busy so the girls can get away," I said. "*I'm* the diversion. You need to find Camila and get out."

"I won't leave you," she said again, her tone firmer.

"Find her, Kate." Opening the door, I ran out, not giving her an opportunity to fight my decision.

Shooting my gun down one floor, the sound reverberated through the whole shaft. "You sons of bitches want a piece of me?" I shouted. "Come find me."

As they rushed up the stairs, I took off in a sprint toward the upper floors. I made it to the tenth floor before running out of steam. Astaroth hollered inside my head, urging me to let him free, promising to give me the strength needed to escape.

Fucker didn't realize I couldn't just hear his thoughts, but I could sense his intentions as well.

If I let him out now, I feared this would be the last time I'd have full control of my body. Choosing to take my chances with my own strength, I exited the stairwell and ran straight into a wall of men staring at me down the barrel of their rifles.

"I think I may have gotten off on the wrong floor," I said, palms up, offering them a lopsided grin.

No one laughed.

"Lower your weapons," an all too familiar female voice said, chilling my blood.

As if they were one solid organism, the men all lowered their guns and stepped to the side, plastering their backs against each of the two walls. Striding down the middle of the wide hallway, and flanked by two of Hell's unholy princes, Pestilence and Death, Edith emerged, her long, red velvet robe trailing behind her.

The next thing I knew, someone struck the back of my head with something hard and everything faded to black.

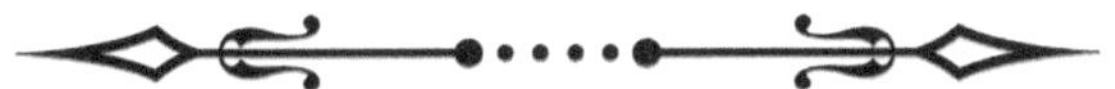

When I came to, I sat on a metal chair, wrists bound behind my back, ankles tied to the legs.

"Jackson Cornelius Constantine," that female voice uttered. "Your actions have cost us more than a year's worth of trouble."

A throbbing headache threatened to split my skull open. Brain still swimming with fogginess from the hit I'd taken to the head, my vision struggled to focus on the individual standing a few feet from me. But I didn't need to see her clearly to know who she was. I even painted her blurry face with the memory of her permanent scowl.

I didn't want to be here. Fuck, I'd rather be pierced in the gut by that scorpion and rot than take my mother's scolding.

I took a deep breath. "I know how long it's been, Mother. Eighteen months, to be exact." My mouth was so dry and every word uttered scraped my throat. I wet my lips. "Every single day has been torture. Having a Horseman trapped inside your body can do a real number on your sanity."

Edith's body remained unmovable, her face a canvas of pure apathy. Dark hair dulled by grays sat atop her head in a tight bun. My vision finally cleared, and I was able to appreciate the sharpness of those eyes now lined with new wrinkles that didn't suit her well. She looked worn, her patience stretched thin. And I was the reason for her year's worth of *trouble,* as she called it.

I should've been proud of myself—causing her all that grief was some fucking achievement. But I wasn't able to conjure a single ounce of glee because, despite my best efforts to fuck up her little operation, that stupid little boy still existed inside me.

The one who always looked for validation, for approval. For love from the woman who'd birthed him.

"I should kill you for your insolence and count my losses." The disgust in her eyes cut me deeper than a dagger, slicing right through my heart. But I didn't show it. I would never let her see how sharp her blade really was.

I let my lips curl into a practiced grin. "We both know if you'd wanted me dead, I wouldn't be here. I'd be rotting somewhere in the sewers or gnawing at someone's throat like one of the infected. Yet, here I am, alive and insolent. And there you are, bitchy and displeased as ever."

The corner of her lip lifted into a snarl. "You ungrateful, pitiful excuse for a son. After everything I taught you, everything I sacrificed, you still think this is about *you.*"

"Nah. I've always known I never mattered much to you; I was simply a means to an end. A sack of flesh to serve as a vessel for one of your demon pets. The only thing you've ever truly cared about is power."

"I cared about your father's vision," she said. "He gave up everything so you could have the honor of carrying through with our people's plan for the new world order. He gave his life for the cause, and you spat on his sacrifice the day you walked away from your duties."

Edith rarely talked about my father. I'd been too young when he bled dry for a ritual that had failed. Whenever I asked about it, Edith would become even more volatile toward me, so I learned to accept the short answers and did my best to move on. The fact she was mentioning him now meant she was trying to chip at my defenses.

But I refused to give her the satisfaction. Ignoring the comments about my father, I said, "Bringing damnation to this world is not exactly *honorable*."

"Salvatore Constantine was a great man. I only wish you'd been more like him."

Fervent as ever.

"Too bad I didn't know him well because just like the absent mother you were, he wasn't really there for me, either. But is this why you've tied me up, *Mother?*" I asked, pronouncing that last word like an insult. "To talk about a dead man? Isn't this conversation a couple decades too late?"

The scowl etched on her face deepened.

As much as I enjoyed irritating her with my quips, I was getting bored. And I hadn't forgotten Kate and Hank were somewhere in this building. I needed to find a way to get free from these chains.

I didn't even have a clue how long I'd been unconscious. I looked around slowly, trying to decipher where I was. My stomach clenched when I recognized the 102nd floor observatory of the Empire State Building. I sat with my back to the tall glass panes encircling the room that showcased a three-hundred-and-sixty-degree panorama of New York City—though, at the moment, everything was pitch-black except for the looming full moon partially obstructed by dark clouds.

My mother stood with her back to the metal and glass elevator, her eyes trained on me, gaze unwavering. "What brings you here, Jackson?" Edith asked, oblivious to the storm churning in my chest. "I'd hoped it had been because you'd finally come to your senses and returned home, but then I was told four of my men were found dead and most of my girls were missing."

I sucked in a deep breath. "Aww. You were really hoping I'd come back *home* to you. That's touching."

Edith's hardened expression softened, and the tiny hint of a smirk ghosted across her thin lips.

I knew that look. It was the look of a viper about to strike.

Fuck, that wasn't good. Not good at all. If I knew anything about this woman, it was her determination to break her opponents and grind them to a pulp. Fear rang hard in my chest. There was only one thing that could break me.

I gulped hard, blood rushing so fast that my temples throbbed.

With a nod, she signaled some type of command to one of her minions. The man radioed another, then the gears and pulleys inside the elevator shaft began to move. I held my breath as we all waited for the elevator to rise, my heart lodged in my throat.

When the doors opened, everything inside me turned to frost.

Beleth and Chemoth—the Horsemen of Death and Pestilence—marched out. Dressed in his black robe, Beleth carried Kate's limp body draped over his massive shoulder. Obscured by his hood, the only visible features on his face were his glowing red eyes.

I clenched my jaw as I watched the wretched creatures strap her body to a metal, X-shaped St. Andrew's Cross. I'd not seen when Edith's men had assembled the damn thing, and the thoughts running through my head of why they'd brought that contraption in here had me drenched in cold sweat.

Once secured, Beleth pulled her head up, revealing a freshly bruised eye, busted lip, and blood dripping down her chin. Kate seemed dazed, almost unconscious. And the knowledge these vile creatures had put their hands on her made me roar with the rage of the demon living inside me. I yanked on the chains wrapped around my wrists, muscles ready to rip through my skin. "Mark my words," I gritted through clenched teeth, "you will fucking *die* for what you did to her." I didn't care that she'd heal soon enough; those fucking assholes would pay for every ounce of pain they'd inflicted on her.

Edith laughed. "Another lesson lost on you. Love is weakness, Jackson. I thought you would've learned that by now."

"Fuck you," I gritted. "If those monsters touch her again, I swear I'll kill you first."

"According to the Horsemen," she went on, as if my threat meant nothing, "that woman carries a hybrid child—a child with the blood of angels and demons flowing through its veins. Do you know what that means? She's the one who will birth our king, Jackson. Despite all your transgressions against your family, despite your hatred for who you were born to be, you delivered her straight to us."

The rage brewing inside me threatened to snap my spine in half. I should've never agreed to this fucking rescue mission. Kate was too important. Bringing her had been a mistake I would regret for the rest of my God-cursed life. Mikha'el had been right in trying to stop her, and I'd been the fucking idiot who'd gifted her to these demons. But if my child was Samael's vessel, then Edith already had what she needed. Why did she have me chained up?

"What do you want from me?"

"The amulet you stole." She glared at me. "Where is it?"

Fuck. If that was my bargaining chip, then we were royally screwed.

"I don't have it."

The amusement she'd played across her features dissolved into wickedness. "Where. Is. It?" she repeated, her lips taught.

"I. Don't. Know." I'd had it when I ran out on the summoning ritual, but I had gaping holes in my memory of that day. I didn't have it with me when Astaroth caught up with me. There was only one explanation. "I spelled myself to forget."

Her palm collided with my cheek so hard, the sting spread across my face like a spiderweb. Tasting the tang of iron in my mouth, I spit out blood, my top lip already swelling.

"You stupid, *stupid* fuck," she barked, her mouth practically frothing with anger. "Why the hell would you do that? Do you understand how long our people have searched for the stones? How much of our own blood we spilled stealing them back?"

"I'm the one who stole it, Mother. I'm quite familiar with its history."

"Fuck!" Her scream reverberated through the room. She turned toward Beleth. "Is there a way to reverse that kind of spell?"

Beleth stepped forward, his hard steps *thudding* against the tiled floors. Pulling down his hood, I was struck by the absence of my friend. The demon had been fully restored to his angelic glory, shedding any sign his body had once belonged to Sam. Though beautiful, he no longer carried the golden glow of his heavenly brethren. This monster belonged to a different king. Skin pale as moonlight contrasted with a long mane of black curly hair that cascaded to his shoulders. He assessed me with those glowing red eyes and their intensity made me drop my gaze.

"I can't restore his memory," he said. "But Astaroth might be able to track the stone's signature."

"You don't think I've tested that, asshole? It doesn't work," I spat, peering back up at him. "And thank fuck for that."

"Vapid mortal, with the aid of my stone and Chemoth's, Astaroth's power will be amplified." He leaned down, his cold breath inches from my face. "Tracking the Fire Stone will not be a problem. And once we have it, his body will be restored and you will be no more."

"Good luck summoning him through," I said, baring my teeth. "I have him locked up. Not to mention, you're still missing Famine's stone, or did you forget your brother is dead?"

"We felt our brother's death," Chemoth snarled. "And we know who took the stone. Destroying that rebellious group will be like stomping on vermin."

Edith stepped between me and Beleth. "You think you're so clever. So in control of the situation. But you've forgotten I know your weakness." The veiled threat in her words traveled down my spine like an icy claw. "I never wanted you, you know that?" she hissed. "But your father convinced me to keep you. I was right about you, though. You're still a worthless lump. I should've listened to my instincts and flushed your bloody clot of cells down the drain."

She was trying to piss me off, to rattle me enough to weaken the locks to Astaroth's prison. "But, *Mother,* if you'd done that, then I wouldn't be here to crush your plans to rule the world."

Eyes anchored to mine, she smiled, cold and calculated. "Beleth, as long as you don't harm the fetus, you and your brother can do as you please with that woman. Oh, and make sure my son has a prime view of the spectacle." She cupped my chin. "Wouldn't want you to miss a single moment as my demon pets take turns defiling your precious Kate."

Nostrils flaring, I yanked on my restraints, growling at her so violently, she stumbled back. "Don't do this, Mother. Kate hasn't done anything wrong. She's innocent in all of this."

"*Innocent*? Jackson, she killed Malphas. You think his brothers don't want their pound of flesh?" Turning on her heel, her robe swooshed at her feet as she walked away without saying another word to me. "Get me when it's done," she said to one of her guards before jumping into the elevator.

I fought against my restraints and two of her men struggled to keep me from tipping on my side. "I'm going to kill you for this, Edith," I shouted before the doors closed, making sure she read the certainty in my eyes. "That's a fucking promise!"

Her lips twitched as the elevator doors closed, hiding her face from view, and leaving my fate and Kate's in the hands of the Horsemen of Death and Pestilence.

Chemoth grabbed Kate by the hair, raising her head. "Wake up, Daughter of Eve. This will be more enticing when your screams fill the room."

The rage tears burning in my eyes had me seeing double as Kate opened her lids and stared at me in confusion.

For though we walk in the flesh, we are not waging war according to the flesh. For the weapons of our warfare are not of the flesh but have divine power to destroy strongholds.

2 CORINTHIANS 10:3 - 4

CHAPTER 17

KATE

EARLIER...

hit. Jax literally gave me zero chance to go after him. I growled and plastered my back against the wall as the group of guards ran after him. Every muscle in my body wanted to bolt through that door, but I had to believe Jax could take care of himself.

My mission was Camila.

Hank let out a low whine, his tail wagging.

"I know, buddy. I don't like this either, but we can't go chasing after him right now. And since when are you so fond of Jax?" I couldn't see much in the dark hallway, but I knelt and ruffled his ears. "Did that big goof grow on ya?"

He whined again.

"Yeah, buddy. Me, too."

I stood and peeked through the small square window in the door, then ducked when I saw a guard come down the stairs. Dressed in civilian clothes, he had a rifle strapped to his back. His walkie went off, and a muffled voice echoed in the stairwell, "We've got the asshole. Find the woman."

The air thinned around me and I couldn't breathe. Could they've been talking about me and Jax or the two Marines? Fuck. Either option sucked balls, and I couldn't stand around sequestered on this floor waiting to find out. I needed to find Camila and Jax, and then get us the fuck out of there.

The guard chuckled as he replied, "Fucker is gonna get his balls ripped off by the boss lady. I'll sweep the vault area, see if I find signs of the bitch."

I sucked in a steadying breath as his footsteps faded down the shaft. *Time to roll.* I reached into my pants pocket and pulled a ripped piece of cloth from Camila's rag doll and let Hank sniff. "Find," I whispered to him as we stepped out from the shadows and into the stairwell. Liling said Camila was probably still on the basement level, which was only a couple of floors up.

We took off in a sprint while still staying light on our feet. Once we entered the basement floor, all I saw was a labyrinth of hallways and doors. The sounds of mechanical gears could be heard vibrating through the walls. Hank sniffed every corner and crevice as I kept a watchful eye for any guards. Sweat beaded on my forehead and dripped down the front of my chest, drenching my white T-shirt. Footsteps sounded from around a corner, and I had to hide behind a wall, but Hank kept going.

Shit. Once he was on the trail, he wouldn't relent. When I pulled out of my hiding spot, Hank was nowhere to be found. I clenched my jaw. Slithering down more poorly lit hallways, I finally spotted Hank right as he stopped by a door. He sniffed, then pawed at the door and whined.

Gotcha.

I hurried up to him and gave him a huge rub between the ears. I had no idea what I would find on the other side, but I didn't have a lot of time to consider the risks. The door was locked, so I used my sword to hack off the padlock. Bursting through, I aimed my gun and held my sword out, ready to slice through fresh meat, but all I saw was Camila huddled in a corner, arms wrapped around her legs, shaking.

Completely barren, the room didn't even have a bucket for her to relieve herself. One bulb hung from the ceiling, giving off a pale dim light. Big, round, sodden eyes looked up at me as I stood by the entrance with Hank at my side.

"Kate?" she said in a tiny voice.

"Yes, honey." I ran to her and helped her up, wrapping her in a huge hug. "I'm so happy to see you. Are you okay?" I held her face in my hands. "Did those monsters do anything to you?'

She shook her head. "They put me in this room after they brought me here, but I haven't seen anyone since."

I hugged her tighter. *If those beasts had touched her…*

I didn't even want to think about what I would do. Kid had seen enough horrors as it was. Still, the fact that they'd separated her and kept her isolated meant they'd probably intended to use her as a bargaining chip in exchange for me. It also meant someone would be coming to collect their pawn soon.

"We have to get out of here." Grabbing her hand, I guided her out of the room, but a bullet rang out, hitting the doorframe as we exited. Motherfucker. I turned and found some asshole pointing his gun at me from down the hallway.

"Idiot," a second guard cried out, knocking the one who'd shot me upside the head. "We need her *alive*, asshole.

Returning fire, I urged Camila to follow Hank, who I'd ordered to run in the opposite direction. "Go, go, go!" Reloading my gun, I shot another round toward the guards, then took off after Camila and Hank.

Clever boy that he was, Hank guided us back to the stairwell that led to the sub-basement—the floor where the vault was housed and the entry into the wind tunnels. Without him, there was no way we would've found our way back. We slammed through the service door and sped down the stairs, the two guards at our tail.

I didn't spare a look behind me. They weren't firing at us, which meant they needed us alive, especially if I supposedly carried Samael's vessel. Hank ran past the vault and down the long corridor that led to the entrance of the tunnels. "Keep following Hank," I hollered, my voice echoing off the walls.

Reaching the ventilation maintenance access, we descended to the tunnels and were stopped in our tracks when we spotted a person sprawled on the floor in the middle of the tunnel.

Fuck. I recognized that body. Tavs.

Heaps of debris scattered the floor, as if part of the tunnel had collapsed. That's when I spotted the crushed scorpion underneath the rubble. I ran to Tavs. She lay on her back, a large chunk of concrete crushing her legs. I figured she was dead until I saw the slightest rise and fall of her chest.

"Shit, Tavs. You're alive."

She wheezed, then coughed out blood. "My… med pack," she said, shakily pointing to a military backpack just out of reach. When I handed it to her, she reached inside for a syringe. Morphine.

"Tavs, I can get help."

"My legs are crushed, Kate. We both know I won't be walking out of this one."

Footsteps and voices sounded from behind us. The guards were catching up.

She reached into her pack and retrieved a grenade. "Get the girl out of here. I'll hold them back."

"Tavs, no—"

"You have no other option. Let me do this. It's my duty. *Please.* Let me die on my own terms, with honor."

"Fuck," I screamed. There was no way I would allow those monsters to recapture Camila, but I couldn't leave Jax behind, either. I took the girl by the shoulders and played my only card. "Listen to me. I need you to run through this tunnel until you get to the sewer entrance. You need to get as far away as possible. Hank will guide you. Get to the church and alert the others." But as I uttered those words, I realized the guards weren't her only threat. Scorpions or other deadly monsters possibly skulked in those sewers, not to mention the devoured or nightcrawlers patrolling the streets.

I couldn't let her go unarmed. I reached for my sword and was about to hand it to her when I remembered Jian's words in the tunnel. Something about his men being zapped when they'd tried carrying my sword.

Damnit. Perhaps it was too powerful for anyone not anointed, unless…

Shit. I hoped I knew what I was about to do. Slicing my hand open with the blade, I dipped my fingers in the beads of blood. Using it to draw the sign of the cross over her forehead, I said, "With this blood, I anoint thee. Use this blade in my name.… and… may any fiend that comes across it turn to ash. Amen."

I shook my head. That was the stupidest anointing in the history of anointing, but by God, I hoped it worked. Handing it to her, I said, "Hank will protect you, but don't be afraid to use it, okay? Give it to Mikha'el. He'll know what to do."

Her body trembled. "What about you? I can't do this by myself."

"I'm not done here. And yes, you can." I turned to Hank. "Listen, buddy. I know I always ask you to stop being a hero, but right now, I'm going to need you to be the bravest pup you can be."

Hank tilted his head. He knew a command was coming.

With my nose to his, I said, "Find Mikha'el. Protect Camila."

Without giving myself a chance to change my mind, I sent them running, my heart shattering into a million pieces as I watched them disappear down the tunnel, knowing I might have just sent them to certain death in those sewers.

"What's the plan?" Tavs asked, looking up at me with a strained gaze.

I knelt beside her and took her hand in mine. "I'm going after Jax. Once I'm at a safe distance, use your grenade to collapse the tunnel. We need to give Camila and Hank the best chance at getting away."

"Copy that."

"Tavs…" I said, squeezing her hand one last time, "thank you for your service."

"My pleasure, ma'am." She took off her dog tags and handed them to me. "Please make sure Chaz gets these. He's the only family I've got left."

I put them around my neck and tucked them under my shirt. "I'll make sure of it."

Then she gave me her rifle. "Now go kick some demon ass."

Strapping the rifle over my shoulder, I took off toward the sub-basement entrance, hoping to intercept the Devil's Army guards. After winding through the tunnel for about fifty yards, the ground beneath my feet shook with the rumble of the explosion from Tav's grenade, making me lose my balance. Stumbling a few steps, I managed to find my footing as my hand connected with the wall for support.

I took a moment to silently thank her for her bravery. Hopefully, her sacrifice would earn Camila and Hank the time needed to get out of the sewers.

Bullets rang out as I approached the entrance to the sub-basement, tearing into the tunnel walls. I ducked under a stack of wooden boxes, which appeared to be filled with artillery. I returned fire, but without a clear vantage point, I was aiming blindly. They shot back, but their bullets went wide.

These assholes weren't trying to kill me.

"Daughter of Eve," a deep, growly voice uttered.

Fuck. Only two types of creatures had called me that—angels and demons. And without my sword, I was practically defenseless against them.

"We don't mean to harm you."

Sure.

"Listen, asshole, we both know what you mean to do with me, and I'm quite certain it constitutes harm."

"You are surrounded, Kate," a female uttered. "There is no escape. We can do this with as little bloodshed as possible or as much as you like, but if you want to see my son alive again, then I suggest you drop your weapon and walk out with your hands above your head."

Son? Edith?

"How do I know he's still alive?"

"I guess you're just going to have to trust me."

Trust her? From what Jax had said about her, that was the last thing I should do. But what other options did I have? I was not going to get through the collapsed tunnel behind me and the only other escape route was clogged by the Devil's Army. Even if there was a way out, I was not about to leave Jax behind.

Dropping the rifle and my handgun, I walked out of my hiding spot, hands up as she'd commanded. "I want to see him."

About fifteen weapons snapped in my direction as I stepped out from behind the stacked boxes. Flanked by who I could only imagine were the two remaining Horsemen, Edith walked toward me. With a red flowing robe draped around her in sensual waves, her movements held the fluidity of a snake. As she drew nearer, I marveled at the resemblance between her and Jax. Same colored eyes, same shaped nose. Yet her expression held no warmth or humor the way Jax's did. Her eyes were devoid of sparkle and her mouth curved into a distasteful frown.

She eyed me from head to toe, scrunching her nose. "So, you're the woman carrying Astaroth's spawn?"

"Jax's child. *Your* grandchild."

"Let's refrain from calling it that, shall we? That thing growing inside you is Samael's vessel, nothing more."

Even though Jax and Edith shared similar physical features, that's where the resemblance ended. This woman was colder than the Arctic.

"Where's your Empyrean weapon?" she asked.

"Far from your reach."

Her lip lifted at the corner, but it wasn't quite a snarl or even a smirk. "Seize her." Then she turned and walked away. "Prepare the cross," she said to someone as the two Horsemen approached me. "I believe my son will need a bit of... *motivation* to start talking."

"Wait... no—" But it was too late to protest. The two creatures closed in on me. I tried punching my way out of their hold, but I only managed to earn myself a punch to the face.

Total lights out.

The next time I opened my eyes, I was strapped to some type of metal contraption that looked like an X, my ankles and wrists secured at opposite ends of each other like a starfish. Someone was holding my head up by my hair. When my vision finally focused, I saw Jax tied to a chair a few feet in front of me.

"Jax?"

A surge of panic crawled over my skin when I saw the terror on his face.

"Keep your eyes on me, angel. Okay? Don't look anywhere else. Just keep them on me."

Didn't he know telling someone not to look at something was like telling them to do the opposite? But it wasn't like I would've been able to avoid looking at the two massive demons standing before me. Death and, who I could only surmise, was Pestilence, disrobed, their brutally beautiful bodies on full display, horrific and glorious at the same time. Standing completely nude before me, the demons were the embodiment of lust and sin.

Tearing my gaze from their very male bodies, my eyes darted around the room, trying to situate myself. Only floor-to-ceiling panes of glass surrounded us, opening to the darkness outside. Was this the 102nd floor observatory? And why the fuck was I tied up like this? Fright climbed up my esophagus and I wanted to gag. Why the hell were these creatures standing before me naked, their monstrous dicks engorged, their eyes feral with the type of hunger that had me frantically yanking on the binds around my limbs.

I was completely immobile. I turned to Jax again. "Jax, what is going on?"

Before he could respond, one of the guards stepped forward, using a knife to slice my T-shirt down the middle. "Your little boyfriend over there thinks he can keep the Fire Stone from us, so Death and Pestilence are going to take turns fucking you in every hole until he lets Astaroth through."

Body trembling, I shot my gaze toward Jax.

"In order to complete Samael's summoning," he said, his voice so gruff, I could barely recognize it, "they need all four stones. They're going after Jian's group for Famine's amulet, and Astaroth is the only one who can track the Fire Stone."

"But if Samael breaks through…" A weight settled in my stomach, and I felt like I would vomit. "He'll take our baby, Jax. He'll destroy what little hope remains. Humanity will be lost."

"We have no other option. I can't let them hurt you, angel."

"No. *No.* If Astaroth pushes through one more time, you'll be lost, Jax. Think of our ba—"

Death's hand came down hard across my face and blood flew from my mouth. The blow was so hard, it felt like he'd crushed my skull. With the intense ringing in my ears, I could hardly make out any other sound.

"Silence," he bellowed, his voice sounding muffled to my ringing ears. "We've wasted enough time with these mortals." He ripped off my shirt and terror rushed up my throat in a screech.

But my screams were nothing compared to the roar that burst from Jax's chest. He made the glass panes rattle in their frames. He was allowing Astaroth's power to push through, and the thought of losing him to that monster splintered through my bones.

No matter how much pain they could inflict upon me, how they planned to rape me, they couldn't kill me. I carried the vessel to their king. Jax didn't need to sacrifice himself for me. He didn't need to sacrifice this world. "Jax, no." I begged. "They need me. I'll heal."

"I'd rather risk damning this world to Hell than allow these monsters to defile you, Kate."

"You'll be sacrificing yourself and this world for nothing. Regardless of what you do, they'll still use me to bring Samael through."

"I'm sorry it had to be this way, angel. Just know that I love you and I'm doing this for us." He closed his eyes and before I could take my next breath, he broke through his chains, flinging each of the guards standing at his sides across the room. The Horsemen shook with anger, their faces aghast as they watched Jax draw symbols in the air. Words in a tongue I did not recognize spilled from his lips.

Death rushed toward Jax, his footsteps so heavy that the building trembled beneath his feet. He reached for Jax's neck, holding him up like a rag doll. "Imbecile."

Jax's feet dangled as he tried to pry the monster's hand free from his neck.

"You think he *scares* me?" Death mocked. "I welcome the opportunity to fight against the false king's fallen warrior once again."

Fallen warrior? Did he mean Mikha'el? Had Jax summoned the archangel?

"Come forth, brother. Your destiny awaits," the beast hissed.

A choking cough escaped from Jax's lips.

My breath caught as silent tears ran down my cheeks. It was as if time stood still. This couldn't be it. I couldn't lose him.

Jax's gaze flashed toward me, and I swore I heard his unspoken words as his eyes shut closed.

I love you, too, I mouthed back, but it was too late. The room went completely silent, and the demon dropped Jax's limp body on the floor.

"Rise, Astaroth. Come, take what is yours."

Jax's body convulsed, and the sound of breaking bones made my stomach clench. His muscles expanded, ripping through his shirt. His vertebrae became more pronounced, almost like bony spines protruding down the length of his back. Black, claw-like nails extended from his fingers and a growl rumbled from his chest. I couldn't stand watching his body transform, watching Astaroth pollute Jax's body with his demonic essence.

When the transformation was complete, Astaroth rose, and I gasped at how much taller he now stood. His skin had paled to an ashen tone, and when he turned toward me, his glowing red eyes matched those of his brothers.

But unlike the other Horsemen, Astaroth wasn't restored. Without the amulet, he remained cursed, corrupting Jax's body, mutating him into something grotesque. A mouth full of pointed, black teeth grinned at me, icing my blood.

He exchanged words with Death in the same language he'd spoken before, then stalked toward me. His sordid gaze traversed every inch of my body, his mouth practically salivating. The conversation we'd had back in that courtyard repeated in my mind, making my stomach churn with disgust.

As if hearing my thoughts, Astaroth reached for my face and grabbed my cheeks in his clawed hand. Ripples of dread shot through my body. He chuckled, the grating sound scraping against my skin. "I promised you insufferable agony, *angel.*" He inched closer, the stench of his breath almost knocking me unconscious, those sharp teeth dripping with something vile.

I spat in his face. "Do your worst, *beast.*"

He grinned, licking the saliva off his face with a reptilian tongue.

My lips parted in a silent gasp. This transformation was worse than anything I'd seen before. I couldn't find any signs of my Jax inside this abomination. I clenched my jaw, trying to keep the tears burning behind my eyes from cresting. This monster would not get that from me. Peering into his unholy red eyes, I searched their gaze for a glimmer of hope, for anything that told me the man I loved was still alive somewhere deep inside.

"Jax, please," I whimpered, my emotions betraying me.

The demon trailed a clawed finger across my jaw, down my neck, and further down. My body trembled, chest heaving as he reached between my breasts. My nostrils flared with each heated breath I took, but I wasn't scared. The fire burning in my veins was a promise, an oath to make these fallen angels pay for all the carnage they'd caused. To exact my revenge for the ones they took from me.

His finger hooked into my pants as he licked my face with that disgusting tongue. I held my breath and closed my eyes, imagining another world. A world where the sun shone over a peaceful morning, where I scrambled eggs over the stove in our kitchen. Where Jax flipped pancakes over the griddle and coffee brewed, the aroma of freshly ground beans wafting around me. I shut off the burner and wrapped my arms around his waist, resting my face on his back. He smelled divine, like a mix of fresh linen, coffee, and him. Just him.

Then… giggles. Childlike giggles as a little boy ran into the kitchen, a Superman action figure in his hands, soaring through the air as he rushed to save the world. I knelt and looked into his ocean-blue eyes. He smiled and my heart doubled in size.

He was mine. That little boy was mine, and I loved him. I loved him, and I hadn't even met him yet.

But as I took him into my arms, the sun eclipsed. Outside our kitchen window, the sky burned and the world fell to ash. His body disintegrated in my arms, leaving only plumes of smoke in its wake. Jax was gone, my home was gone, and only a scorched earth remained.

A pounding storm drummed inside me.

I refused to accept that fate. My world would not end that way.

I opened my eyes with a new energy surging through me—not one governed by hate or revenge, but by pure, all-consuming, blinding love. My fingers tingled, a spark of light emitting from the tips. Astaroth must have noticed the same thing, and he took a step back, a cloud of confusion swirling over his head—over the entire room.

All three Horsemen and the half dozen guards in the room stood like stone statues with their jaws slack as they stared at me.

That's when I realized my fingers weren't the only things shining brightly. My entire body was aglow with a light as bright as the sun. Power swam through my veins, and I yanked on my restraints, freeing myself from the bindings as I fell to the ground on bended knee. Snapping my gaze up at the beasts still staring at me, I puffed a breath to blow a strand of hair away from my face.

They'd taken my weapons, but that didn't mean I couldn't fight, right? *Hopefully, that one Krav Maga course I'd taken while still at the force would come in handy.* Plus, they couldn't use their weapons on me. After all, I was still carrying their demon king's vessel.

The first guard rushed me, but I quickly sidestepped him, then used the butt of my palm to jab up on his nose, breaking it. He fell backward, disoriented.

The next guy came at me, but I pushed on his chest and a blast of energy shot through my arms and into his body. The man flew across the room, hitting the glass so hard, his bones *crunched* and the pane splintered into a ripple of cracks.

What the…

I looked at my hands, shock and awe weaving through me. Strange markings lit up under my skin, running the length of both my arms. Each symbol glowed as if liquid sunlight ran through my body.

Incredible.

Walkie-talkies crackled, and I heard the remaining guards call for back-up, but in the background, gunfire blasts mixed with the sounds of men shouting. "Under… attack. Repeat. We… under… attack."

Had the Guardians come?

The short distraction had cost me dearly. All three Horsemen surrounded me. The look in their eyes didn't spell hunger or wickedness, though; it spelled frustration and immense anger. I carried the one thing that mattered to them the most—their salvation and their freedom from imprisonment. As much as they'd threatened me with pain, they couldn't harm the child growing inside me.

Which meant they couldn't harm me.

And that pissed them off.

I rolled my shoulders and cracked my knuckles. "What's it gonna be, boys? Who's gonna go first?"

Snarling, Death stalked forward. As I rounded up for a punch, the glass walls exploded inward with a blast that almost knocked us off our feet. Broken shards intermixed with rain as a whoosh of air filled the room, accompanied by the distinct sound of flapping wings.

In unison, we all pivoted to the gaping hole where the glass panes should be. Looking every bit like an avenging angel, Mikha'el hovered outside the Empire State Building's 102nd floor observatory, rain soaking his dark hair. His white and gold leather armor hugged every muscle of his body, and those immense, bronze-colored wings gleamed as water beaded on their surface. Each flap of his wings sent a wave of wet wind through the observatory.

Talk about making an entrance.

Showoff…

His gaze met mine. '*I came as fast as I could.*'

"Thanks," I replied with a smirk. "But I did have things under control."

"I'm certain of it, but I figured you might want this back." He pulled out my sword and relief welled inside me. Camila and Hank had made it out of the sewers. With a mighty swing, he flung it toward me, the sword spinning in the air before landing perfectly in my hand. All the symbols running the length of my arms lit up as soon as I wrapped my fingers around the hilt and the blade sparked to a white-hot flame.

Time to slice up some demon flesh.

Death spread his own wings, a set of bat-like monstrosities covered in a smoky substance. He spun toward the gaping hole and charged, shouting something that sounded like Mikha'el's name. He leapt into the air, colliding with the archangel and sending the both of them spiraling down.

My heart sank. "Mike!"

But as quickly as they fell, they flew back up, demon and angel battling midair, their wings a tangle of light and smoke.

Astaroth and Pestilence swung back toward me. But as Pestilence took a step forward, Astaroth said, "No, she's mine. Take care of the archangel. He's been stripped of his holy weapons."

Like his demon brother, Pestilence sprouted black wings out of nowhere and flew out into the night. My chest tightened as I silently uttered a prayer, hoping Mikha'el was as fierce a warrior as legends claimed.

I turned to Astaroth and swiped my sword. "Guess it's just you and me, lover boy."

"We both know you won't use that on me."

We pivoted around each other, forming a circle. "I wouldn't be so sure about that."

"Stop playing games. Just grab her already!" one of the guards shouted as he stood by the elevator doors. "We've got to go. There isn't much time. The Guardians have infiltrated the building."

Astaroth turned toward the guard and grabbed him by the neck. With one flick of his wrist, the man's vertebrae snapped. "I don't take orders from *you*."

The rest of the guards aimed their weapons. "Cool it, sunshine," one of them said. "We're on the same side here."

A bark echoed up the emergency staircase in the middle of the room.

Hank?

Gunfire erupted from inside the shaft, along with my German Shepherd and a face I was so relieved to see. "Chaz!" I shouted from across the room as the Marine shot another round of bullets down the staircase. The guards turned and fired at him, but he ducked behind a steel pillar. Sparks flew as the bullets ricocheted off the metal beams.

Hank ran toward one of the guards, but the man already had his scope trained on my dog. On instinct, I dashed toward the guard and leapt at him, spinning once in the air before coming down hard with my blade, cleaving the asshole straight down the middle. Blood misted the air as his bloodied corpse split in half.

A shot rang out, and I flew back as a bullet hit my shoulder and I fell with a grunt.

"Kate, are you okay?" Chaz yelled.

"I… think so."

"We need her alive, you worthless lump of flesh," Astaroth hollered as a body flew across the room and toward the broken windows. The man fell over the side of the building, his screams fading as his body raced toward the ground.

My gaze shot up toward the demon, my wound already mending itself. "Um… thank you for the assist?"

Growls echoed up the stairway shaft.

"Hope you have holy water stashed somewhere, because we've got company," Chaz said.

The hairs on my skin raised. Nightcrawlers. "They took all my weapons, including my vial of holy water."

Chaz spoke into his walkie. "*Padre*, need some help in the observatory. Over."

A staticky voice came through his walkie that sounded like Father Ortega. "Taking heavy fire. Over."

"If we don't get some holy water, then Kate, Hank, and I are about to become demon chow. Over."

"Copy. I'll see what I can do. Over."

Heavy rain whipped inside the observatory, and my breath hitched when I saw two nightcrawlers walk up the staircase. The last remaining guard jumped into the elevator and disappeared as the beasts stepped onto the floor. Growling, they bared their giant fangs, but Astaroth commanded them away from me. Instead, they focused their attention on Hank.

Bastard.

Hank bared his teeth, refusing to back down from the challenge.

"Hank, no!" I pushed back to my feet and aimed my weapon at Astaroth's neck. "Call them off. Now."

"Put the sword down. You know you don't have what it takes to kill me."

"The hell I don't. Call them off or I swear, I will slice your head clean off your neck."

The nightcrawlers closed in on Hank, pushing him closer toward the edge of the broken windows.

Chaz shot at the beasts, trying to divert their attention from Hank, but the bullets simply bounced off their hide.

Fed up, I sliced the sword against Astaroth's chest. "Call them off!" He moved away, but I still managed to cut his flesh. He hollered as the blade singed his skin.

Hank growled, and the beasts seemed to be torn between Hank's assertion as alpha and Astaroth's command.

My heart raced as I watched Hank's back paws graze the jagged end of the broken window. But he continued to growl.

Astaroth's red eyes glowed brighter. "Drop the sword and come with me, or I will have them tear him to shreds."

"Kate, don't. You can't trust him," Chaz said.

I inched away from Astaroth and toward the beasts. If he wasn't going to call them off, then I had to do something.

Suddenly, the beasts began to howl in pain, their skin sizzling as rain hit their hide.

Holy water?

Father Ortega had transformed the rain into holy water. But no matter how much they burned, the beasts wouldn't relent. Thinking he probably had the advantage, Hank charged, and my blood turned to ice. I ran toward him, but Astaroth tackled me to the ground, making me drop my sword. I watched in terror as one of the beasts whipped their tail, and Hank latched on. The hellhound let out an ear-piercing yowl, and as he tried to shake Hank off, the beast slipped and fell off the side of the building, taking Hank with him.

My world came to a screeching halt.

I was unable to find breath. Everything moved in slow motion. I was unable to move, unable to utter a single word.

No. This couldn't be happening. Hank. God no, not Hank—

Chaz ran toward the remaining beast, a military knife glinting in the rain. The Marine leapt onto the beast's back and stabbed its neck. Blow after blow, Chaz hacked at the monster, blood spurting in all directions.

I simply stared in shock. I tried to convince myself I hadn't just watched Hank fall off the side of the 102nd floor of the Empire State Building. Tried to convince myself this was all some nightmare. But when Astaroth's breath brushed against my hair, reality rushed in. Red-hot rage burst from me, and I knocked the demon off my back.

He flew against one of the remaining glass walls, and I jumped to my feet, sprinting toward him. The symbols over my skin flared to life and power unlike anything I had ever felt flamed inside of me as I delivered punch after punch.

There were no words to utter, no snarky remarks. I didn't even bother grabbing my sword. Fuck it, I was just going to pummel this beast to death with my bare hands. He'd taken

Jax, and then he had taken Hank. With tears cascading down my face, I screamed with every punch, and he grunted with every blow, but the asshole didn't hit me back. He couldn't. Because I was meant to carry their fucking king.

"Hit me back, you fucking coward. You said you would cause me *immeasurable* pain, so fucking do it. Hit me!"

The blow shot across my chest before I knew what happened. I flew across the room and landed hard on my back. Astaroth's body descended on top of me before I had a chance to catch my breath. His hands wrapped around my neck, and he squeezed so hard that all I saw was a blinding light behind my eyes.

"You insipid human. I am no coward. I am *War*. I don't care who you are. I don't care that you carry Samael's vessel inside you. Your death will be mine to claim."

I clawed at his hands, but he was too strong—even with my angelic powers, I was no match for his strength. His fingers felt like iron bars pressing into my windpipe. A numbness spread over my body. My legs no longer kicked, and my fingers could barely hook around his. He was going to kill me. This beast trapped inside Jax's body—the demon inside the man I loved—was going to be my end.

And I welcomed it. If this was how my story ended, then so be it. I had nothing left to fight for. And as my hands fell away from his, a set of blue eyes appeared before my mind. Then a face. A child. He smiled at me. "Fight, Kate," he uttered, cupping my cheeks in his little hands. "Fight!"

I snapped awake, managing to open my eyes into slits.

"Fight, Kate." Chaz's voice reached my ears from a distance.

From the corner of my eye, I spotted the Marine crawling toward me. His clothes were torn, bloody gashes carving across his face and body. He held something out to me. The hilt to my sword. "Take it, Kate. Kill him."

I couldn't feel my body, couldn't summon a single ounce of strength to fight.

"Do it for your child, Kate. Do it for Jax!"

For Jax... for our child. I needed to live for them. For humanity's last hope.

All the hate, all the regret, all the pain. None of it mattered now.

Only love. That was all I had left. And I took every ounce I possessed and infused it into my muscles. I extended my hand out toward Chaz and wrapped my fingers around the hilt. The sword's power lit through me like lightning racing through my veins. Fuck. I knew what I had to do and a part of me feared I wouldn't be able to.

Jax had made me promise. I couldn't let him down. Astaroth's hands squeezed my neck tighter and hot tears swelled in my eyes. "I'm so sorry, Jax." With one last heave, my world shattered as I jammed the blade straight through Astaroth's heart.

The hold around my neck loosened as he let go and I unleashed a guttural scream that shook the heavens. I plunged the blade deeper, all the way to the hilt, making my body tremble with the torment of what I'd just done.

Holding on to the sword, War's gaze latched onto mine. Horror. Shock. The look in his eyes lasted two beats before their red glow faded, and all I saw were Jax's blue eyes.

Jax...

He fell onto his back, the sword still plunged in his heart. Coughing, I scurried to my knees and leaned over Astaroth—no, over Jax's body. All evidence of the demon's possession bled away.

"Oh, God." I went to pull the sword out of his chest, but Jax managed to raise a hand and put it over mine.

Blood gurgled up his throat and spilled at the corners of his mouth. "Don't… angel. It's no use."

"You can heal. You've done it before," I whimpered, tears mixing with the whipping rain as I ran my fingers through his hair.

He cupped my cheek. "Not this time."

I cupped my hand over his. "I'm— God, I'm so sorry, Jax."

"I know, angel," he said, reaching up to wipe my tears, but it was of no use because they only came harder. "It's okay. You did the right thing." The blood seeping from of his wound spread around me.

God. There is so much blood.

The hollowness in my chest threatened to choke me. "You can't leave me, Jax. I can't raise this child on my own. Not in this world."

Skin growing paler, his hand fell to the floor as more life seeped from his wounds. "I will be with you always. If there is anyone I know who can kick demon ass, it's you, baby girl. You gotta keep fighting, angel. Promise me… you'll keep fighting."

I nodded, a lump forming in my throat.

His lips twitched with a sorrowful smile. "It's amazing, Kate. The love inside. You take it with you."

Even dying, the goof couldn't stop quoting movies. I laughed as I furiously wiped at the tears streaming down my face. "I love you," I whispered, practically breathless. God damn it, I loved him more than I thought possible in this world. In this short amount of time.

His lips parted with one last breath and then he was gone.

I didn't think I could feel this kind of pain ever again, but I was wrong. So wrong.

Removing the blade from his body, I pulled him into my arms and rocked him as every part of me cracked. And I screamed, wanting the sky to burst. Needing God to hear my anguish.

To hear the sound of my heart breaking. Of my soul dying.

This poor man called, and the Lord heard him; He saved him out of all his troubles. The angel of the Lord encamps around those who fear Him, and He delivers them.

PSALM 34:6 - 7

CHAPTER 18

KATE

Wind and rain whipped around us with fury, but I didn't care. I held on to Jax's body by the edge of the skyscraper's broken windows, weeping into his neck as I prayed.

Prayed with every thread of my soul, every pulse of my heart, for this nightmare to end. For the agony tearing me up inside to cease. For the strength to rise above this rubble. For hope. And for one last chance to make things right.

Laying Jax back onto the floor, I wiped a wet tendril of his hair away from his face. The world felt so silent without his jokes, so dark without his smile.

But losing him wasn't the only thing clawing at my chest. I looked over to the gaping hole of shattered glass and everything inside me trembled. *Hank.* My poor boy had tumbled off the edge trying to protect me. Hank had died fighting, but I knew it was the only way he would've wanted to go.

Fresh tears ran down my cheeks and I buried my face in my hands, pouring my soul out. "Please, God. If You're listening, if there's a part of You that still cares… please—" my voice cracked against my sobs, "just take this hollowness from me. Please."

"Kate," A hoarse voice sounded behind me, but I didn't have the will to turn around. Didn't have the desire to even breathe. "Kate," the male voice said louder, and I realized it was Chaz calling to me. "Look out the window, Kate."

With a heavy breath, I wiped at my tear-stricken face and peered out into the soggy, grey night, the storm quieting to a drizzle tapping on the exposed metal frames. Looking like he'd been through Hell and back, Mikha'el hovered right outside the building. Gently flapping his wings to keep himself aloft, he looked like the warrior he was described to be. His wounds bled with the golden hue of his ichor, and his torn armor was splattered with the Horsemen's dark blood. And in his arms…

In his arms, he held Hank.

A tired smile traced across his lips. "Did someone lose a dog?"

I gawked at him, too stunned to move. To even blink. "Hank?"

Can this be real?

His ears perked and he whined in the archangel's arms, shivering from the soaking rain.

Breaking out of my stupor, I jumped to my feet. With shaking hands, I reached out toward Hank, my heart ready to explode. "Buddy, you're *alive!*" I looked at Mikha'el. "How? He fell. No one could have survived that."

Holding his injured arm, Chaz peered over the opening. "Lucky son of a bitch. They must've been working on the building right before shit went down."

I followed his gaze through the misty rain and spotted the scaffolding surrounding the observatory ten feet below. Farther down, on the eighty-second floor open-air observatory, people shouted commands.

Mikha'el flew inside and placed Hank on the floor. My arms wrapped around his furry neck in less than a breath. The heaviness clenching around my heart loosened its grip and this time, the tears that flowed were imbued with gratitude. So much gratitude. "Oh, Hank. I thought I'd lost you." He licked my face, slobbering me with doggie kisses. I looked up at the archangel. "Thank you so, so much."

"Thank the wooden boards that broke his fall. All I did was grab him and fly him up. Brave beast. He was just sitting there on his hind legs, waiting patiently."

"And the nightcrawler?"

Mikha'el's lip curled into a snarl. "The hellhound wasn't as lucky."

Hank limped toward Jax's body and licked his cheek, as if trying to wake him up. A knot formed in my throat while I watched him nudge Jax's face.

Mikha'el knelt beside Jax, placing his golden bow on the floor. Soft murmurs in a language I couldn't understand poured from his lips.

"What do your words mean?" I asked.

He glanced back at me. "It's a prayer for his soul."

Sitting on my knees across from Mikha'el, with Jax's limp body between us, my insides twisted once more. I said a silent prayer too, though I wasn't sure anyone was even listening. "Can't you heal him?" I asked.

"He's gone, Kate." Mikha'el's eyes softened over me, their fiery glow dimming. "I don't hold that kind of power; only the higher spheres have authority over death."

My lips trembled as I held back more tears. Why did things have to be this way? It just wasn't fair. "He didn't deserve to die. Jax never wanted this. He tried to stop it."

"His soul wasn't pure, Kate, but he was a good man. His love for you was untainted, and he would've done anything to protect you and your unborn child. I'm sure the scales will tip in his favor." His words were meant to comfort me. To make me feel better that perhaps, God would have mercy on Jax's soul, and he wouldn't end up burning in the pits of Hell where Samael would exact revenge on Jax for sabotaging his plans.

But it only sliced me deeper. If God didn't have mercy on the world, then how could I believe He'd have mercy on Jax?

I looked down at Jax's solemn face and sighed, hoping he was at peace. "He knew Astaroth would take over his body once he let him through, but it was the only way he could break free from the chains." Lifting my gaze to the archangel, I added, "And he did that so he could call upon you."

Mikha'el stood, his towering frame looming over me. Rain fluttered off his wings—reminding me of a swan on a riverbank—before he tucked them away behind his glamor. Strapping his bow over his back, he said, "Jax did the right thing, Kate. Your exact location was heavily concealed with wards. Though I knew you'd come here, I couldn't detect you, and when I saw you'd given your sword to Camila, I thought we might have lost you. Without the summoning spell Jax cast, I would've never known you were up here. Those demons would have done unthinkable atrocities to you or taken you away to a different location."

A shiver ran the length of my back as I recalled the feral look in the Horsemen's eyes. If Mikha'el hadn't shown… "What happened to the Horsemen?" I asked, remembering both Death and Pestilence had gone after him.

"I took out Chemoth, but without an Empyrean weapon, I only managed to send him back to Hell. In the fight, his amulet fell and Beleth swooped in to take it. Possessing both stones amplified his power, and I wasn't able to fight against him. Then, when Astaroth died, he used his abilities to rift between planes."

"Rift?" Chaz asked.

Mikha'el lifted one shoulder. "Kate would call it teleporting, as she so aptly put it once when she wondered if angels had the ability to do so."

My blood buzzed with alarm. "Where could he have gone? Do you think he knows the location of the Fire Stone? Astaroth said something to him when he came through."

"I don't know, but rifting uses a lot of power. If he does it again, I should be able to track his location. If he is going after the Fire Stone, then hopefully, we can intercept him before it's too late."

More shouts echoed from below. From the sounds of it, the Guardians were rounding up Edith's men.

"It's a good thing your friends were already on their way," Chaz said, stepping forward and peering below at the commotion taking place on the eighty-second floor. "When I emerged from the sewers with the girls, it wasn't long before we ran into the Guardians. Then Camila and Hank showed up shortly after, and she told us what you did. What…" he lowered his chin and heaved a giant breath, "what Tavs did."

The weight of Tavs' dog tags still hung around my neck. I lifted them off me and handed them to him. "She wanted you to have these. Said you were the only family she had left."

Taking them from me, he hung them over his own dog tags and kissed the name plate before letting them settle on his chest. "She was mine, too."

Heavy footsteps echoed up the staircase, and the three of us turned in unison, weapons pointed at the entrance. A wave of relief blasted through me when Father Ortega popped up, heaving heavily as he scaled the last step. Clint, Trinidad, and several other Guardians followed behind him. Taking a second to catch his breath, he said, "Those cursed devils cut the power to the elevator."

"I feel ya, *padre*," Chaz said. "I was in the elevator with Hank when the assholes cut the power. Got to the eighty-second floor, but we had to trek up the rest of the way on foot."

Father Ortega was about to say something else when his gaze fell upon Jax's body, then turned up to meet my eyes. The mark of true sympathy crossed his face, and it was enough to send another score of aches rumbling through my heart.

"Kate, I am so sorry." He immediately rushed toward us and took me into his arms as I stood, offering me a touch of solace. After a brief moment, he took a knee beside Jax and made the sign of the cross over his body. "Oh, merciful God, we humbly beseech Thee on behalf of Thy servant Jax, which Thou hast called out of the world. That Thou wouldst not deliver him into the hands of the enemy, nor forget him forever, but command that he be taken up by Thy holy angels and borne to our home in paradise. That having put his hope and trust in Thee, he will not suffer the pains of Hell, but may come to the possession of eternal joys."

I placed a hand on his shoulder and softly uttered, "Thank you."

Right then, a majestic horn reverberated through the heavens, followed by a light so bright, I swore the sun had fallen to the Earth. We inched closer to the broken windows and gazed up into the sky as the brilliant sheen sharpened.

That's when I realized it was more than a bright light. It was an angel with wings so white, they cast their own illumination. "Hail, Daughter of Eve," she said with an ethereal, yet commanding voice. "I come to you with tidings, for you have found great favor with the Lord." Looking down upon me with eyes made of liquid gold, her snow-white hair billowed in the wind as her immense wings flapped elegantly through the air. Skin dark like a sea of onyx shimmered with a glow of its own. She was nothing short of magnificent, and when she spoke, her melodic voice flowed like the airy tunes of a flute.

"Gavri'el," Mikha'el uttered as he fell to one knee and bowed his head.

"Commander," she greeted him. "It is good to see you."

"You as well, emissary."

"Rise, warrior." Gavri'el drew an enormous, gold and silver broadsword out of thin air. The metal glinted as if made from the light of the sun and moon. "There is much to be done."

Pushing to his feet, Mikha'el took the weapon, his eyes shimmering with euphoria. "Emrandael..." he whispered with reverence as he took the sword. "Does this mean..."

"God's legions await your orders, commander. It is time to take up arms with your brethren."

She flew inside the observatory and gently lowered to her feet, shifting her attention to me. "Kathrine, you fought bravely today. Your sacrifice has not been overlooked," she said while placing a hand on my shoulder. "But this war is far from over."

I shook her hand off. "Bravely? Never in my entire life have I fought with so much fear in my heart. Have you any idea how much this war has already taken from me?" The angel stayed quiet. "I did not *willingly* give up anything today. I *lost*." I pointed to Jax's body. "He's the one you should be praising. He sacrificed himself to protect me and our child. Where is his favor from God?"

Mikha'el stepped forward, perhaps sensing the turmoil trying to break through my chest. "Kate, please. Listen to what Gavri'el has to say."

"Gavri'el, is it?" I said, looking up into her glowing eyes. "You're God's holy messenger, aren't you? Perhaps you can bring Him back my message. Tell Him I don't need His favor. What I need is my family back."

The gold in her eyes cooled to a crystalline amber. "Your husband and daughter did not meet an untimely death, Kathrine.

It was their fate to leave the world of men when they did, but Jax—"

My chest puffed with a hearty breath. "What about Jax?"

"Jax was *your* fate, Kathrine. And so is the life you carry inside you."

Her words sent a ripple of shockwaves through my veins. All I could do was stare at her impossibly beautiful face. This was Gavri'el—one of the few angels spoken of in ancient scriptures, besides Mikha'el. According to those teachings, she carried the word of God; and now she spoke to me about my fate. This moment was too surreal for words. And the fact she mentioned Jax and our baby as being my fate reminded me of all the biblical stories Grams used to force me to read. Gavri'el had been present during some of the most important and iconic moments in Abrahamic faiths.

A heaviness settled over my heart as I considered the weight of her words.

Her gentle smile soothed the erratic beating of my heart, and I slowly released the massive breath I'd been holding. She turned toward Jax's body and glided to his side. Kneeling beside him, she placed her hand over his heart. Words spoken in the same tongue Mikha'el had used earlier spilled from her lips, igniting her palm in a warm glow.

I gulped and turned to Mikha'el. "What is she doing?"

"Kneel," he murmured, then raised his voice to the group assembled in the observatory. "All of you, kneel."

No one disobeyed, except for me. A pit settled in my stomach. "I need to know what she's doing."

"She's invoking the Holy Spirit, Kate."

"Why?"

He took a knee and looked up at me from his lowered position, eyes pleading with mine. "Kneel, Kate. You're about to witness a miracle."

This time, I listened and did as he said. My heart raced a million miles a second as I watched God's holy messenger pray over Jax's body.

"There is no greater act of love than self-sacrifice," she said in English, looking directly in the face of everyone in the room. "This man willingly gave his life for those he cherished, and thus, has earned God's favor." Her eyes fell to his face and a soft smile played on her lips. "You will enter the Lord's kingdom, Jackson Cornelius Constantine, but not today. For your work on Earth is not yet complete. Through the power of the Almighty God and the Holy Spirit, I grant thee dominion over death."

A blast of powerful light shot through her hand and into Jax's body. The energy wave surged through the room, shaking the construction beams and rattling the frames. The glass shards littering the floor turned to dust and blew off the edge, taken away in the wind.

My entire body pulsed with rapture, and I swore my soul vibrated within me.

The angel sang a verse of praises, and leaning over Jax's face, she whispered, "Breathe, Son of Adam. It is time to return to the living."

With a loud gasp, Jax opened his eyes and everyone in the room gasped along with him. Heart lodged in my throat, I jumped to my feet and ran to him, awe and disbelief lacing through my entire being. But time moved so slowly, and it felt like I was trudging through molasses. When I finally reached him, I slid my hands under his head and placed it on my lap, pulling his hair away from his eyes, which shone bright blue, though hazy with confusion, as he blinked. "Jax. Oh, my God. You're… *alive*."

With a shaky hand, he reached up and pulled a strand of my hair behind my ear. "Angel?"

"Yes, baby. It's me. How do you feel?"

He groaned, "Like I died and came back to life."

I laughed. "That's because you *did* die and came back to life."

"Wait. I did die, didn't I?" Slowly sitting up, he rubbed at his now healed chest, his shirt ripped where the wound should be. "You stabbed me… I was cold and then… and then there was nothing." Jax looked around the room, taking note of the familiar faces and the not-so-familiar one staring down at him. "I don't think we've met."

"I am Gavri'el, Virtue of the Second Sphere and the Lord's emissary. And you, Jackson Constantine, have been reborn."

"Holy shit. *The* Gavri'el?" Jax choked on his own saliva as he shot to his feet, but he wobbled, struggling to stay upright. Father Ortega and I helped to steady him.

"She brought you back," I said.

He turned to me, eyes big as saucers. Running his fingers through my hair, as if he was touching me for the first time, he said, "I thought… I thought I'd never see you again."

"Your sacrifice was noble, Son of Adam," Gavri'el answered, calling back his attention. "Which is why God has granted you this favor. But your work here is far from complete."

Facing the angel, he took a minute to balance on his feet. His chest puffed and the muscles in his jaw twitched as if he was holding back from breaking down. "I know I'm not worthy of His love or forgiveness." His voice trembled as he reached for my hand and squeezed gently. "But I will do everything in my power to earn this second chance. Tell me what is asked of me?"

She turned to everyone in the room, all still on bended knees. "Stand, Guardians. It is I who should kneel before you." She went down on one knee and said, "You've all fought with honor tonight. With faith in your hearts, despite our absence. Despite our failure to protect your kind. Tonight, you rejoice, for you have won this battle, but your toughest fight still lies ahead. Samael will not stop until he fulfills what he believes to be his destiny, and you must do everything in your power to ensure he does not fulfill that goal."

I placed a protective hand over my belly, already anticipating what the angel would say next.

"Katherine, Jax, your son is the key. He must be shielded from Samael and his army at all costs."

Son? Had my visions been real?

"Your child will have the power to bring destruction or salvation," she continued. "But the path he chooses will depend on you."

"How?" I asked.

"The power living in his veins will be strong enough to unite your people once again, to bring forth healing. But in the wrong hands, he will be used as a lethal weapon against you. Guard him from those who wish to take him from you. When the time is right, I will call upon you, upon him. Until then, you must protect each other. Protect him. But above all, love one another. It is your greatest weapon against the false king."

I appreciated her warnings, but a part of me couldn't help but wonder why it had taken this long for her to come, for God to send us help. "Why now, Gavri'el? Why is God sending us this message of hope after everything that's happened? After leaving us here to die like this?"

"The mysteries of His love for you are not mine to unlock, Katherine. One day, His answers will be revealed, but even I am not privy to that holy secret. All I can tell you is that He has not forsaken you. More angels are coming. Samael's army might be weakened right now, but they are far from defeated."

"What of the Horsemen? Are they all dead?" Jax asked, rubbing his chest as if searching for any trace of Astaroth.

Mikha'el swung his Empyrean sword over his back. "Chemoth has been cast back to Hell, but Beleth still lives. He has the Air and Water Stones in his possession. We believe he is going after the other two stones."

Jax took a deep breath, furrowing his forehead as a thought seemed to cross his mind. "The Fire Stone, the Horsemen said they were going to use the combined power of the Air, Water, and Earth stones to amplify Astaroth's ability to track the Fire stone."

I grabbed Jax by the shoulders. "Did he tell them anything?"

He lowered his chin and shook his head in disappointment. "When he took over, it's like he obliterated my consciousness. All I remember is letting him punch through, then waking up to see your face before I died."

"You must remember something, Jax. Where could you have hidden it?"

"I don't know, Kate. The spell I used is irreversible."

Dressed in black fatigues, a large, golden cross dangled from Father Ortega's chest. "The Earth Stone is secured back at the church. The Light Reformation Group brought it to us shortly after your party left for the tunnels, just as Jian had instructed. If Death needs the combined power of the stones to track the Fire Stone, then he'll need to take the Earth Stone first."

Jax shook the priest's hand. "Thank you, Father. That should buy us some time to uncover the location of the Fire Stone."

Father Ortega clapped a hand over Jax's shoulder. "I know we didn't start off on the right foot, but I'm glad you're back, son."

Jax nodded his appreciation.

"Jax," Mikha'el said, his dark hair whipping in the wind circulating through the observatory. "You must've left yourself a clue. Even though the spell is irreversible, if you left any unintended breadcrumbs, we might be able to follow them, or at least piece together where you could have hidden it."

"Think, Jax." I took his hands in mine and squeezed. "Back at the church, you told me when you saw Death take over Sam's body, you freaked out. And when Astaroth came for you, you ran. Where did you go?"

Jax pulled his hands from mine and paced in the center of the observatory. "I ran right out of the building and slammed into a couple pushing a stroller. The man, he got so pissed, he tried to hold on to me, but Astaroth crashed through the doors, and I was able to get free." Jax paused to look at me, a grim shadow swirling inside his gaze as if he'd just stumbled upon a crucial detail. "Roger," he said slowly, weighing my reaction to his revelation. "The man's name was Roger."

The hairs on my arms stood like needles. *Could it be?*

Eyes wide, his body shuddered as he released a shaking breath. He stepped closer to me and took my face in his hands, gaze roaming every inch of my features as if he was seeing me for the very first time—seeing me differently. "It was *you*," Jax said smiling, his voice a soft whisper. "I can't believe it. That day, when Hell broke loose and I ran, I ran into *you* and Roger. God. It's always been you, Kate. We've been connected from the beginning."

Chills scaled down my back. He was right. How had I not pieced that together when he first told me the story. Roger had been so angry, but when the demon shot through the entrance, we took Isabella to safety, and I began to work on helping the wounded Astaroth had left in his wake.

"Kate, I'm so sorry."

I wrapped my arms around his neck and inhaled the warm scent of his skin. "No need for apologies. That's the past now, Jax. Everything happens for a reason. If anything, it's more proof of what Gavri'el said." Taking a short step back, I peered up into the depths of his blue eyes. "You're my destiny. We were meant to be in each other's lives one way or another. Despite the horrors of that day and everything that followed, it's also tragically beautiful in a way. I'm glad it was me. Glad it was us. Now, I need you to think harder. Where did you go after that?"

"Everything is so fucking foggy. I remember a cab. Racing through the city. Astaroth chasing after me. His skin burning in the sun. The stench. God, the stench. But I can't recall where I was headed. Fuck. *Fuck*." Jax hit the butt of his palm against his forehead several times. "Think. Think, dammit." Then his eyes shot up. "Kids. There was a group of kids crossing the street. The same kids I saw every day when they were on their way to school."

I shrugged. "What does that mean?"

"Downtown. I headed downtown."

"What's there?" Father Ortega leaned against one of the exposed beams and crossed his arms. "Why would you drive into the middle of the city if you were trying to get away from the Horseman?"

"My studio apartment. That's where I must have gone. If there are any breadcrumbs, as Mikha'el says, that's the only place I can think of where we'd find them."

"You didn't go back after everything hit?" I asked.

"My mother knew where I lived. That's the first place she would've looked for me."

"The place is probably trashed," Clint said, joining the conversation. I'd forgotten we weren't the only ones in the room.

"Clint is right," Jax said. "If not by the Devil's Army, then by scavengers."

"It's worth the try, though," I said. "We can't leave any stone unturned."

"I can mount a search team," Clint said. "I know the area very well and can get us in with minimal risk from the hellhound nest down there."

Jax ran a hand through his wet hair. "Let's go, then."

Father Ortega put a palm on his chest. "Wait. My fighters are tired. Let's follow the emissary's advice and rest for the night. Plus, the hellhounds don't come out during the day and the infected are less active."

Mikha'el expanded his wings, their luminosity pulling everyone's attention. "I must gather the Lord's legions. We may have defeated this sect, but the Devil's Army has members across all nations. With both the Water and Air Stones, Beleth will be able to temporarily open the gates long enough to bring forth some of the lower circle demons. Once he regroups, he'll be coming for the Earth Stone."

His wings fluttered as he looked at me, perhaps sensing the uneasy energy crackling inside my heart. Mikha'el had been pivotal in our fight against the Horsemen. He'd sworn to protect me, and now that I had another life to worry about, I needed him even more.

He knelt in front of me and took my hand, those impossibly bright eyes glowing with an internal fire. "I pledged my sword to you, Katherine. I will not break my vow to protect you. I will return with my army, and we will crush Samael once and for all."

When he stood, I wrapped my arms around him. "Thank you for everything. Don't take too long, okay? I don't know how angel-time works or whatever, but please, hurry back."

"I promise to return as soon as I can, Daughter of Eve."

Gavri'el opened her wings as well, preparing to take flight, but first, she turned to the group. "Children of the Light, we leave you now, but we do not leave you without hope. We will return with your holy weapons and with God's legions to fight alongside your warriors. Until then, you must hold your defenses." She nodded toward me. "And protect that child with all your might."

Jax held my hand as we all watched the two angels take to the heavens and disappear with a crack of thunder and a whoosh of energy that blasted us all.

I guess that's what he'd meant about rifting.

Once the angels were gone, a Guardian came running up the stairs. "Father," the woman panted. "You're going to want to see this." Then she turned to Jax. "You, too."

Blessed are those who mourn, for they
will be comforted.

MATTHEW 5:4

CHAPTER 19

JAX

Some of the engineers who had been a part of the Light Reformation Group joined the Guardians when they stormed the Empire State Building. Thankfully, they were able to get the elevators working again. We were escorted to the basement floor and to one of the rooms that had been used by the Devil's Army as a holding cell.

We stood outside the door as the Guardian explained what had happened. "We found her a couple of blocks from here, trying to get away with a few other guards. They'd been cornered by a horde of the infected. We weren't able to get to her companions in time, and quite frankly, we probably wouldn't have cared what happened to her until we realized who she was."

"Speak plainly, Cassie. Who did you bring back?" Father Ortega asked as he wiped sweat off his face with a handkerchief.

Cassie looked at me before she said, "Edith."

A muscle in my jaw tightened. I rotated my shoulders, rolling off the tension climbing up my neck. I moved to barge through the door when the Guardian stopped me. "Wait. There's something else. She's been bitten and the infection is spreading fast. I don't know how long she has before she turns."

"I still want to see her. Alone."

"She's been secured to a metal cross that had been in the room. You should be safe but take my gun just in case. We'll be out here if you need anything."

Kate reached for my arm before I went in. "Let me come with you."

"Kate, I don't know if it's a good idea. She's infected. Not to mention, she could cast a spell of some sort. I don't need her trying to hurt you or the baby."

"I will be fine. She is not going to hurt me or the baby. She's tied to that cross. She can't use her hands to draw sigils. Trust me, she ain't moving, so long as she's tied to that thing."

"Her tongue is poisonous, Kate."

"I don't give a damn what she has to say. But I'm not letting you go in there alone. We do this together or not at all."

I puffed a breath of defeat and let my shoulders relax. "You win, angel. You win."

Once we stepped through the door, Edith lifted her head and curled her lips up in a snarl. Her gums had begun to turn black, and her eyes were already bloodshot. Ropes of darkened veins scaled up her neck and bled into her face.

"Well, if it isn't my disappointing lump of a son and his fucking *whore*," she growled.

I racked the slide of the pistol and pointed it at her head. "Insults at me, I'll take. But you will not disrespect her."

Kate held on to my arm. "It's okay, Jax. I don't care what she calls me."

My hands tightened around the grip. "But I do."

"Devil's horns, Jackson," Edith said. "You were always so soft. It's why your father couldn't stand you. He thought you were *weak*."

"You don't plan to quit, do you? Even facing death, you continue with your vitriol."

"I've made peace with my maker, Jackson. Go ahead and kill me. I've entrusted my soul to my king. You'll be sending me home."

"You're so sure he'll welcome you with open arms after your grand failure?"

She coughed so hard it sounded like she was hacking out a lung. Black blood dribbled out of the sides of her mouth as the infection continued to ravage her body. "But that's where you're wrong, again. I didn't fail. That cunt carries his vessel. It's only a matter of time before the rest of his army comes for you." She turned her eyes toward Kate. "There is nowhere you can hide from us."

"He will never have my son. I won't allow it."

"You stupid bitch." Edith laughed. "Your son has been marked. There is no escaping his fate." As she continued to cackle, her body convulsed and she thrashed against her restraints.

"She doesn't have much time left, Jax. I can heal her."

I craned my neck toward Kate. "Heal her? For what? There's no curing her toxic soul, Kate."

"Then why are we here, Jax?"

"Because I wanted her to see my face. To know it was I who pulled the trigger." I turned back to the monster who was my mother and drew closer, gun still pointed at her head. "Then again, I could just absolve you of your sins, Mother, and steal your dream of going to Hell. Or maybe I should let the infection take you and have you spend the rest of eternity as a walking corpse."

Her cloudy eyes widened at my words. There were no more quips or insults. For the first time ever, she was listening. "That's right, Edith. I paid attention. You thought I was a useless lump, but I paid really close attention to all those teachings. Without a true death, your soul will linger in limbo."

"I always knew you were a coward. It's no surprise you'd fail, even now."

"You'd think that, wouldn't you? But you see, I said that I *could*, not that I *would*. I told you I would kill you if you hurt Kate, and I intend to keep that promise. What you don't understand is that I know what awaits you. I've been there; I've seen it with my own eyes. There's no welcoming committee, Mother. Samael hates humans above all else, and there's a special place there for people like you. Have fun burning for all eternity. Oh, and do me a favor, when you see him, tell him Jax Constantine is coming for him. Because he won't be able to hide from me, not even in Hell."

Then I pulled the trigger, and she was gone.

My lower lip twitched as I watched her body fall limp on that cross. Even now, even after everything she did, a part of me wished things would've ended differently.

Her soul would not rest in peace, and I was afraid neither would mine.

"You did what you had to do, Jax," Kate said, squeezing my hand.

I gulped hard, swallowing a resigned breath. She was right. The world would never be safe with Edith around.

*You make known to me the path of life;
in your presence there is fullness of
joy; at your right hand are pleasures
forevermore.*

PSALM 16:11 ESV

CHAPTER 20

JAX

As we'd discussed, Clint took us through downtown Manhattan the next day. To my surprise, my old place wasn't as trashed as we'd expected. Looked like someone might have been squatting there for some time, but there was no sign they were living there now.

We looked for hours, trying to find those breadcrumbs, and we were ready to give up when Kate stepped on the broken DVD case for one of Scarlett Johansson's older movies and picked it up.

"Hmm. I never saw this one," she said.

"Never saw what?" I asked as I looked over her shoulder.

"Vicky Cristina Barcelona."

For a second, all I did was stare at the cover, trying to recall what the movie was about, and then it was like a gear knocked into place in my head. "The breadcrumb."

Kate turned toward me. "What?"

"That's it. That's the breadcrumb. Oh, my God. I can't believe it." I spun in place, holding my head in astonishment. "Mikha'el, you fucking genius!"

"Jax, what is going on? What breadcrumb?"

I turned toward Kate and took the DVD from her, tapping on the cover. "Barcelona. That's where the stone is."

"How can you be sure?"

"Because that's where the Sagrada Familia is—the biggest Roman Catholic church in Spain. Which also happens to be headquarters for the Eastern House of the Guardians."

"Are you certain?"

"I mean, I have no idea how I could have gotten it there, but it's the only thing that makes sense. Hiding it with the Eastern House would ensure it was as far away from Astaroth, and in a place designed to keep demons out. What could be safer?"

Kate dropped her gaze. "Spain? How the heck are we supposed to get there? Not like we can just jump on a plane and fly there."

The plan was to wait for Mikha'el and his army to return, then have him rift us to the Sagrada Familia, but days turned into weeks and there had been no sign of the angels. We'd begun to worry help was not coming.

Kate had also begun to show more prominently. It was clear the baby was not going through a normal gestation, as Mikha'el had predicted. We'd also started to see an increase in *d'shiad* activity, as well as different kinds of monsters that were starting to sprout from the shadows.

Seemed Beleth had managed to open the gates long enough to bring forth more demons. The scorpions we'd seen in the tunnels were teddy bears compared to the new creatures prowling the streets.

Even though the church was heavily warded, New York City was not a safe place for Kate, especially so close to giving birth. It was decided we would need to leave, at least until the baby was born and the Guardians had managed to clear the city.

Kate recalled the conversation we'd had with the boat people back when we first met. They'd told us about a sanctuary up north, some type of community that had managed to flourish behind a walled compound. After careful consideration, we decided we would find our way to the sanctuary and await Mikha'el's return there.

Father Ortega agreed to let us leave, provided we took all the girls we'd rescued from the Devil's Army and gave them a new home in the sanctuary. Several Guardians would be coming with us for protection. He also told Kate they would resume the research into the healing properties of her blood once the baby was born. Given the complexities of her pregnancy, they decided it was safer to wait until after the birth. We'd waited eighteen months for a cure; we could wait a couple more.

After securing two school buses and loading them up with supplies, we slept our last night at the church.

Kate and I lay in bed, both of us staring at the ceiling, both of us unable to sleep. Hank lay sprawled at the foot of our small bed as if he owned it. He had his own bed on the floor, but he refused to use it.

"You think we'll find the place?" Kate whispered in the dimly lit room.

"I don't know, angel. All we can do is hope."

"What about Mikha'el? He's been gone for over a month. What if he comes back and we're not here?"

"He's an archangel sworn to protect you. He will find you in any corner of this world. I'm certain of that. Plus, you've got me. I'm sworn to protect you as well. Or am I not good enough anymore since I no longer have superpowers?"

She nudged my arm. "Shut up. You know that's not it. I'm just… I'm just worried they're not coming back. That something happened."

I turned on my side to look at her. She lay propped on a pillow, hand on her round belly, blanket at her feet because she was too hot. "You're so beautiful, you know that?"

"You're so full of it. I'm a blimp. And stop trying to change the subject."

"I'm not. And you're the most beautiful blimp I ever did see, baby girl."

She turned her gaze toward me, and I swore if her eyes were made of lasers, I'd be fried meat right now. I raised a brow. "You know, there are other ways I could get you to relax and forget about all this angel nonsense."

"Oh yeah, and how's that?"

"Remember that time I showed you how to eat an Oreo the right way?"

She smiled.

"I knew that would get you back on my side." I whistled and snapped my fingers, stirring Hank from his deep slumber. He raised his head, ears flopped.

"Down, Hank," I said. "You need to sleep in your bed tonight."

He side-eyed me, then plopped his head back down.

"Hank," I said more firmly, but he just huffed.

I turned to Kate and crinkled my forehead, urging her to please tell her adorable yet very annoying dog he needed to sleep in his own bed tonight. I wanted my baby mama tonight, and I was not budging.

"Hank," she crooned, smiling. And all she had to do was gesture with her head that she wanted him off the bed, and he obliged with minimal protest. He burrowed under a pile of blankets until all we could see was his tail. Good. The privacy was much appreciated. I didn't need an audience for what I planned to do.

"He hates me," I said.

"No. He just doesn't like sharing me with you sometimes."

"Well, too bad." Shifting her toward the middle of the bed, I leaned in and kissed her. Her lips tasted like honey, and the instant her tongue brushed against mine, liquid fire spread through every part of my body. "Fuck, Kate, I don't think I could ever get enough of you, angel."

She moaned into my mouth and the sound vibrated all the way down to my cock.

"Even when I look like a refrigerator?" she whispered against my lips.

I shook my head and grinned. I wasn't gonna fall for that one again, so I ignored her absurd comment and simply raised her shirt over her bare, and now, larger, pregnancy breasts—as she called them. God, how could she think she was anything other than a complete goddess? My gaze traveled down the length of her body, making sure to absorb every inch of her curves.

I kissed my way down her neck and lowered my tongue to her breasts, taking each nipple into my mouth until they were hard as pearls. She arched her back slightly, and her soft moans fanned my ego.

"That's it, baby. Let go." Trailing a line of kisses over her baby bump, I paused for a second to marvel at the miracle growing inside her. Who would've guessed Jackson Constantine would soon be a father? Certainly not me.

Kate squirmed under me, and I knew she was growing inpatient. I gently peeled off her underwear and spread her thighs open. Shit, she was already glistening, and I hadn't even touched her yet.

"Jax," she moaned, and I knew what she was asking. But it wouldn't be me if I didn't offer a little torture first—and only because it made her pleasure better.

"Not yet, angel." I circled the little bundle of nerves right at the apex of her sex, making sure to use her lubrication to wet her entire slit. Her hips raised a little off the mattress as her breath hitched.

"Jax, please."

"Please, what? Tell me what you want."

"You know what I want."

"I want to hear you say it."

"Your tongue, you devil. I want you to lick me. To make me come in your mouth."

Damn if those words didn't sound so fucking sexy coming from her lips. After getting her to the edge with my thumb, I finally brushed the tip of my tongue against her swollen clit and basked in the sounds of her ecstasy. God, she tasted divine. I opened her folds wider, completely exposing her to my mouth.

I lapped at her until she gave me her release, and with it, all her stress and torment. For those sacred moments, all that existed was us in that room and the pleasure I was giving her. It was like I was worshiping my goddess at her temple.

Once she came down from her high, I asked, "Can you take a little fucking?"

She laughed, and that rumble touched me in all the right places. "I can take a whole lot of fucking."

I took her from behind, soft then savage, until her screams reverberated off the fucking church walls. I wouldn't be surprised if Heaven heard them, too. And when her body asked for a small reprieve, I let her straddle me, and by God, watching her naked body move over my cock in small circles had me nearly coming inside her.

But I wanted to prolong this for as long as I could.

She didn't know it, but I needed her tonight as much as she needed me. Tomorrow was totally unknown, the road ahead a blank map. I couldn't tell her I was scared. That a part of me worried we weren't making the right decision.

But those were problems for tomorrow. Tonight, it was only about us.

She grabbed her breasts and pinched her nipples as she worked herself to another orgasm, riding my cock like she owned it—because she fucking did.

"Fuckin hell, angel. You're going to make me come if you keep moving like that."

"But that's what I want. I want to feel you coming inside me. Filling me."

I grabbed her hips and pushed down as I thrust up harder and harder. "Fuck, Kate."

She lowered down to my chest and took my mouth in hers. "I love you," she panted over my lips.

And it was all I needed to come undone for her. With one final thrust, I gave her all of me, every ounce of my soul. "I love you, too, angel," I said, breathless and spent. "More than you will ever know."

She fell asleep in my arms shortly after, while I traced my fingers over her back. I refused to close my eyes. I wanted to treasure this moment for as long as I could—this moment where we were just a man and a woman, and our love was enough to grant us redemption.

*The book has ended, but
Kate and Jax's story has not.
Stay tuned for more…*

ACKNOWLEDGEMENTS

OLIVIA BOOTHE

There are so many people who I want to thank for helping bring Afterworld to life, especially Victoria. Without her, there would be no Kate, Jax, or Hank. When I first bought the book cover, I had a vague idea of what I wanted to write, but it wasn't until I met Vic and we started talking about writing that I realized that together we could accomplish something great. We are so proud of this book and hope you will enjoy reading it as much we enjoyed writing it.

Afterworld is everything I could've hoped for and more. What started off as an idea for a standalone novel, has sparked a new series I never saw coming. And I can't wait to share this journey with you all.

But we couldn't have done it without our support network. I'd like to thank my beta readers for reading through our draft and providing such valuable feedback. Brittany, David, Sara: I'm so happy to have you as part of my tribe!

To my husband: Thank you for being my guy-in-the-chair, my unofficial personal assistant, and my accountant. And for always supplying me with my writing essentials—gum and iced-coffee. Without you, I couldn't run this biz.

To my boys who love to read and keep begging me to please let them read this book. One day, my loves. For now, just know that everything I do, I do for you. Your love of books and stories have inspired me to write you a fantasy that you and your kid friends can enjoy. Stay tuned for that…

Last but not least, I'd like to thank you, my readers—old and new. This writing journey wouldn't be possible without you. Thanks for keeping me in my happy place, my writing chair, crafting new worlds and adventures.

Love always,
Liv

The writing process of Afterworld started from a loose idea, a lot of improvisation and no plan forward whatsoever. To be able to pull off a fully finished and coherent storyline that I myself fell in love with is something I have Olivia Boothe to thank for. She has been the most amazing author to work with. I was on board with the idea the moment Olivia threw me the suggestion to co-write on 17th May 2021 (and yes, I scrolled up our Instagram chat to find the exact date). The very same day is when our brainstorming started. Plotting started way later. We had what we considered half a book ready by the time we actually started planning as to where this story was headed. The book ended up growing longer than either of us expected, but I wouldn't take back any part of it. Without Olivia, this book wouldn't be what it is.

My partner has had to put up with me constantly in my head, figuring out the next scene, or worse yet, eyes glued to the screen in sheer concentration. The time's he'd ask, "What are you writing now?" while I silently blush behind my hands were countless. Without his love and support, wouldn't be able to write the same.

Throughout the writing there have been many other people involved in the process, beta-readers, our editor and formatter without whom this book would've turned out differently. Jessica's enthusiasm and love for the story was the best kind of feedback I could've wanted given and it was a joy to read her comments. I'd like to thank Garima for her input. I loved the way Debbie devoured the story and how her opinions changed after she dove deeper in. Without Silvia, we'd been unable to see through our wonkier sentences and Giulia has made the most beautiful design.

And lastly, I want to thank you, the reader, for taking the time to read this book. You're the reason we've written it

ABOUT THE AUTHORS

Olivia Boothe

Author of Contemporary Romance, Paranormal Romance, and Romantic Fantasy.

Born in Colombia and raised in New Jersey since the age of eight, Olivia always dreamed of becoming a storyteller. Now, she's the author of the seductive and emotional contemporary romance duet, **Chronicles of a Dancing Heart: Wicked Dance & Wicked Embrace** & co-author of the **Amazon #1 Best Selling Paranormal Romance, Eternally Yours.**

If you enjoy deadly-hot romance novels with deep, layered plots, she's your gal. Because it's not just about the first kiss and the happily ever after, it's about everything in between.

FUN FACTS

When not locked away in her writing tower in the wee hours of the night, Olivia works a government 9-5 job and manages a house full of males (a husband, three sons, and a doggo named Hunter). On occasion, she summons her tribe for a night of wine and shenanigans. Dark chocolate is her kryptonite, she hates/loves to ugly cry during movies, and is a die-hard Bon Jovi fan.

To read more from Olivia, visit her website:
https://oliviaboothe.com

Victoria Liiv

Victoria Liiv is a writer, reader, nature lover and traveler at heart. She has been traveling through magical worlds since a very young age and wants more than anything to share the wonder with everyone else eager to escape from all things mundane. Let it be a magical adventure through slowly darkening Earth or a soul crushing fight for survival and love while the world burns. Sometimes all it takes is a little bit of romance.

She self published her debut novel Through Hell & Highwater on 2020 when the pandemics keeping her isolated gave her the reason to follow her dream of becoming an author. She hasn't looked back since.

Afterworld: Road to Redemption is Victoria's second novel. She is grateful for the opportunity to be able to co-write it with Olivia.

This February 2023, she'll also be releasing Treasure Me, a contemporary romance, as part of Tease Me box set.
With many more ideas and characters keeping her awake at night this is only the beginning of her writing career.

In her everyday life she found the magic in her partner, who gave her courage to move out of Estonia, the country she was born in, to an equally small but more known The Netherlands. He was also the one who encouraged and supported her throughout the writing process of this novel.

If you enjoyed this novel, please consider leaving a review at Amazon and/or Goodreads, even if it's only a line or two. Your review will make all the difference and is very appreciated.

www.vicwritesbooks.com

Instagram: @vicwritesbooks
Facebook: @vicwritesbooks
Tiktok: @vicwritesbooks
Twitter: @liiv_victoria

TABLE OF CONTENTS